A PLACE
TO CALL
HOME

BY DEBORAH SMITH

From Bantam Books

A PLACE TO CALL HOME

SILK AND STONE

BLUE WILLOW

MIRACLE

FOLLOW THE SUN

THE BELOVED WOMAN

A PLACE TO CALL HOME

DEBORAH SMITH

BANTAM BOOKS

NEW YORK · TORONTO · LONDON · SYDNEY · AUCKLAND

A PLACE TO CALL HOME
A Bantam Book / August 1997

Grateful acknowledgment is made to StoryPeople for permission to reprint excerpts from "High Places," in *Mostly True: Collected Stories & Drawings*, by Brian Andreas. Copyright © 1993 by Brian Andreas. Reprinted by permission of StoryPeople, 216 West Water Street, P.O. Box 64, Decorah, Iowa 52101.

Library of Congress Cataloging-in-Publication Data

Smith, Deborah
    A place to call home / Deborah Smith.
        p.   cm.
    ISBN 0-553-10334-2
    I. Title.
    PS3569.M5177P53   1997
    813' .54—dc21

Published simultaneously in the United States and Canada

PRINTED IN THE UNITED STATES OF AMERICA

BVG   10 9 8 7 6 5 4 3 2 1

AUTHOR'S NOTE

John Power arrived in America from Donegal, Ireland, in 1761, married Rachel Duvall of Greenville District, South Carolina, and together they raised a dozen children. Their adventurous youngest son, James Power, a veteran of the War of 1812, made his home in the wilderness of north Georgia after the 1826 Georgia land lottery opened the Creek Indian territory south of the Chattahoochee River, not far from a tiny pioneer settlement known as Marthasville, which later became known as Terminus, and later still, Atlanta.

James Power was a blacksmith, surveyor, judge, and ferry barge operator who hunted and traded with his Cherokee Indian neighbors across the river. He married an Irish girl, possibly a recent immigrant, whose name and fate are not known. Their only son, Samuel Wesley, was born in 1830 and served in the Confederate army during the Civil War. Four years after General William Tecumseh Sherman commandeered Powers Ferry (prior to the Battle of Atlanta) the first of Samuel Wesley's six children, Samuel Adam, was born.

Samuel Adam Power died in 1908 when his youngest son, William, was still a baby. William married Agnes Nettie Quarles the day after Christmas in 1926. In their wedding photograph they are a handsome young couple, she in a pale, simple dress with her dark hair pulled back by a small barrette, he in a dark suit with a rosebud pinned to the lapel. He sits and she stands beside him with her arm draped gently around his shoulders. His hands, clasped around one updrawn knee, are large and strong, a workingman's hands. He and she are smiling.

Their first daughter in a family of four daughters and four sons is Dora Power Brown, and she is my mother. She grew up playing in the river bottoms James Power farmed more than a hundred years before. When I was a child, my brother, sister, and I spent nearly every Sunday and holiday there, in the company of our grandparents, three aunts, four uncles, and fifteen first cousins.

This book is dedicated to them, for the memories and expectations, shared joys, sorrows, and strengths, and to my husband, Hank, and to my Dad. A family whose heart is as deep as its heritage.

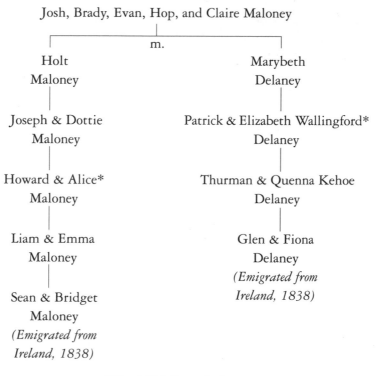

Josh, Brady, Evan, Hop, and Claire Maloney

m.

Holt
Maloney

Marybeth
Delaney

Joseph & Dottie
Maloney

Patrick & Elizabeth Wallingford*
Delaney

Howard & Alice*
Maloney

Thurman & Quenna Kehoe
Delaney

Liam & Emma
Maloney

Glen & Fiona
Delaney
*(Emigrated from
Ireland, 1838)*

Sean & Bridget
Maloney
*(Emigrated from
Ireland, 1838)*

*The "Old Grannies"

A PLACE
TO CALL
HOME

Part One

FOR HE COMES, THE HUMAN CHILD,

TO THE WATERS AND THE WILD

WITH A FAERY, HAND IN HAND,

FROM A WORLD MORE FULL OF WEEPING

THAN HE CAN UNDERSTAND.

—W. B. YEATS

PROLOGUE

$\mathscr{I}$ planned to be the kind of old Southern lady who talked to her tomato plants and bought sweaters for her cats. I'd just turned thirty, but I was already sizing up where I'd been and where I was headed. So I knew that when I was old I'd be deliberately *peculiar*. I'd wear bright red lipstick and tell embarrassing true stories about my family, and people would say, "I heard she was always a little funny, if you know what I mean."

They wouldn't understand why, and I didn't intend to tell them. I thought I'd sit in a rocking chair on the porch of some fake-antebellum nursing home for decrepit journalists, get drunk on bourbon and Coca-Cola, and cry over Roan Sullivan. I was only ten the last time I saw him, and he was fifteen, and twenty years had passed since then, but I'd never forgotten him and knew I never would.

"I'd like to believe life turned out well for Roanie," Mama said periodically, and Daddy nodded without meeting her eyes, and they dropped the subject. They felt guilty about the part they'd played in driving Roan away, and they knew I couldn't forgive them for it. He was one of the disappointments between them and me, which was saying a lot, since I'd felt like such a helpless failure when they brought me home from the hospital last spring.

My two oldest brothers, Josh and Brady, didn't speak about Roan at all. They were away at college during most of the Roan Sullivan era in our family. But my two other brothers remembered him each time they came back from a hunting trip with a prize buck. "It can't hold a candle to the one Roan Sullivan shot when we were kids," Evan always said to Hop. "Nope," Hop agreed with a mournful sigh. "That buck was a king." Evan and Hop measured regret in terms of antlers.

As for the rest of the family—Daddy's side, Mama's side, merged halves of a family tree so large and complex and deeply rooted it looked like an overgrown oak to strangers—Roan Sullivan was only a fading reflection in the mirror of their biases and regrets and sympathies. How they remembered him depended on how they saw themselves and our world back then, and most of them had turned that painful memory to the wall.

But he and I were a permanent fixture in local history, as vivid and tragic as anything could be in a small Georgia community isolated in the lap of the mountains, where people hoard sad stories as carefully as their great-grandmothers' china. My great-grandmother's glassware and china service, by the way, were packed in a crate in Mama and Daddy's attic. Mama had this wistful little hope that I'd use it someday, that her only girl among five children would magically and belatedly blossom into the kind of woman who set a table with china instead of plastic.

There was hope for that. But what happened to Roan Sullivan and me changed my life and changed my family. Because of him we saw ourselves as we were, made of the kindness and cruelty that bond people together by blood, marriage, and time. I tried to save him and he ended up saving me. He might have been dead for twenty years—I didn't know then—but I knew I'd come full circle because of him: I would always wait for him to come back, too.

The hardest memories are the pieces of what might have been.

1

*I*t started the year I performed as a tap-dancing leprechaun at the St. Patrick's Day carnival and Roanie Sullivan threatened to cut my cousin Carlton's throat with a rusty pocketknife. That was also the year the Beatles broke up and the National Guard killed four students at Kent State, and Josh, who was in Vietnam, wrote home to Brady, who was a senior at Dunderry High, *Don't even think about enlisting. There's nothing patriotic about this shit.*

But I was only five years old; my world was narrow, deep, self-satisfied, well-off, very Southern, securely bound to the land and to a huge family descended almost entirely from Irish immigrants who had settled in the Georgia mountains over one hundred and thirty years ago. As far as I was concerned, life revolved in simple circles with me at the center.

The St. Patrick's Day carnival was nothing like it is now. There were no tents set up to dispense green beer, no artists selling handmade 24-karat-gold shamrock jewelry, no Luck of the Irish 5K Road Race, no imported musicians playing authentic Irish jigs on the town square. Now it's a *festival*, one of the top tourist events in the state.

But when I was five it was just a carnival, held in the old Methodist campground arbor east of town. The Jaycees and the Dunderry Ladies' Association sold barbecue sandwiches, green sugar cookies, and lime punch at folding tables in a corner next to the arbor's wooden stage, the Down Mountain Boys played bluegrass music, and the beginners' tap class from my Aunt Gloria's School of Dance was decked out in leprechaun costumes and forced into a midyear minirecital.

Mama took snapshots of me in my involuntary servitude. I was not a born dancer. I had no rhythm, I was always out of step, and I disliked mastering anyone's routines but my own. I stood there on the stage, staring resolutely at the camera in my green-checkered bibbed dress with its ruffled skirt and a puffy white blouse, my green socks and black patent-leather tap shoes with green bows, my hair parted in fat red braids tied with green ribbons.

I looked like an unhappy Irish Heidi.

My class, all twenty of us, stomped and shuffled through our last number, accompanied by a tune from some Irish dance record I don't remember, which Aunt Gloria played full blast on her portable stereo connected to the Down Mountain Boys' big amplifiers. I looked down and there he was, standing in the crowd at the lip of the stage, a tall, shabby, ten-year-old boy with greasy black hair. Roan Sullivan. *Roanie.* Even in a small town the levels of society are a steep staircase. My family was at the top. Roan and his daddy weren't just at the bottom; they were in the cellar.

He watched me seriously, as if I weren't making a fool of myself, which I was. I had already accidentally stomped on my cousin Violet's left foot twice, and I'd elbowed my cousin Rebecca in her right arm, so they'd given me a wide berth on either side.

I forgot about my humiliating arms and feet and concentrated on Roanie Sullivan avidly, because it was the first close look I'd gotten at nasty, no-account Big Roan Sullivan's son from Sullivan's Hollow. We didn't associate with Big Roan Sullivan, even though he and Roanie were our closest neighbors on Soap Falls Road. The Hollow might as well have been on the far side of China, not two miles from our farm.

"That godforsaken hole only produces one thing—*trash.*" That's what Uncle Pete and Uncle Bert always said about the Hollow. And because everybody knew Roanie Sullivan was trash—came from it, looked like it, and smelled like it—they steered clear of him in the crowd. Maybe that was one reason I couldn't take my eyes off him. We were both human islands stuck in the middle of a lonely, embarrassing sea of space.

My cousin Carlton lounged a couple of feet away, between Roanie and the Jaycees' table. There are some relatives you just tolerate, and Carlton Maloney was in that group. He was about twelve, smug and well-fed, and he was laughing at me so hard that his eyes nearly disappeared in his face. He and my brother Hop were in the seventh grade together. Hop said he cheated on math tests. He was a weasel.

I saw him glance behind him. Once, twice. Uncle Dwayne was in charge of the Jaycees' food table and Aunt Rhonda was talking to him about something, so he was looking at her dutifully. He'd left a couple of dollar bills beside the cardboard shoe box he was using as a cash till.

Carlton eased one hand over, snatched the money, and stuck it in his trouser pocket.

I was stunned. He'd stolen from the Jaycees. He'd stolen from his own *uncle*. My brothers and I had been trained to such a strict code of honor that we wouldn't pilfer so much as a penny from the change cup on Daddy's dresser. I admit I had a weakness for the bags of chocolate chips in the bakery section of the grocery store, and if one just *happened* to fall off the shelf and burst open, I'd sample a few. But nonedible property was sacred. And stealing *money* was unthinkable.

Uncle Dwayne looked down at the table. He frowned. He hunted among packages of sugar cookies wrapped in cellophane and tied with green ribbons. He leaned toward Carlton and said something to him. From the stage I couldn't hear what he said—I couldn't hear anything except the music pounding in my ears—but I saw Carlton draw back dramatically, shaking his head. Then he turned and pointed at Roanie.

I was struck tapless. I simply couldn't move a foot. I stood there, rooted in place, and was dimly, painfully aware of people laughing at me, of my grandparents hiding their smiles behind their hands, and of Mama's and Daddy's bewildered stares. Daddy, who could not dance either, waved his big hands helpfully, as if I was a scared calf he could shoo into moving again.

But I wasn't scared. I was furious.

Uncle Dwayne, his jaw thrust out, pushed his way around the table and grabbed Roanie by one arm. I saw Uncle Dwayne speak forcefully to him. I saw the blank expression on Roanie's face turn to sullen anger. I guess it wasn't the first time he'd been accused of something he didn't do.

His eyes darted to Carlton. He lunged at him. They went down in a heap, with Carlton on the bottom. People scattered, yelling. The whole Leprechaun Review came to a wobbly halt. Aunt Gloria bounded to her portable record player and the music ended with a screech like an amplified zipper. I bolted down the stairs at that end of the stage and squirmed through the crowd of adults.

Uncle Dwayne was trying to pull Roanie off Carlton, but Roanie had one hand wound in the collar of Carlton's sweater. He had the other at Carlton's throat, with the point of a rusty little penknife poised beneath

Carlton's Adam's apple. "I didn't take no money!" Roanie yelled at him. "You damn liar!"

Daddy plowed into the action. He planted a knee in Roanie's back and wrenched the knife out of his hand. He and Uncle Dwayne pried the boys apart, and Daddy pulled Roanie to his feet. "He has a knife," I heard someone whisper. "That Sullivan boy's vicious."

"Where's that money?" Uncle Dwayne thundered, peering down into Roanie Sullivan's face. "Give it to me. Right now."

"I ain't got no money. I didn't take no money." He mouthed words like a hillbilly, kind of honking them out half finished. He had a crooked front tooth with jagged edges, too. It flashed like a lopsided fang.

"Oh, yeah, you did," Carlton yelled. "I saw you! Everybody knows you steal stuff! Just like your daddy!"

"Roanie, hand over the money," Daddy said. Daddy had a booming voice. He was fair, but he was tough. "Don't make me go through your pockets," he added sternly. "Come on, boy, tell the truth and give the money back."

"I ain't got it."

I was plastered to the sidelines but close enough to see the misery and defensiveness in Roanie's face. Oh, lord. He was the kind of boy who fought and cussed and put a knife to people's throats. He caused trouble. He deserved trouble.

But he's not a thief.

Don't tattle on Carlton. Maloneys stick together. We're big, that way.

But it's not fair.

"All right, Roanie," Daddy said, and reached for the back pocket of Roanie's dirty jeans.

"He didn't take it," I said loudly. "Carlton did!" Everyone stared at me. Well, I'd gotten used to that. I met Roanie Sullivan's wary, surprised eyes. He could burn a hole through me with those eyes.

Uncle Dwayne glared at me. "Now, Claire. Are you sure you're not getting back at Carlton because he spit boiled peanuts at you outside Sunday school last week?"

No, but I knew how a boiled peanut felt. Hot, real hot. "Roanie didn't take the money," I repeated. I jabbed a finger at Carlton. "Carlton did. I *saw* him, Daddy. I saw him stick it in his front pocket."

Daddy and Uncle Dwayne pivoted slowly. Carlton's face, already sweaty and red, turned crimson. "*Carlton,*" Uncle Dwayne said.

"She's just picking on me!"

Uncle Dwayne stuck a hand in Carlton's pocket and pulled out two wadded-up dollar bills.

And that was that.

Uncle Dwayne hauled Carlton off to find Uncle Eugene and Aunt Arnetta, Carlton's folks. Daddy let go of Roanie Sullivan. "Go on. Get out of here."

"He pulled that knife, Holt," Uncle Pete said behind me.

Daddy scowled. "He couldn't cut his way out of a paper sack with a knife that little."

"But he *pulled* it on Carlton."

"Forget about it, Pete. Go on, everybody."

Roanie stared at me. I held his gaze as if hypnotized. Isolation radiated from him like an invisible shield, but there was this *gleam* in his eyes, made up of surprise and gratitude and suspicion, bearing on me like concentrated fire, and I felt singed. Daddy put a hand on the collar of the faded, floppy football jersey he wore and dragged him away. I started to follow, but Mama had gotten through the crowd by then, and she snagged me by the back of my dress. "Hold on, Claire Karleen Maloney. You've put on enough of a show."

Dazed, I looked up at her. Hop and Evan peered at me from her side. Violet and Rebecca watched me, openmouthed. A whole bunch of Maloneys scrutinized me. "Carlton's a weasel," I explained finally.

Mama nodded. "You told the truth. That's fine. You're done. I'm proud of you."

"Then how come everybody's lookin' at me like I'm weird?"

"Because you *are*," Rebecca blurted out. "Aren't you scared of Roanie Sullivan?"

"He didn't laugh at me when I was dancing. I think he's okay."

"You've got a strange way of sortin' things out," Evan said.

"She's one brick short of a load," Hop added.

So that was the year I realized Roanie was not just trashy, not just different, he was dangerous, and taking his side was a surefire way to seed my own mild reputation as a troublemaker and Independent Thinker.

I was fascinated by him from then on.

The world in general didn't even know that Dunderry, Georgia, existed. I searched for us on the enameled globe in the living room and we weren't there. We were barely findable on the creased, coffee-stained road map of Georgia that Mama and Daddy kept in the glove compartment of our station wagon; Atlanta rated a fat star and Gainesville was marked with a circle. But Dunderry was only a black dot. We lived an inch to the left of Gainesville and an inch and a half above Atlanta.

We had peace and quiet, a beautiful little courthouse square with tree-lined streets, and sweet, handsome, old homes, big farms tucked in broad, lush valleys, and cathedral-like mountains around it all, to keep us safe.

Our ancestors would still have recognized the town they'd founded, despite electricity, paved roads, indoor plumbing, and monuments to five wars—including the one that left a dozen young Dunderry men dead in far-off states and gave us, in return, four anonymous Yankee soldiers whose graves at the edge of the First Baptist Church's cemetery had become a tourist attraction.

I asked Mama, who was a Delaney by birth and a Maloney by marriage—in other words, she stood proudly at the crossroads of the two oldest families in Dunderry—if we were as small as the map said. "Don't you worry," she told me. "If you study an ant under a magnifying glass, it's as big as an elephant. Size is all in how you look at things, and we're very big."

I pointed out that Hop had held a magnifying glass over an ant in the front yard once and after a minute in the sun it had looked like a Rice Krispie with legs. Mama studied me the way she did when I stumped her and then she told me to stop thinking so much.

But I decided we'd better be careful how we looked at ourselves.

Mama's great-grandparents, Glen and Fiona Delaney, immigrated from Ireland in 1838, the same year as the Maloneys. But they were educated shopkeepers, born and raised in the city of Dublin, while the Maloneys were descended from illiterate tenant farmers in the Irish backcountry. More important, the Delaneys were Protestant and my father's ancestors, the Maloneys, Catholic. Glen and Fiona established Dunderry's first dry-goods store and the first bank and built the first two-story house in town, and Glen was elected the first county magistrate. He and Fiona supported the Union during the Civil War, and their two oldest sons served in General Grant's army. The Dunderry Home Guard retaliated by looting the dry-goods store and burning the Delaney buggy shed. A Maloney, my great-great-grandfather Liam, was the Home Guard's captain.

So pride, class, religion, and politics kept several generations of Delaneys and Maloneys from intermarrying, even as they all gradually turned into prosperous Methodist Democrats. It took more than a hundred years until Mama and Daddy broke the stalemate.

Great-Grandfather Howard Maloney built the house I grew up in, on the foundation of a log cabin his grandfather Sean had built. It is where my

Grandpa Joseph Maloney and his five brothers were born, and where Daddy and all six of his brothers and sisters were born.

Each generation added to it like a hope chest; by the time my brothers and I were born (in the hospital at Gainesville, except for Brady, who came two weeks early in an upstairs bedroom with Mama screaming, "Holt, get me an aspirin!") the house had ten bedrooms, four bathrooms, and three chimneys, and its bottom-level additions sprawled from a two-story center inside wide porches, front and back. It sat in the center of the Estatoe Valley with round, green mountains rising on all sides. There was not another house, the light of another window, or the soft white smoke from any other chimney in sight. We were a kingdom of our own making.

Mama ran our household like a business. Spick-and-span, no room for messy customers. Beds made, fresh flowers in the vases, meals on time, clothes mended, silver polished, toilets sparkling, floors waxed, rugs and drapes vacuumed to the dustless sheen of old velvet. She marshaled doctors' appointments, school activities, and homework. She pickled and preserved, canned and baked; she sent old chairs to be reupholstered and antique mirrors to be resilvered. The land was Daddy's but the house was hers, and everything that went on in it was under her dominion, and we'd better not forget that.

Daddy took her on a second honeymoon once to tour the California wine country. She broke out in hives, and they had to come home two days early. "I couldn't stand all that relaxation," she said.

When I was a girl, my British-born Grandmother Delaney (I never called her Grandma—she considered it coarse and disrespectful) and my Great-Grandma Maloney lived with us. I learned the fine points of stubbornness and pride from them. Daddy said the Old Grannies could worry the horns off a brass billy goat, and Mama said anyone who lived in the house with her Mawmaw and Daddy's grandma could qualify as a saint. Or a lunatic.

Great-Grandma Maloney was a frisky eighty-eight, while Grandmother Delaney, as she herself reminded us often in her delicate English accent, was a very, very frail seventy. Frail like a cedar stump. Virginia Elizabeth Wallingford Delaney dyed her gray hair a flat, unrelenting nut-brown color and wore it pinned up with a hairpiece of coiled brown braids at the crown, which, combined with her pointy-tipped bifocals, gave her the look of a strangely youthful, squinting, grandmotherly queen.

She never sat outdoors without a broad-brimmed hat to shade her complexion, which remained, despite jowls and a few age spots, as milky and smooth as a porcelain doll's. She wore slender, pale dresses with a small cameo brooch anchoring a lace handkerchief to her right shoulder, and if anyone failed to jump up fast enough when she asked for something, she hooked the offender with the brass, goosehead handle of her mahogany cane.

She always reminded us that she had been only seventeen, an orphan consigned to an English boarding school, when she met Grandpa Patrick Delaney in London during the First World War. She said he was a dashing American infantryman who carried racy postcards of French cabaret dancers in his pockets and regaled her with stories about his Southern homeland. She married him and crossed the ocean with visions of antebellum plantations in her head.

She never quite forgave Grandpa Patrick after she discovered that her new home was a mountain town fed by dirt roads and the big house a drafty Victorian shared by Grandpa's overbearing parents and two spinster sisters, Vida and Maedelle. Grandmother Elizabeth was appalled when her female in-laws dipped snuff, wore their stockings rolled down, and drank their tea cold.

It didn't soothe her when Grandpa Patrick built her a large, lovely house on a hill just off the courthouse square, or when he bought her a shiny black Model T to drive, while most of the neighbors were still dependent on mule-drawn wagons. She wanted electricity; instead she had kerosene lamps and a woodburning cookstove. She wanted trolleys and cabs and trains; instead she had a dusty car that blew its tires on the rutted mountain roads.

She recalled trips to Atlanta, not because they were grand adventures that included stays at the finest hotels and shopping sprees at Rich's department store, but because on one horrifying occasion the car broke down on a muddy road miles from the city; she and Grandpa had to camp in a gully overnight. A moonshiner drunk on his own corn whiskey crept out of the bushes and offered to buy her from Grandpa for two dollars and a jug.

Somehow Grandmother Elizabeth survived for the sake of four sons and four daughters. She actually thrived because the ladies in the county considered her to be an expert on all matters of fashion and decorum, and after Grandpa Patrick became president of Dunderry Savings and Loan her social dominance was cemented. She won prizes for her needlepoint, she wrote articles on etiquette for the newspaper, and she was in high demand for poetry readings, which she conducted with the drama of a Royal Shakespearean.

When I was four, Grandpa Patrick had a series of strokes that crippled him. She moved him into a downstairs bedroom at our house and for the next year I watched her care for him tenderly, night and day, her frailty forgotten. After he died she channeled all her fierce, lonely energy toward aggravating Great-Grandma Maloney, who had the bedroom across the hall.

It was an old feud, birthed in their youth, nurtured in their prime, and still sizzling like banked coals in their old age.

Great-Gran's first name was Alice, but she was named after a Confederate general. Alice Stonewall McGinnis Maloney. Her husband, Howard Maloney, died of a heart attack twenty years before I was born. He and Great-Gran had already turned the farm's management over to their son, my Grandpa Joseph, by then, but Great-Gran still ran the whole operation. By the time Grandpa Joseph retired and Daddy took charge, she still hadn't mellowed much.

My brothers and I called her Stonewall behind her back. It suited her aura of command, especially the way she drove a car. She'd learned to drive when there was no traffic and no rules. Center lines didn't mean a thing to her. At almost ninety years old she might have given up driving except for the fact that her independence nettled Grandmother Elizabeth, who'd quit driving in her late sixties after a hip operation made her right leg stiff.

Great-Gran's hair was a thin cap of blue-white spit curls above a thick face enormously wrinkled and weathered. She wore stern-looking brown dresses and thick-heeled flat shoes, was almost six feet tall, and weighed two hundred pounds. She had grown up in the last decade of the previous century on an enormous cattle farm fifty miles north of Dunderry. Her mother was a transplanted Vermont Unitarian who preached and ran the first mountain school for black children; her father was a Confederate veteran who'd lost an arm during the battle of Kennesaw Mountain when he was twelve.

She met Great-Grandpa Howard at a Sunday social sponsored by the North Georgia Young Ladies' Academy, where she was a teacher. In yellowed photographs she is a tall, big-boned, unsmiling young woman with masses of dark hair piled in a Gibson Girl bouffant, dressed in one of those tightly corseted, pigeon-postured black dresses with puffed shoulders. An old maid at twenty-six.

She married him a month later and moved to our land in the Estatoe Valley of Dunderry County to raise children and eyebrows: she wore overalls at home, and she could milk a cow faster than any man; she marched for women's suffrage at the state capitol years before the female vote had any chance in Washington; and she threw an egg at Great-Grandpa's cousin,

Dr. Arnold Kehoe, when he gave a speech condemning birth control. As the decades passed she worked against prohibition and for civil rights. She also organized most of the women's clubs in the county.

She was the empress of all she surveyed, except for Grandmother Elizabeth.

When Grandmother Elizabeth married Grandpa Patrick and came home with him from England, she immediately usurped Great-Gran's place as the most interesting woman in Dunderry, and became, once and for all, the only permanent thorn in Great-Gran's side.

Their bitter rivalry was clinched on April 4, 1920, the day Great-Gran hosted the Methodist Ladies' Auxiliary Garden Luncheon. A majority of Methodist ladies deserted Great-Gran's head table to huddle excitedly around Elizabeth Delaney, their exotic new member, asking her opinion on matters of taste, decorum, and all things British. Great-Gran stewed in furious silence. Someone asked Grandmother Elizabeth if she was related to any royalty. That was the last straw.

"Royalty, my hind foot," Great-Gran announced to Vida Delaney, loud enough for everyone to hear. "If she hadn't married your brother she wouldn't have a pot to piss in or a window to throw it out of."

Grandmother Elizabeth, livid with insult, drew herself up to her full five feet three inches and declared, "You are a shabby, mannish, jealous clodhopper. I shall never forgive you."

Thirty years later, in 1950, Mama eloped with Daddy the night after her high school graduation ceremony. It was a scandal—Elizabeth Delaney's smart and beautiful daughter, Marybeth, who had just received her acceptance letter from a Methodist women's college, and Alice Maloney's favorite grandson, Holt, who rode a motorcycle and wore a black leather jacket, had dropped out of Georgia Tech, and was working at the Maloney chicken houses and as a lineman for the power company. Elizabeth Delaney threatened to have Holt Maloney arrested for seducing a minor. Alice Maloney tried bitterly to have the marriage annulled.

But Mama and Daddy were already expecting my brother Josh. So that was that. For better or worse, the Delaneys and the Maloneys were shackled together by marriage. Grandmother Elizabeth and Great-Gran Alice remained dedicated to making each other miserable, and with both of them living with us, they sometimes made us miserable, too.

Great-Grandma Alice's son Joseph and his wife, Dottie, lived a two-minute walk away, in a small house they built after they turned the big house over to Mama and Daddy, probably to escape the Old Grannies.

Dottie Maloney was still young at sixty, a hearty, thick-bodied, red-haired tower of feminine strength who wore slacks and beautifully embroidered sweaters, a smart woman who tinkered successfully in the stock market and kept the farm's business accounts and played tennis and loved opera. I adored Grandma Dottie, but Grandpa Joseph was my dearest mentor. People said he and I were a lot alike, temperament-wise, though sometimes I wasn't sure they meant it as a compliment. He could be honest to the point of embarrassment.

Grandpa was a broad, strong old man, planted solidly on the ground. He moved like a bear, and he was completely bald except for a monk's fringe of white fur around the base of his skull. He could predict the first frost of fall to the day and tell you how much it was going to rain over the summer by listening to the frogs sing. He planted by the moon and astrology signs, and his stalks of corn grew at least twelve feet high.

He was also an amateur and very low-rent comedian. "Pull my finger," he'd say. And as soon as I did, he'd fart loud enough to scare the dogs. I'd roll on the floor, laughing.

Grandpa served in World War II—hand-to-hand combat fighting on some of those godforsaken jungle islands in the Pacific, shaking with malaria, his boots rotting off his feet in the damp, fetid heat. During the war Grandma Dottie moved my daddy and the rest of the children to an apartment in Atlanta so that she could work at the Bell Bomber plant.

When they came back home after V-J Day, the farm had just about sunk to nothing. Grandpa limped from a piece of shrapnel embedded permanently in one hip. He and Grandma were broke and would ultimately have seven children to raise. Holt—my daddy—was the oldest, and he was only sixteen. The Latchakoochee Power Company hadn't gotten very far before the war; almost everybody in the mountains was still in the dark.

Grandpa Joseph put together a crew that included Daddy and most of the men in the family, who were almost as broke as Grandpa was. They went into the contracting business and installed power lines all over our part of the state. They made a small fortune. And Grandma Dottie, who knew about money and investments because her daddy was a banker in Gainesville, began nurturing that fortune on the stock market.

Which was the main reason we had, as people said, more money than we knew what to do with. Around us were our fenced pastures, our broad fields, five large barns, various storage sheds, and ten long, low chicken houses, which produced fifty thousand fryers at regular intervals throughout the year.

So there we were—one great-grandmother, one old grandmother and one youngish grandmother, one beloved grandfather, Mama and Daddy, Hop and Evan, and Josh—after he came home from Vietnam—and Brady, visiting from college every month or so. Plus a hundred head of Hereford beef cattle, a dozen dogs, five cats, a housekeeper, ten hired hands and a foreman, tons of pumpkins, corn, and cabbages, and me.

Not to mention my thirteen Maloney and Delaney aunts and uncles plus their spouses, my three dozen first cousins, Mama's and Daddy's numerous cousins of various degrees, and other assorted relatives, in-laws, and friends, who came and went as if our home were a train station at the center of the universe.

In the long run, Roanie Sullivan never had a chance. From the start, he was only one against many.

He and his daddy lived in a trailer down in Sullivan's Hollow among junked cars and appliances and piles of rusty tin cans, beside a gully filled with half-burned garbage. Big Roan only had one leg; the other was a metal contraption—so I'd heard, because I'd never gotten a peek at it. Evan and Hop insisted the metal leg had all sorts of weapons built in it—a bayonet and a poison-dart gun and a razor-tipped claw—and that Big Roan Sullivan could whip it off and throw it like a spear. I never had the gall to ask Mama and Daddy if any of that was true.

The Sullivans didn't have People—none that anyone knew of, anyway. Grandpa said Big Roan had rambled into town a year or two before the Korean War. He was an edgy hot-rodder who took a job at Murphy's Feed Mill and threw beer cans out the window of the room he rented from Old Maid Featherstone.

Daddy and Mama were already married and expecting Josh, but Daddy enlisted for the war because that's what Maloneys have always done, and several of our relatives enlisted, too. But all of them, Daddy included, spent the war stateside, keeping the Commies at bay by fixing army jeeps and cleaning latrines.

Big Roan Sullivan, who was Irish but didn't have the luck, got drafted and was immediately carted off to the front lines. He came back to Dunderry because he'd had no place else to call home, and because it was as good an address as any for his disability check. He'd lost most of his right leg when he stepped on a mine.

Daddy said he'd been surly before, but after the war he turned mean—a mean drunk, a condition that took some work, since the county was dry then. Because Big Roan was a war hero Grandpa Joseph Maloney deeded him two acres in the hollow east of our farm. The Masons and the VFW bought him a used house trailer and an old truck.

Daddy and his brothers drilled a well for him and built a bathroom onto the back of the trailer. The Kiwanis donated the tub and toilet. The Latchakoochee Power Company ran the electricity and gave Big Roan six months' free service. Dunderry Gas donated and installed a propane tank. Mountain View Telephone ran the phone lines and donated a phone.

The Ladies' Association planted a lawn, and Mama set out a few of her rose shrubs. All five members of the Dunderry African Men's Association (one of whom was a relative of ours, but my family didn't talk about that in public back then, and not much now) brought out a tractor and dug Big Roan a garden patch. Barker Murphy offered him his old job at the feed mill. He was prayed with, and for, and over, by every minister in the county, including the priest from our tiny Catholic chapel.

The salvation of Big Roan Sullivan was the biggest civic project since a tornado scattered the county courthouse to kingdom come, but unlike the courthouse, he couldn't be rebuilt.

He let the lawn and the garden patch go to weeds. The roses shriveled, the trailer began to look like a garbage can, and Big Roan kept the truck working just well enough to drive to the grocery store and down to Atlanta twice a week for liquor.

He stumped around the town square on his metal leg most nights, drinking and pissing in the flower tubs and shouting nonsense—"To hell with all you coward sons of bitches! The whole country can kiss my ass!"— until the sheriff's deputies hauled him off to jail to dry out.

"That's why I can't laugh at Otis on *Andy Griffith,*" Grandpa Joseph said. "There's nothing funny about a town drunk."

At least one part of Big Roan still worked, and it attracted a certain kind of girl, mostly the kind who would have lived on the wrong side of the tracks, if we'd had tracks. He laid rail until Mother Nature called his bluff and word got around that Jenny Bolton was pregnant. Jenny, by all accounts, was a pretty little brunette, only about seventeen, but beaten-looking already. She'd arrived the year before with her brother and his wife, tenant farmers from south Georgia looking for a new stake.

The three of them shared a two-room log cabin on a cattle farm owned by Daddy's first cousin, Charley O'Brien, and when people figured out who'd knocked her up, they organized a righteous group, mostly made up of my relatives, who dragged Big Roan over to the O'Brien farm and made him own up to his part. Today we'd call it an intervention. In those days they called it a shotgun wedding.

Jenny moved to the Hollow with Big Roan, but when it came time for the baby to be born, he was passed out, drunk, behind their trailer. Mama felt sorry for Jenny and had been checking in on her nearly every day. Mama found her curled up and crying in the trailer's tiny, dirty bed. Daddy hurried over to the Hollow and carried Jenny out as if she were a kid herself. He and Mama drove her to the hospital in Gainesville as quick as they could, but the doctors had to deliver the baby by cesarean—he was so large and Jenny was so small. When Mama asked her what she wanted to name him, she gasped out, "Roan, Junior, please, ma'am," then fell asleep for the next twelve hours.

Everyone called the baby Roanie to distinguish him from Big Roan. Five years later, right about the time I was born, Jenny caught pneumonia and died. She had given all her willpower to Roanie, I think. There was a lot of talk about taking him away from Big Roan, but people were squeamish—a man had an ordained right to his own seed, especially if he'd already sacrificed a leg for his country.

And so, in the way even good people have of turning their backs when problems are messy, my family let Roanie grow up the way he did.

I figured his situation this way: I came into the world to take care of him for his mama.

No one else wanted to.

2

When I started the first grade at Maloney Elementary School, Roanie was already in the sixth. I watched him from a distance with horrified curiosity.

"You stay clear of Roanie Sullivan," Mama warned me. "He had head lice last spring."

Maloney women are known for their red hair. Bunch us up and we look like a fistful of lit matches. I had a glorious head of hair—dark red, long, and curly. The thought of lice setting up shop in it was enough to convince me. Head lice meant you'd have to have all your hair shaved off, and it meant you were the lowest of the low, because decent people didn't get lice.

Besides, Roanie always looked dirty, and his jeans were too long one week and too short the next. He was big for his age but wiry-thin, with huge gray eyes looking out of a tight face. His brown-black hair was shaved down to nubs except for a greasy patch at the top of his forehead. His crooked tooth gave him a sinister expression when he opened his mouth. I wanted him to talk right and have his tooth fixed, so he'd be respectable.

Evan, who was in the same class with him, told us Roanie stories at supper.

"He smells like that old garbage hole in the Hollow," Evan would say, "and Miss Clark makes him sit off by himself sometimes. He chews his fingernails right down to the pink parts. Man, his lunch bag is so greasy, Mama could fry chicken on it."

Somebody was always messing with Roanie; he was like a scab the other boys couldn't stop picking. *White trash. Pig shit. Smells like a toilet.* He'd fight anything, anybody—older, taller, or heavier, all comers—and about half the time he got the living daylights beat out of him. It wasn't unusual to see Principal Rafferty dragging Roanie down the hall to have the nurse stitch up or ice down some part of his face.

His fury and isolation and status as a worthless outcast fascinated me because I was his opposite—the pampered darling of a prosperous clan. I had a vast number of kinfolk who really *were* kin, not just names but a daily part of my life. At school I couldn't spit gum without hitting someone related to me.

But Roanie and I had one thing in common: my foibles, too, were no secret. If I got into trouble for talking in class, or traded my lunch money for another kid's forbidden pack of Twinkies, or was caught scribbling knock-knock jokes on the wall of the girls' bathroom, the trespass traveled the family grapevine faster than a monkey on pep pills.

I couldn't imagine someone who broadcast his notoriety without benefit of three dozen cousins to transmit for him. *That* was power. At the same time, I felt sorrier for Roanie Sullivan than I'd ever felt for another human being in my life.

I knew I could count on Grandpa Joseph to have respect for an underdog.

Grandpa never bragged about how much money he'd made or how many Japanese soldiers he'd killed during World War II; he wouldn't talk about the war at all. He wouldn't even watch John Wayne war movies on TV.

One time he took me with him to eat Saturday breakfast at the Dunderry Diner, and I sat in the center of a rump-sprung vinyl booth, surrounded by him and his cronies, and somebody brought up the war in Vietnam, and the other old men started talking big—wipe out the Commie gooks, drop the bomb on 'em and fry their little godless, slanty-eyed behinds, that kind of stuff. Josh had just come home from Vietnam, so I guess they expected Grandpa to agree with them.

"Shut up," Grandpa said suddenly. "Those Vietcong are damn sure mean, but they fight for what they believe in and they die for it, and I've got more respect for 'em than I have for any of you old loud-mouthed bastards." And he got up furiously and took me by one hand, and we went home.

"Distance makes killin' sound too clean and easy," Grandpa said. I guess he'd never forgotten about killing Japanese soldiers during the war. "You need to look a man in the eye," he told me, "and see his fear, and watch him bleed, and watch him die. There's a balance to that. Accepting responsibility. You'll know what it means to take another person's life."

So I knew you had to respect the people you fought, and be grateful you'd come out on top, and just hope you were as lucky the next time.

I figured that was how Roanie thought of us.

He didn't let people catch him standing beside the road at the Hollow. I guess he knew how he looked, waiting for the school bus by the lopsided mailbox in front of that awful sinkhole with its junk and garbage-filled gully and rusty trailer.

But there was another reason, too: my older cousins, Arlan and Harold Delaney. They were already in high school, old enough to drive, and if they caught Roanie by the Hollow's mailbox, they'd take a whack at the mailbox with a baseball bat. When they could catch him, they took a whack at Roanie, too.

I missed the bus one morning in May. I was in a mood, an ill mood as usual, as Mama called it, because I'd spilled a whole pot of hot grits on my skirt while I was helping her make breakfast. It was thundering and pouring rain outside, weather that made my curly hair explode in fuzz. I knew I looked like cotton candy with a face. Mama braided my hair four different ways and finally slicked it down with hair gel. "Now I look like a greasy Brillo pad," I sobbed, and hid in my bathroom.

So I missed the bus.

Grandpa was the only one who could stand me when I was being a brat, so he drove me, Hop, and Evan to school. I sat glumly beside him in the front bucket seat of his Trans Am. That was Grandpa. He didn't drive an old-man car, he drove the latest-model black Pontiac Trans Am with mag wheels and an air scoop on the hood.

So there we went, skimming between the forest on either side of Soap Falls Road, rain drenching everything around us, Grandpa humming along with a Tammy Wynette song on the radio, me wrapped in a pink plastic raincoat and a pink scarf protecting my hair, Hop and Evan wedged together in the Trans Am's small backseat. We rounded the curve at Sullivan's Hollow and saw Arlan and Harold's souped-up truck speed off.

I shrieked. "They got Roanie again!"

"Those skinny-assed shitbirds," Grandpa said under his breath.

Roanie was hanging on to the mailbox in that downpour. He had no raincoat, no umbrella, no nothing except a plastic garbage bag pulled tight around his shoulders like a cape. His books were scattered in the weeds, and the way he and the mailbox leaned, it wasn't clear which one was going to fall down first.

But as soon as he saw another car he turned, staggered, fell, got up, and ran down the Hollow's mud-slicked driveway. The last I glimpsed of him he was wobbling into the woods on the next hill.

"*Grandpa,*" I begged. "Grandpa, *please* stop."

Grandpa pulled off to one side.

"Aw, come on, Claire," Hop protested from the backseat. "You can't catch him."

"He'll smell up the car," Evan said.

"Grandpa," I said again. "Nothing could stink worse than Hop's sausage breath."

Grandpa studied me with his head tilted. "Roanie's your fish, Claire. If you want to reel him in, you'll have to get out in the rain and do it yourself."

I guess he was testing me to see what I was made of. Vanity or valor. I gave Grandpa a level look. "I'm already fuzzy and greasy. Might as well get wet, too."

I pushed my door open. "Hold on, sweet pea," Grandpa said, but I was already out. I trudged down the muddy road. "Roanie!" I yelled. Rain whipped water into my face. I slipped on the mud and sat down hard. "Roanie, come here! We'll give you a ride to school! It's okay! I swear!"

Grandpa stood beside me, cupping his hands to his mouth. He could have yodeled Moses down from the mountain. "Cooome ooon, Roooanie!"

Silence. Stillness. We called for ten minutes.

I knew Roanie was watching us from somewhere in the dripping green forest on a ridge above the Hollow. I could feel his gaze in the goosebumps on the back of my neck. But he wasn't coming back.

"All right," Grandpa said wearily. "We can't get that cat out of his tree." He gently pulled me to my feet. All my pent-up misery curled out in small, choking sobs. I was muddy, I was soaked, and I was still better off than Roanie. "He thinks we're jinxed," I cried as Grandpa guided me back to the car. "Every time he has anything to do with us something bad happens."

Grandpa patted my shoulder. "We're not jinxed. We just live on the opposite side of the fence. We're as strange to him as he is to us."

I turned toward the woods again. "You come over and see us!" I yelled. "I'm leaving a gate open for you!"

When I was in the second grade, Neely Tipton made my life a constant, daily hell. He was a year ahead of me, the third-grade bully—a walking, talking stereotype of a future football gorilla—and he made a game of slipping up behind me, hissing "Bony Maloney," yanking my hair so hard, my eyes watered, then running before I could turn around.

I knew, of course, that Evan or Hop would cheerfully strangle Neely if I asked them nicely, but one of the lessons I'd already learned, being the only girl in a house full of brothers, was to keep quiet and get even. I was both a girly-girl and a tomboy—the first because Mama was so pleased to have a female child that she exaggerated my differences, the latter because—poor Mama—Hop and Evan treated me like a baby brother who just happened to have long hair and an innie.

The only problem with Neely was that he moved too fast for me to smack him. I began to get twitchy about it, always looking over one shoulder with a fist curled against my stomach.

But he learned his lesson one day and he never laid a hand on my hair again.

It started like every other Neely-dreading encounter. At recess I edged warily out a doorway to the playground. He was lurking behind the open door, and the next thing I knew my head jerked and I flew backward like a calf hitting the end of a rodeo rope. I landed on my back on a concrete stoop and lay there, gasping for air, my jumper hiked up to my panties, the crown of my head burning as if I'd been scalped.

"Bony Maloney, I *gotcha*," Neely yelled. Dazed, I propped myself on my skinned elbows just in time to hear Neely's footsteps crunching quickly on the graveled rain-drip bed beside the building. Then I heard a whump and looked over to see Neely bounce off the brick wall and sit down hard.

Roanie towered over him, cool as a cucumber. "You mess with her again," Roanie told him calmly, "and I'll jerk your butthole through your mouth."

I stared at Roanie with stunned wonder. Neely began snuffling. I got up, wobbled over proudly, and punched him in the side of the head. Personal revenge, better late than never.

Roanie looked down at me with his eyes half shut and glittering. Maybe he expected me to ignore him or insult him or run like a squirrel. "Thanks, Roanie," I said very carefully, because I couldn't quite forget those head lice he'd had the year before.

"I seen you, and I heard you, that time at the Hollow," he said. "You ain't like nobody else in the whole world." Then he just shrugged and walked away.

That was the day I began to love Roanie Sullivan.

·   ·   ·

The realization that I was in love was something I weighed against Maloney romantic tradition, which, to me, was majestically powerful but might be bad for a person's teeth.

Sean and Bridget Maloney. Romantic Irish names. But there was nothing romantic about the two old people, my great-great-great-grandparents, who stared down at me from massive portraits that hung in the main hallway of our home. I was afraid of them—that gray-bearded Irishman and the solemn, thin-faced Irishwoman with her hair in white ringlets who had birthed twelve children and buried six of them with her own hands.

Daddy assured me people just didn't smile for pictures back then. Smiling wasn't proper, and besides, a lot of old people were missing a couple of their front teeth. But I was convinced that my ancestors thought I wasn't up to the job of being a Maloney. They'd crossed an ocean. They'd carved a thousand-acre farm out of the Estatoe Valley wilderness. They'd named a town and helped build it. They were giants.

And they were still close by, under timeworn tombstones on a knoll behind the house, surrounded by their lost babies and surviving children, the wives and husbands of their children, their grandchildren, and assorted others—a sprawling, granite town of dead Maloneys. On Halloweens my brothers and cousins and I huddled among them, telling one another ghost stories that seemed all too real. Uncle Bert jumped out of the shadows one Halloween, wearing his preacher's robe and a Nixon mask.

Most of us, me included, wet our pants.

So a person was better off keeping romantic information to herself around other Maloneys, because the dead ones had stern, unsmiling expectations and the live ones might scare the tea out of you when you least expected it.

What took place the next spring later became known among my relatives as The Day We First Saw It Coming. It had to do with me, Roanie, the McClendon sisters, Easter, and evil.

3

*T*he McClendon sisters lived in a cluster of shabby little houses and trailers in the woods north of town, on a dead-end dirt lane named Steckem Road. I had access to a spectrum of lurid, half-baked gossip, so I'd done my share of snickering over Steckem Road's whispered nickname. *Stick 'Em in Road.*

I knew it involved men and women and their private parts, plus I had a vague idea about what was being stuck where. I also knew, from remarks I overheard at home, that if any of my brothers ever so much as set foot on Steckem Road, Mama and Daddy would skin them alive.

Mama would have skinned her brother Pete if she could. It was a well-known fact, even among us kids, that our Uncle Pete Delaney spent half his time with the McClendon sisters on Steckem Road. I had heard enough about his notorious habits to know he was the shame of the Delaneys. That might explain why his boys, Harold and Arlan, were so mean. Embarrassment makes some people use hatefulness as a protection.

There were four sisters—Daisy, Edna Fae, Lula, and Sally. Daisy was the oldest, about thirty-five when I was seven, though her bleached yellow hair and the hard lines around her mouth made her look older. She had a husband, but nobody had seen him in years. She had two nearly grown sons who'd already run away from home and two scraggly, half-grown girls whom my Uncle William Delaney, the county judge, and my Aunt Bess Maloney, the county social worker, had sent to live elsewhere for reasons nobody explained to me.

Daisy spent most of her time with Big Roan Sullivan. In some strange way I think she loved him.

Edna Fae and Lula had had a whole pack of husbands, and the latest models looked like stray dogs waiting for a better offer. "You could throw a handful of marbles at Edna Fae's and Lula's tribe of children and not hit two that have the same daddy." That's what Grandpa said.

Sally McClendon was sixteen, the youngest of the sisters. She'd already dropped out of high school, and her main hobby was stealing makeup and perfume from my Aunt Jean's Dime to Dollar Store, and I couldn't fathom why she didn't just buy the stuff, it was so cheap. But worst of all, Sally had a baby. A son. I couldn't understand where she'd gotten him, with no husband around. I had heard that Sally was Uncle Pete's favorite McClendon sister.

My Aunt Dockey Maloney said the McClendons were evil.

"Evil exists to teach us the difference between right and wrong." That's what Aunt Dockey told us, and she, being Uncle Bert's wife, and him the minister of Mt. Gilead Methodist, was as good as a preacher herself, so she ought to know.

"God presents us with choices," Aunt Dockey lectured at Sunday school and family get-togethers and any other time she had an audience. "He says, 'Now here's this path and here's that path. Here's a sin and here's a virtue. And if we choose according to His commandments, we never go wrong.'"

Aunt Dockey made righteousness sound like comparison-shopping at a mall. So I understood why our town needed the McClendon sisters. They were a lesson in what happened when people ignored God's shopping list. They survived on welfare checks and odd jobs, doing laundry and cleaning houses for people in town, supplemented by what they earned from the men who visited them. Uncle Pete, I decided, was just plain strange for wanting anything to do with such women.

When I was older, I understood that the McClendon sisters were poor, uneducated, and abused. But at seven I only understood that they aroused both pity and disgust in my family. Polish those feelings with well-intentioned religion and you get charity.

That's how Easter got tied in with the whole mess.

I'm ashamed to admit that I already thought of Easter in terms of goodie baskets and egg hunts and frilly new dresses, not of solemn celebrations of Jesus ascending to Heaven. The mountains were speckled with white dogwood blossoms and the soft green palette of new leaves, the yards around our house burst into patches of yellow jonquils and red azaleas; the air smelled sweet and warm-cool, and the bugs hadn't come out yet. There were calves and chicks and kittens and puppies to play with, and a whole new clan of wild, gray Peter Cottontails bouncing across the long driveway between the front fields, and the fields began to trade the empty brown surface of winter for a primer coat of green stripes.

I couldn't be solemn. I was Mama and Daddy's only daughter; I was the Easter princess. Everybody got new clothes to wear on Easter Sunday, but mine were special. Mama bought me a pale pink dress with imported lace at the neck and a skirt so ruffled that it stood out from my waist like a shelf. I had new white patent-leather shoes and sheer white knee socks with pink roses embroidered on the ankles and a broad-brimmed white straw hat with a pink ribbon that trailed halfway down my back.

The Saturday before Easter was egg-decorating day. If there's one thing you have on a chicken farm, it's eggs. The Monday after Easter, by the way, was egg-salad day.

We spent the whole Saturday in the kitchen, boiling eggs and dipping them in vinegar-scented pastel baths. Josh and Brady were too old and serious for egg decorating; Hop and Evan hung around but wouldn't admit they wanted to participate, but Mama, Daddy, the old folks, and I decorated up a storm. No Fabergé designer for Russian royalty was ever more intense about egg art than we were.

We put some of the eggs in a dozen small Easter baskets along with candy and Bible pamphlets. Those baskets were for the poor McClendon children of Steckem Road. Aunt Dockey and Mama and some other church ladies delivered the baskets to them every year.

I raced downstairs in my nightgown on Easter morning. And there, in the center of the library table in the living room, sat my personal huge, pink Easter basket exploding with pink cellophane and pink bows and a soft pink poodle doll. Mama and Daddy peeked at me from the doorway.

I said dutifully, "Thank you for the poodle doll," then shoved it aside and went for the good stuff—foil-wrapped marshmallow eggs, and marzipan chickens, and a giant chocolate rabbit with yellow marzipan eyes, all nestled in a bed of green cellophane grass. I tore the rabbit from his plastic wrapping and examined his molded perfection with my fingertips. I could already taste his richness, imagine his hollow innards, his delicious shape.

Evan strode into the room dressed in his blue Easter suit and white silk tie, his red hair slicked down, his white Bible in one hand. He was only twelve, but he was going through a holier-than-thou phase.

"This isn't what Easter is about," he announced. "I think we should wait."

"Evan's right," Mama allowed. "Claire, don't eat that candy until after church."

I had the rabbit halfway to my mouth. Oh, temptation. Oh, interrupted greed. Oh, the sin of chocolate lust. Oh, bunny.

"Claire," Daddy warned, drawing my name out.

"Oh, *dammit*," I blurted out.

Doomed. Doomed the second that word passed my lips. The Lord had not risen so that Claire Maloney could say "dammit" over a chocolate rabbit.

Which is why I had to sit out the Easter egg hunt and donate my beloved basket, chocolate rabbit and pink poodle and all, to the McClendon children of Steckem Road. And I had to go there, too, with Mama and Aunt Dockey and the other ladies, on Easter afternoon, to see why I should be humble.

The McClendon place reminded me of Sullivan's Hollow, with paper trash littering a bare-earth yard shared by a half circle of tiny, dilapidated houses and rust-streaked trailers. There were no flowers and no shrubs, and the forest cast long shadows on two ancient sedans with bald tires and duct tape plastered over their broken windows. Skinny dogs crept around, shy and standoffish, like the children. The porches sagged with junk. Edna Fae's latest husband was stretched out on a couch under a tree. His mouth was open. He snored. His shirt was unbuttoned and he had one hand jammed down the front of his jeans.

"May the Lord bless us for our bounty and help us help those who cannot help themselves," Aunt Dockey said as she pulled up the parking brake of her Cadillac.

"Amen," Mama said.

"Please wash this place clean of sin," intoned Sarah Kehoe, Mama's first cousin, from the backseat.

"And please punish men who have ten dollars to waste," added Mama's older sister, Irene.

"That's all it costs Pete each time?" asked Ruby O'Brien, Daddy's cousin-in-law. I adored Cousin Ruby. She ran a dress shop and let her children draw on their bedroom walls. She was a little flighty and always blurted good questions in front of us kids.

"Let's change the subject," Mama said, glaring at Ruby. "Claire, you stay by the car. Hand out a few eggs if you want to. We'll get the Easter baskets out of the trunk after we're done inside."

"Yes, ma'am." I was relieved. I wouldn't have to go into one of those foul-looking houses with them. Wouldn't have to sit in a prayer circle.

"Talk to those kids about Jesus," Aunt Dockey told me. "And make them say 'Please' and 'Thank you' for the Easter eggs. Teach them some manners."

"Yes, ma'am."

We got out, and the ladies made a fuss over the rag-tail boys and girls, who shuffled their feet and didn't answer but darted excited glances at me in my ruffled pink splendor and at the basket of Easter eggs I lugged from the backseat. I was glad I hadn't worn my hat. I suddenly felt embarrassed, and depressed, and a little foolish.

Edna Fae and Lula and Sally strolled out to meet us. They were dressed in tight jeans and tight low-cut blouses, with lots of makeup on their faces. Sally had already been inducted into the McClendon big-bleached-hair club, and she had the kind of body that looked like ripe cantaloupes were stuffed in a thin paper sack. Edna Fae and Lula were intermediate versions of Daisy and Sally. Together the four of them would make a Dorian Gray gallery—Daisy's tough, worn, cemented sensuality, Edna Fae's and Lula's fading freshness, and Sally—I knew exactly what Sally would look like eventually, after too much hard living had sucked the juice out of her.

I was so busy staring, I nearly dropped my basket of Easter eggs. "Well, ain't you pretty?" Sally said to me in a sly, boisterous way. She leaned too close to me and grabbed a handful of my long hair and stroked her fingers through the curls, all the while staring into my face. "You look just like a strawberry shortcake with blue eyes. Them eyes. Bright as sapphires. You just take in the whole world with them eyes, don't you? What you thinkin', little queen?"

I was thinking, You mess with my hair again and I'll give you a tittie twister, but I was already on thin ice with Mama, so I kept quiet.

Besides, Mama sidled over and got between us. Polite but cool as a little brown-haired lioness in a mauve suit and pumps. She didn't say a word, but Sally backed off. Sally was scared of Mama and Mama's sisters.

"Where's Daisy?" Aunt Dockey asked. "Isn't she going to participate in our prayer meeting?"

"Aw," Edna Fae said, lighting a cigarette and nodding toward one of the houses. "She ain't up to it."

Lula giggled and covered her mouth.

Aunt Dockey got a flat-lipped, squinty look on her face and stared hard at the house. "I see. I'll speak to her later."

Mama took her box of charity food from the trunk, then bent close to my ear and whispered fiercely, "You stay by the car. Stay away from Daisy's house, or I'll skin you alive."

Whoa. I was in the same league with my brothers. I nodded.

And then, unhappily, I was alone in the yard with a dozen grimy, bare-foot kids ranging from my age on down to some who were barely old enough to walk, all of them staring at my basket as if they'd like to knock me down and take it.

"Y'all want to hear about Jesus?" I asked. Silence. I sighed. "Y'all want some Easter eggs?" Quick nods and outstretched hands.

I fished among the hard-boiled eggs and found the candy ones first, because every kid knows the real eggs are a disappointment once you get past the decorations. But the McClendon children didn't care. They snatched candy eggs and real eggs with the same fervor, and admired them with wide eyes, and touched the decorations, and then tore off the wrap-pings and peeled the colored shells with dirty fingernails, and ate slowly, relishing every bite.

I was doubly ashamed of myself and mad at this awful place, this sad place and its left-out children, and I knew, for certain, that the McClendon sisters only put up with a bunch of praying rich women so that their kids could get a little free Easter loot. They were bartering with us, the same as they did with the men.

And I thought about Roanie, who was so proud, and how his daddy was so mean, nobody had ever dared go down to Sullivan's Hollow to bribe him with Easter eggs. I was glad—shivering, goose-bumped thank-ful—that Roanie hadn't been turned into a charity exhibit like the McClendon kids.

I heard a car coming down the dirt road, the rumble of an unmufflered engine, and lo and behold, as if he'd materialized from my thoughts, Roanie drove his daddy's beat-up truck into the yard.

My mouth fell open. He was only twelve years old! Yet he rolled that vintage rattletrap into the yard and jerked it to a stop, and he pushed the door open and climbed out. Then he froze, staring at me with an almost painfully surprised expression. His T-shirt was dirty and his bare ankles showed between his jeans and his worn-out tennis shoes.

He was only twelve, and he'd driven to Steckem Road to visit the awful McClendon women. "What are you doing here?" I demanded hoarsely.

My accusing tone stamped the surprise out of his face. All emotion receded behind a flinty mask. At that moment the front door of Daisy's house banged open.

Daisy ran out wearing a bra and a pair of cutoff jeans, her gold-plated hair tangled around her face. One of her eyes was swollen shut. "You come git him, Roanie! You come get that son of a bitch outta my bed! I ain't gonna put up with his shit no more!"

The kids scattered like roaches when a light's turned on. I stood rooted to the spot, fascinated and afraid. Roanie walked into the house with his fists clenched beside him and his head down. Daisy flew in behind him, cursing.

Oh, Mama, come out here and bring your pistol. That's what I tried to shout, because I knew Mama had put her little .32 revolver in her purse, but my mouth wouldn't work and neither would my feet. I was all ears, listening to Daisy's muffled voice and the crashing noises, and then the low, slurred boom of Big Roan Sullivan's voice. "Git out of my face, bitch, or I'll hit you again."

The door slapped open and Big Roan staggered out, lopsided on his metal leg, bare-chested, the waistband of his tan trousers hanging unfastened beneath his hairy beer gut. He was huge and black-haired and had a jaw like a bulldog's. His bloodshot eyes settled on me and I froze. "Don't need no Maloney starin' at me," he said loudly. "Hymn-singin', Bible-thumpin' hypocrites—don't you look at me, you little fluffball."

I backed against Aunt Dockey's car and gaped at him. He staggered down the steps toward me.

"Leave her be, Big Roan," Daisy ordered. "She's just a little girl."

"Shut up." He limped forward, swinging his arms. "See that youngun over there?" Big Roan swung a hand toward a barefoot baby boy with light brown hair. Sally must have seen him from the other house, because she bolted outside and snatched the baby up.

"Big Roan, you stop!" she yelled. "He ain't yours. Don't you mess with him!"

He grunted at her. "I ain't got nothin' to mess with, you bitch. Gov'ment sent me off to fight and left me poor." Big Roan swung toward me again. "Your daddy and his kind—gov'ment sent them where they'd be *safe.* I done their dirty work for 'em." He slapped his metal leg. "I come back, what do I get? A little piss-wad of gov'ment money and a free shit-hole for a home. You quit lookin' at me! Quit it!"

Roanie ran out of Daisy's house and down the warped wooden steps.

He got between me and Big Roan. "Go on," Roanie shouted. "Get in the truck."

"Get out of my way, boy!"

"It ain't her fault she's rich," Roanie said. "She ain't done nothing to you."

"Boy, when I want you to talk to me, I'll beat some talk out of you!" Big Roan pointed at me, then at the baby boy in Sally's arms. "Cain't let a poor girl alone, can you? Cain't even admit you done it. Just shit on her and her kid and pretend he ain't worth nothin'."

"You're just mad 'cause he's too good to be *yours*," Sally screamed.

I thought I'd swallow my tongue. My knees shook. They were all crazy. Big Roan jabbed his finger toward the little boy. "That youngun, you know what he is? You ask your Uncle Pete. That there's your fine Uncle Pete Delaney's thrown-off bastard!"

My Uncle Pete's? Daisy got between Sally and Big Roan. "Big Roan, keep quiet!" she mewled. "You want to git us all in trouble?"

Roanie made a sound like a wounded dog and shoved his daddy. Big Roan lost his lopsided balance and sprawled on the ground. Roanie stood over him. "Git up," he said between clenched teeth. "Git *up*."

"Don't gimme no orders, boy!" Big Roan swept one thick arm out. He caught Roanie around the ankles and jerked his feet out from under him, and Roanie went flat on his back. The breath gushed out of him and he gasped. Big Roan rolled onto him in a flash, pinning him by the throat. "Don'tcha gimme orders, boy!"

Roanie coughed and struggled, latching both hands around Big Roan's wrist. "Let him go!" Daisy shrieked. "You're chokin' him to death!"

"Ain't gonna gimme no orders!"

I had a mean arm. A strong arm, honed by baseball-playing brothers who'd taught me to throw. I didn't think, I didn't breathe, I was blind with sheer rage and terror. I snatched a hard-boiled Easter egg from my basket and drew back like a major leaguer. I beaned Big Roan right between his shoulder blades.

He kept one hand on Roanie's throat but twisted on one hip and glared woozily at me over his shoulder. I drew back another egg and edged toward him. "*You let him go!*"

"Whadtha hell?" Big Roan mumbled.

I hit him right between the eyes.

They don't call them *hard*-boiled eggs for nothing. If he hadn't been drunk, it might just have dazed him. As it was, his eyes rolled up and he slumped backward.

I had killed him. On Easter. I was sure.

Roanie got up slowly. His face was tinged with blue and the skin of his throat was dark red. He gasped for air and hunched over. A thin, watery stream of vomit dripped from his mouth, and he dragged an arm across his lips. But he managed to keep his head up and he scrutinized me with his unwavering gray eyes.

"That's for Neely Tipton," I told him, saving him a thank-you. "And for everything Arlan and Harold do to you. Now we're even."

He nodded weakly.

The battle had only lasted thirty seconds. By now Mama and everybody else had run out to us, and Edna Fae McClendon's lousy husband straggled over, and he and Edna Fae helped Roanie drag his father to the truck and hoist him into the back.

"Did I kill him?" I asked Mama tearfully.

"No," she said, putting one arm around my shoulders. She held her revolver in her other hand. "I'm afraid not."

"Mama, he said Sally got her little boy from Uncle Pete."

Mama's mouth flattened. Color zoomed up her cheeks. "There's some things we don't talk about."

"But Uncle Pete comes down here to visit Sally all the time! I heard all about it and—"

"*Claire Karleen.* What your uncle does when he visits is nobody's business and nothing but gossip. Forget about it."

Roanie didn't say a word. He climbed into the truck's cab. Twelve years old and hauling his drunk, passed-out daddy home on Easter Sunday, humiliation stretching every inch of his face. I couldn't let him go like that. I sprinted around to the trunk of Aunt Dockey's Cadillac. The lid wasn't fastened. I shoved it up and grabbed the giant chocolate rabbit from my basket. Mama had wrapped it in wax paper.

I ran to the truck as Roanie cranked the engine. He stared at me warily as I leaped up on the sideboard. I thrust the rabbit into his lap. "You take this," I said, crying. "This is from me to you. It's not 'cause it's Easter, and it's not 'cause of Jesus, and it's not for charity. It's because I *like* you. You take this rabbit and you eat him!"

He swallowed hard. He shrugged. I struggled not to pull back from the stink of vomit and garbage and unwashed clothes.

After he drove away, I handed out Easter baskets to that pack of quiet, fearful McClendon kids. Sally ran into her house carrying her little boy. Uncle Pete's son. My cousin. It was true. We couldn't talk about it, but it was true.

I didn't make even one of those McClendon kids beg me for some Easter eggs with a "Please" or a "Thank you." I was so ashamed of all of us.

One of Daddy's cousins, Vince O'Brien, Ruby's husband, was the town sheriff. Ruby told him what had happened and he sent a couple of deputies over to the Hollow to make sure Big Roan hadn't killed Roanie later. But Big Roan was still asleep in the back of the truck. The deputies said Roanie had taken off into the hills, anyway. He'd learned when to disappear.

I was much praised and told that I'd done a good, Christian deed, like David with Goliath. Evan tried to read me the Bible story, but I told him to shut up and leave me alone, I needed to think.

I had too much, and Roanie had nothing. From that day forward I vowed to save him from the evil that pervaded our lives.

·4·

I didn't get to see Roanie much for the next couple of years, especially after he entered Dunderry High, but I heard about him regularly.

"Roanie Sullivan showed up at school with a big knot on his forehead," Hop told us one night. "I heard he caught Arlan and Harold knocking his mailbox again and they took a swing at him."

"Do something, Mama," I begged. "They'll bust his brains out."

Mama sighed and looked at her mother. But Grandmother Elizabeth insisted Arlan and Harold would have turned out gentler if their mother, Uncle Pete's wife, hadn't died young. They were her grandsons after all. "Men need a full-fledged mother in attendance throughout their childhood in order to refine them," Grandmother Elizabeth said unhappily.

Great-Gran Alice snorted. "Pete's a no-account, and *you* raised *him*."

Grandmother Elizabeth began to cry. Mama patted her hand and eyed Daddy. "I've talked to Pete until I'm blue in the face. Will you try again?"

Daddy sighed. He was close with Mama's other brothers but barely tolerated Pete. "He doesn't listen. There's not much I can do if Roanie won't name names, and Big Roan doesn't care."

"Roanie's bound to drop out of school pretty soon," Evan predicted. "Nobody could put up with the kind of crap he gets." Evan almost wished he'd quit school, I believe, because Evan had had asthma when he was little and remembered being teased about his wheezy frailness. He could sympathize.

I was furious. At the next family get-together I went up to Arlan and

Harold. "I hope you die and buzzards eat your guts," I told them. "I hope you get sick and your peters fall off." They laughed.

But Roanie hung on as tenaciously as bitterweed in a cow pasture. He had no money for nice notebooks or pens or field trips down to Atlanta for the symphony or the Fernbank science museum—the sort of things I and mine took for granted. He could never afford lunch in the school cafeteria, and he never had money for even the bare necessities to play a sport, although the coaches avidly wanted his big, aggressive self on their teams. He took as little as he could to get by. Some time later, when I got to know him, I understood.

"The only things you can count on keepin'," he told me, "is what you think inside your own head."

He dropped out of high school only once, in the early spring when I was nine, after Big Roan robbed Uncle Pete's store.

The Auto Supply was in a low concrete building that Uncle Pete had erected on a back street in town, across from the lot where he sold used cars. We pretty much rolled up the sidewalks at six in town, so there weren't many people around after dark.

Big Roan, drunk as usual, drove his truck through the Auto Supply's big plate-glass window one March night, then loaded up with oil filters, radiator hoses, a CB radio, and a new set of tires. But the store had its own peculiar alarm system—Dot and Rigby Boyles, retired Baptist missionaries who lived next door to the Auto Supply with their ten dachshunds.

The dachshunds barked, the Boyles called Sheriff Vince O'Brien—and Big Roan was in jail within thirty minutes. Uncle William Delaney sentenced him to two months. Since Roanie was only fourteen and had no other relatives, my Aunt Bess and a couple of other social workers went down to the Hollow to collect him. He sprinted into the deep forest on the ridge above and refused to come back. Daddy and Sheriff Vince tracked him for a few days, without any luck.

I walked over to Grandma and Grandpa Maloney's house. "Roanie'll starve," I moaned to Grandpa Joseph.

He laid a finger to his lips. His eyes gleamed. "No, he won't. I know where he is."

Ten Jumps Lake had belonged to Maloneys for as long as anyone could remember. It was nearly a mile off an old paved road that intersected Soap Falls above the farm. The lake was small and rimmed with high ridges, and the only way to get there was by a narrow trail that crawled around steep hillsides and turned into a mud bog where it crossed creek-fed bottoms.

Grandpa said the lake was named for a Cherokee legend about a warrior who once crossed it in ten jumps, using the backs of giant turtles as stepping-stones. He had helped his great-uncle Harvey build a two-room hunting cabin there decades ago, and because Harvey was a retired navy man who owned a salvage business on the Georgia coast, the cabin was an odd, landlocked creation made of timbers from an old yacht, with a chimney of smooth, round ballast stones that Harvey collected from the wreck of an eighteenth-century schooner. One of Harvey's nieces had inherited the land and the cabin from him, but she lived in Minnesota, and we'd never met her. Grandpa paid the property taxes for her every year.

Grandpa parked his truck behind a grove of thick green laurels and we crept along the lake's edge. The cabin's broken-out windows and the black rectangle of its doorless doorway gaped at us across the water through large oaks and ferns as tall as I was. "There's nothing else like it in the county," Grandpa whispered. "It's a boat in a strange harbor, but it's right where it belongs."

"Is Roanie in there?"

"Yep." Grandpa pointed. "He fishes for brim in the lake. I've come across his trail a dozen times since he was little. I've seen him out on the porch a time or two, but I never let him know."

"Why?"

"It's the only safe place he's got, sweet pea. He's like a wild animal in a burrow. If he thinks we've found his den, he might not come anymore. But I think he's got more than he bargained for this time, with his daddy in jail."

"Daddy and Cousin Vince'll carry him off someplace if they find out!"

"I know. Maybe that'd be the kindest thing for him, but I just can't abide it." He touched the tip of a thick forefinger to my nose. "This is our secret. Your grandma's the only other soul who knows."

I nodded avidly. Then we went back to the truck, and Grandpa took out a big cardboard box packed with food, and we left it on the lake bank in front of the laurels. Grandpa tore a sheet of paper from a notepad in the pocket of his overalls and gave me a pencil, and I wrote, Roanie, IT IS OKAY TO EAT. MY GRANDPA says don't worry. WE WON'T TELL. Your friend, Claire.

"If he trusts anybody it's only you," Grandpa said.

When we went back the next day, the box was where we left it, but the food was gone and Grandma Dottie's plastic serving containers were there, rinsed and stacked. I was so proud I put long letters to Roanie in every box after that.

We left food every day for a month—Grandma's baked hams and roasted chickens, casseroles, and slabs of cakes and pies. At first she sent the food in leftover margarine tubs, but as Grandpa proudly returned the washed tubs, she began substituting her good Tupperware. By the time Big Roan was released from jail and Roanie reappeared at school, he'd earned full Tupperware trust.

"Wherever the boy was hiding," Daddy mused after he saw Roanie in town, "he looks like he lived off the land pretty well. I have to give him credit."

"You should, son, you should," Grandpa said.

Christmas in town was overwhelming and wildly uncoordinated and so bright it hurt my eyes, and I loved it. The Ladies' Civic Association ran the Christmas festival, and Aunt Irene, Mama's older sister, ran the association.

Every store owner in town put up decorations right after Thanksgiving. When I was little that meant miles of metallic garland, glowing plastic Santas, fake snow applied to the windows, and strings of lights that draped the big elm trees around the square as if some giant, addled spider had woven multicolored webs around them. At the center, on the lawn of the courthouse, sat a log manger with a life-size nativity scene cut out of plywood. If any civil libertarian had complained about the nativity being on public property, he would have been hunted down like Santa's reindeer during bow season.

On a Saturday night in the middle of December, hundreds of people congregated on the square to listen to a choir from one of the churches and watch a parade and the arrival of Santa and the official lighting of the giant cedar tree beside the courthouse steps.

We Maloneys and Delaneys got there early and commandeered a whole corner where Main Street splits to make a loop around the courthouse. I stood, warm in my nice wool coat and pants in the crisp air, jostling excitedly against my brothers and cousins, as the choir of Mt. Gilead Methodist burst into "Jingle Bells" from their platform in front of the Chamber of Commerce offices and the parade started coming toward the square, led by Aunt Irene dressed as an angel, her big wings made of chicken wire covered in white muslin. I looked behind me for no particular reason and met

Roanie's eyes. He was standing by himself in the shadows under the tin awning of the dime store. He was watching me.

I was nine, short and plump. He was fourteen, tall and lanky. His hair lay in thick, dark hanks pushed behind his ears. He looked ragged and grimy in faded jeans and a thin denim jacket with two of the brass buttons torn off. His shoulders were hunched against the night air. His eyes were cool and silvery, like the metal garland stapled to a store window behind him.

I pretended he was a young cowboy who'd wandered in off the range. Lonesome. So broke he could only spend a nickel with his silvery eyes. His grime came from dusty trails, not a dirty trailer. He had lost his buttons wrestling a rustler.

With that romantic image to bolster me, I wormed my way unnoticed to the back of the crowd and leaned against an awning post with my sweaty hands hidden in my coat pockets. He studied me with a slight wariness in his mouth and eyes. The mystery of the frontier made my heart race. "Howdy, pardner," I drawled.

He could be the stillest human being, but it was the stillness of a cat watching a bird. I'm sure he weighed the consequences of speaking to a prissy, precocious little girl who had sadistic cousins and whose attention might get him in trouble with her overprotective parents and about another two dozen righteous Maloneys who might turn around at any second and see us.

"Funny little peep," he said eventually.

"So are you," I said back. "Funny *big* peep."

"Look like a red-haired elf."

I took that to be some kind of invitation, so I inched closer. My head barely reached the chest pocket on his jacket. "I expect to grow."

He stared straight ahead. "Aw, you ain't too bad."

"You aren't either."

"Sure know how to scribble words."

I beamed at him.

The parade began. The big red hook-and-ladder truck from the fire department crept by, with a dozen volunteer firemen sitting on top. They flung candy into the crowd. A miniature bag of butterscotch drops bounced off my head and Roanie caught it. He cupped that little bag of candy in his palm, studying it, running his thumb over it as if it were gold. Then he offered it to me. "Hit you first," he said.

"Huh? You caught it. It's yours. I don't like butterscotch." Which was a lie, but I wondered if that bag of candy was the only Christmas present he'd get. He shrugged but carefully tucked the bag in his chest pocket.

"I can't see the parade," I said coyly. "Think I'll climb up on the windowsill."

"You'll fall off and bust something."

"Nah. I'll hold on to you." I grabbed his sleeve and he stiffened. He stared at my hand on his arm, then looked furtively around as if to ward off anyone who accused him of provoking me. I clambered nimbly atop the wide wooden sill of the dime store's window and perched there. I planted my hand on his left shoulder. "Now you don't move and I won't fall."

"This ain't so funny. Get down and let go."

"It's okay. It's my idea. Look!" I pointed to Aunt Irene, who was passing the corner, her chicken-wire wings bobbing wildly. "My Aunt Irene looks like a big ol' white goose!"

"Git down," Roanie said again in a low voice.

At the front of the spectators, I saw Mama's head dip. She searched for me around her legs, then pivoted quickly and looked through the crowd. When she spotted me with Roanie, her eyes widened and her mouth popped open and she stared. She tapped Daddy on the shoulder and he turned, too. I grinned at them. His red brows arched, then he rolled his eyes. Mama frowned hard. He took her by one arm and spoke closely in her ear, and she exhaled with her lips pressed together. They faced the parade again.

"See?" I chirped to Roanie, whose shoulder felt like a clump of rock under my hand. "Nobody minds."

After a moment he said darkly, "You don't know nothin'."

I thought I knew everything and started to tell him so, but the high school band marched by and drowned me out with "O Little Town of Bethlehem," followed by Uncle Dwayne and Aunt Rhonda Maloney, playing Joseph and Mary. Decent people didn't talk while Joseph and Mary were going past. Uncle Dwayne was dressed in blue sheets and looked biblical with his long red beard. Aunt Rhonda was dressed in white sheets and looked nervous, because she was trying to hold a baby-doll Jesus while balancing sideways on the small brown mule Uncle Dwayne was leading.

Next the Three Wise Men came along, riding skittish horses with their western saddles peeking out from under the Wise Men's robes. I leaned over and whispered hotly to Roanie, "I know plenty. I know you oughta tell somebody when Arlan and Harold beat up on you. They'd get in trouble."

"Rich boys ain't never gonna get in no trouble."

"They're not rich! Uncle Pete spends all his money on stock-car racing."

"You don't know nothin'," he repeated.

"You know what?" I said grandly, changing the subject. "You could cut some holly or mistletoe at the Hollow and bring it over to Mama, 'cause she uses it in her decorations, and she'd pay you with a box of homemade Christmas cookies."

"Yeah. Sure."

"She would!"

"I ain't been invited."

"I'm inviting you!"

"*You don't know nothin'.*"

"You say that one more time and I'll pull out all your hair! If you still got those nasty lice, I'll yank them out, too!" What a terrible thing I had blurted out. How thoughtless and cruel. His angry, accusing eyes shot to mine and I nearly swallowed my tongue. "I didn't mean it. Roanie, I didn't—"

My plea was cut short by a collective gasp in the crowd. I heard someone yelp, "Oh, my God, somebody stop him."

Big Roan had joined the parade.

He limped up the middle of Main Street, apelike and huge, a necklace of garland hanging down his plaid shirt and baggy overalls. Greasy dark hair stuck out from his jowly face. He sashayed and twisted his butt. His mouth was screwed down in sarcastic contempt. He staggered through the Girl Scout troop. They dropped their troop banner and scattered like green leaves in a windstorm. Big Roan plowed ahead, waving a beer bottle. "Y'all want to see Santy Claus?" he bellowed. "I'll drop my pants and y'all can kiss him on both cheeks!"

Then he threw the beer bottle. It hit one of the Wise Men's nervous horses on the rump. The horse bolted and collided with Aunt Rhonda's mule. Aunt Rhonda fell off. The mule jerked away from Uncle Dwayne and darted ahead. The high school band split down the middle, and my cousin Aster toppled over with her tuba. The mule raced by the fire truck and the firemen accidentally pelted it with a handful of candy, which made the mule accelerate. It careened past Aunt Irene and clipped one of her angel wings, and she spun sideways like an out-of-control airplane.

My feet were frozen to the windowsill. People were screaming. Daddy and some other men ran out in the street and grabbed Big Roan. He went down swinging and hit Daddy in the face.

I squealed with outrage and fear. Suddenly I realized that I was standing on the sidewalk, that Roanie had pulled me off the sill and set me there, and that I was by myself.

He'd melted into the shadows, or evaporated from shame.

The Atlanta newspapers and TV stations ran stories about the Dunderry Christmas parade. We were funny, small-town, mountain people. We were quaint. We were humiliated.

Daddy had a broken nose. Big Roan was sentenced to three months in jail. My whole family, both the Maloney and Delaney sides, swore no Sullivan would ever cross their doorsteps. I was the family goat after word leaked out about my hobnobbing with Roanie during the parade. Mama was widely advised to keep an eye on me, as if I might grow up to join the circus or vote Republican.

Cousin Vince went after Roanie full-bore this time and caught him before he could get to Ten Jumps. Uncle William signed the court order, and Aunt Bess sent him off to a state boys' home in Atlanta. Aunt Bess told everyone it was a relief to know that Roanie Sullivan would be safe and well fed during Christmas.

Grandpa was right. Some brands of kindness are hard to abide.

5

*A*unt Jane, who ran the Dunderry Library, said the finest writing grew out of terrible pain and suffering over the human condition. That must be true. I was desperate to console Roanie during the month he spent away, and the springs beneath my mattress were lined with letters, poems, and stories I'd scrawled since Christmas. I'd spent more time inside my room than out.

"Why, sure, you can send some of your writings to Roanie," Mama said carefully, when I asked her. "But I'd have to check your letters for, hmmm, spelling and grammar first."

I hadn't fallen off the turnip truck yesterday. I knew what Mama really meant. My letters would end up looking like some of the ones Josh had written home when he was in Vietnam. Full of blacked-out lines and pruned thoughts. "I'll think about it," I told her.

I got the idea for my disastrous Roanie Sullivan poem by reading books that were bad for me.

Our house was filled with books. The ones that were good for me were downstairs in the living-room bookcases, the shelves crammed with encyclopedias, agricultural textbooks, and leather-bound classics like Shakespeare and Dickens. The coffee table nearly sagged with Mama's huge picture books about art. But the *real* library was in Mama and Daddy's bedroom.

Pyramids of paperbacks were stacked on the floor under their polished, cherrywood nightstands. Daddy's side was wild territory inhabited by testy gunslingers and four-armed aliens and tough detectives who liked their gin cold and their babes hot. Mickey Spillane and Louis L'Amour. Robert Heinlein and John D. MacDonald. Man Stuff.

Mama's collection was more varied but no less woolly—Tolkien and Vonnegut, Lillian Hellman and John Le Carré, and stacks of fat, luscious historical romance novels, bursting with adventure and passion, heavy on medieval England, which Mama, proud of Grandmother Elizabeth's homeland, considered part of our family heritage.

I snuck their paperbacks into my bedroom and worked my way through the ones that were particularly shocking and not totally bewildering. So my imagination ran to hard-boiled detectives and space monsters and adventurous medieval ladies, all of whom, to my astonishment, were absolutely determined to have sex.

Sex was not spoken about in our house. It was not joked about, even by my brothers, not in front of me anyhow. Body parts and bathroom noises, yes. Merged body parts, no.

After my awful Steckem Road visit I demanded my older girl cousins explain *exactly* why everyone called it Stick 'Em in Road. They told me, and their description was so graphic, so gross, and made the whole sex thing sound so embarrassing that I looked at them shrewdly and said, "Anybody with more sense than a rock wouldn't waste their time doing *that*."

What I knew of romance I learned from watching old movies on TV and studying Mama and Daddy.

Mama had big blue eyes and a butt that was the envy of every woman in town—shaped like an upside-down Valentine heart. Daddy liked her fanny so much, he patted it whenever he thought nobody was looking. He would give her a wicked grin when we caught them doing stuff like that.

Daddy was one of those nearly fat-free men with ropy muscles and hands that could bend steel cable. He had long, lean arms and skinny legs, and he carried what little fat he did have in his belly, a hard little mound above his belt buckle. I would thump it. It felt like the rind of a ripe watermelon. Mama called it his spare gas tank, and she liked to rub it. When he was sitting at the table, Mama would walk by and trail one fingertip through the soft hair at the base of his neck.

The contrast was clear—sex was something sweaty and naked and embarrassing, not to mention highly regulated and often forbidden, but romance was lovely and polite and involved admiring each other with your clothes on.

So that was the kind of romance Roanie and I would have. I resolved to explain my intentions with a series of poems led by a polite ode to his worthiness.

I taped the first poem to our refrigerator in a prominent spot between the Farmers' Bulletin calendar and a snapshot of Mama, Daddy, me, and my brothers in the lobby of the Atlanta Civic Center when we went to see the touring company show of The Sound of Music.

> Roanie, Roanie,
> He's no phony,
> Got a pair of big cojones.
> He'd fit right in
> With us Maloneys.
>   by Claire

Cojones was a term I'd discovered in one of Daddy's detective novels. I judged its impressive power by the way it was used in the book. I waited to see who'd notice the poem first.

Aunt Arnetta was as nearsighted as a mole. She wore thick glasses with bright orange rims or prescription sunglasses with Day-Glo blue reflecting lenses, which made her look like a big, blue bottle fly. She was a hefty woman, a no-nonsense woman with a fashion sense that favored brown with hints of more brown.

Her allegiances were rock-hard: God, church, children, job, bingo. I think thieving, weasel-inclined Carlton was an embarrassment to her, and probably the reason she was so hard on everyone else.

Uncle Eugene, who owned a local car dealership and was umbilically tied to a TV set in his spare time, was way down on her list of priorities. She worked for a state agricultural agency as a home economics expert.

She had come over to drop off a new brochure on no-salt cooking, because Mama was worried about Great-Gran's blood pressure. Aunt Arnetta tromped into the kitchen, where I was lounging at the table pretending to read a Reader's Digest. It was a freezing day in early January, and a streak of cold air seemed to follow her across the warm room.

"You'll ruin your eyes holding that magazine up like that," she said to me. "You're a bookworm. You better practice good habits, or you'll end up with bad eyes and stooped shoulders."

"Oh. Okay. Yes, ma'am."

She breezed past me, and I was afraid she'd go through to the back hall and miss the refrigerator completely. But she zoomed in on my poem like a radar and halted. I watched her lean forward. She leaned back. She took off her glasses and cleaned them on the lapel of her brown blazer, put them back on, and leaned forward. She quivered.

"CLAIRE KARLEEN MALONEY, what is this filth?"

Aunt Arnetta tore my poem off the refrigerator and whirled around and slapped the paper on the table. My mouth went dry. "It's a poem!"

"You're writing poetry about . . . about Roanie Sullivan's *privates?*"

"What? Huh? No, it's about his cojones!"

"Privates," Aunt Arnetta repeated, shaking the paper under my nose. "Male organs. Gonads. Testicles." Her voice rose on each word, and when I stared at her in blank horror, she finished loudly, "His *balls.*"

I shrieked. *That's* what the men in Daddy's books meant when they said somebody had big cojones? "I didn't know! I thought cojones were *muscles! Big, strong muscles.*"

"Oh, I'll just bet you didn't know! A smart girl like you! Let me tell you something, Missy Claire, if you lay down with pigs, you'll get up muddy! You don't have the good sense to keep your distance from that lowlife Roanie Sullivan! Well, I'll just put the lid on this pot right now! I'm telling your mama and daddy that that junkyard dirty-fingered hillbilly white-trash troublemaker is inspiring you to write dirty rhymes!"

I leaped up. "No! It isn't his fault! I read about cojones in a book!"

"There's not one book in this house that discusses the male privates in those sorts of lewd terms!"

Aunt Arnetta had no idea. "It's not Roanie's fault! Don't say anything to Mama and Daddy! I was just trying to show everybody what I think about him!"

"You're sweet on him! Lord have *mercy*, this is worse than I thought! Nine years old and running after white trash! Claire Karleen Maloney, you put that boy out of your mind! There's no way on God's green earth this family'll ever let you take after that Sullivan boy! He's bred to be thick-blooded and mushy-minded, and he won't ever amount to a hill of beans! In another few years he'll be lyin' around on welfare breeding a shack full of younguns with some whiffle-tailed girl! Your folks'd just as soon lock you in the cellar and throw away the key than see you fall under his filthy-mouthed spell!"

By the time she finished I was over my shock and well on the way to a tantrum. Never talk back to your elders. Never. I knew that, but since I had a ruined reputation now anyway, I might as well go whole hog. "Go worry about Uncle Eugene's cojones!" I yelled. "Daddy says he can't find 'em anymore because you keep 'em in your jewelry box!"

No tomato ever turned redder than Aunt Arnetta's face at that moment. She stuttered something and her eyes gleamed with magnified tears behind her glasses. She slapped the no-salt brochure down on the table and went to look for Daddy.

Oh, what a mess. I got lectured on all sides and punished—I lost my weekly allowance for the rest of the month and had extra work added to my regular household chores—but worse, everyone decided I had absolutely no sense at all where Roanie was concerned.

To top things off, Aunt Arnetta was mad at Daddy for months. Daddy told me not to *ever* repeat anything he said about her and Uncle Eugene again. Uncle Eugene's missing balls—like my devotion to Roanie—was the kind of embarrassment the family swept under the rug.

I took all my writings outside and buried them behind one of the barns. A person can never be too careful with her privates. Especially if she isn't certain what they are.

Roanie came home finally, along with Big Roan. We heard Big Roan stayed down on Steckem Road with Daisy McClendon most of the time. That's why Aunt Dockey and Mama didn't go over there the next Easter. They sent Uncle Bert and Daddy to deliver the Easter baskets.

I don't know what kind of Easter Roanie had that spring; Hop and Evan saw him at school and said he was even more of a loner than before. I tried to talk Hop into giving him my Easter rabbit and a note I'd written; I wanted him to know I was sorry Aunt Bess had sent him away and that she'd meant well by it. But Hop said the family doghouse only had room for one Maloney at a time and he didn't want to be stuck in it, too.

Hop did try to talk to Roanie for me eventually, but Roanie just stared at him as if he were an enemy.

I guess, at that point, we were all enemies to Roanie.

That September I finally learned, firsthand, why Sean and Bridget Maloney hadn't had enough teeth for a smile. Love is hard on a smile. It will knock your teeth right out.

Our whole clan went to every high school football game but especially to the first one of each autumn. That night was one of those delicious, barely past summer evenings when the warm air has spicy currents in it and the moon rises full and ripe over trees flecked with the first few hints of gold and red.

Along with related families, such as the Kehoes and the O'Briens, Maloneys and Delaneys provided about half the team, plus a good portion of the marching band and the cheerleading squad, too. Josh had been a star quarterback in his day, and Brady a pretty fair place-kicker. Now Hop was a tackle, Evan was a tackle, Harold and Arlan were tackles. Maloney and Delaney boys were part of a long tradition of running over people.

The Dunderry High School stadium squatted solidly on the side of a hill facing a football field ringed with a slate-gray running track. Huge moths swarmed in the hot white beams of overhead lights and danced in the glow from the concession stand beyond the track's far turn.

It didn't take light to draw me down to the track. The lure of candy would do it. I was a moth after sugar. I flew with a small, flashy gang—we thought our wings were five feet wide and bright orange, but I'm sure to everyone else we were just giggling, nickel-size flutter-bys.

"I'm going to be a cheerleader when I get to high school," Rebecca announced as we sashayed along.

"Me, too," Violet chimed.

"Not me, I don't care," I said. I'd already flunked out of the small-fry-league cheerleading tryouts three years in a row. Something about wanting to add new moves each time I performed a routine. Cheerleading was serious, regimented business. They would take away your pompom license if you improvised.

"I'm not gonna be a cheerleader." Tula Tobbler spoke up firmly. "I'm gonna be Alvin's manager."

We all looked askance at Tula. Elfish, with skin the color of chocolate, she stared back at us from under a stiffly styled cap of black hair with bangs and curved-under ends that wouldn't so much as flex, even in a strong wind. No Afros for Tobbler children, because Tobblers were big on conservative traditions, just like Maloneys.

In fact, though nobody talked about it, Tobblers *were* Maloneys. The doors to our two worlds might be connected by no more than a single hinge, but we were connected nonetheless. When people looked at a dark-skinned Tobbler, they might not see even the hint of it, but he was there, deep in the Tobbler past, a great-great-uncle of mine, a red-haired, pale-skinned Maloney.

A roar came up from the packed stadium behind us and the band blared the Dunderry Panthers' fight song, and we all turned to watch an enormous, long-legged receiver spike the ball in the end zone.

Alvin Tobbler, Tula's brother, was the brightest football star, black or white, ever to carry a pigskin across green Dunderry grass. "See?" Tula said, grinning. "Alvin's gonna play for a big college and then he's gonna play for the grown-up teams one day. And he's gonna be rich. And I'm gonna tell him what to do with his money."

We all nodded solemnly and walked on. Any dream was possible for Tobblers, because they had some mix of African and Irish magic in them, and if you doubted that, all you had to do was go where we were headed and see it up close.

Next to the concession stand, Tula and Alvin's grandpa worked at a small card table piled with apples. This was something he volunteered to do at every game, his way of cheering for Alvin.

Boss Tobbler was an apple man. His orchards stretched across stair-stepped hills outside town, and every Tobbler in the county worked for him in the autumn, harvesting apples and selling crates filled with apples from a roadside warehouse, plus every homemade apple concoction known to humankind—cider and fried pies and bread and jellies and cookies, to name a few—there was no end to the Tobbler apple kingdom.

His first name really was Boss. He was short and muscular, with patches of tight gray hair on his thick forearms but not a speck on his head, and when he took off the limp fedora he wore year-round, his scalp gleamed like an eight ball. He'd been a sergeant in a black platoon during World War II, he'd won a Purple Heart, he had a year of divinity-school training, and he was a deacon of Dunderry's African Methodist Church.

He and Grandpa Joseph had hunted and fished together since they were boys. They'd both served in the war, they both hated stupidity and meanness, and they were both as sweet as honey, once a person got inside their hive. Grandpa called him Boss T. Everybody else called him Mr. Tobbler, with an emphasis on the mister.

A fantastic aroma rose from the apples and the melted caramel bubbling in a stew pot on a hot plate. A small crowd watched, awed, and as we sidled up to its edges, a familiar sense of awe settled on us, too.

Mr. Tobbler rolled the crank handle on an apple corer. Curlicues of red apple peel dropped to a mountain of apple peelings that covered his shoes and climbed halfway up his pants legs. He popped the peeled apple from the corer's clamps, deftly sliced it into pieces with a razor-sharp paring knife, spread the slices on a paper plate, and dribbled liquid caramel over them.

Then he presented the plate to a waiting member of his audience, a man who stood way back as he tucked a dollar into the coffee can on a stool in front of the table, a man who reached for his caramel apple very carefully, because nobody had the courage to stand inside Boss Tobbler's circle of helpers.

Hundreds of yellow jackets flitted around him. They crept over the apple peelings, they swarmed lazily around the corer, they perched on his shirt and his hands, they clung to the wiry tufts of brindled hair on his thick forearms.

But they didn't sting him. They never did, according to local legend. He'd made some kind of magical, dignified peace with the small, hurtful creatures and they knew it. And they respected him.

"Granddaddy," Tula said softly. "Will you fix us some candied apples?"

Mr. Tobbler nodded solemnly. "But I'm not gonna let y'all stand back like babies anymore." He slid a fresh apple into the coring vise. The yellow jackets hovered over his hands like the tiniest fairies. "Y'all are half grown now. You know there's nothing to be afraid of. Fear is what stings. Come on. Come close."

Rebecca and Violet refused to budge, but I edged forward and Tula did, too, because I guess she knew we had a double dose of magic between us. I moved in slow motion, my heart in my throat. Yellow jackets feathered our wrists, our hands; one lit on the nail of my forefinger and sat there calmly, rubbing its head with one tiny front leg, like a cat cleaning itself.

I expected to feel needle-hot stingers at any second.

"Now there, they know you got good hearts," Mr. Tobbler whispered as he handed us two filled plates. "They know you'll share with 'em." Victory! I sighed with relief as we backed away. My personal yellow jackets left my skin delicately.

"Wow," Rebecca murmured.

Violet had her hands clamped to her mouth. She just stared at us. We said our thank-yous and dropped two dollars in the can because Mr. Tobbler donated the money to the school's booster club.

And then the four of us retreated hurriedly. Even Tula looked happier once we were out of yellow-jacket range. "No problem," I lied proudly. "I wasn't scared a bit." I popped a caramel-soaked slice of apple into my mouth, chewed it, swallowed, and looked around to see who might be admiring me.

There was Roanie, standing just inside the shadows on the side of the grassy hill above the concession stand.

I halted. Whether his gaze was admiring or not, I couldn't tell. I could never quite tell what he was thinking behind those gray wolf eyes, his scrutiny as sharp as a ten-penny nail. He stood with his hands in his pockets, one long leg angled out to the side. *I like the shadows, I want to be right here, don't mess with me,* everything about him warned.

At fourteen he was as tall as a grown man and about as wide as a board. He was stuck with cast-off jeans and work shirts from the Dunderry Civitans Thrift Shop, and his enormous, patched, red-flannel shirt was instantly familiar. Grandma Dottie had donated a bag of Grandpa's work shirts to the Civitans. It looked like a tent on Roanie, but I considered it a good sign.

"Come on, *come on,* Claire," Violet urged nervously, tugging at my arm.

"Why's he looking at you?" Rebecca whispered. "He oughta know better than to look at a Maloney."

"He knows I'm not gonna sting him."

Tula grabbed my sleeve. "He sure might sting *you.*"

But I knew that wasn't true. Hypnotized, I climbed the hill toward him, every step catching the breath out of my lungs. Roanie straightened, his head came up, and he frowned.

Rebecca called, "We better go tell Aunt Marybeth! Claire? We gotta tell your mama!" From the corner of one eye I glimpsed her and Violet and Tula take off toward the stadium.

"Get on back," Roanie called out, glancing around uncomfortably. His voice was deeper than I remembered from Christmas. I wanted to shout, *I grew two inches over the summer,* but my mouth wouldn't work. "Git," he ordered firmly. "Little peep, I don't want no trouble."

My heart broke. I stopped. When his expression grew darker, I spouted, "I'm not scared of yellow jackets. How come you're scared of *me?*"

"It ain't right, you chasin' after me," he said gruffly. "You're just a half-pint. You ain't got no idea how it looks. Go on."

"You're not so old!"

"Hey!" a voice called behind me. I turned. My cousin Carlton, who was a senior that year, so big and fleshy even the football coaches had given up trying to sweat a game out of him, was glaring up the hill at us. A half-dozen of his cronies were with him. They weren't football-burly types either, but they were big enough, and mean enough, in a crowd.

"Get down here, Claire," Carlton yelled. "Leave that white trash alone."

Nothing, no one, could have changed my mind then. I plowed uphill and planted myself beside Roanie. I realized later, when I replayed the whole mess in my mind, that the instant I stepped out of the light and into the shadows with him, he went on guard in some new way, braced against the world beyond us both, his hands clenching by his sides.

"I said . . ." Carlton tilted his head back and raised his voice, "leave that white *nigger* alone!"

Carlton uttered the word that separated one small part of the Maloneys from the rest. A word so petty and disreputable that it wasn't allowed in our house, not ever, for any reason. It was a fighting word to whomever got hit with it, black or white, and Grandpa always told my brothers and me that if we ever used it toward any soul, we could never look the Tobblers straight in the eye again.

I dropped my plate. "You gonna take that? *You go knock the chickenshit out of him!* I'll tell everybody why you had to do it."

"Get out of here, Claire." Roanie's voice was low, dangerous. The look he focused on Carlton could raise bruises. "I pick my own fights."

"But . . . but you *can't* let him call you names like that! You never let anybody do that! What's the matter with you? Go on! Smack him! I know you're not scared of *Carlton*. You're not scared of anybody!"

What a little idiot I was, weighing my pride against his, not understanding what I added to his misery. I don't know what he would have done—probably just turned and walked away—if Carlton hadn't suddenly strode up the hill. "I swear," Carlton hissed at me, "at the rate you're going you'll end up down on Steckem Road with the McClendon whores."

He grabbed my arm. I lurched back and kicked him in the shins. He gasped a shocked sound. *Whaaaf*. Then he shook me by the arm, hard, just once.

Because then Roanie was on him.

There are boxing fights and there are dog fights. One is careful and cushioned and mostly sane, the other is a wild, tearing, close-in jumble of fingers that claw into soft spots and bare-knuckled fists that land with cracking thuds.

That's what Roanie gave him, driving him down the hill, Carlton falling, trying to punch back, yelling. If it had ended there and ended quickly, it would have been as brutally neat as a big dog snapping at a fly. But Carlton's slack-jawed friends joined in. One on one they'd never have had the guts to tangle with Roanie, but they had enough courage among them to gang up on him.

So there he was, struggling inside a circle of swinging fists and knees, his head jerking back as a fist slammed into his jaw, his body bowing forward as someone punched him in the stomach. Grown men ran toward us, yelling at the boys to stop it. Mr. Tobbler bolted from behind his table, thick arms pumping, yellow jackets parting like a cloud around him.

But I couldn't wait for reinforcements, Roanie was getting clobbered. I launched myself down the hill, scrambled atop Carlton's bucking back, and sank my teeth into the nape of his neck. He squealed like a hog and shook me off.

I fell under the moving pistons of arms and legs, a hard shoe stepped on my hand, and then, as I tried to get up, Carlton drew back his fist and my eyes crossed as my whole horizon filled with fist, just before it crashed into my mouth.

I woke up with my head in Mama's lap, Mama yelling for Daddy to get a cup of ice, and blood streaming down my chin. I was dimly aware of a large crowd around us and of the band playing the fight song again, somewhere where people were still watching the football game.

I lay there on the shadowy hillside, addled, shivering, and moaning, my mouth on fire. Mama dabbed my lips with the hem of her skirt. Roanie, I thought woozily. What happened to Roanie? I looked up into Grandma's calm blue eyes. "Marybeth," she said, "she's lost a couple of teeth."

"Oh, my lord!" Mama cried.

Teeth? Something like hard pellets tickled the back of my throat. I retched onto Mama's lap like a cat coughing up a hairball. Two bloody specks fell out. I touched my tongue to the aching top gap in my once-precious smile, went "Aaaaah," with embarrassment, and collapsed on my back.

Grandma plucked my teeth up and wrapped them in a handkerchief. "They'll go back in," she promised Mama.

"Oh, her smile, her smile," Mama cried. "When I get my hands on Roanie Sullivan—"

"Woanie!" That was the best pronunciation I could manage, as I struggled upright.

I saw him not far away, hunched on his knees with his arms braced on the ground in front of him. Grandpa and Mr. Tobbler squatted beside him, holding his shirttail—the tail of Grandpa Maloney's own cast-off flannel shirt—to his mouth. Blood soaked it, trickling slowly down his chin and falling in terrible, bright red splatters on the legs of his jeans.

Grandpa and Mr. Tobbler were talking to each other in low, grim voices, nodding like horses pulling a heavy load in tandem. Roanie lifted his head and looked at me. Above the shirt's crimson material, inside the grimace of his lips, I saw the dark gap where his snaggletooth had been.

So we'd both had the smile knocked out of us.

"Your toof," I said sadly. Half fainting and hurting from the nose down, I opened my mouth and showed him my more humiliating gap, but the horror in his eyes shut my mouth and brought tears down my face. "Woanie dida dah anythang wong," I announced loudly. "Carltoh dah it."

Mama dragged me against her and wrapped her arms around me. "Hush, honey, hush."

Daddy ran up the hill, dropped to his heels, and thrust a paper cup filled with ice into Mama's hands. His face was as red as his hair; his eyes flashed furiously. "Dathy," I begged, "Carltoh started it. He gwaffed me. Woanie hif him. Carltoh knoffed me in tha mouf."

"Hush," he soothed. "You're not making any sense, baby."

Daddy pivoted toward Roanie and snatched him by one shoulder. "I don't care how bad hurt you are. You tell me why you got my daughter into a brawl, or I'll break what's left of you."

"Dathy!"

Roanie's eyes flared. He shook his head. Flecks of blood flew everywhere. He wheezed, banding one long arm around his ribs. "I ain't never gonna let nobody hurt her—"

"Not let anybody hurt her?" Daddy shouted. "What do you think you just did to her?"

"Son, back off," Grandpa ordered. "It wasn't Roanie's fault. It was Carlton's, goddammit. Boss T saw the whole thing."

Daddy sat back, his mouth flat with concentration. "That right, Mr. Tobbler?"

Mr. Tobbler barked out the truth. He told him about Carlton's insults, and when he said the words "white nigger," laying them off his tongue with the military dignity of an old warrior, Daddy's shoulders drew back. "That Carlton, he punched your little girl in the mouth," Mr. Tobbler added grimly. "He did it deliberately, too. Holt Maloney, you want to break heads, go break your nephew's."

I felt Mama catch her breath. She and Daddy looked at Roanie. Daddy lifted a hand toward him. "I . . . I . . . listen, boy, I—"

But Roanie shrugged away, tried to get up but sat down hard, wiping his mouth with one hand, the other clamping harder across his ribs. He swayed. "None of you got to worry about Claire when I'm around. I ain't gonna hurt her somehow. I know what you been thinkin' and I ain't that way. I wouldn't a-laid a hand on nobody 'cept Carlton was hurtin' her. I . . . I won't let nothin' bad happen to her. Not ever. No matter how it looks to y'all."

"*Woanie*," I mewled.

He tried to get up again. He couldn't without help.

Daddy took him by one arm, Grandpa by the other. Help was what he got, whether he wanted it or not.

Hurt, distrustful, and trapped, he had no choice. Neither did I.

So that was the night, that warm, yellow-jacket-charmed night in September, when Roanie began to be part of my family.

We were taken to my Uncle Mallory Delaney's office. The doctor. Nothing wrong with me except busted teeth and some bruised fingers, nothing wrong with Roanie except a busted tooth and a cracked rib.

Then, at Uncle Cully Maloney's office—the dentist—my two teeth were painfully cemented back in place, and Roanie's gap was measured for a permanent bridge.

Finally, we took Roanie under our own roof, at the farm. Mama put him in a spare bedroom. Daddy tried to phone Big Roan but couldn't find him, either at the Hollow or at Steckem Road. He was off drinking somewhere. Big Roan wouldn't have cared, anyway.

There was a haunted, awestruck glimmer in Roanie's eyes that night. It wasn't easy for him to trust good luck or Maloneys. In the morning, the bedroom window was open and Roanie was gone.

I took a strong leap of faith myself and told Mama and Daddy about Ten Jumps. Daddy and Sheriff Vince caught him there.

$\mathcal{C}$arlton was in the hospital in Gainesville with a broken jaw, a few stitches here and there, an ice pack on his testicles, and a bandage on the back of his neck.

Aunt Arnetta was determined to punish Roanie. She filed charges.

"I'm sorry," I heard Sheriff Vince tell Mama and Daddy that night. "I caught him, and I've got a job to do as sheriff. He just can't run around loose anymore. Big Roan doesn't want to take responsibility for him, and there's nowhere for the boy to go."

"Bring him here," Daddy said. "We'll take him in."

Faith. It had worked. I was awestruck.

"Holt, I won't have that boy around Claire!" I heard Mama from my crouched vantage point outside the living room's double oak doors, despite their being closed. Hop and Evan squatted beside me like big, redheaded chimps. We traded spooked glances. I shivered and leaned closer to the crack between the doors. "We still don't know much about him," Mama went on. "Claire has some kind of foolish crush on him. Oh, God, Holt, what if he's a pervert?"

"Then he'll be a *dead* pervert," Daddy answered firmly. There was a long silence punctuated by Mama's sniffling sounds. I peered through the crack and saw Daddy hugging her. Then he said, "If I thought there was anything sinister about the boy, I wouldn't let him set a foot on the place."

"How do you *know* there isn't?"

"Because he's never laid a hand on any of the girls at school. Never spoken badly to any of 'em. That's what Evan and Hop say."

Evan whispered behind me, "Yeah, but they won't go near him. He stinks."

"*You shut up,*" I whispered back.

"There are other females besides the ones at school," Mama said. "There're those McClendons."

"Roanie doesn't hang around his daddy's women. Believe me, I'd have heard about it. Sex talk travels, Marybeth."

"Uh-huh. I guess you and your brothers discuss something besides the weather during those Saturday gabfests at the feed store."

"Hoo! I'd like to be a fly on the wall when you and your sisters get together. My ears'd burn and fall off."

More silence. My face felt red-hot. Sex talk. Burning ears. Perverts. My feelings for Roanie. It wasn't fair to connect all that together. I knew Roanie was no pervert, because I had a clear definition of what one was. Long before I was born, Great-Uncle Victor Delaney moved away to Ohio and married some woman the family never got to meet. Great-Uncle Victor died young and left her all his money, and decades later, when she got old and sick, a doctor undressed her and found out she was a *man.*

Great-Uncle Victor was a *pervert,* everyone said. Or else really dumb.

"What're we going to say to the family?" Mama's voice again. Calm or resigned. "Irene still cries when anybody mentions the Christmas parade."

"Don't visit the sins of the father on the son. That's what we'll say. Roanie can't help what he comes from. I feel bad for the boy. I think you do, too, hmmm?"

"Of course I do."

"We should have stepped in when he was born, Marybeth. Or when his mother died." Daddy's voice was low and serious. "All that noble talk about Big Roan having a right to raise his own son—hell, Big Roan hasn't *raised* him, it's a miracle the boy's not a thief or a dope addict. I say the boy's got something good inside him, something strong enough to give him a chance. We can't turn our backs on him again."

"But, Holt, no child grows up around that kind of meanness without learning meanness himself. He's got no solid foundation. Push him and he might fall the wrong way. I just don't want Claire in his path if he does."

"Claire's a little girl. *He's* fourteen years old. He's got bigger fish to fry. Good lord, hon, when a boy's that age he's looking *up* the female ladder, not down it. I can't see any sign that Claire's anything but a pesky little kitten to him. Same way she is to Evan and Hop."

Pesky little kitten. I was crushed.

"Besides," Daddy continued, "I'll read him the riot act. 'You act like a gentleman around the ladies on this farm, or I'll break your neck.'"

"All right," Mama answered, sounding tired. "But I'm going to figure out some way to clean him up. Start with the outside and work my way in."

I gasped. This was unbelievable. This was wonderful. This would split the responsibility for Roanie among me and Mama and Daddy, because what they'd offered would upset every Maloney and Delaney in the county.

"Claire, Claire, what do you look so worried about?" Mama asked that night as she sat beside me on my pink-ruffled bed in my pink-ruffled bedroom.

"Mama, Roanie isn't a pervert."

"Somebody," Mama said darkly, "was listening outside the living-room doors."

"I know he'll do fine. Big Roan can't take him back, can he?"

Mama looked at me sadly. "Big Roan said he doesn't care where Roanie lives as long as Roanie sends him some money."

A mixture of sorrow and relief burst from me in a long breath. "Big Roan doesn't want him," I said. "He never wanted him." I perked up. "But I do!"

"When Roanie gets here," Mama said slowly, eyeing me, "I expect you to treat him the same way you treat your brothers."

I whooped. Brother, my hind foot, I thought, but didn't say it. I told her about Roanie knocking Neely Tipton down for me when I was just a kid. She mulled it over with a troubled expression in her blue eyes, one hand stroking the tiny gray streak in the swath of hair splayed over the shoulder of her silk robe. She had Delaney hair, glossy brown, fine and straight, and she wore it pulled back with headbands or tiny barrettes. She was deceptively delicate-looking, like her mother, and loved delicate things. She always wore a pair of diamond-stud earrings Daddy had given her, even when she was dressed in jeans and an old T-shirt, hoisting heavy pots in the kitchen or digging in her flower beds or herb garden.

"Claire," she said finally, gently. "What is it you see in him?"

"He's my project. Nobody else likes him. He's different. So am I."

"How are you different?"

"I gotta move all the time. I gotta think. Everybody else is like, Well, that's just the way things are. But why are things one way and not the other? Why are there so many rules?"

"So decent people can live together in peace."

"Why? We've got lots of peace around here. More than enough."

Mama sighed. She bent over me and smoothed the backs of her work-hardened fingers down my cheek. "Try to understand something. You're a very pretty little girl. You're a *perfect* little girl, and before long you'll be a perfect young lady. And I want you to grow up that way and go to college and get some perfect job and marry a perfect man and have perfect little babies. Now that's a good row to hoe, but it's a straight row, and you can't look away from it for a minute."

"You think I wanta marry Roanie? Ugh! I don't want to marry any-body! I don't even want to kiss a boy!"

"Okay." She smiled and blew out a long breath. "That's fine with me."

"So don't worry about me liking Roanie *that* way. I just think we can hoe along together."

That set her back. She stared at the pink-carpeted floor for a while, rubbing her jaw and sighing. She cleared her throat and looked at me solemnly. "He's hoeing in a whole separate garden."

"Huh?"

"You'll understand when you're older." Frowning, she kissed me good night and turned out the light.

I dreamed fitfully. Hoes. Rows. Gardens. Roanie. And how I would not act like a girl anymore, perfect or otherwise.

He was coming to live with us. That was all that mattered.

I had plans.

Daddy and Grandpa went up to town the next morning and got Roanie out of jail. Then they gathered up his belongings at the Hollow and brought him to me.

I'm sure that's not how they looked at it, but that's how I saw the situation.

Coming back to Maloney territory as our charity case must have been the hardest thing he'd ever done. When I spotted Daddy's car from my writing roost in the loft of the main barn, I nearly fell over the loft stairs hurrying to get down. Roanie eased out of the car and stood defensively at the end of the dirt drive between the front fields, where the hired hands were loading bright orange pumpkins onto the tractor wagons. He stood with purpose; he stood with stern self-respect, as if he expected even the pumpkins to carve themselves into gaping jack-o'-lanterns as he passed by.

I brushed hay from my jeans and sweater with one hand, checked my sore, reset teeth, and picked up a curly-tailed black puppy as I ran out of the barn. Puppies are always good conversation starters.

Mama strode from the house and cut me off. Daddy and Grandpa nudged Roanie forward, but he stopped again under our oak trees, looking grim and uncertain. Our fat dogs gathered around as if he were a pork haunch at a barbecue. I planted myself beside Daddy and looked at Roanie squarely. But he refused to look at me.

"If you live in my house," Mama said, "you live by my rules."

"I come to say . . ." Roanie cleared his throat. "I come to say I ain't gonna take no charity."

"Glad to hear it. What else have you got to say?"

"Y'all paid for the doctor. Y'all paid for my tooth. Now I gotta live here. But I *ain't gonna take no charity.*"

"All right," Mama retorted. "How are you going to pay us back then?"

My heart was beating so fast, I thought I'd explode. A red stain crept up Roanie's face. "I'll figure out something."

"I've got twenty bucks!" I announced. "You can have it!"

"Claire," Daddy said in a low voice. He pointed a warning finger at me.

"But, Daddy—"

"I . . . I'll do some work for you, Mr. Maloney. Anything you want. However much it takes."

Daddy sank his hands in his pockets and studied the ground. He squinted in thought and pursed his lips. I wound two fingers in one of his belt loops and tugged like a hungry trout. Daddy studied me somberly, then looked at Roanie. "You'll stay in school, you'll do chores just like Claire and my boys, and you'll work like a field hand. And I'll pay you a salary. You'll earn your keep."

I searched Roanie's face desperately. He looked stunned.

"Well?" Daddy said.

"Yeah. Yessir. You bet. Sure. Thanks."

"It's hard work. And I don't stand for any excuses."

"You won't get no excuses from me. I swear to God."

"Don't swear," Mama ordered. "That's my first rule."

"Yes, ma'am!"

For the second time in my life I saw a smidgen of real satisfaction in Roanie's eyes. The first had been when he looked at me after knocking Neely Tipton down.

I waved him toward our grand, friendly house. When I set the puppy down, it ran straight to Roanie, tail wagging. "I *said* you'd be welcome!" I bellowed. I had a long memory regarding arguments. A Maloney family trait.

The expression in his eyes was half tragic, half hopeful. He just looked at me and shrugged.

Roanie came from the Hollow with so little. Just himself, a box with his clothes and shoes in it, a grainy snapshot of his mother, and a yellowed paperback book with lots of folded page tips. Mama gave him a bedroom downstairs, next to Hop's and Evan's rooms. She told him he'd share the bathroom across the hall with them. Clean up after himself, wash the tub, the same as them.

Before he set up housekeeping I left a little wicker basket on his bed, with a bottle of bubble bath in it and two of my personal soaps, which were shaped and smelled like rosebuds. It was my last chance to go into his room. I'd been forbidden to hang out there, the same as if he were a brother.

This rule had been established after I unearthed a stack of *Playboy* magazines under Hop's bed and an even bigger stack under Evan's. Whew. Naked women and jokes I didn't understand. I was disgusted and enthralled for hours until Mama caught me. The *Playboys* went in the fireplace, Hop and Evan were condemned to scrub every toilet in the house for a month, and they swore they'd hang me by my hair if I ever set foot in their rooms again.

So I loitered respectfully outside the door to Roanie's room, watching him carefully place his ratty, cast-off clothes in the closet and the dresser, and my attention zoomed in on a book lying on the bed's quilt. *The Power of Positive Thinking* by Norman Vincent Peale.

"Is that your special book?" I asked.

"Yeah."

"You like to read?"

"Yeah."

"Good! We've got lots of books. We read all the time. You can have all the books you want around here."

"I know."

"So what's in that book of yours?"

"Deep thoughts."

"Like what?"

"Like 'Always look on the bright side.'"

"Of what?"

"Everything."

"Good. Now you're on the bright side, aren't you?"

He stopped what he was doing, a pair of cracked leather shoes hanging in one of his hands, an oversize T-shirt with a torn sleeve hanging in the other. His face was pale, with blotches of red on his cheeks. I noticed the fine dark hair on his jaw and upper lip. "My old man is something else, ain't he?" His voice was gruff. "Real concerned."

"Are you sorry? Did you want to stay with him?"

"No."

"Did you want to go on hidin' at Ten Jumps?"

"No."

"Okay. Then you're gonna live with us. Okay? *Okay?*"

"Yeah."

"Forever."

He shook his head. "I don't know about that, Claire. I don't know how to live with nice people. I don't want to make no mistakes." He paused. "I ain't got noplace else to go if this don't work."

"Hey, boy," I said with tears catching at my voice. "You're doing fine. I'll help you! You can ask me any questions you want to! I'll help you figure out how to act!"

"Little peep," he tossed back.

"Smile," I ordered.

He did, slowly, awkwardly, because he hadn't had much practice. He had his new tooth, and it was a fine tooth, straight and even with the rest. I studied him and tried to appear nonchalant. He looked great. Handsome. He had a better smile than Donny Osmond and all four of the Bee Gees put together. "Yeah, you look okay," I pronounced casually. "Don't get a big head over it." But I was so pleased I couldn't say another word.

Hop and Evan hooted when they found my bubble bath and soaps beside the can of manly Boraxo on their bathroom shelf. But when Roanie came to dinner he was suddenly, sparklingly clean. He'd cut his hair, and his cheeks looked as if he'd scrubbed them nearly raw. He had a rose scent, as if he'd washed himself, clothes and all, in girl soap.

He sat across from me at the dining-room table, stiff, quiet, his gray eyes alert and amazed. He handled the white stoneware dishes—which were just everyday china—as if breaking a piece would send him straight to hell. He laid one of Mama's red-checked cloth napkins on his lap, watching me carefully as I placed mine on my lap, as if taking his cue. I think if I'd tied the napkin around my head like a scarf, he'd have done the same.

I learned later that the water pipes to his daddy's trailer had frozen and burst one winter years before and Big Roan never fixed them. He'd slapped together a wooden outhouse behind the trailer. Big Roan didn't have a washing machine, either, and he'd been barred from the laundromat in town since the time he was caught pilfering socks from someone else's dryer.

So I finally knew the reason behind Roanie's shameful appearance and bad odor. That night I sat guiltily in my warm bubble bath in my personal boudoir with its frilly pink trimmings and heat lamp, thinking about all he'd been through.

If cleanliness was next to godliness, Roanie wanted us to know he'd christened himself.

By the way, he and I named the puppy. I think that puppy recognized the kindness in him the way I did. It was his dog, I decided. I asked Daddy for an okay and he agreed. So Roanie and I named it General Patton. Not Patton, not General, but General Patton. We conferred a high rank and a tough pedigree on it.

It was Roanie's dog, after all.

$\mathcal{N}$ever argue with a drunk, a skunk, or a redheaded woman, Grandpa always said, probably because most Maloney women were redheads and he liked to annoy them. But I was proud to be taken seriously.

Now I had Roanie. Now he was safe, like a caterpillar wrapped in a cocoon. All he needed was peace and quiet and time to grow a set of wings. My poetic comparisons stopped there. I couldn't imagine my personal, homegrown butterfly ever deserting me for open sky.

I loved my folks and my brothers and my grandfolks for treating Roanie with respect, because I could see him absorb our respect like a sponge. Mama was so good with him.

"Roanie! Would you do me a favor? Go through this closet and see if there's anything you can wear. Every time Josh and Brady come home from school they leave behind so much it looks like we own stock in a department store. This closet's gonna explode if you don't clean it out."

"Roanie! You need a wristwatch. Here, try this one on. I bought it for Hop, but he doesn't like the band. If you like it, you keep it."

Daddy and Grandpa supervised other parts of his education, talking to him about manly things like tractor maintenance and how to barbecue pork ribs just right. Hop and Evan teased him the way boys do. *Man, you look ugly today.* And *Don't let Claire boss you around. She'll have you wearin' pink sweatsocks.* At first his mouth tightened and he stared at Hop and Evan angrily, but then he began to realize they liked him. Boys insult one another to prove they're on the same wavelength. The first time he grinned at one of their insults, I knew he'd figured it out.

But then he crossed paths with Renfrew.

Mama trusted only one other person to run her house—Sugar MacFarland, who was Old Maid Featherstone's younger, widowed sister. We never thought of her as our housekeeper because her loyalty was only to Mama. My brothers and I called her Miz Mac out loud, but after I saw a *Dracula* movie on TV I knew what her real name had to be, and it was the only way I could think of her after that. *Renfrew.* Dracula's devoted, bug-eating assistant.

Renfrew was a short, thin, wiry-tough woman with no butt and no bosom and lips so narrow and flat you couldn't have slid a penny through the slot. There was something about her that made me think of mushrooms and old newspapers. She wasn't old, she didn't have any gray hair, but what hair she did have was a thin cover of washed-out brown hanks and she skinned it up under one of those spidery mesh hairnets, which she stretched so tightly, the web's hub made a dark splotch on the center of her forehead, like the hypnotizing ruby at the center of a swami's turban.

She cleaned toilets and waxed floors; she shucked corn and plucked chickens. Mama paid her well, but she had a hard life, and she wasn't going to take any nonsense from us kids. Renfrew wouldn't bite us, but if she caught us on the wrong side of daylight she'd inform Mama instantly. Or as soon as Mama came out of the pottery room.

Mama had a pottery studio off the kitchen; it was a wonderful, earthy place, with brown potter's clay staining the bare wood floor, the walls, the potter's wheel, the kiln, the old portable radio hanging from a metal hook by one window. The shelves were filled with finished pieces and greenware. Mama shut the door and turned on the radio and worked at her hobby there, and it was her sanctuary. When Mama was in her pottery room, no one was allowed to disturb her. Renfrew practically guarded the door.

And when trouble arose, Renfrew dealt with it.

"Gimme that underwear, you wild-eyed tomcat," I heard her hiss one afternoon.

I ran to Roanie's door. He was on one side of his bed, Renfrew on the other. He clutched a pile of dirty clothes to his chest. I hurried to him. "What's wrong?"

"Ain't no lady gonna wash my clothes for me," he said angrily.

"Boy, you can't keep hiding your dirty dainties under your mattress!" Renfrew retorted. "I'll skin you and throw away your hide!"

He squinted at her. "I'll wash 'em myself!"

"No, you won't!"

I grabbed his pillow, tugged the pillowcase off, and handed it to him. "Put 'em in here and then Ren—Miz Mac can stick the whole bunch in the machine without looking at 'em."

Scowling, he stuffed the pillowcase, clamped the open end shut, but couldn't quite seem to hand it over. I eased my fingers under his, pried, tugged, and he finally let go. Renfrew snatched it from me, hissed at him again, and scurried from the room.

His shoulders slumped. "I cain't get the hang of this."

I whispered to him about my private name for Miz Mac, and finally he began to smile.

After that, she was Renfrew to him, too.

That was the kind of secret that made him feel at home.

My family was defined by food. Food meant competition and compliments. Every weekend we held our own informal county fairs, with unspoken prizes judged by empty bowls and naked platters speckled with crumbs.

We had feasts: deviled eggs, baked chicken, roast beef, fried trout; heaping bowls of collards and peas and sliced yams swimming in butter; biscuits—an art form—and soft yeast rolls, and corn bread; bowls of homemade chowchow, casseroles steeped in Velveeta, and canned cream soup; coconut cakes, apple cobblers, pecan pies so rich they puckered the tongue, and molded gelatin salads filled with submerged green grapes and cherry pieces and pineapple chunks, as colorful as a stained-glass window. All of it washed down with sweet iced tea and hot coffee and soft drinks.

The women set it out on the kitchen table with practiced modesty and a quick, furtive darting of eyes—an "Oh, I just threw it together" coupled with the brass pride of secret recipes and personal techniques no gourmet chef could have bested. We all suspected, for example, that the quality of Aunt Lucille's potato salad was defined by the exact, crisp, finely chopped celery in it—I swear she must have measured each piece with a ruler.

I think Roanie was stunned by our vittle-heavy gatherings. I could sense his isolation, his ingrained mistrust of the bounty. At the long, laden kitchen table we fed one another and knew we could count on one another; we knew where we belonged. Roanie didn't have that kind of kin, that satiating surplus. He'd never really eaten.

So he kept out of sight whenever our temperamental relatives came around; Arlan and Harold and Carlton taunted him, I learned from Hop and Evan a long time later, but he just had to take it—he wouldn't fight, because he was sure he'd lose his home. So on the weekends, when there were big gatherings of Maloneys and Delaneys for Sunday dinner, I never saw him.

"You know where Roanie Sullivan's pay is headed, don't you?" Aunt Irene demanded of Mama. She and Aunt Jane and Aunt Lucille were gathered on the front porch in rocking chairs, the aunts lined up on either side of Mama like sentries flanking a prisoner. I hid between the azalea shrubs and the jasmine trellis at one end of the porch, listening.

Roanie had been with us exactly one month. I couldn't hang around with him. I couldn't follow him all over the farm. He had work to do, and I had orders.

"He's giving your good money to his old man," Aunt Irene said, thumping her glass of bourbon on the arm of her rocker. "That's the only reason Big Roan lets him stay here. To turn over the money."

I thought of Mama's older sisters as old, but they were only in their forties, prime, pretty, brown-haired Delaney women. They were small-town society queens, like Mama and Grandmother Elizabeth, very sure of their place in the world. Sure that Daddy had gone crazy and taken Mama along for the ride.

"Big Roan bought Daisy and Sally McClendon some new clothes," Aunt Jane peeped. "*Both* of them. He's fooling with *both* of those McClendon sisters. *At the same time.*" Aunt Jane was a small, twittery woman. I'd always known her to be open to new ideas and large thoughts. She ran the library with a magnanimous love for books and people who loved books. She'd introduced me to the fantastic worlds of C. S. Lewis. She let me check out more books than the limit. "Daisy came to clean house for Lilah Johnson yesterday, and she was wearing a new sweater, and she told Lilah her 'man friend' gave it to her."

"Everybody knows Daisy's still stewing around with Big Roan," Aunt Lucille added helpfully. "And now with the extra money he's getting from Roanie, he can keep Sally on his line, too. I'd bet you a dime that little boy of hers is his."

"We *all* know who fathered that baby boy," Mama said impatiently. "I'd do something about it if I thought it wouldn't tear the family up. Get that baby. Raise him decently. He's Pete's son. *We're his aunts.*"

"Marybeth, I swear I don't see much that reminds me of Pete when I look at that baby."

"You see Delaney bloodlines, if you look close."

"Well, there's no proof, and Sally won't give him up, anyhow, and you're right—no Delaney would set foot in this house again if you and Holt took in the baby. And you'd break Mawmaw's heart. Good lord, you've caused enough gossip by taking in Roanie Sullivan."

"Roanie's a good boy. He can give his pay to his daddy if he wants to. In a way, I respect Roanie for that. Not deserting his daddy."

Aunt Irene snorted. "You're just supporting Big Roan's whores."

"No, we're giving Roanie half a chance to make something of himself."

"The boy's a lost cause. Bad breeding. Bad influence. Lucille knows."

I could see Aunt Lucille, who taught social studies at the high school, nodding. "Quiet as a clam. Careless hygiene. Barely gets by, gradeswise. Touchy. He's got a junkyard-dog look in his eyes, Marybeth. Mark my words. He'll slit somebody's throat someday."

"Well, I wouldn't blame him if he did," Mama retorted. Mama could change her tune when she was provoked. "He's been treated like pond scum by this town for his whole pitiful life. We ought to be ashamed. If that chicken comes home to roost, it'll be on all of our doorsteps."

"Marybeth!" Aunt Jane chirped. "You've got to think about our Mawmaw!" As if she and the other sisters spent much time thinking about Grandmother Elizabeth, I fumed. They were usually glad to let Mama take care of her. "What if Roanie Sullivan knocks our Mawmaw in the head? Or does it to old Granny Maloney?"

"Then I'd have one less mean-tempered old lady to put up with."

"Marybeth!"

"Oh, he's not a thumper or a throat cutter," Mama added with some disgust. "For goodness' sake."

Aunt Irene said sternly, "Holt's gotten more than a few hard comments in town. They've been telling him to think twice about his good-hearted nonsense. Pete's furious. He says he might as well turn over the key to the Auto Supply so Big Roan won't have to break a window to rob it next time. He says at least he'll know where to look for his merchandise."

Mama snorted. "I bet Pete didn't say that to Holt's face."

"Well, no, but—"

"Well, what about Dwayne?" Aunt Jane asked. "He's hardly speaking to Holt. He says Rhonda still has nightmares about the Christmas parade."

"Dwayne hardly speaks anyway," Mama said. "If he didn't have to talk to customers at the pharmacy, he wouldn't talk at all."

Aunt Lucille cleared her throat. "I have to tell you, Marybeth, I don't want Violet visiting Claire over here, not with that Sullivan boy around. I don't want her writing any pornographic poetry, if you know what I mean."

There was an awkward silence. I bit my tongue. Violet was my best friend, a deceptively wispy little soldier who would go anywhere or try anything as long as I promised it wouldn't get us in too much trouble.

"I don't want my Aster around him, either," Aunt Irene added with misty anger. "She nearly gave up the marching band after . . . well . . . the Christmas parade."

"Claire had good intentions with that poem," Mama said in a thready tone. "Just a bad choice of words."

"Marybeth, be serious." Aunt Lucille scowled and then was quiet. I felt disappointed in her. She looked stern and inflexible, her back straight as a fence pole in her tailored blue pantsuit with the bell-bottomed trousers.

"Marybeth, I'm all for Christian good works," Aunt Lucille continued finally. "But the most Christian thing you and Holt could do for Roanie Sullivan would be to ask Bess to file an order for him with the courts. William would send him to a foster home for good. He'd be with his own kind. They'd keep him until he turned eighteen."

I felt sick to my stomach. Oh, please. Mama and Daddy wouldn't change their minds, would they?

"Ship him off?" Mama said evenly. "Turn him over to a bunch of strangers and let 'em lock him up in something no better than an orphanage for juvenile delinquents? There's nothing Christian about that."

Aunt Irene snapped, "You let 'em have him before. After that . . . that . . . after my poor parade—" Her voice broke and trailed off.

"We were wrong," Mama said. "Now, listen, sisters. I've prayed and taken counsel from my inner voice—"

"Oh, Marybeth, sometimes you sound no better than a hippie!"

"My conscience," Mama corrected. "And it tells me that Roanie has a good heart, and Holt thinks so, too. The boy works hard and learns fast. I say he'll be just fine."

I loved Mama for that, but I had a job to do. I pulled a long, fat lizard from the pocket of my overalls and set it on the porch's edge. I'd dug it out of its bed under some leaves behind the calving barn. The cool October weather made it sleepy. The warmth of my pocket had charged it up. I blew on it and it scurried toward Aunt Jane's tennis shoes.

Aunt Jane peeped loudly when it zipped over her toes.

Aunt Lucille shoved her chair back.

Mama raised her loafers and let it pass.

Aunt Irene stomped on it. "Got the little heathen," she said.

I felt bad about that poor lizard for a long time.

I had to get some things straight between Roanie and me. In private. That was difficult to accomplish, since Daddy rarely let him out of his sight and swore that if he caught me alone with Roanie he'd hang me up by my heels until I turned the color of my hair.

He never did anything like that to me or anybody else, but my brothers and I were all sure he might.

We had ten farmhands, eleven once Roanie came to work for us. Daddy treated all of them the same—like privates in his own personal army.

In that pecking order, Roanie was a raw recruit still in boot camp. I had to make him go AWOL to talk to him.

Roanie and Nat Fortner were in one of the chicken houses the next afternoon, shoveling litter from under the long rows of hen cages. Litter is a polite Southern name for the gooey grayish slop chickens contribute to the creation of fertilizer. The toilet aroma of two thousand well-fed hens will burn the hair out of your nose. But the strange thing is, if you grow up with it, as I did, the smell becomes familiar and pleasant. I shoveled my share of chicken litter.

I tromped up the center aisle of the chicken house, surrounded by a symphony of clucking, pooping hens in rows of cages, and halted before Roanie and Nat. They hoisted loaded shovels over the sides of a small tractor cart. Roanie's jeans and old shirt were covered with the sweat-caked dust of dried chicken dung and the tall rubber workboots Hop had loaned him looked slimy. General Patton sat in a corner, wagging his curly tail. When Roanie saw me, he idly brushed a tiny white feather from his chin. I went, "Brrruck, cluck cluck," and smiled at him.

His eyes gleamed. He seemed happy in all that chicken shit. It was a step up for him. He nodded but didn't speak. I'm sure he was afraid to say a word to me until he had the rules down pat.

"Hi, Missy Claire," Nat thundered, grinning. "What you want?" Nat was gap-toothed, skinny, and white-blond. He'd worked for us since he flunked out of school in the eighth grade and he was about thirty now. He had a slow smile and the brain to match. Not much of a threat.

"My mama wants Roanie to come to the house," I lied smoothly. "She wants him to try on a pair of Josh's coveralls."

"Oh, me," Nat said, frowning and shaking his head. "Mr. Holt told me to learn him this job."

I squelched a laugh. Anyone but Nat could have qualified for a doctorate in shoveling in five minutes. "Okay." I started to walk away. "I'll go back and tell her you won't let him go."

"Oh, no! No, that ain't right! But . . . but you have to ask Mr. Holt. Or your grandpa. Or somebody. Not me."

"Everybody's out in the back fields except you." I sighed. "I'll just go tell Mama that you don't want to do what she said."

"No, no, no!" Nat grabbed Roanie's shovel. "You go on, Roanie. But come right back. Come right back."

"I will," Roanie answered, eyeing me with a slight, puzzled scowl.

I whistled under my breath as we left the chicken house. I'd shoved my long hair under a baseball cap. I had no breasts or any hint they'd rise anytime soon, so I thought I looked outstandingly boyish in a floppy gray sweatshirt, baggy jeans, and dirty tennis shoes.

Roanie measured his long strides to my short, swaggering ones but stayed a half-step behind. "What are you doing?" I demanded.

"Keepin' my distance. Tryin' to figure out if you made up a story to get me out of there. I don't want to get in no trouble."

"Made up a story? Boy, are you suspicious."

"I'm an expert on liars. I know when I hear one."

"Then why'd you come with me?"

"Why'd you ask me to?"

"I don't know. I don't speak to boys. Waste of time."

"What am I, huh?"

"Oh. Oh, shut up."

He halted. "I gotta get back to work. Don't make up little-girl games no more. I ain't no little boy, and this ain't no game to me."

"Wait! I've got to ask you something." I looked at him hesitantly. "Do you . . . do you give your money to your daddy so he can spend it on whores?"

His face darkened. He looked away. "I give him money and he goes off to spend it. I get left alone. That's how I want it."

"But it's not fair."

"I like it here. Don't care what it takes to stay."

"But it's your money. You could buy things you've always wanted."

"I already did. In a way."

"What?"

He looked at me for a long minute. Just looked. Then his gaze moved over the hills, the wooded mountains behind them, the wide, clear blue sky, our grand old house and the oaks and flower beds and fields and outbuildings connected by fine gravel roads—all of it—until, full circle, he came back to me. "I like it here," he repeated.

"Okay." I thought for a moment, then pulled a moist wad of tobacco from my back pocket. "Want a chew?"

He bit his lower lip and squinted at me. "Nooo."

"Well, I do. Josh taught me. Him and Brady do it. So do Evan and Hop. Me, too. All the time." Lies, lies, and damn lies. Josh had let me try a chew once, and I'd spent the next two hours rinsing my mouth out.

"Go ahead," Roanie said.

I gnawed off a large, nasty bite and tucked it inside one cheek. The acrid juice immediately seeped over my tongue and I thought I'd gag. I launched into a long, rambling monologue about my non-girl exploits. The pet grass snake I'd had until it slithered out of its mason-jar home and nested in one of Great-Gran's bedroom shoes. My status as a substitute catcher for my brothers' pitching practice. The fact that I'd clipped the hair off two Barbie dolls to see if it'd grow back. Things like that.

"Yeah," he said slowly, studying me as if I'd lost my mind.

"So don't go treating me like some kind of girl." I accidentally swallowed some juice. My stomach lurched. "You'll just get laughed at."

"Well, I'll tell you somethin', Claire. I can't treat you like no boy."

I liked it when he spoke my name. It gave me a fluttery feeling. Or maybe that was the tobacco. "Why not? You scared to?"

"Nooo. I just like things the way they are."

I glared up at him. "You treat me like a girl and I'll laugh at you."

His face became somber. "Don't do it. You ain't like nobody else."

My heart melted. "Okay, I won't laugh at you. But I—I go anywhere I want to around here, and I don't want Mama coopin' me up because she's scared."

"What's that supposed to mean?"

I rolled my eyes. "Oh, she's just a worrier. But I know you're not gonna grab me or knock me in the head or something."

He went as still as a statue. "She thinks I *would*?"

I inhaled sharply and choked on tobacco juice. "Uh, no. No, no, she just—"

"I ain't *ever* hurt a girl," he said furiously. "I ain't ever done nothin' to a girl. I don't want no girls hangin' on me. I ain't gonna end up bein' a daddy to babies I don't even want to take care of. Somebody sticks you with a baby, you gotta do the right thing. Any man don't do right by a baby, he's not worth spit."

"You're talkin' about my Uncle Pete," I said slowly. "That's what you mean, isn't it? It's true. Sally McClendon's baby belongs to him."

He was silent. His jaw worked. Then he said, "I'm talkin' about *any* so-and-so that lets a baby grow up without a good daddy. *Hey.* I ain't the kind your mama ought to worry about. Go on now. Go back to the house 'fore somebody catches us and thinks ol' nasty Roanie Sullivan's fixin' to eat you alive."

"Oh, *shitfire,*" I said. I marched away a couple of steps and hiked up the legs of my jeans a couple of inches and spit a stream of tobacco juice to prove I could do it.

Don't ever try to spit tobacco juice when you're upset. Inhaling and spitting are mutually exclusive. It felt as if the whole wad went down my windpipe and got stuck there. I gagged and choked, clutching my throat, struggling to breathe. I thumped my chest. Watery goo spewed from my nose and mouth. But no tobacco.

"Take a breath!" Roanie yelled.

Well, I would have, if it had been that simple. Bright firefly lights speckled my vision, and I sank to my knees. Something hit me hard between the shoulder blades. Roanie stood over me, one hand drawn back. "Breathe!" he ordered hoarsely.

I tried frantically, shaking my head.

Roanie picked me up and ran toward the house, me kicking and flailing in agony. When he reached the edge of the backyard, we both fell sprawling on the lawn. Mama and Grandma Dottie ran out. Grandmother Elizabeth and Great-Gran Alice peered excitedly from the back windows. Anyone might have misinterpreted the sight of Roanie Sullivan covered in chicken litter and pounding my back except he hit me one more time, knocked me flat, and the clump of tobacco popped out. I sucked in deep gulps of air.

"Undo her jeans!" Grandma ordered. "Get some air into her belly! She's purple!"

Mama dropped beside me, rolled me over, and yanked at the fastenings. The next thing I knew, Roanie jerked my jeans over my shoes and flung them—and my tennis shoes—behind him.

Total humiliation. I lay there in a sweatshirt and pink panties. Roanie turned his back.

He, undoubtedly, was a gentleman.

And I, undoubtedly, was not.

Mama sagged. "Where did you get that tobacco?" she demanded.

I coughed and gasped. "From H-Hop's dresser drawer."

Roanie pushed himself to his feet and said with his back still turned, "'Less you need me to do something, I'll go on back to work, Miz Maloney."

"Hold on." Mama flipped a dishrag over my panties and went to him. "What were you doing out here when you were supposed to be working?"

"I just . . . just come outside for a minute."

"Then you can just come in the house and wait for Mr. Maloney. Explain to him why you can't follow simple instructions."

"Mama," I tried, my head and stomach reeling, "Mama, it was my—"

"Be quiet, young lady. You're in enough trouble."

I began to cry, small, choking sobs of frustration. It was all my fault.

Nat, drawn by the noise, hovered a few yards away, shifting from one foot to the other and shaking his head. "I'm sorry, Miz Maloney, I shoulda gone with her to get them coveralls for Roanie."

Mama looked at me shrewdly. "I see," she said. She marched Roanie and me indoors.

Still woozy, I lay on the living-room couch with an afghan over my legs, and Roanie sat gingerly on the edge of a straight-backed cane chair beside the piano, moving his big-boned bare feet occasionally, as if the softness of the Oriental rug beneath them was a remarkable sensation. Mama had made him leave his dirty galoshes on the back porch.

I watched his tense gaze travel slowly around the large room, taking everything in as if he might be seeing it all for the last time. It was home to me; I tried to picture it through his stunted view—the handsome, plush furniture, the crammed bookcases, the wide stone fireplace, the fine lamps, and the console TV and stereo case stuffed with record albums. Astonishing luxury.

Mama had draped a soft blue bath towel over Roanie's knees, and he wiped his big hands on it. They were smeared with some of my regurgitated tobacco. I thought of that intimacy as a sort of bonding ritual, my bile-soaked embarrassment drawing the misery out of him.

But his eyes were bleak.

Mama entered the room. He stiffened, staring straight ahead. She laid a folded heap of brown material on the piano bench. "Those are the coveralls I wanted you to try on," she said.

He looked at her incredulously. "But—"

"Mama, he didn't do anything wrong." I was begging.

"Oh, I've already figured out who's to blame." Mama squinted at me.

I held my breath. Mama studied Roanie with a kind of sad, thoughtful frown between her slender brows. "You go take a bath," she told him. "Change into those coveralls. All right?"

"You mean I ain't in trouble, ma'am?"

"Good lord, no. Claire'd probably be a lot worse off if you hadn't been there to help her. Thank you." She gave me a look that said, *If you weren't already sick* . . . , then strode from the room, flicking her fingers across the front of the slim denim skirt she wore, as if shooing her own doubts away.

I said cheerfully, "See? Mama doesn't think you're gonna eat me alive."

"I hope not. You'd stick in my craw if I tried."

"Then I'd just whack you on the back until you spit me out."

He didn't know what to say to that, I could tell. I smiled with smug confidence.

We were giving each other breathing lessons.

8

*A*fter that, against the advice of everyone else in the family, Mama
and Daddy trusted him in my presence unwatched. So I rambled around
with him every day, talking his ears off. I gained a certain mystique in the
fourth grade at school. To my female cousins and girlfriends Roanie exuded danger like a musk; I basked unafraid in the shadow of his reputation,
so I was widely admired and gossiped about for taming him, as if I'd adopted a wolf.

Aunt Lucille eventually relented and let Violet wander outside with me,
and so I coaxed her down to the equipment shed one Sunday, where Roanie
was rebuilding a tractor engine. He was great with mechanical things; he'd
had to learn in order to keep Big Roan's truck running.

Violet was stiff with apprehension. Red hair stuck out from under her
sock cap, as if she'd been electrified. I led her into the huge, oil-perfumed
building. Roanie's face and hands were streaked with grease. He looked posi-
tively wicked, with a camouflage army coat pulled back from his chest and
his gray eyes glinting in the raw glare of two work lights clamped to the tractor's steering wheel. Sitting among engine parts on a tarp, with General Patton
curled up beside him, he surveyed me and Violet somberly. I pointed at him
as if I'd trained him. "Say something," I commanded.

"Boo," he deadpanned.

Violet ran all the way back to the house.

"You scared her," I said furiously. "I wanted you to make a good
impression!"

"You wanted to show off," he corrected smoothly, wiping his hands on a greasy rag. "But if you go get her and bring her back, I'll tell her I was just kiddin'."

"Why don't you come with me and say so in front of everybody? Then you could get something to eat. You could sit at the kitchen table."

"No, I couldn't. That's for family. Besides, I don't want a bunch of people starin' at me and whisperin' about me."

"They won't do that. I won't let 'em."

"I wish you was in charge of the whole world, Claire. I really do."

"Please come to the house," I repeated wistfully.

"Boo."

"Oh, *boo* yourself. You don't scare me at all."

"You scare me," he said darkly. "How about that?"

"I do not. How?"

He didn't answer immediately. He wiped greasy wrenches and rearranged engine parts; his gloomy and unfathomable silences were as deep as a well. Then, " 'Cause you'll grow up one day and be like everybody else."

"I will not." I had no idea what he meant, but I was certain of my uniqueness. "I'll never be scared of you, and when I grow up, I'll have my own house and you can sit at my table anytime you want."

He looked at me seriously. "I'll have a house, the best house in the world, and you can sit at *my* table."

"All right. Whatever. Shake on it." I stuck my hand down. He encased it carefully in his tough, greasy fingers, and we closed the deal.

I never understood my feelings about Sally McClendon. She gave me the creeps, and I was jealous of her because she had breasts and I didn't yet, but I also felt sorry for her. The collision of emotions left me nearly tied in knots.

I saw her again, up close and personal, one autumn afternoon. I was sitting on the counter at Uncle Eldon Delaney's hardware store, waiting for Daddy to come out of a back room, where he and Uncle Eldon had started debating saber saws and ended up debating politics. It had been a subject of fine controversy all fall, since our own Governor Carter was known to have aspirations for the White House.

I could hear their exasperated voices from the back of the store.

"I'm still a Talmadge Democrat," Uncle Eldon thundered. "Carter's so far off center he's not much better than a socialist."

"Oh, hell," Daddy shot back, "you wouldn't know what a socialist was if one walked in here and hit you with a hammer."

"I know the damn Democrats don't say anything worth listening to anymore."

"Are you telling me you'd vote *Republican?*"

"You bet I am!"

"Good lord!"

I shivered. Vote Republican? We'd have to do a lot of cleanup work at the family cemetery plots—all those Maloneys and Delaneys knocking up clumps of grass as they whirled in their graves.

So I sat there, frowning, idly drumming my heels against the counter's thick, sturdy side. I liked being different, but I didn't like startling changes. This store and this counter were over a hundred years old. The counter was built of burnished slabs of extinct chestnut, each one two feet wide, from a tree that must have been majestic to behold. The cash register that sat at the opposite end of the counter had belonged to Great-Grandfather Thurman Delaney. It was the Victorian cathedral of cash registers, decorated in brass curlicues, with tall price tabs that popped up smartly, like wooden targets at a carnival shooting gallery, when Uncle Eldon pressed the enameled keys.

But I sat on the counter among stacks of magazines with slinky Cher on the cover and a wooden bowl filled with smiley-faced Have A Nice Day pins, and a tray of mood rings. I slid one on my finger, scrutinized the murky oval plastic jewel against my skin, and waited to see what my mood was.

I was just murky.

One of the broad wooden doors swung open so hard the window-panes rattled. Sally marched in, her thighs bulging in tight jeans, her bosom bulging in a tight sweater, her red platform shoes thudding uneven-ly on the wood planks. Her hair had grown blonder and bigger every year, her mascara heavier, until at eighteen she looked like a big-haired yellow raccoon.

She teetered right up to me and stared into my eyes. "What's a little pink sugar baby like you gonna do for a boy like Roanie?"

"Well, I got him a good home and a straight front tooth, for one thing. And he doesn't belong to you anyhow."

"He will when he's a little older. You'll see."

"You've got enough boys. Big and little. What do you need with anoth-er one?"

"There ain't any others like him. Y'all are just gonna mess him up, give him big ideas and then knock him flat."

I had a horrible thought and immediately gave voice to it. "Mind your own business! He doesn't want to make babies with you or anybody else!"

"Babies. *Babies?* Little queen, I don't want no more babies. One lap rat from your kin is enough."

"That baby doesn't even look like my Uncle Pete! You better watch it. If my mama knew for sure, she'd come get him."

"If your mama knew the whole story, there'd be hell to pay that you ain't got no idea about."

"What's that supposed to mean?"

She leered and leaned closer. "Your folks are blind as bats when its suits 'em. Roanie'll be sorry he trusted 'em, someday. He's just playin' along to get money. That's how people like him and me get what we want."

I picked up a Have A Nice Day pin, bent the pin out, and thrust it under her chin. I whispered to Sally, "You want a prick? I'll give you a prick."

Her eyes widened. She backed off. I think she wasn't so much scared as amazed.

The shop's door opened again suddenly and Big Roan glared inside. I heard footsteps coming from the back room. Daddy and Uncle Eldon.

"Get your ass out here," Big Roan said to Sally in a low voice. "Truck with my money and I'll take it out of your hide."

"Roanie's money," she retorted, but she slunk away, throwing dark looks at me over her shoulder and bitter ones at Big Roan. I stared as he slammed the door behind her. As they walked off, I ran over and watched through a window, him limping, her wiggling. He dug one hand under her fanny and squeezed so hard she nearly fell off her shoes.

"Who was just in here?" Daddy asked, marching up to me with a red-faced Uncle Eldon still muttering about politics behind him.

"Sally McClendon."

Daddy scowled. "What did she want?"

"Uh . . . uh, I guess she'll come back later. I think she was looking for a screw."

That just popped out. I froze my face in neutral innocence. Daddy squinted hard at me, but Uncle Eldon started pounding the counter and talking about Governor Carter again, so Daddy was distracted.

I dragged the mood ring off my finger and stuck it back on the tray.

The plastic stone had gotten darker, a lot darker.

I tracked Roanie down as soon as we got home. He was in a storage shed, stacking sacks of fertilizer. I tiptoed up behind him, latched a thumb and forefinger in the seat of his jeans, and pinched hard muscle with all my strength.

He dropped a sack and whirled around, one fist rising like a sledge-hammer. When he saw who'd attacked him, he dropped his arm by his side, but his dark brows drew together in a formidable **V**. "What do you think you're doin'? You keep your hands to yourself!"

"You keep your hands to yourself!" I yelled. "Don't you mess with ol' big-tittied Sally McClendon, or the next time I'll sneak up on you with a pair of pliers!"

"Who says I done anything like that?"

"She says you belong to her!"

"Well, she's lyin'!"

"Did you . . . did you . . . have you ever . . ."

"No, I ain't, not ever! And I ain't talking about this kind of stuff with you! Now haul your little monkey fingers out of this shed!"

"That's all I wanted to know," I said sweetly. "Because I do believe you."

"Well, thank ya so much. You got a nasty mind for a little girl."

Oh, this was war. "Sally's busy, anyhow!" I taunted. "She was with your daddy and I saw him squeeze her on the butt!" The look on his face. Oh, the awful shame that colored his rawboned cheeks. I willed my mean-spir-ited news back into my mouth the instant it left, but it was too late. He sat down on a stack of fertilizer bags and stared at the dusty floor.

"I . . . I . . . maybe I made a mistake," I lied quickly. "Yeah, I, uh, I didn't see—"

"Yeah, you saw." His voice was so low.

"Well, he was just being friendly, I guess. I mean, 'cause Sally's not his girlfriend or anything. I mean, he's like, uh, a daddy, and she's kinda young, uh, and besides, Daisy's his girlfriend." I halted and studied him miserably. "Isn't she?"

"Yeah."

"Are you . . . you're not, uh, upset 'cause you like Sally? Like she's your girlfriend—"

"Claire, for God's sake, *she ain't my girlfriend*."

"Oh, yeah. Okay." I swallowed sickly. Then, in a small voice, "Is she Big Roan's girlfriend, like, uh, Daisy is?"

"Yeah."

"Well, oh, my, oh, shit." I sat down on the floor by his feet. "It's all right," I said finally, and I patted the toe of his workboot. "I won't tell anybody."

"Everybody knows." He just sat there, staring into space.

I kept patting the toe of his shoe. Small caresses, careful ones, through the hard leather.

No wonder he didn't want anything to do with girls who were old enough to do it with. Big Roan might have gotten there first.

Every year I made the mistake of naming the newborn calves and making pets of them, and I always picked a favorite, and the next year, without fail, we ate him. My bad luck was uncanny.

That fall the future contents of our meat freezer was a steer I called Herbert. Herbert the Hereford.

I knew, of course, that the cute red-and-white Hereford bull calves had one purpose—to grow up, grow fat, be castrated, and be killed before their meat turned tough. Either we ate them or someone else would. When they were stocky yearlings, Daddy sold them to a slaughterhouse broker, and they were loaded into huge stock trucks and disappeared forever.

Herbert was like all of our de-balled bovines—placid and unsuspecting, with dark, gentle eyes and the sweet scent of ruminated grass on his breath. He'd been spindly when he was young. I'd helped feed him special formula from a big, rubber-teated bottle. I'd scratched him between the eyes when the summer flies were after him. I'd laugh and tell him, "Herbert, you're gonna taste good." Because I admitted that after Herbert was dead I'd stop thinking of him as Herbert. He'd become a steak.

So I understood the facts of a steer's life completely and could joke about it with the same bawdy humor as my brothers, except for the countdown hours on the day of the butchering and then I was grief-stricken.

On Herbert's execution day I hid in the loft of the main barn and cried my eyes out.

Roanie found me up there, lying flat on my stomach between pyramids of baled hay, my head buried in my arms. He carried General Patton up with him and set him down next to me. General Patton snuffled my hair and whined. I sat up quickly, wiped my eyes, and looked at Roanie sadly. "Daddy's fixin' to shoot Herbert. I can't watch."

"That's what I figured. Grandpa Maloney told me that's why you went running out here. I told him I better keep you company."

"Thank you."

"I gotta go down in a minute. Supposed to help with the skinnin'."

"Yeah. Me, too."

"You, too?"

My mouth trembled, but I shrugged. "I'm not a sissy."

He nodded solemnly. "Yeah. I know."

"I've seen all sorts of dead things. I've seen Grandpa chop off chickens' heads. Boy, do chickens flop around. Then you dunk 'em in hot water and pick all the feathers off, and you clean 'em out and cut 'em up, and pretty soon they look just like chickens in the grocery store."

"Yeah. Then you don't have to think about how they got that way."

"Josh shot a bunch of squirrels once. We ate 'em. He gave me their tails. I made a necklace out of 'em."

"Squirrels are tough to eat."

"Aunt Arnetta hunts. She sits up in a deer stand and shoots at anything that moves. Daddy says Uncle Eugene won't even go outside in the fall. 'Fraid she'll plug him." I studied Roanie carefully. "You go hunting?"

"Yeah."

"Grandpa doesn't hunt anymore. Josh quit after he came home from Vietnam. And Daddy stopped because Mama said he couldn't put any more stuffed deer heads on the living-room walls. She said it was getting to where she couldn't read in there. It felt like she had an audience."

"I don't much like to hunt myself."

"Then why do you?"

He rubbed General Patton's head and didn't answer right away. Then, "Got used to it. It was better than eatin' cereal and bologna sandwiches all the time."

I started to say, *Well, we don't feed you any bologna,* but the distant pop of Daddy's pistol threw me down on the floor again. I pressed my hands to my ears. "Herbert," I moaned.

Roanie put a hand on my hair and stroked it very gently. "It's done with so quick," he offered in a low voice. "Herbert didn't feel no pain." He paused. "So I'd say he had it pretty good."

Roanie had a low standard for happiness. All he asked was that things not hurt.

Daddy loaned him a deer rifle and he went hunting with Evan and Hop, and he shot a sixteen-point buck at dawn in the woods of Old Shanty Pass.

That buck made him a celebrity. To deer hunters, bagging a sixteen-point rack of antlers—which means there are eight prongs on either side—is like bringing home the crown jewels. It had been so long since anyone had seen antlers that big that even Grandpa Maloney had trouble remembering one.

A parade of men and boys stopped by our farm to gaze longingly at the giant spread on the buck's glassy-eyed head, which sat in a place of honor on a workbench outside the barn. "Gut shot or through the heart?" they asked Roanie with the solemn interest of doctors consulting on a patient.

"Through the heart," he answered.

I got my Instamatic and took a picture of Roanie sitting beside the buck's head. I had connections with Mr. Cicero, the publisher of the *Dunderry Weekly Shamrock;* I was secretary of the 4-H Club at school, and Mr. Cicero ran my two-paragraph articles about the club meetings and gave me a byline. So I had established myself as a bona fide member of the press.

"You'll be in the paper next week," I told Roanie proudly.

"Gut shot or through the heart?" he said back. I didn't understand his morbid humor, but I smiled anyway.

Uncle Cully arrived shortly afterward. His expression mournful and awed, he examined the buck's head. Uncle Cully had twenty deer heads on the wall of the waiting room at his dental office. Uncle Cully loved deer heads even more than he loved teeth. "Oh, that's beautiful," Uncle Cully said to Roanie as he caressed the buck's antlers.

Roanie looked at Uncle Cully. "Will it pay the bill for my tooth?" We all stared at him. There was a wave of disbelieving murmurs among the envious hunters.

Uncle Cully's mouth fell open. "Your bill's been paid."

"I know. Will you give Mr. Maloney his money back?"

"You don't have to do that," Daddy said, frowning. "I said you could pay me out a little every week from your salary."

"This tooth thing'll take me forever. I want to get done with it."

Daddy studied him shrewdly. "Don't like to be in anybody's debt, hmmm?"

"No, sir. Ain't nothing personal. Just don't like it."

"All right. I respect that. Cully, is it a deal?"

"Oh, lord, *yes,*" Uncle Cully replied. Five minutes later he left with the buck's head in his trunk.

"I'll still get your picture in the paper," I promised Roanie. "And when we go to Uncle Cully's office, you can say hello to your deer."

He nodded. But I don't think he cared if he ever saw that prize rack of antlers again. It had served its purpose.

"I give the boy credit," Mama said that night, with no small amount of respect in her voice. "He knows what he wants."

I felt proud. Roanie was always smarter than anyone but me expected. He was the only person I've ever known who got Uncle Cully to fix a tooth for one buck.

9

Grandmother Elizabeth and Great-Gran Alice weren't afraid of Roanie like the aunts were. They weren't afraid of anything except each other's opinion. They hated the idea that whichever of them died first wouldn't get the last word on the other.

On a frosty Saturday not long before Thanksgiving, Roanie was thrust into the middle of the granny wars.

It started at breakfast. Our family meals, even the most ordinary ones, were crowded events, and breakfast was eaten at the long oak table in the center of the kitchen, which was a kingdom of its own, big and sunny and cluttered, with squeaking wood floors and tall white cabinets and scarred Formica counters. This was a room of serious purpose; there was an industrial-size, steel-doored refrigerator and broad, squat freezer, two huge stoves, pots and skillets hanging from a wrought-iron rack over the table, a double sink deep enough to bathe a calf in, and Mama's only concession to frivolous convenience—a freestanding dishwasher that sat in one corner, rumbling and swishing in almost constant service from dawn until bedtime.

The basic group that morning included me, Roanie, Hop, Evan, Mama and Daddy, Grandpa and Grandma Maloney—who often walked over for meals—and, of course, Grandmother Elizabeth and Great-Gran Alice, plus the field hands, who could count on sausage biscuits and coffee, which Mama dispensed to them on the back porch off the kitchen.

We were contentedly eating a huge country breakfast of sausage and fried eggs, biscuits, gravy, and slices of the very last of the cantaloupes from the household vegetable patch. I was sleepy, still wearing my pajamas and robe. I sat between Grandmother Elizabeth and Great-Gran Alice, who were still in their robes, too. One of my duties was to pass platters of food between them, so we could avoid their having to utter even a single word to each other.

"I'm going shopping today," Great-Gran announced suddenly. "I'm going to Atlanta. I'm going to Rich's."

This was not a request. It was a decision. It meant someone would be pressed into chauffeur service for a four-hour round-trip drive, and it meant venturing into the seedy, aging heart of downtown Atlanta, because no matter how many bright new Rich's popped up in the suburban malls, there would always be, for Great-Gran, only one true Store.

Grandmother Elizabeth piped up. "I believe I'll go as well."

Forks stopped moving. Coffee cups and juice glasses halted midway to lips. Hop's pet squirrel, Marvin, peeped over the table edge from his perch on Hop's thigh. Marvin sensed trouble. He froze. Roanie was the only one who didn't understand. But he stopped eating, too, and watched warily.

Great-Gran adjusted her hearing aid and arched a white brow. "I didn't invite you, Elizabeth."

"Mawmaw, I'll take you next week," Mama quickly assured her mother. "I promise."

Grandmother Elizabeth dabbed her eyes with a napkin. She could turn her tears on and off like a lawn sprinkler. "How will I do my Christmas shopping if everyone shuffles me aside until it suits their mood? It's all very well for the rest of you to make plans, but I can't depend on my strength to hold out." A single tear trickled down her soft white cheek. "I suppose I'll have to forgo proper gifts now that I'm old and frail. I'll simply hand out cards with money in them. That's what helpless, elderly women are reduced to. I hope you all forgive me."

Great-Gran pursed her lips. "Quit sniffling and mind your own business."

Grandpa held up both hands. "Mother," he said to Great-Gran as if he were still a boy, "I'd rather cut off my own two paws than hear any more of this."

"She started it, Joseph. And I've never backed down from a fight in my life."

Grandmother Elizabeth snapped to attention. "I most certainly am going shopping with you today. I'll take Claire with me to carry my packages."

I felt like Marvin. Afraid to move.

"I'm taking Claire to carry my packages," Great-Gran said.

Grandmother shot back, "Since you're too ancient to drive us to Atlanta, *Alice*, I don't see how you can be in charge. You don't have any say over who accompanies me and carries my packages."

"It's my damn car. Carry your own damn packages."

"I don't wish to be cramped in your small, uncomfortable car. It reeks of that vile tearose perfume you wear." Grandmother Elizabeth smiled around the table. "Now, who shall drive us? Whom shall we honor?"

Excuses gushed out. Daddy and Grandpa had to go to Gainesville and pick up a new belt assembly for one of the mowers. Mama had to get five bushels of overripe apples peeled and puréed for apple butter. Evan was too young to drive, and Hop wasn't experienced enough to be turned loose on the Atlanta freeways. But Grandma Dottie was caught without escape. She knew it, too. I could tell by the trapped expression in her sharp blue eyes. She couldn't think fast enough. "I, well, I . . . hmmm, have to—" she began.

"You're not busy, daughter-in-law," Great-Gran proclaimed. "You can drive us. I'm so sorry Elizabeth butted in. If you can't stand her company, we can tie her to the luggage rack."

"I'm not the annoying old *nanny goat* in this family," Grandmother Elizabeth replied tartly. "We all know who that is."

"All right, all right. Hush, both of you," Grandma Dottie said. "I'll go. I'll drive. But hush!" She lit a cigarette and smoked in disgusted defeat.

Grandpa tried to rescue her. "Well, y'all can't go to Atlanta today anyhow," he said. "I'm not gonna let y'all traipse off down there without me or Holt or one of the boys to go along. It's not safe anymore."

Daddy nodded. "That's right."

"There's our solution," Grandmother Elizabeth announced, gesturing toward Roanie with her cane. "Not a soul will bother poor, decrepit Alice with that brawny young knight by our sides. He can go."

"And when Elizabeth trips over her cane," Great-Gran interjected smugly, "he can tote her like a sack of horse turds."

Run, I mouthed to Roanie. He looked at me with a puzzled frown.

But it was too late.

Grandma Dottie guided her big, gas-guzzling station wagon down the freeway with her right hand clenched, white-knuckled, on the steering wheel and her left hand propped by a narrow opening in her window, a cigarette burning constantly between her fingers. She was as stoic as the Statue of Liberty, torch raised.

Roanie was lucky. He got to sit in the front seat with her. I studied the back of his head, watching its slight movements as he silently absorbed the cluttered urban scenery outside his window. I wondered what he was thinking, what he saw in apartment buildings and skyscrapers, warehouses and billboards, if the city promised him something I couldn't fathom. I'd heard Daddy assure him, before we left, that he'd get paid the same as if he'd spent the day working at the farm.

"But this trip ain't work, Mr. Maloney," Roanie had replied.

"Believe me," Daddy had answered drily, "it'll be a chore."

It certainly was, for me at least. I was the backseat buffer zone between Great-Gran and Grandmother, and I sat there in stiff misery, my hands wadded together in the lap of my pinstriped shirtdress, my feet sweating in knee socks and loafers, my shoulders hunched inside a thick blue sweater. I wished I were fireproof.

"And, of course, as secretary for the British Magnolias Association, I had a place of honor at the gala following the premiere," Grandmother Elizabeth was saying. "So as she and Laurence Olivier—of course, he was only Mr. Olivier then, he hadn't been knighted yet—as she and Mr. Olivier moved down the receiving line, I put out my hand and said, 'Miss Leigh, it is so nice to welcome you to Atlanta,' and Vivien grasped my hand and gave me the sweetest smile. 'Oh!' she said to me. 'To hear a voice from home! How kind of you!'"

This was Grandmother's *Gone With the Wind* story, which she told and retold at the drop of a mint julep. How she and Grandpa Delaney had attended the movie's world premiere in 1939; how magical the Loew's Grand Theater had been, fitted with an antebellum facade and klieg lights sweeping it; the crowds, the dignitaries, the flashing camera bulbs, Margaret Mitchell signing *"To Mr. and Mrs. Delaney, Best Regards, Peggy Mitchell"* on Grandmother's theater program; and the silk-and-taffeta gown Grandmother had worn to the ball afterward, and Grandpa Delaney as handsome as Clark Gable in his formal evening clothes; how Grandmother had written two full pages for the *Dunderry Weekly Shamrock* about that glorious night; and how everyone, *everyone*, in town had sworn that she, Elizabeth Delaney, had looked as beautifully English and Southern as Vivien Leigh, Scarlett O'Hara herself.

Grandmother finished her story and took a tortoiseshell compact from her purse, patted her coil of fake, brown braids, smoothed her red lipstick, and studied her soft, aged face as if Vivien and Scarlett still looked back at her.

Her story fascinated everyone except Great-Gran, who despised it. Grandmother knew Great-Gran did, too. As predictably as could be, Great-Gran stared out the passenger window on my right as if pretending that she'd turned her hearing aid off. But she muttered in a stage whisper, "Crazy as a damned bedbug."

"I beg your pardon?" Grandmother said.

"Vivien Leigh." Great-Gran snorted. "She went crazy as a bedbug before she died."

"She most certainly did not."

"And Margaret Mitchell was a mousy little toot who wouldn't say peep to a pigeon. She stole the whole plot of that book from old war veterans who told her stories when she was growing up. And you, you old liar, you signed your own program and just told everybody she autographed it."

Grandmother Elizabeth took a long, loud, quavering breath. "Stop the car, Dottie. Let me out. I'd rather walk."

Grandmother always demanded to be let out at some point on a car trip with Great-Gran. In the rain, in the snow, in the middle of a city, in the middle of the mountains. We were zooming forward at seventy miles an hour on two lanes of the in bound expressway, surrounded by cars and tractor-trailers.

"Let me out, Dottie!"

Grandma Dottie took a drag from her cigarette and aimed a forceful stream of smoke out the window. "I'll think about it," she muttered, "when I get to the next exit."

"Set the yakkety old flirt on the street," Great-Gran ordered. "She wasn't invited anyway."

"I know when I'm not wanted," Grandmother said, her lips trembling.

Great-Gran hooted. "Good. Get out."

I was learning the art of distraction. I leaned over the front seat. "Grandma? How about we go to the bakery at Rich's and buy some éclairs?"

"You betcha, sweet pea," Grandma Dottie said.

I poked Roanie on the shoulder. He swiveled his head toward me. "They're named after me," I teased solemnly. "E-Claires."

A tiny smile crooked one corner of his lips. He shot a glance at the sullen backseat grannies and opened his mouth to say something, but Great-Gran proclaimed suddenly, "They're Jewish, you know."

I looked back at her. "Éclairs are Jewish?" I asked carefully. I didn't know much about Jewish people or their food, so anything was possible. At least it was a change of subject.

"No," Great-Gran said. "The Rich's department-store people are Jewish. Hungarian Jews from way back."

"Oh? Okay." I prodded Roanie's shoulder again. "That doesn't mean they were hungry," I said in a droll tone. "It means they came from *Hungary*."

"They're real nice people," Great-Gran added. "Real humanitarians. Good to everybody. You'd never think they used to be foreigners." She paused. "Unlike some people I could name."

"One of my aunts was Jewish," Grandmother Elizabeth retorted. We all knew that. Some of the Maloney kin whispered about it as if it were some mysterious shame. I couldn't connect this vague infamy with Grandmother. Aggravation, yes. Shame, no. "Polish and Jewish," Grandmother elaborated. "A quite sturdy combination."

Great-Gran sniffed. "Oh, *la-di-da.* In a minute you'll claim you're related to Jesus Christ Himself."

"Don't be sacrilegious."

"Jesus and Vivien Leigh."

"Dottie, stop the car. *I want to get out.*"

Grandma Dottie drove faster.

Rich's department store in downtown Atlanta was a dream castle, a social touchstone for generations. You could furnish your whole house there. You could buy books and jewelry and linens and fine underwear. You could eat lunch in the tearoom. You could buy a cake. You could shop on credit, lots of credit, and if you came back, ten years later, with an outdated blouse in a dusty, faded-green Rich's box and said, "I'd like to return this, please," they'd take it back.

Black or white, rich or poor, city or country, we all had a Rich's. The grand, massive, dignified downtown store was beginning to lose its luster when I was a girl, but it still had years to go before everyone agreed that no one shopped there anymore.

Grandma parked the car and locked it. We were alone in the shadowy, concrete womb of the store's parking decks, a vulnerable troupe walking slowly, Grandmother Elizabeth tottering along with her cane and Great-Gran moving with the heavy-footed pace of sore knee joints. She planted a hand on my shoulder and leaned on me. I wished she'd give up a little pride and buy a cane.

A subtle but intense change had come over Roanie. I'm sure Daddy and Grandpa Maloney had told him that his job was to protect the family's womankind. He scanned the long, dimly lit parking lanes relentlessly and walked as if balanced on the balls of his feet, his arms spread slightly away from his body. He looked gracefully threatening, so quiet and controlled.

A shiver ran down my spine. I wasn't just scared of the parking deck, of muggers and rapists and all the other human monsters who lived in cities, according to every account I'd heard at home. No, I was a little scared of Roanie, or at least awed, and strangely giddy inside—it was a confusing mixture, somehow involved with being female.

When we were finally inside the store, breathing in its soft lights and scents, its safe, nicely dressed people and beautiful merchandise, I still watched Roanie and felt, somehow, that trouble was brewing.

We were in Men's Accessories when it happened.

The Old Grannies tired quickly. They settled into their standard shopping routine, which meant that Grandma Dottie convinced a salesman to let us drag a pair of chairs from a dressing room so that Great-Gran and Grandmother could sit, like solemn judges, while we presented merchandise to them for their appraisal.

Grandma Dottie smartly stationed them at opposite sides of the department, then, sighing, she escaped to the restroom for a few minutes, leaving Roanie and me on duty. Back and forth we went, ferrying neckties, driving gloves, pullover sweaters, and bottles of cologne, which the grannies examined shrewdly. The goodies that passed muster were stacked beside their chairs; the others we carefully put back in place.

There were only a few other shoppers in the department; the ones I noticed most were a well-dressed couple with a skittish blond boy who was maybe four years old, who darted through the racks, skewing suits sideways on their hangers. His daddy had a squeaky-sharp, impatient look that set my teeth on edge. "Be careful!" I heard him snap at the woman as she helped him try on a tweed jacket. "You caught the lining on my watch. Pay attention." The woman smiled too quickly and apologized. I couldn't imagine Daddy speaking to Mama that way or her giving him a meek look if he had.

The harried salesman, who looked stern and prim to me but was probably no more than twenty-five, fawned over the man and followed the little boy around, straightening the clothes he dislodged, not once asking the kid's parents to make him behave. And when the salesman wasn't trying to baby-sit, he dogged Roanie's footsteps, frowning at him, even though Roanie wasn't doing a thing.

Roanie's expression grew darker every second. I positioned myself near him and made jokes and silly comments, trying to lighten him up, but a muscle flexed in his cheek and he didn't answer. I couldn't figure out what was going on until Grandmother Elizabeth crooked a finger at the clerk. He went over to her and bent down, oozing attentive charm, and I heard her whisper, "Dear young man, if you're worried about shoplifting, I advise you to stop following my helpers and concentrate instead on that elderly lady across the way. She's quite senile. She has a habit of hiding merchandise in her coat pockets."

The salesman's jaw fell open. He tightened his tie. I was furious. So he thought Roanie might steal something. He wandered toward Great-Gran, his eyes shifting uncertainly from her back to Roanie. I stepped in front of him and said in an angry whisper, "My grannies are crazy, but they don't steal, sir. And neither does my . . . my *boy*. You leave him alone or he'll beat your butt."

The clerk wiped his glistening forehead. "I should never have quit bartending school," he said under his breath, and then he went over to the cologne counter and shuffled invoices. I think he gave up. He was hiding from us all.

Grandma Dottie returned. I filled her in on the situation—Grandmother trying to cause trouble for Great-Gran, the salesman making Roanie feel like a thief. She shut her eyes for a second, rubbed her temples with her tanned, tobacco-stained fingertips, then said, "Keep moving, sweet pea. Let's get done and go *home*. I have a headache."

What happened next happened so fast.

The little blond boy scooted past us. His mama touched peach-colored, manicured nails to her throat and called softly, "Jimmy, honey, *slow down*," and then the daddy stepped out of an aisle and snared the little boy by his shirt collar. "I *told* you to stay out of the way," the man said loudly. And then he shook the boy hard, and the boy gave a loud, terrified shriek. "Be quiet," the man ordered, but the kid shrieked louder and the woman threw out her helpless hands toward him, and the man drew back one of his and slapped his son hard in the face.

The blow tumbled the little guy backward and he fell. He curled up, sobbing, on the carpeted floor.

I stared in unabashed shock. I had seen Mama smack Brady across the legs with a forsythia switch once for saying "fuck." Daddy had given me a few openhanded swats on the fanny over the years, but the occasions were so rare that each one had the power of legend. I had cousins who laughed about the ritualized whippings some of my aunts and uncles dished out for various transgressions. But I'd never seen anything like this, this sudden and untempered violence against a small child.

Grandma Dottie laid a hand on my shoulder. I could feel her trembling, and when I looked up at her, she was staring at the man with the compressed fury of a slow-burning firecracker. *Do something*, I screamed inside.

The kid's mama gathered him up and glanced around, blushing, avoiding our eyes. "Take him somewhere," the man told her. "You're in charge of him. I can't shop with him underfoot. Go on."

"I'm sorry," his wife murmured. "He's just tired."

The man noticed us watching him. "You have nothing better to look at?" he snapped.

"Nothing worse," Grandma Dottie answered stiffly.

He turned his back and began flipping through a rack of dress shirts. His wife carried the little boy away. His whimpers faded slowly.

"I saw it," Great-Gran said behind us. "It was an abomination."

"I saw it first," Grandmother Elizabeth added. "Any man who treats his child that way should be horsewhipped."

They stood there alongside Grandma Dottie, muttering and slinging darts at the man's back with their gazes, but they didn't *do* anything, and I was locked in my own steaming, silent world of unanswerable questions. *Why couldn't we do something? Shouldn't we say something? Tell somebody?*

It happened so fast. Violence is easy; justice is hard. Roanie, accustomed to one but not the other, strode across the aisle and shoved the man on the shoulder. I've never forgotten that sight: Roanie, a shabby, lean, fourteen-year-old boy, aiming a murderous stare at a grown man. A gangly young wolf confronting a pampered spaniel. Roanie's face was contorted. He was almost crying, I decided later. "You son of a bitch," he said.

"Hey," the man said, stepping back. "Leave me alone."

"Goddamned bully."

The man held up both hands. "Listen, I don't have to take this kind of crap."

"How'd you like it if somebody slapped you?"

"Don't threaten me, hillbilly."

Roanie hit him. Punched him right in the jaw. The man's arms flailed, and he fell against a rack of pinstriped suits and sank between two of them, as if he'd been swallowed.

I screamed. Then I broke from Grandma's grip and ran to Roanie. I dodged in front of him and peered into the suits. The man half lay, half sat, moaning. Blood trickled from his lower lip. "Hit him again, Roanie!" I yelled.

The salesman ran over, his mouth gaping. "Cool it, cool it, kid," he said, keeping his distance from Roanie. "I've called the security guards!"

Oh, no. I switched from attack to retreat. Pushing Roanie was like pushing a brick wall. I plowed into his chest like a bulldozer. I threw my head back and looked up at him pleadingly. His eyes were glazed, his mouth drawn back in a snarl. "Roanie, it's *Claire*. Hello, hello. *Look at me.*"

"Don't you never hit your kid again," Roanie hurled over my head at the man. "It ain't right. It ain't fair."

"Roanie, I know," I begged. "Come on."

"Assault," the man groaned. "I'll have you arrested."

Suddenly Grandma Dottie was beside us, thrusting an arm around us both. "Roanie," she ordered in a low, fierce voice, "you and Claire *go to the parking deck. I'll bring up the rear with the Old Grannies. Go on now. Go.*"

But people had gathered. A pair of security guards ran up. I latched my arms tightly around Roanie's waist and held on to him. I wanted to cloak him, make him invisible. *I know why he's like this. We all know. Big Roan hit him that way. When he was too little to hit back. And no one did anything to stop it.*

"Call the police," Grandmother Elizabeth piped up. I heard her delicate, righteous voice. Eyes shut, I could feel Roanie's heart pounding under my ear. "We'll just see who deserves to be arrested," she said. "I'll tell them exactly what happened."

"So will I," Great-Gran said loudly. "Let's get the law in on this. I saw a grown man knock a baby five feet across the floor."

"Oh, yes, I certainly saw that, too." Grandmother Elizabeth again. "We're in perfect agreement."

I think the world stopped turning.

To make a long story short, the man quit muttering about having Roanie arrested when the Old Grannies launched into the full story of why Roanie had hit him. The salesman, when prodded, confirmed their account. The store's security guards scowled and shifted their feet, obviously wishing we'd all just go away. Finally they let us.

And we got out of there. It wasn't dignified, it wasn't much of a victory, not with me sealed to Roanie's side and holding on to him like a vise, Grandma Dottie pushing us, him dragging his feet, the Old Grannies bringing up the rear in slow tandem.

I couldn't change the future for a little blond boy and his cowed mother any more than I could change the past for Roanie. All I had was the satisfaction of his long arm curled around me, our togetherness in trouble, and the righteous support of two very old grannies and one younger one.

Grandmother and Great-Gran discussed the fight with great relish all the way home. They sat in the backseat close together. I sat in the front between Grandma Dottie and Roanie. I had to know something. I whispered to him, "If some, uh, criminal tried to *get* me—you know, in a bad way—what would you do to him?"

He didn't hesitate. He didn't so much as bat an eyelash. "I'd try to kill him."

I wound my chubby, determined fingers through his and held on. His skin was sweaty and cold. I didn't realize it then, but he was scared sick that he'd proven himself unredeemable, like Big Roan. That he'd get sent away for what he'd done.

Of course, that didn't happen. Daddy lectured him on the consequences of settling arguments with his fists, but it was a mild lecture, no worse than one of my brothers would have gotten. And then Mama sat him down at the kitchen table and wrapped the swollen knuckles of his right hand in a dishtowel packed with ice and insisted he stay put while we set the table and put out the food for dinner.

Hop and Evan came in and Grandpa Maloney—they wanted every detail of the Rich's fight. Roanie still looked as if he expected to be electrocuted. We presented a peculiar mood—all of us gazing at him speculatively, Great-Gran nodding, Grandmother Elizabeth smiling at him coyly behind her thin, blue-veined hand.

"You're a hero," I blurted out. "Heroes have to sit at the table and get admired."

He drew back instinctively. "But I didn't *change* nothin'."

"You tried," Grandma Dottie said firmly. "Which is more than most people can ever claim. More than we had the gumption to do. And I want to apologize to you for not doing more sooner. About similar matters. All right?"

"Fix your plate, Roanie," Mama ordered with brusque diplomacy. "Dinner's getting cold."

Great-Gran and Grandmother Elizabeth were syrupy-sweet to him and endlessly discussed his deed. And I promised him that the next time we went to Rich's we'd get ourselves that bag of éclairs.

"Oh, yes," Great-Gran said. "I have to go back next week and do my shopping all over again."

"Well, I have to go, too," Grandmother Elizabeth said in an edgy tone.

"Not when I go, *Elizabeth*."

"Whenever I wish to, *Alice*."

Roanie ate, and listened, and endured. Just like the rest of us. I grinned at him.

The world is spanned by small bridges between people. He'd crossed another one.

$\mathcal{T}$hanksgiving. To me it was a good all-around holiday, though it couldn't compare to Easter and Christmas since I didn't get any presents out of it. Thanksgiving meant football bowl games, turkey and dressing, and a house crammed to the rafters with relatives visiting from out of town. Thanksgiving was our big homecoming holiday.

"Turkey leg?" I asked Roanie. He sat in the loft of the big barn, near its open door, with General Patton sitting beside him. I plopped down beside the two of them, pulled a turkey leg from a box full of food I'd put together, and thrust it under his chin.

We looked at each other like old married people who can't bear to be separated but sometimes can't bear each other's company either. "Why do you always track me down during family things?" he asked. "I just ain't gonna be part of it, okay?"

"I just decided I'd eat up here. Oh, so you're here, too. Well, my goodness. So shut up and let's eat."

So we did. Romance is simple when you don't discuss it.

From the barn loft we had a front-row, upper-level seat for the annual Thanksgiving Day Maloney-Versus-Delaney Touch Football Game. We leaned against the opposite sides of the door frame, our blue-jeaned legs stretched out on the matted hay. The air was cool, the sky was blue, the mountains in the distance blazed with color. "Now this is a good holiday," I told Roanie.

"Yeah," he answered quietly. "This is how I pictured it bein' over here."

Below us on the mown, brown autumn pasture, the family gathered in lawn chairs and on blankets. Daddy had marked off goal lines with lime. There was a lot of yelling and running and good-natured insults, which was why it was so much fun to watch.

The oldest player was Mama's Uncle Winston, who had brindled gray hair and a belly like a walrus. The youngest were Hop and Evan, who were stocky enough to make me think of future redheaded walruses.

Josh and Brady were home from college, so they were down there, too. And there was Mama's cousin, Stuart Kehoe, the mayor, and his wife, Noona, the county tax assessor, and Mama's cousin Randy Pinkett, the county commissioner, and his wife, Edythe, who sold Avon products and real estate. Plus a lot of relatives Roanie already knew too well, including Uncle William, Aunt Bess, Uncle Pete, Pete's sons, Arlan and Harold, Uncle Dwayne and Aunt Rhonda, Uncle Eugene and Aunt Arnetta, and Carlton.

I decided to tell him about the out-of-town relatives he had no reason to avoid. "That's Sonny Delaney," I said, pointing. "He lives up in Blairsville. He's a state senator. If we need something from the government we just give Sonny a call. He's big friends with Governor Carter."

"He knows the *governor?*" Roanie asked slowly.

"Oh, sure." I pointed again. "And that's Grandpa's brother Mack. Great-Uncle Mack Maloney. He lives up in Tennessee. In Nashville. He's a professional guitar player. You can hear him in the background on some old Elvis songs."

"He knows *Elvis?*"

"Oh, sure. Well, he used to anyhow. Before Elvis went to Las Vegas. And that's Uncle Ralph Maloney over there. He's a lawyer in Atlanta. If you want to know how to kill somebody and get away with it, ask Uncle Ralph. That's what Daddy says. And over there, sitting on that quilt, that's Great-Aunt Sue Maloney. She was in the Peace Corps. She lived in Africa for two whole years. She met President Kennedy, too. Well, not while she was in Africa. After she came back."

"I'm gonna be bigger than any of them," Roanie said suddenly.

"What?"

"I said, *I'm gonna be bigger than anybody around here.*"

"What's that supposed to mean? How come you look mad? I wasn't bragging."

"People'll look up to me. People'll hang all over me to do whatever I want. I swear. You wait. You'll see."

I was flabbergasted, and a little upset. My family ran or owned or had influence over almost everything that mattered in the county. Underneath our blooms we were tough vines. Nobody could pull us down, nobody could pull us out by the roots, and nobody could get a foot in edgewise if we didn't budge. Maybe that was the main reason people like Roanie had it so hard.

But Roanie was part of us. He belonged to us. He belonged to *me*. He shouldn't talk as if he wanted to cut us down to the ground.

I pretended to watch the football game but snuck bewildered glances at his hard profile. He's a lot older than me, I thought with sudden awareness and sorrow. And sometimes he's so far away, I can't bring him back.

We were at the flea market down by Murphy's Feed Mill. Mr. Murphy had outfitted one of his warehouses with a hundred wooden stalls and on weekends people came from miles around to deal with vendors who sold everything from junk to, well, *good* junk. Mama liked to hunt for books and pottery; I liked to hunt for Beep.

Beep Murphy was Mr. Murphy's oldest son. He was a grown man, really, but he was retarded, with round, small, Mongoloid features that made him baby-faced forever. He walked around in overalls and a thick sweater, smiling endlessly as he swept floors and cleaned the portable toilets outside the building and picked up trash, which he deposited in his white plastic bucket with flower decals on it.

He loved kids because he *was* one at heart, and he knew which ones of us he could count on. When he spotted me, he ducked out a side door. "Come on," I said to Roanie.

"What for?"

"We gotta catch Beep. You've never chased Beep?"

"Nooo."

"Come on!" I ran outside. It was a bright, clear, cold December day. I dodged among the cars and trucks parked on the graveled apron around the warehouse. "Beep, Beep, *Beep*," I called as I searched each lane. I rounded the end of a car.

"BEEP!" Beep bellowed back at me. He was crouched beside the fender. He pounded his trash can with one hand. We both burst out laughing.

"How you doin', Mr. Beep?"

"Beep."

Roanie walked up beside me. Beep grinned up at him. "Beep."

"Say it back," I whispered.

"I don't think so," Roanie said with some dignity.

"BEEP," Beep said insistently.

"Say it back, Roanie. Or he'll follow you around till you do. That's part of the game."

Roanie was silent, frowning. "Beep." It was the flattest *beep* I'd ever heard.

But Beep nodded and laughed, satisfied. He sprang to his feet. "Beep!" he tossed over one shoulder as he lumbered back into the warehouse.

"Now you're a member of the Beep Society," I told Roanie seriously. "You've been *Beeptized.*"

"And I thought I'd missed out on a lot," he answered drolly.

"You don't like Beep?"

"Feel sorry for him. He acts like a fool. People make fun of him."

"I wasn't making fun of him."

"I don't mean you. I just mean in general. He doesn't know how to fight back, so he plays along."

"No! He's happy."

"He's not in on the joke."

"Sure he is. He likes it."

His face tight with anger, Roanie leaned against the car and shoved his hands in his jeans pockets. "I saw him in town once. Waiting outside the grocery store while his old man was shopping. Four or five boys decided to have a little fun with him. Got in a circle around him, called him names. Called him an idiot, said he was stupid. He started cryin'."

I felt bad, but I didn't know what to say. Roanie knew how Beep must have felt because he'd been singled out for mean treatment himself. I wanted to squeeze one of his hands in sympathy or hug him, but I knew, too, that he wouldn't like that in public. And not much in private, of course. It was as if touching and being touched were dangerous in some way, and I don't mean because of boy-girl regulations. "I didn't do anything about it," he added dully. "There was so many of 'em. I just watched. I hated it."

"That's how I felt when you were getting beat up on at school," I said. "And at Easter that time, and the Christmas parade last year, and when Aunt Bess sent you away." My voice cracked. He was looking down at me now, not angry anymore, but somber and gentle. "I couldn't do anything," I rushed on, swallowing hard and fighting a tremor in my lower lip. "When I told on you last fall and they caught you over at Ten Jumps so you couldn't hide anymore, I felt awful. I did it to help, but I was scared it was wrong. I'm sorry. I'm sorry."

"You did all right. Did plenty. More'n anybody."

"No, I didn't. What?"

"Gave me a reason to keep trying."

"Trying to do what?"

"Not give up."

I brightened. "Really?"

"Don't get a big head over it."

I punched him on the arm. "Now you're teasing me!"

"Beep," he said darkly.

"Shitbird!"

We started inside the flea market, but an old sedan pulled past us into a parking space. Peeling paint. Missing hubcaps. Duct-taped windows. Yep. A McClendon car. Sally climbed out. She was dressed in a fuzzy white jacket and tight jeans and fuzzy white boots. Her hair was piled up in a curly yellow topknot. She spotted us and looked Roanie up and down with her black-mascaraed eyes. Maybe she'd never seen him in nice clothes before.

Roanie pushed me ahead of him, on into the warehouse. I dug the heels of my loafers into the ground and twisted away. "What are you doing? I want to talk to her."

"No, you don't."

"I don't like the way she eyeballs you. I'm gonna tell her to mind her own business."

"She's all bark and not much bite," he told me grimly. "If you want to feel sorry for somebody, feel sorry for her."

That shut me up.

"You're a good baby-sitter, Roanie," Sally called, grinning at him as she sauntered over. "We miss havin' you around."

Baby-sitter. I wanted to pull out her fuzz one clump at a time. Roanie clamped a hand on my shoulder. "I got tired of draggin' my old man home when you and Daisy kicked him out. Y'all oughta kick him out for good."

Sally stopped in front of him. Her grin faded. "You ain't ever coming back to see us, are you?" she asked in a small voice.

"I can't change what goes on down there, but I don't have to be part of it."

"You're not like your daddy." She tossed that off with a thin smile. "He cain't stay away. Cain't keep his pants zipped neither."

Roanie turned me around and nudged me toward the door. His face was red. "Claire, go inside. I'll be along in a minute."

I pivoted and glared up at him. "Oh, no. I'm not budging."

"*Claire.*"

"No."

Sally seemed to have urgent words burning inside her. She edged closer to Roanie. "He's a dog, but lots of the fine men around here ain't any better. It's gonna catch up one day. Be hell to pay. One of these days I might
just move on. I saved that money you gimme."

Money? Roanie had given her money?

"I ain't like you, Roanie," she went on sadly. "I ain't foolin' myself." She
reached out and smoothed the collar of his jacket.

Roanie shook his head. "There's people who'll give you a chance to do
better. But you gotta meet them halfway."

"What?" She pointed at me. "Her and her kin? They're lyin' to you.
They don't give a damn about you. Her people ain't nothin' special. Her
Uncle Pete'll fuck anything that stands still long enough. And he ain't the
only one."

I screeched wordlessly and lunged at her with one hand drawn back in
a fist. Roanie grabbed me. Picked me up without a word, circling my waist
with one arm and lifting me, dangling, off my feet. I swung my arms and
kicked. Sally laughed. "Don't be jealous, queenie. Roanie got away before I
had a chance. You take care of him, you hear?"

"Put me down!" I shrieked as Roanie carried me away. He took me
inside and ducked into a corner hidden behind the stalls. He set me down.
"Cool off."

"What's she talkin' about?" I demanded. "*Did you give her money?*"

"Yeah, I did."

"Why?"

"Because she needs the help, Claire."

"*Why?*"

"Like I said about Beep, I can't stand by and just watch somebody get
kicked in the teeth."

I took several deep breaths. "I'm trying to feel sorry for her," I told
him. "I really am. But I need to go pull some of her fur out first."

He leaned toward me. His harsh eyes burned into my defiant ones.
"She gets hurt in ways I never had to put up with. You get it? By the time
she wasn't much older than you, she was scared of men. *Scared.* That's why
she acts like she does."

I looked at him with slowly dawning horror. "She shoulda asked for
help."

"Like me? I wouldn't a-taken help if it hadn't been for you. She don't . . .
she *doesn't* have anybody special like you."

"Beep?" Beep said, poking his head around a corner and shaking his trash bucket at us.

I ran to Beep. I threw my arms around his stout waist and hugged him hard. He looked stunned. "Beep," he purred, and awkwardly patted my back.

I turned and met Roanie's shrewd, troubled eyes. "I care," I said slowly. "And don't you forget it."

I told Mama that Sally had hinted about leaving town someday. I thought Mama might be relieved to know. I was wrong.

"That baby of hers isn't some stranger," I heard Mama crying to Daddy late that night as I hid on the back stairs with Roanie. "Poor little Matthew. None of us even talk about him as if he has a *name*. I don't even know whether Sally named him after Matthew the apostle or Matt Dillon on *Gunsmoke*. What kind of life will he have if Sally decides to run off with him?"

"I'll tell you what'll happen if you try to take him away from her," Daddy said quietly. "We'll have to go to court, and no judge is likely to see it our way. She's the baby's mother. She's got rights."

"Oh, Holt! From all I've heard she's no better than a cat! When some new tom yowls at her, she'll forget she ever had a baby."

"Hon, even if we could adopt Matthew, we'd never get your brother to admit to anything. What would you do? Force Pete to take a blood test?"

"We could. Ralph told me he could get a court order—"

"Set my brother against your brother? Good God, hon, you want to do that to the family? What about your mother? She's old, and Pete's a misery to her as it is. You keep pushing the idea that Matthew's his little boy, you'll break her heart."

I listened to Mama crying as Daddy murmured soothing sounds to her. I looked at Roanie, who stared into space, frowning. I could never get him to talk about his mood that night.

I realized much later that there's nothing worse than realizing the limit of good intentions.

11

*T*he trouble with Roanie was that he didn't know his *place* yet; he had been pulled up by the roots too many times. There was a lot of talk about *place* in my family. It was no small matter to know your place in the world, and I don't mean in the way spiteful people talk about *keeping some-one in their place*, I mean the sense of belonging. A place at the table. A place in a family. A place on the land. A place in the heart.

That might be a very Southern concern—places. Aunt Jane was founder and president of the Eudora Welty Literary Society, which met at the library every Tuesday night, and it was a telling fact that she named her book lovers' club after a Southern writer who'd said we had a profound sense of place, that our feelings were all tied up in place.

Roanie had a place in our family, as far as I was concerned, and a deep, secure place in my heart, but he needed something else and I couldn't decide what it was, until the day Grandpa took us up to Dunshinnog Mountain to gather mistletoe.

Dunshinnog towered over the eastern edge of our valley like the king of all mountains. Maloneys had owned it since the very first pioneer land-grant years, which was amazing when you considered the frugal choices old Sean and Bridget Maloney had to make to survive and prosper in the parceled-out wilderness.

After all, Dunshinnog wasn't valuable farmland, like the valley. You could only look at it, and love it. I thought that bit of appreciation said a lot about the hearts of those old ancestors of mine, that they must have been romantic, even without their teeth.

The mountaintop was wide and almost level, with a natural meadow at one end. We skirted patches of pine trees that stairstepped down the easiest side, the west, where some long-dead Maloneys had once built terraced pastures for cattle. I could find the foundation of a house and barns on a low ridge, but only because I knew where to look.

Otherwise the mountain was covered in old hardwood forest, and each spring we gazed up at its white clouds of dogwood blooms and then the pinkish clusters of laurel. In autumn it blazed with red and gold. In the early winter, when Roanie and Grandpa and I went there, Dunshinnog was a spartan world of somber gray. Small herds of deer roamed it, and raccoons, and wild turkey. Hawks hung over it on a clear day, and we saw an eagle once. There was even a bear or two left when I was a girl, though we never saw one.

But *foxes* were the mountain's barter in local legend, foxes and the whimsy of Irish tall tales. Like Mr. Tobbler and his yellow jackets, we chicken-farming Maloneys had long ago made peace with our enemies in trade.

"Tell Roanie how Sean and Bridget named the mountain," I said to Grandpa during the long hike.

Grandpa grinned. "The *sidhe* are in charge up there."

"Irish fairies," I explained to Roanie, who arched a dark brow but didn't dare laugh.

"The *sidhe* helped foxes slip down into the valley at night to steal Maloney hens," Grandpa went on, with grand drama in his voice. "And the foxes were good at it, too, because the fairies put gloves on their paws, so no people could hear 'em sneak in or out of the chicken coops." Grandpa raised his stubby hands and wiggled his fingers. "Every night the fairies would take the blooms off the flowers and put 'em on the foxes' paws, and when the foxes came home to the mountain every morning the fairies put the blooms back on the stems, so a person could never catch on to the magic."

"Foxgloves," I interjected helpfully. "That's how come foxglove flowers are called foxgloves. Except you can see the fairy handprints inside the flowers. The little speckles. That's the only way you can see what the fairies have been up to."

"Claire," Grandpa snorted, "hush up and let me talk. When you're old you get to tell all the whoppers. It's my turn right now."

"Oh. I'm sorry."

"So Sean and Bridget, being from the old country, they knew the only smart thing to do was honor the fairies and the foxes, just grant 'em their due and be glad for God's bounty to share." Grandpa finished with a majestic nod. "So they named the mountain *Dun-sionnach-sidh,* which was Irish for the 'fortress of the foxes and fairies.'"

"But that big name was a mouthful," I told Roanie solemnly. "And hard to spell, too. So it ended up being Dunshinnog. There. What d'ya think?"

Roanie mulled it all over for a second. If he'd laughed at the story, he'd have lost a lot of ground in Maloney territory that day. "Makes sense to me," he said.

The green mistletoe hung in the tops of the tallest trees like remnants of forgotten summer. Grandpa pulled a sawed-off shotgun from his backpack. He and Roanie took turns shooting into the branches. Clumps of mistletoe fell into the lower ones and Grandpa hoisted me up to retrieve it. Hunting mistletoe was a great game. We stuffed most of it into a sack, but I kept a sprig for myself.

I held up my personal commission in mistletoe. I had traditions, too. "I've got a smooch craving," I announced.

Grandpa laughed. He bent down and I held the mistletoe over his head and kissed his cheek, and he kissed mine. Then I looked at Roanie. I felt a little sad and giddy, the way I had in the parking deck at Rich's, and I couldn't understand why. I just knew I had to kiss him, too. "Com'ere."

He shifted uncomfortably and stuck his hands in his pants pockets. "Get it over with," Grandpa said, laughing harder. "It's something Claire has to do every year."

Roanie dropped to his heels. My hand shook. I held the mistletoe above his dark hair and quickly pecked a spot on his jaw. His skin was so warm. "Now you gotta do me," I ordered in a small, reedy voice. He'd never kissed me before, and I wasn't certain he'd do it then. "Come on, come on," I squeaked impatiently. "Get it over with."

He turned his face toward me. His winter-gray eyes met mine for an instant. "I think you're some kind of fairy yourself," he teased. Then he brushed his lips across my forehead. I shut my eyes.

I felt as if I were on fire and I could fly.

"Let's take in the view," Grandpa said. He led us through a meadow to a smooth shelf of silver-gray granite that jutted from the mountain's brow like the brim of a cap. The world as I knew it was spread out below us—the Maloney fields and pastures, our big house with its wide porches and triple chimneys, our barns and long, low chicken houses, and the small house where Grandpa and Grandma Maloney lived. In the distance we could even see the narrow paved ribbon of Soap Falls Road peeping through the trees. It was as if Sullivan's Hollow didn't exist, because it was the only place we couldn't see from Dunshinnog.

"This is a good place," Roanie said gruffly. "This is above everybody. This is a great place. Yeah. I can believe there's magic up here."

Grandpa performed the little ceremony his own grandpa had taught him, as his grandpa had been taught by his grandpa, the ritual stepping back through the generations to Sean Maloney himself. He took an Irish pennywhistle from the pocket of his shirt, maneuvered his thick fingertips over a half-dozen small holes in its shiny tin barrel, fitted the tip in his mouth, and played "Amazing Grace."

The sweet, haunting song surrounded us and was picked up by the wind, singing out toward the valley. Goosebumps crept up my arms. *I once was lost but now am found, was blind but now I see.* Roanie's eyes gleamed, his lips parted in absolute wonder.

He became, on that mountaintop, a boy who found magic and history, who joined a tradition that could fill empty places deep in his heart. The *sidhe* had given my fox a view of the world, they'd given him to me; our paws were slippered in their magic. We could come and go as we pleased, together.

Dunshinnog was our special place from then on.

Josh and Brady were home from college for the Christmas holidays. They were he-men, cool and handsome, with coppery shocks of hair and beautiful smiles. They had thick muscles on their shoulders and tight bellies that didn't flinch when I socked them during wrestling matches. They drove swell sportscars and dated beautiful college girls who sucked up to me shamelessly because I was Josh and Brady Maloney's little sister.

Josh was twenty-five—four years older than Brady—but both of them were seniors at the university because of the years Josh had spent in the army after high school. He had served two tours as an M.P. in Saigon.

I remembered vague, troubling currents of the fear in our home, of everyone huddling around the living-room TV to watch the news each night, of seeing Mama cry as she packed boxes and letters to send to Josh, and of myself somberly including my fingerpainted portraits of the farm and the family, so he'd know we were okay. Painted in broad strokes, maybe, blotchy and runny, but okay.

I found out later that Josh had spent most of his time breaking up bar fights, patrolling whorehouses, and dragging soldiers out of opium dens. There was a lot he wouldn't talk about, a lot that worried Mama and Daddy about him. He was not just my oldest brother, he was my *old* brother, ancient around the eyes, and he didn't laugh much, and when he did talk it was mostly about politics.

Brady, on the other hand, took nothing seriously. Brady had big dreams, trendy dreams. He played the drums about as well as a trained monkey, but he had organized his own rock band in high school. Daddy had let him hold concerts in one of the fields. Brady ran a few electrical cords out there and built a stage out of packing crates, but no more than twenty of his friends showed up at any given event. Brady's music was that bad.

Mama's favorite pet terrier, whose name was Jawbone, chewed through an extension cord one night. The concert ended abruptly with Jawbone's sizzling yelp and the last squawking guitar chord of a Rolling Stones song. Jawbone was never quite the same after that, and Mama lowered the boom on Brady's dream of becoming a rich and decadent rock star. At the university he majored in business and was president of his fraternity, and when he wasn't talking about girls, he talked about money.

Brady didn't seem to notice Roanie one way or the other. Josh seemed to avoid him. Josh swung me up on his back and walked down to the creek one afternoon. "What are you after, baby sister? You want another brother?" he asked.

"Huh?"

"Roanie."

I chortled. "He's better than a brother. I can order him around."

Josh and I squatted on the creekbank. He stared into the cold silver water. "It's easy to get confused about people," he said in a patient, big-brother tone. "Sometimes you make a friend for the wrong reason, because you feel lonely. And when you stop feeling lonely you don't need that friend anymore. That's not fair to the friend, is it?"

I had never imagined Josh feeling confused about anything in his entire life. "I'm not lonely. And there's nothing wrong with Roanie."

"When I was in Vietnam, I made friends with a lot of people who had different ideas from mine. I started to talk like them and act like them and think like them. When I came home, it was hard to stop being that way. I had to work at it. Sometimes I still have to work at it."

"What kind of weird friends did you *have?*"

Josh scrubbed a hand over his face. A fine bead of sweat slid down his temple. It was chilly outside, but Josh always looked as if he were putting out some fire in his mind. "The point is, sis, you can hurt people by making friends with them for the wrong reason. And you can hurt yourself, and you can hurt your family."

I considered that in bewildered silence. There was no point trying to explain to Josh. Some people, Grandpa said, spent all their time cussing the dark when all they had to do was light a candle.

The Christmas parade went off without a hitch that year. But Roanie didn't go, even though I begged and argued, and I was mad at him through the whole event.

I heard the next day that he asked Sheriff Vince to send a deputy over to Steckem Road the night of the parade. Roanie and that deputy sat in a patrol car and made sure Big Roan didn't leave Daisy's house.

$\mathcal{I}$ reached a new level of self-control that Christmas. I was always the first one up on Christmas morning, *always*, and my first act was to fly downstairs in my nightgown and robe and fuzzy pink bedroom slippers, when the pale light of dawn was just shading gray outside the windows and the house was filled with magical, expectant silence. I would open the double doors to the living room and slip inside, alone.

But this time I hurried downstairs and tiptoed along the back hall to Roanie's door, and with every shred of willpower I could muster, I knocked softly and persistently, whispering, "Roanie, *wake up*," until he finally opened his door a few inches and looked down at me in sleepy confusion, a quilt wrapped around him.

"What's wrong?" he asked immediately.

"Nothing. It's *Christmas*. Come with me."

"Wait. What?"

"Oh, you don't *know*. I forgot. You don't know what that *means*." I cast furtive glances up and down the quiet, dark hall. "Come on!" I whispered urgently.

"Hold on. I gotta get dressed."

"No, no, no. Nobody gets dressed right away on Christmas." I peered through the opening at him, eager to see what kind of pajamas he slept in. Above the quilt I saw the frayed neck of a gray sweatshirt. Below it I saw bleach-stained gray sweatpants with a hole in one knee and sagging white gym socks, thin at the toes. "You look swell," I swore. I grabbed the edge of the quilt and tugged. "Come on. Hop and Evan'll crawl out in a few minutes and then everybody'll wake up. We don't have much time."

Frowning, he slipped down the hall behind me. I led him to the front of the house and stopped before the doors to the living room. "Now watch," I whispered. Holding my breath, I turned the long brass handles and eased the doors open so they wouldn't creak.

It was like looking through a mirror into Wonderland.

Glowing and winking with lights, the Christmas tree shimmered next to the fireplace, where a low fire crackled. By that age I knew, of course, that Santa hadn't plugged the tree in or built the fire, that Mama had slipped down thirty minutes ahead of me and done it, but I didn't say so to Roanie, who needed to see the wonder that Santa left behind.

The brightly wrapped presents stacked around the tree's base by mere mortals had mushroomed into a bonanza during the night. That whole corner of the room burst with packages. The soft voices of some Christmas choir purred from the stereo receiver.

I heard Roanie's quick intake of breath behind me. I looked up at him hopefully, and the expression on his face was open and easy. "Come on," I urged. He edged into the room with me. I pulled him to the hearth. "Look." An empty, milk-stained glass sat there, and a china plate dotted with crumbs from Mama's cinnamon cookies. "Of course Daddy ate 'em," I allowed solemnly. "But I used to think it was Santa."

"I never thought I'd see nothing like this. 'Cept on TV."

"Oh, it's real. Sit down. Sit on the hearth. I get to open one present before everybody else 'cause I get up first. So you get to open one of yours, too. It's okay."

He stared at me as if I were joking. "I got presents?"

"Of course." I shuffled over to the tree and pushed the stacks aside and crawled behind them, then popped up with a deep, rectangular box wrapped in red foil paper and topped with a fluffy gold bow. "This is from me."

I held it out anxiously. He was absolutely still for a second, then he angled carefully behind the tree and dropped to his heels. When he stood, he held a tiny box in his hand. It was wrapped in green paper printed with tiny red bells. There was as much Scotch tape on it as paper, and the green bow was bigger than the box.

"I got this for you," he said in an offhand way. "The grannies helped me pick it out." He shrugged. That shrug told me it was important.

I felt as warm as a light on the Christmas tree. "*Gimme.*"

We traded, then sat down side by side on the hearth. "Open yours first," I ordered, though my fingers automatically began prying at the tape on his gift to me.

He was so careful with the paper on his gift, not wanting to tear it, I guess. I shifted my feet and squirmed. He opened the box and took out the blue pullover sweater I'd gotten him. He examined it the way he'd dealt with the wrapping paper, tenderly, uncertainly, drawing his fingers over the thick cable knit. "It's new," I blurted out. "I mean, that's why it's still got that tag on one arm. So if it doesn't fit right or you don't like it, you can exchange it for another one."

"No moth holes," he said. "Smells new. I like it."

"Put it on."

He let the quilt fall around his waist and donned the sweater over his sweatshirt. He looked bulky, but fine. "I was gonna get you something fun," I said, hedging against any nonchalance in his reaction. "Like a hunting knife or something. But Grandma Dottie said you'd like this." I sighed. "Clothes aren't much fun, though."

He looked at me. "It's the first *new* anything I ever got, Claire. It's great."

I grinned. "Well, I knew you'd like it."

"Open yours."

My fingers moving as fast as ants at a picnic, I ripped the paper and bow off the tiny box on my lap and flipped the top off. Inside, on a bed of white cotton, lay an enameled green shamrock pendant about the size of a dime. It hung from a thin gold chain.

"Oh!" I loved jewelry the way Hop's squirrel loved nuts. Mama limited my collection to a few delicate necklaces and a silver wristwatch and a pair of clip-on earrings with a single pearl on each of them. Otherwise I'd have decked myself out in every dime-store bauble my allowance could provide. "It's beautiful!"

The necklace was just long enough for me to squeeze it over my head without unfastening the clatch. I put it on and freed my tangled hair, then closed one hand over the shamrock. "It's the very *best* Christmas present I've ever gotten." I looked at him with my heart racing. "I love you."

"Ssshh," he said, glancing around as if we weren't alone. "I know how you mean it, but nobody else would."

"Say it back to me anyhow. Say it."

"I don't think it's a good idea to say it."

"Just say it's forever."

He looked at me without blinking. "It's forever," he admitted softly.

• • •

The day was a whirl of visitors. Roanie watched from the corners, absorbing it all with the quiet intensity of an animal that had been caged too long to step out quickly just because someone opened a door for him.

I had to admit, finally, that I was glad he kept to himself, because some of the things that went on that day shook my optimism a little.

My cousin Aster, the one who got knocked over with her tuba the Christmas before, was the leader of the female anti-Roanie faction. She was one tough bloomer. Sixteen, chunky even by our well-fed standards, with fat, sturdy legs that angled in at the knees, she still wore braces on her teeth. It takes a tough girl to play the tuba through a wire grill. She wore her brown hair long and straight with the ends permed to a fare-thee-well. And she wore blue eye shadow. She was a sight.

"Where's your boyfriend, Claire?" Aster taunted. She had wandered into my bedroom, where Violet and Rebecca and I were examining our presents.

"Let me see that necklace," Aster said. She bent down and snagged my shamrock with her fingers.

I pushed her hand away. "Hey, that's personal."

Aster snorted. "It's cheap. If you think it's green now, wait a couple of months."

"Oh, go away," Rebecca said. "We don't want to know what you think."

I gave Aster a sour look and tucked my necklace inside the collar of my red Christmas sweater. I sat cross-legged on my bed, cradling the small portable typewriter Mama and Daddy had given me. Aster leaned against the canopy post and waved a hand at me. "What are you going to be? A secretary?"

"No, I'm going to be a writer. And someday I'm going to write about you. So watch out."

"You're spoiled rotten. I guess Aunt Marybeth just doesn't care what people think. If you were being raised by my mama she wouldn't let you accept a piece of junk jewelry that Roanie Sullivan probably stole from some dime store."

I looked her right in the eye. "Why don't you pull your butthole over your head 'cause you're full of shit."

Violet and Rebecca gasped. It suddenly dawned on me that I almost never said "shit" in front of anyone but Roanie. "Shithead," I added cheerfully.

Aster gaped at me. "I guess you learned that from Roanie Sullivan."

"No, I thought it up on my own."

"That boy is just plain trash. He'll chase whores exactly like his daddy does. I wish he'd just leave."

"I wish *you'd* just leave. He's fine. We all like him. I like him."

Aster smirked. "So you're going to be a writer and a whore?"

Violet and Rebecca clamped their hands over their mouths. Not over their ears, of course—they wanted to hear every filthy word. They just didn't want to take the chance that what they heard would go in one way and pop out the other.

I smiled at Aster. "Sure! I'll be the biggest whore in Dunderry! But at least I won't waddle around knock-kneed, suckin' on a tuba."

"I can imagine what you *will* suck on," Aster retorted. She stalked out of the room.

Angry and embarrassed, I shrugged. Her eyes huge, Violet lowered her hand slowly. "What do you think she meant by *that*?"

"Aw, who cares?"

Rebecca, blushing, cupped a hand to Violet's ear and whispered something. Violet's nose wrinkled and she stared at me. "Oh, my."

We sat there in frazzled silence. They studied me furtively, as if a river of shocking plans ran beneath my familiar surface. My shamrock pendant felt hot against my chest. "Oh, I'm not going to be a whore," I assured them. "I was just kidding."

"Then don't say the *s*-word again," Violet begged.

Rebecca leaned toward me eagerly. "What else did Roanie Sullivan teach you?"

"*He did not teach me to say it.*"

"I think it'd be exciting if he stole that necklace just for you," Rebecca added.

"*He didn't steal it! He doesn't steal!*"

Rebecca and Violet traded solemn looks. "I think it's exciting," Rebecca repeated. "After he gets a driver's license, I bet he'll steal a car."

I was so angry I almost said "shit" again. But that was when I realized that everyone measured Roanie by the yardstick of my indecencies.

Considering my natural inclinations, he was under more of a burden than I'd ever realized.

We went to church that night.

Roanie in church. Wearing a sharp blue suit of Josh's and a wide, pinstriped tie of Daddy's. He was a sight that made more heads swivel than a Ping-Pong match.

He sat there in our pew with all the animation of a bump on a log, but he was a handsome bump. "Sing," I whispered during "O Holy Night," elbowing him in the side.

"I ain't no singer," he whispered back. "And you sing loud enough for the both of us."

"'I am not a singer,'" I corrected. "'You *are not* a singer. *We* are not singers.'"

"Right." His lips quirked. "You ain't no singer neither."

Daddy asked him, after we got home, if he thought he'd like to take Bible study and be officially recognized at the altar sometime. Be saved, Daddy explained. Getting saved was like trying out for a football team. God's football team. It meant you were willing to play by the rules.

"I've done been saved, Mr. Maloney," Roanie answered quietly.

Daddy, bless his gruff heart, let it go at that.

On New Year's Eve I heard Josh's and Brady's deep voices in the hall outside my door. I could smell intrigue like a mouse smells cheese. I went over to my door and cracked it open an inch, then listened.

"I thought we might have to tackle him."

"Did you see the look in his eyes? When Dad told him about talking to Aunt Bess and Uncle Billy? Yeah, I was sure he was about to bolt before Dad explained why they were filing papers in court."

"The kid's tough."

"He's not a kid. He hasn't been a kid for years."

"Yeah, well, this ought to be interesting."

"Mama says he'd fight tigers to protect Claire. I'd say she's right."

"Hey, listen to the way the Old Grannies talk about him. I think they've got a crush on him, too."

"Yeah, what a gas."

Roanie. They were discussing Roanie. I popped out of my room and stared at them. "What's going on?" I demanded.

Josh shot a startled look at Brady. "Little pitchers have big ears."

"You're talking about Roanie. *What's going on?*"

They traded careful, adult glances. I gave them a dirty look and ran downstairs, my heart in my throat.

Mama and Daddy were sitting at the kitchen table, their faces serious. I halted. "What's going on with Roanie?"

They traded solemn looks. Then Daddy waved me over and curled an arm around my waist. "We made sure Roanie's not ever going back to the Hollow. It's permanent, sweetie pie."

"You mean Roanie can live here forever?"

Daddy studied me as if something about my reaction worried him. I could barely breathe. "That's what I mean, sugar."

"Y'all promise?"

"Promise," Daddy said. Mama crossed her heart and held up two fingers. "We signed some papers at the courthouse."

I ran outside. It took me a while to find Roanie. He was out in a back pasture, sitting on a knoll. "I heard," I said, flopping down beside him. "You're permanent!"

"Ain't that something," he said, his eyes glowing. "You was right."

I touched his arm carefully. "I love you, boy."

He looked away. Then back. "I love you, too," he said. "Don't tell nobody."

Just before sunset, Roanie and I walked up to the top of Dunshinnog. We lit some bottle rockets and watched them burst against the cold purple and rose streaks of the evening sky.

Standing beside me with his head thrown back, Roanie was quieter than usual. I looked up at him and the expression on his face made my chest feel full.

He would not, could not sing in a church, but he was singing then without a sound. He'd grown up in Sullivan's Hollow, about as low as a person could get. He loved high places.

The Great Monopoly Game of February established what I'd suspected for a long time: When it came to land and money, Roanie was as flint-eyed as any Maloney or Delaney.

All of the Atlanta TV weathermen said it was too warm for an ice storm, but Grandpa Maloney knew better. "It'll be icier than an Eskimo's nose hairs," he warned as Daddy and Mama loaded Great-Gran Alice and Grandmother Elizabeth into the car that Saturday morning for a trip to Atlanta. The Old Grannies were determined to see Carol Channing in the road show of *Hello, Dolly!* They'd have crossed the Arctic in a dogsled to see Carol Channing.

"We'll be back before the roads close," Daddy said. "I'd rather risk frostbite than tell the Old Grannies Carol Channing's a no-go."

"Son, you're going to think you're at the Ice Capades," Grandpa promised.

But off they went. Hop and Evan were over in South Carolina for a weekend teen retreat sponsored by the church. They'd asked Roanie to go with them, but he backed out. Said he had a term paper to work on. But maybe his decision had something to do with the dull picture I'd painted of those church shindigs. "You'd have to do Bible study and eat stale hot dogs and then pray a whole lot," I explained. I just forgot to mention that teenage girls went to the retreat, too.

At any rate, Roanie and I stayed home with Grandpa and Grandma Maloney, and just as Grandpa predicted, by four o'clock the farm was covered in a white crystalline layer of sleet and the state patrol had closed all the roads. Grandma and Grandpa settled in at our house, with me, Roanie, General Patton, the rest of the dogs, all the cats, and Marvin the squirrel curled up by the living-room fireplace. Daddy called and told Grandpa that he, Mama, and the Old Grannies were stuck at a hotel for the night. When he got off the phone, Grandpa turned to Grandma Dottie, chortling. "That'll teach him. Mother and Elizabeth are arguin' over the price of room service."

I couldn't have been happier. Roanie and I watched television and made popcorn. We trudged outdoors with Grandpa and nearly froze helping him feed the livestock. General Patton chased Marvin without much serious intent. The cats thought of Marvin as a small, long-tailed kitty that hid pecans in the upholstery. The dogs, other than General Patton, were too lazy to care.

The electricity went out shortly after dark. We ate some sandwiches. Grandpa went to sleep in the recliner with a blanket wrapped around him and a cat asleep on his stomach. Grandma lit a pair of kerosene lamps on the library table, cracked her knuckles, and asked slyly, "Who's ready for a game of Monopoly?"

"Not me," I said immediately. "She's a shark," I whispered to Roanie. "She'll win all your money and giggle when you ask for a loan."

Roanie was great at Monopoly. He always won Hop's and Evan's money before they could bat an eyelash. I sold everything and took wild chances, but Roanie held on to his real estate like a miser.

"I'll play," he said with a wicked smile.

So Grandma and Roanie sat across from each other at the table, the Monopoly board spread out between them like a battlefield, the light of the fire and lamps flickering on their steely eyes. I watched from a couch, snuggled in a quilt and yawning. "She never loses," I murmured, and then I fell asleep.

When I woke up, shivering, it was early morning. The fire was out, the lamps were out, General Patton was balled up inside the circle of my arms, and Grandpa was snoring.

"One more game," I heard Grandma say hoarsely. "Best four out of five. You can't quit now. I deserve a rematch."

I blinked, scrubbed my face, and rose on one elbow. Huddled at the table, bleary-eyed, Roanie propped his head up on one hand and looked at Grandma. "I'm so sleepy I can't even find Park Place anymore," he croaked. "Give it up, Miz Dottie. You can't beat me."

"One more game." She crouched at the table, her brindled red hair raked into wild rows.

"I'm sorry. I just can't do it."

"I'll fix some coffee. You're a fair businessman, Roanie Sullivan. Don't begrudge me one more rematch. Okay, here's my deal. If you keep playing, I'll explain high-yield bonds again."

His head bobbed. "Okay," he murmured.

She staggered out of the living room. "Y'all are nuts," I announced. "Pretty soon Marvin's gonna try to hide y'all in the cushions." Roanie dragged himself out of the chair, sat down on the floor next to me, and leaned heavily against the couch with his eyes shut. "Just tell her you're pooped," I said. "She'll understand. Sort of."

He yawned. "She promised she'd teach me about the stock market. I want to . . . know." His head lolled against General Patton. He breathed slowly, sound asleep.

I glanced around furtively, then stroked his hair with my fingertips so he wouldn't feel it. Roanie had an avid interest in money. That was the Irish in him, Daddy said. He'd already opened his own savings account at the bank. Every week he divided the money he earned into three stacks—one that he put in an envelope and stuck in his daddy's mailbox at the Hollow, one he took to the bank, and a very small one he kept for himself.

Grandma came back soon and woke him up. She made him drink two cups of coffee. They played Monopoly until Grandpa woke up and we had to go back outside to feed everything again. Then she made Roanie play Monopoly some more.

When Mama and Daddy and the Old Grannies got home that afternoon, they found Roanie asleep on the living-room floor and Grandma asleep on the couch. Both of them were clutching Monopoly money.

We all agreed: Anybody who shut out Grandma Maloney at Monopoly was destined for great things.

I was destined for greatness too, I decided. I planned a great leap forward into the publishing world beyond my small fame as the 4-H Club correspondent for the *Dunderry Weekly Shamrock*.

"We Want Your Hometown Stories," said the headline in one of Mama's ladies' magazines, the kind that told ladies how to make a perfect custard and have shapely thighs, and had Mary Tyler Moore on the cover as a role model for ladies who wanted to star in a TV show but still be a nice person, too.

The magazine offered fifty bucks for hometown stories. Fifty bucks! Why, I was full of stories. Driven by the urgency of confidence, I secretly tapped out five pages, single-spaced, on my new typewriter. Using grand metaphors and as many adjectives as I could find in the big leather-bound thesaurus in the living room, I related how Roanie shot a deer to pay Uncle Cully. I threw in lots of asides about Grandpa shooting Japanese soldiers and Daddy shooting my beloved Herbert. My theme, I decided, was that people in my hometown felt sad every time they shot something. Therefore we were nice people, like Mary Tyler Moore.

I was very professional. I circled my typos and winnowed them down to only a couple dozen or so in the second draft I typed. I composed a cover letter that said, essentially, *I know you'll love this. Please send cash,* and signed it, *Yours Most Truly, Claire K. Maloney,* at the bottom in red ink. Then I folded the finished masterpiece into a sharply creased five-by-four-inch wad and put it in a pink notecard envelope embossed with my return address in gold ink.

The magazine's offices were in New York. I wrote the address in gold ink, too. Those people in New York would be impressed. Two stamps, for extra insurance, and then I furtively stuck the envelope in our mailbox while I was waiting for the school bus one cold morning.

And the answer came right back. A stern, flat letter in a stern beige business envelope. Thank goodness I retrieved the mail that day as I had on every day since I mailed my story, so no one knew.

> *Dear Miss/Ms./Mrs. Maloney:*
>
> *Your writing lacks maturity and polish. The single-spaced format and numerous typing errors made your submission nearly unreadable. Your story was more than twice the stated word limit. I cannot return your submission, as you did not include an SASE. Most of all, as a person of Japanese descent, I found your analogy regarding Japanese soldiers and cows somewhat offensive. Best of luck with your future projects.*
>
> *Jane Takahashi, Editorial Assistant*

I was flattened. I tore up the rough drafts of my story and burned the pieces. Either Roanie smelled the smoke or sensed my misery. He found me huddled behind a chicken house with ashes scattered on my jeans and my face swollen from crying.

"What's the matter, Peep?" he asked anxiously, squatting beside me with his arms propped on his knees.

"Nothing." Professional humiliation required solitude.

He squinted. "I'll just hang around and see what you set fire to next."

"No, go away. I'm thinking."

He sat down regardless. "Why don't you think out loud? Pretend I ain't here."

"*Am not* here. I can't pretend that well. I can't . . . pretend at *all*." I let out one of those involuntary huh-huh-huh sounds of a stifled sob. And then, heartbroken, I poured out the whole, devastating tale as he listened somberly. "I can't type like a real writer," I moaned. "I've got no taste. I insulted a Japanese lady. I didn't know I was supposed to send a SASSY. I don't even know what a SASSY is."

"You wrote about me?" he asked.

I wiped my eyes. "Well, yeah, but don't worry. I changed your name. I changed all the names."

"What name did you give me?"

"Dirk DeBlane." His brows shot up. I cringed. It had sounded romantic at the time. Like one of the knights in Mama's romance novels. "You hate it," I said sadly.

"Nah. I, uh, I *like* it. Nobody ever wrote a story about me before." He mused over the name, nodding. "Why'd you write about me that way?"

"Because it's . . . romantic." My face burned. "I'm almost ten. Mama says I can start dating boys when I'm sixteen. So you only have to wait six years to go out on a date with me. But we can be romantic *now*."

"Why, thanks," he said drily.

"Well, you'll be busy anyhow. You'll go to college."

"Maybe. Haven't made up my mind about college."

"Of course you'll go. And then I'll go to college, and after I get out, we'll go off and see the world together. Like my cousin Lisa. She went to England for a year."

"Whatever you say, Peep." Sometimes he could be so *old*, so patient and serious, that I felt like a fly buzzing around him.

I ducked my head and scrutinized him from under my brows. "But I guess we'll have to get married then. So we can save money on hotel rooms."

"I plan to make a lot of money," he said, raising a determined gaze to me. But one corner of his lips crooked up. "We could afford two rooms. We wouldn't have to get married."

"I guess that'd be okay. As long as you don't marry anybody else."

"Don't plan to."

"So you don't need any girlfriends, right? I mean, you've already got me."

"Cool off. I'm not gonna ask no girls out anytime soon. That takes money. And a car. Girls ain't easy to fool with."

"Girls *aren't* easy to fool with," I corrected sternly.

"That's right." He laughed.

"Look, I'm not *stupid*. I watch how you look at the girls who hang around Hop and Evan. I watch how they look *back*. I've noticed. They've got boobs and I haven't. But I *will* get some. You just wait."

He scowled. "You ain't—you *aren't*—a girl. You're Claire."

"Why do you have to look at them?"

"They're fun to watch. But too much trouble." He emphasized *trouble*.

"Yeah. I'm not any trouble. And I'm a lot of fun."

"It's not the same." His eyes narrowed. "There's some things you and me ain't gonna talk about. This is one of 'em. Don't go around tellin' people I'm your boyfriend. It's not that way, and you'll get me in trouble."

"What way is it?"

He studied me for a minute, very still, absorbing me. "You know what you are?" he said softly. "You're everything good I can imagine."

"What?" I leaned toward him, warm inside, dry behind the eyes, distracted.

"You don't see things the way other people do. You gave me a chance when nobody else would. People will listen to what you've got to say someday. Maybe not them people at that magazine, but people who know what's worth listening to. Don't you give up. You keep writin'. The rest of us don't have a voice unless you talk for us."

I nearly burst with fledgling, adoring hope. I burrowed my head on his shoulder and cried some more. He put his arm around me. "When you're old enough I'll try to live up to ol' Dirk," he said.

"Look at him," I heard Aunt Lucille whisper to Mama one Friday night. They were seated at a table in the high school cafeteria. The band was holding its first spaghetti supper of the year to raise money for new uniforms. Aunt Lucille and Mama didn't know I was standing behind them. "He's just a square peg in a round hole, Marybeth. Look. There he goes. Fixes his plate, takes it outside, sits in the cold by himself."

"He's just shy," Mama told her.

"When y'all bring him with you to my house, he wanders off alone. Same at Irene's. Same at Jane's. Same everywhere he goes. Then Claire traipses off after him and they huddle like two old hens on the same nest. The family comes to visit y'all, he's nowhere to be seen. And neither is Claire. What in the world do those two *do* together?"

"We work on his talkin'," I announced. They turned around in their chairs and looked at me. "I'm teachin' him to congregate his verbs."

"Conjugate," Mama corrected.

"Well, that's very nice of you," Aunt Lucille said with some exasperation and not much sincerity, I thought. "But maybe Hop and Evan could do that, so you could spend more time with your own friends."

"I don't mind. I like conjugating."

"Roanie needs to make some friends his own age, Claire. You know, you're like a little sister to him. Before long he won't have time for you. He'll be going out on dates. He'll have girlfriends."

That wouldn't happen. I just wouldn't stand for it. It was unthinkable. "I don't see why," I told her. "He won't conjugate with anybody but me."

Aunt Lucille made a sputtering sound and looked at Mama. "*Claire*," Mama said.

Aunt Lucille smiled nervously. "Claire, you save a nickel for every boy you like between now and the time you settle on one to marry and you'll be rich. I promise."

"If I'm rich, I won't get married."

"Oh, yes, you will."

"Well, then, I'll just marry Roanie."

Aunt Lucille stared at me. Mama shut her eyes with a kind of resigned effort, then waved me outside.

I went gladly. I didn't realize it yet, but I had a knack for putting the kibosh on conversations about Roanie. At least the ones that took place where I could hear them.

14

*R*oanie's fifteenth birthday was on the last day of March. Nobody'd ever celebrated his birthday before. We only heard about it because he mentioned the upcoming date to Grandpa.

Grandpa was the official driving honcho for my brothers, coaching them for their driver's tests and seeing that they got their licenses. He'd taken Evan to get a learner's permit in September; since then, Evan had backed Mama's Thunderbird into Grandma's station wagon, sideswiped a stop sign with Daddy's truck, and run over the lilac bush in Aunt Irene's front yard. Then he backed up and hit her birdbath, too.

Grandpa had just recently recovered his sense of humor as a driving tutor.

"Roanie says he turns fifteen on Saturday," I heard Grandpa tell Daddy. "I told him I'd take him to the state patrol next week to get his learner's permit." Grandpa chortled. "We need another chauffeur around here. Even the Old Grannies won't ride with Evan."

Fifteen. Birthday.

I conferred with Mama. "Oh, my lord," Mama said sadly. "Your daddy and I should have remembered." They'd been on hand, of course, when poor, struggling Jenny Sullivan gave birth.

Fired with regrets and determination, Mama made a huge layer cake covered with white icing and blooming with blue sugar roses and fifteen blue candles. I *had* to make an artistic contribution, I told her, so she filled one of her cake-decorating cones with green icing and I wrote, *Happy Birthday, Roanie,* across the top of the cake.

My icing script looked like the work of a tipsy garden snail. Mama said, kindly, that it gave the cake a certain character, but she turned *Roanie* into *Roan* with a dab of white icing. "He's getting too old to go by Roanie," she explained.

I didn't want him to get that old. I had no corresponding name change to look forward to. If I dropped the *e* off Claire, it would still sound the same.

I'd never seen a look on Roanie's face like the one I saw when I carried that birthday cake, candles blazing, out of the pantry and set it in front of him on the breakfast table. Not just surprise or gratitude, but the slow, dawning *glow* of understanding. This was what families were all about—a whole bunch of people who showed you they were glad you'd been born.

"Make a wish and blow out the candles, Roan," Mama instructed.

"Wish for a fire extinguisher," Hop interjected. "Man, if you lean any closer to those candles, you're gonna lose your eyebrows."

"Wish for things to stop getting in the way of my wheels," Evan said glumly.

"No, wish for an early spring," Grandpa said. "That's our only hope for gettin' one."

"Wish for extra rain this summer," Daddy added.

"Wish for my tennis elbow to stop aching," Grandma Dottie told Roanie, smiling.

"I know precisely what I would wish for," Grandmother Elizabeth said, darting a smug look at Great-Gran.

"I wish you'd lay down and die, too," Great-Gran shot back.

"She was special, wasn't she," Roanie said suddenly.

Puzzled silence. "Who?" I asked in a hushed tone.

His somber gaze moved around the table, then stopped on Mama and Daddy. "My . . . my mama. I mean, she didn't hurt nobody—anybody. She would have been a real lady if she'd had a chance. Wouldn't she?"

More silence. Fragile, delicate, like paper-thin glass in our hands. Grandma Maloney raised her fingertips to her lips to catch a soft, sad sound. Mama blinked hard. Daddy and Grandpa got the funny look men get when they don't want anybody to see their feelings. Hop and Evan looked as if they'd been asked to recite a love poem in front of girls. Not comfortable.

"Sure," I said quickly. "She got married and everything. She was a lady."

Mama cleared her throat. "Roan, she was a sweet girl, and she loved you dearly. She did the best she could. She *was* a lady. And I know she'd be proud of you."

After a moment of stillness, his solemn face dappled with the flickering light cast up by fifteen years of uncertainty, he nodded and blew out the candles.

"Did you make a wish?" I asked fervently.

"I forgot."

"Make one quick! Before the candles stop smoking!"

"I, uh, I wish—"

"Not out loud! If you say it out loud it won't come true!"

Hop snorted. "Claire knows all the wishing rules. She's some kind of leprechaun."

"I am not!"

"Tooth fairy," Evan deadpanned. "Elf, troll—"

Roanie blew on the smoking candles. I stared at him. "Did you make a wish?"

"Yep."

"Good. Let me know when it comes true."

"I will," he said quietly.

The spell of the sad mood was broken. Carried away on the smoke. Relief. Movement. I galloped into the pantry and came back with my arms full of presents. He gaped at them. I had to prod him on one arm to make him start unwrapping the boxes.

Mama had orchestrated the gifts with practical matters in mind—a nice leather belt, new socks, a pair of cufflinks, things like that. But I'd persuaded her to let me give him *good* stuff. He unwrapped my gift and examined it with a slight, pleased smile. It was one of those bulky red Swiss Army knives. He pried each section open until it bristled with blades and bottle opener and corkscrew and scissors. It wasn't just a pocketknife to me, it was a symbol. We'd come a long way in five years since the time he'd threatened to cut Carlton's throat. He wouldn't poke a knife at anybody else, but at least if he did, it'd be a nice knife.

"Look," I said. I plucked a metal toothpick from one end of the knife. I cast a dark look toward Hop and Evan. "This is a leprechaun sword." I tapped Roanie on each shoulder. "Now you're Sir Roan. You can kill dragons for King Arthur and go over the rainbow to the Emerald City."

"Oh, Sir Roan!" Grandmother Elizabeth said, and applauded lightly. "Bold knight! Dragonslayer!"

"You've got leprechauns mixed in with *Camelot* and *The Wizard of Oz*," Mama told me.

Well, I knew *that*.

"Yeah, she's the Wizard of *Odd*," Evan teased.

I sighed. Roanie looked at me carefully. "You bring on the dragon, Claire. I'll clean his teeth."

Everyone laughed. Even me.

My tenth birthday, in May, was, above all, a milestone. Roanie left a dozen red carnations outside my door that morning and I thought I'd die from happiness.

I can't quite describe what I must have been to him—innocence, loyalty, acceptance—a bossy little girl he could tease and protect and talk with on some safe level that existed nowhere else in his life. The difference in our ages and our dreams was invisible to me then, because I loved him from a child's viewpoint, without the influence of grim reality or raging hormones.

I'll never know how that might have changed as we grew older. I read *Wuthering Heights* when I was a girl and hated Cathy for her snobbish cruelty toward Heathcliff; I read the book again, years later, and morbidly decided they'd been doomed from the start.

I didn't know it on my birthday, but we'd come just about as far as we were going to go.

15

Our magic stopped working on a Saturday in early June. It was a steamy, turbulent day, with cottonball thunderheads riding the sky above Dunshinnog and the air as rich as soup. I remember the smell of plowed earth, and greenery, flowers, and wind. I remember anticipating the cold, red sugar of the first watermelon we would eat that summer, and the slow drone of bees, and the delicate whir of a hummingbird outside the back porch.

I remember that day in endless, painful detail, how it started and how it ended.

Mama and Grandma Dottie had taken Grandmother Elizabeth shopping in Atlanta. Daddy and Grandpa went to a luncheon for the poultry breeders' association in Gainesville. Hop and Evan went bass fishing with Uncle Winston and his boys. Josh and Brady weren't home from college yet.

Roanie stayed home to tinker with the engine of an old Volkswagen that Grandpa acquired in some barter deal for farm equipment. Grandpa told him that if he got it running they'd sell it and split the profit. Roan regarded that ugly yellow Bug as if it were gold-plated.

As for me, I was assigned to go to the beauty parlor with Great-Gran Alice. She had turned ninety-three, after all. She didn't drive anywhere alone anymore. She shouldn't have been driving at all. She needed help getting out of her boxy blue Chevy, plus she needed a lookout to yell when she swerved too close to any object that couldn't run, like a tree. Riding with Great-Gran was a rite of passage—my brothers had survived until they got their learner's permits, and I was expected to as well.

Soap Falls Road curled through miles of hardwoods and laurel tangled on steep hills. Daddy and Grandpa always insisted that Great-Gran take Soap Falls into town, because there was practically no traffic on it and the hills hemmed her in on either side.

So there we were, hurtling down the middle of the road like a bobsled down a chute, her white gloves lying neatly on the broad lap of her blue dress, the car filled with the scent of face powder and tearose perfume. I was dressed in overalls, a pink T-shirt, and tennis shoes. I clutched a Laura Ingalls Wilder book I'd brought to read while Great-Gran got her hair permed. I wished I could be on the prairie with Laura. At that moment I could have taught Laura a thing or two about plucky perseverance.

A huge chicken truck came around a bend. The driver didn't give—he felt lucky or else he couldn't think fast enough to move tons of steel and chickens onto two feet of road shoulder backed by a slab-faced hill. "*Watch out,*" I yelled.

Great-Gran said, "Wee, laudy," under her breath and peeled off to the opposite side of the road. I crouched low in the seat, frozen inside my overalls, as we flashed by stacks of terrified-looking hens and a Kehoe Poultry Farm sign. The Chevy's right headlight scraped half the real estate off a red-clay bank and we plowed to a stop. White clouds of steam rose from under the hood.

The chicken truck and its driver disappeared around the next curve and didn't come back. Either the driver didn't realize what had happened or he was desperate to get all those shocked chickens to the processing plant before they fainted.

For the next five minutes Great-Gran ranted about the near miss being all his fault. Then she took a nitroglycerin tablet from her purse and put it under her tongue and laid her head back on the seat. Her knobby, blue-veined hands trembled. I was shaking all over. "Great-Gran, you okay?"

"I just need to rest my heart," she said weakly.

"I'll get help!"

I leaped out. I was just glad I still had legs. I looked back the way we'd come. Home? Yes. No—too far. I pivoted and stared at the curve ahead. The Hollow was close.

The Hollow. Big Roan.

I couldn't waste time running home. I ran toward the Hollow.

My mind was blank except for whatever concentration moved my feet. When I reached the driveway, I plowed to a stop by the lopsided mailbox, sucking in deep breaths, wishing an angel would swoop down and go the rest of the way with me, as the preacher at the Methodist tent revivals swore angels would do.

I inched down the hill. I'd never been in Big Roan's yard before, never been inside the awful trailer. His rusty truck was parked catty-cornered to the trailer's wooden steps. I swallowed hard. My Adam's apple felt as big as a softball.

I stepped carefully among rotting bags of garbage, old tires, car axles, a rusty washing machine with the door torn off, and piles of slimy tin cans that seemed alive with maggots. Flies buzzed around me. I smelled the smell Roanie had lived with, the stink he'd carried with him in his clothes, and I tried not to gag.

I climbed the stairs, my steps leaden, opened the warped screen door, and knocked on a wooden one with a cracked peep window. After a minute I knocked again, louder. I heard slamming sounds inside, then uneven foot-steps, and finally Big Roan flung the door open and glared down at me. His dark hair looked slimy, and there were wet stains down the front of his T-shirt. He had his metal leg on, thank God. And his pants. "Whatcha want?" he growled, swaying from side to side. A gust of his fetid breath washed over me.

I want that darned angel to get here.

"Could I use your phone, please, sir?"

"What the hell for?"

"Great-Gran had a car accident up the road. I need to call for help."

Roanie. Roanie'll come get us.

"Huh." He rubbed his beard stubble. When his lips drew back in some-thing like a smile, I saw the white scum on his teeth. His eyes were blood-shot, and there were patches of broken veins on his cheeks like the tiny, lacy fractures in an old plate.

He staggered to one side and I edged past him. There wasn't much more than a dog path between the crummy furniture. A table fan whirred in the nasty air. A baseball game was showing on a little black-and-white TV with bent antennae wrapped in aluminum foil. Beer cans and liquor bottles lay everywhere.

"You scared of me?" Big Roan asked.

"No, sir." I bumped into the arm of a couch and dust motes puffed out. He lurched over to a sagging green recliner and plopped down on it. He didn't say another word, just watched me with his legs spread and the fake one stretched out, straight and stiff, across my path. A dirty-looking black phone sat on a stack of magazines by his chair. There was a picture of a naked woman on the top magazine's cover. I could see her from the waist down, sticking out from under the phone.

I hopped over Big Roan's leg with the speed of a goat.

His slithery gaze stayed on me as I dialed the phone. I clamped the receiver in my hand. Ringing. Ringing. Roan was outdoors. He wouldn't hear. Nobody else was home. I should have run toward home, not to the Hollow. Not to Big Roan's glowering face, his frightening eyes, his disgust.

"Hello?" Roanie answered. There *were* angels.

"Come get us! We had a car accident! I'm at the Hollow! Great-Gran's sittin' in her car! I'm at the *Hollow!* Come get us!"

"Claire, go back to the road," he said immediately. His voice was low, steady, and I realized he was trying not to sound worried, which really scared me. "Go *right now*," he added. "I'll get Grandpa Maloney's car and I'll be there in five minutes. I swear to God. Just hang the phone up and *walk back to the road.*"

"I will! Hurry!"

I carefully set the receiver back on its berth. "Thank you, Mr. Sullivan." My voice squeaked. "I'll wait up at the road. Thanks." I turned. Big Roan stared at me. Suddenly he raised his metal leg and propped the fake foot-shoe on the couch. As if his leg was one of those automatic arms that close off a railroad crossing when a train's coming. He trapped me behind his side of the tracks.

"That was my boy on the phone, wadn't it?" he asked in a low monotone. "You squealin' for him to come get you."

"I—well, I gotta go, Mr. Sullivan."

"No, you stay the hell put. I wanna talk to you." I stared at the way his pants leg hung on the metal limb as if there were nothing but a skeleton's leg under there. "You better put your leg down, Mr. Sullivan." I could barely breathe. "I don't want to climb over it or something. I mean, I might bend it."

He snorted. "Shit." After that, he didn't budge. Neither did I. We gazed at each other for what seemed like forever, him scrutinizing me with hard eyes like wet marbles, me trying very hard to appear unconcerned. I heard the baseball game on TV. I heard the blood throbbing against my eardrums. I counted silently as several minutes ticked by on a clock atop the TV. Finally he leaned forward and whispered, "You turned my boy against me."

Ice in my veins. "No," I whispered. "Nope. Sir. I don't th-think so."

"What's so special about you?" He flung an arm out and plucked at the sleeve of my T-shirt. I flinched. His fingers twisted tighter in the material. "Too good to talk to me, ain't you?"

"I'm talkin'. See? I'm talkin'. But I gotta go. Sir."

"How'd you win him over, fluffy?" He fingered the hem of my sleeve between his thumb and forefinger. "You little pink-faced, redheaded busy-body. You think you're a pretty little thing, don't you?"

Politeness wasn't working. My head reeled from the closeness, the stink, the heat, the terror. I tried sternness. "You let go of my shirt. You put your leg down. *Right now.* Or I'll . . . I'll tell my daddy and he'll come over here and knock the tar out of you."

I was reduced to Daddy threats. But anybody with more sense than a stump knew better than to mess with Holt Maloney's kids.

Big Roan's eyes gleamed. He didn't have gray eyes like Roan's; his eyes were some washed-out color, hooded under puffy eyelids, like the eyes of an alligator submerged in muddy water. He jerked hard on my sleeve. "You ain't no Daddy's girl. You're a little wet-tailed, ass-waggin' bitch." He raised his hand toward my hair.

I punched him in the face.

He bellowed in surprise and grabbed me with both hands. I screamed, kicking wildly, punching in every direction. Grunting and cursing, he dragged me across his thighs. I hit him in the face again, and he slapped me, hard, not just on the face but on the whole side of my head. I slammed into something. There were crashing sounds. I couldn't see anything but stars for a second, I couldn't think, I didn't know where I was.

Then he had me by one arm and I was facedown on the cluttered floor, wedged between the furniture, with him on top of me, mashing the breath out of my lungs. I squirmed furiously, listening to my own high-pitched shrieks. He twisted one of my arms behind me and something tore, something inside my shoulder, and the pain flooded me like a black wave. He jerked the wide straps of my overalls down my arms, he held me down, he pulled my overalls to my ankles. He grabbed me between the legs.

All I knew was that I had been snatched up in the jaws of a nightmare, that the monsters who lived under children's beds and in their closets were real, and that nothing, nothing in my entire life, would ever be the same.

Then there were sounds, there was shouting, Roanie's voice, guttural and wild, like a dog's furious snarls. I don't know what happened exactly. Thudding noises, violence, chaos. I was free, pulled free of the weight, Big Roan grunting, yelling, cursing, Roan's hands on me, dragging me across the dirty floor.

I heard Big Roan bellow, "Goddamn shit, you raise a hand against me and I'll—"

And then the gunshot.

It cleared my mind; it shocked the darkness out of my eyes. Moaning, crying, I rolled over and stared. *Dear Jesus, dear Jesus, dear Jesus.*

I had never seen a person with his brains blown out before.

Roan crawled to me on his hands and knees. I hurt all over. I passed out for a little while. When I came to, we were outside. Roan was hunched on his knees, bending over me. He held one of my hands. He was crying. "Claire," he said. "*Claire.*"

That was the scene that God and Jesus and all the angels—none of whom were dependable, I decided then—looked down on: a nearly grown boy and a half-grown girl with bloody faces, huddled together in the lowest, darkest place in the world, scared and hurt.

Everything else was so quiet.

What happened during the rest of that day was mostly vague and distant to me—the effect of shock, I suppose—like watching a horror movie with one eye shut and my hands over my face. I had never seen Mama and Grandma Dottie in hysterics before. I had never seen Daddy cry from sheer rage. Hop and Evan had never been tearfully sweet to me before, either.

Roanie and I were taken to see Uncle Mallory. Our busted lips, my black eye, my sprained shoulder—I was numb to all the prodding and fixing until Mama and Grandma got me undressed down to my panties and it sank in that Uncle Mallory wanted to look between my legs for some reason. Then I burst into convulsive sobs and had to lie on his table wearing nothing but a paper sheet while Mama cried and held my good hand and he pried around where nobody but me had any right to pry.

When I was dressed again, doped up on some kind of medicine that made me feel fuzzy and limp, my right arm in a sling and my cut lip smeared with yellow antiseptic, Daddy carried me into the waiting room and there was Roanie, his eyes haunted and intense as he stared at me, his lower lip and scraped chin tinged with yellow, too. All I could manage to do was paw my good hand at him, desperately trying to reach him, but when he raised a hand toward mine, Daddy turned away. "Is she all right?" Roanie asked hoarsely.

"Yeah," Daddy answered, but it was a tight word, not what Roan deserved. Daddy's anger stuck in my drugged thoughts.

I was taken home and put to bed in Mama and Daddy's room. Great-Gran had already been put in her bed. Grandmother Elizabeth sat with her and they drank peach brandy. Grandmother held Great-Gran's hand.

Mr. Tobbler came to the house. "Damn white-trash Sullivan," he told my folks, and *he* cried. Renfrew didn't cry. She took over the kitchen and began to cook for the crowd.

Every relative within reach came as soon as they heard. And Cousin Vince showed up before long, and his deputies came, and other men in uniforms, men I didn't know, and they took Roanie into the living room and shut the doors.

I kept trying to ask about him, but my tongue wouldn't work. I sank into helpless, woozy, half-conscious sleep. "My little girl, my hurt little girl," I heard Mama sobbing. "Everybody was right, Holt. Look what it's come to."

"She's a trooper," Daddy answered. "At least she wasn't . . . Big Roan didn't . . ." Daddy's voice trailed off.

"He would have," Mama said. "That must have been what he had in mind. Oh, my God."

"But Roanie saved me, and he didn't do anything wrong," I mumbled over and over to everyone, until finally Grandpa, who had taken charge as calmly as anybody could, came upstairs and, realizing what terrified me, whispered, "Don't worry, sweet pea, Roanie's not going to jail. He did the right thing."

Okay. Then we would just forget Big Roan, we'd get well and go on. Of course. I fell asleep.

"Where's Roanie?" That was what I wanted to know when I woke up. It was after dark.

"He's in his room," Mama told me, smoothing my hair and looking as if she might start crying again at any second. "Hop and Evan are with him."

"I want to go see him. I have to see him."

"Not right now."

"Why not?"

"Vince wants to talk to you," Daddy said gruffly. "If you think you can do it. You don't have to."

"I don't mind. Why are you mad at Roanie?"

"I—I'm just mad in general, honey. Because my little girl got hurt."

"But Roanie didn't do anything *wrong*! He came to help me. It was my fault."

"Oh, honey, it wasn't your fault at all. Don't worry about Roanie right now."

"When can I worry about him?" I was still fuzzy.

"Not ever again, if I can help it," Mama said.

I thought that sounded promising.

Mama helped me put on a nightgown and my pink terry-cloth robe. She gave me a pill. I didn't hurt at all. I felt quite happy, actually. Daddy carried me downstairs. All my aunts and uncles were there and some of my grown cousins. I remember the tearful faces, the strained, angry faces, the sympathetic faces. "Hi. I'm fine," I announced with gauzy determination as we passed through the crowd in the hall. "Roanie's fine, too. We're fine."

"Look at her eye," Aunt Lucille moaned. "And her mouth. Oh, God."

"There's the result of associating with lowlifes," Aunt Arnetta said loudly. "I told everybody nothing good would come of this. But oh, no, would anybody in this house listen to me?"

"Nobody's arguing with you now," Uncle Eldon growled.

I would have. But we went into the living room, and I couldn't think fast enough.

I knew things were bad when I saw Uncle Ralph. If Uncle Ralph had come from Atlanta, we needed lawyer advice. He sat beside us on the couch and told me I was one brave cutie.

Daddy held me on his lap. I clutched Mama's hand. Sheriff Vince sat across from us. He smiled at me and asked me to tell him exactly what had happened. I told him once. I told him again. He made notes.

"Roanie cried," I blurted out desperately. "He cried because he had to shoot his daddy. I know he was sorry."

"Now think hard," Vince said. "What did you hear Big Roan yell before you heard the pistol go off?"

I had already repeated, "'Goddamn shit, you raise a hand against me and I'll—'" twice.

But it dawned on me what he was getting at and what I had to do for Roanie. I stared into space. I pretended to be in deep thought. Then, giving a large and dramatic gasp, I looked Vince straight in the eye. "Mr. Sullivan yelled, 'Goddamn shit, if you turn on me I'll kill *you*.'"

Two words. That was all I had to make up. Vince looked relieved. "You sure about that last part, Claire?"

I nodded fervently. "I forgot before. But now I'm sure."

"There you go," Uncle Ralph announced. "That settles it. There's no question about the justification. That's just added confirmation. Case closed."

"Roanie can't go to jail!" I yelled. "It wasn't his fault!"

"Whoa, whoa," Vince said. "It's all right, Claire. We're just getting all the details. He's not in trouble."

I exhaled shakily. "Promise?" I looked at Mama, at Daddy, at Uncle Ralph. "Promise?"

"I promise, cutie," Uncle Ralph said.

"Everybody promises?"

"He's not going to jail," Daddy said, looking away.

"Mama?"

"I promise," she said, covering her face with one hand.

"Okay. Then I'll go see him now."

"No," Mama said. "He needs to rest."

Something was peculiar. I just couldn't figure out what it was.

I lay in the dark beside Mama in her and Daddy's big bed, staring owl-eyed at the wooden slats in the ceiling. I felt as if I were in a dream, the kind where a person can only think, not move or talk. My small, important lie had settled in my chest like a heavy acorn and I think Daddy and Mama suspected it.

Josh and Brady arrived from the university about midnight. I heard the clocks chime twelve and the soft, deep song of their voices downstairs. They and Daddy and Grandpa Maloney went over to Uncle Bert's farm to have some kind of powwow.

Roanie will absolutely stay here forever now, I thought as I fell asleep. Because Big Roan's gone and Roanie did the right thing. And we're fair.

I didn't suspect it then, but fairness had nothing to do with it.

$\mathcal{S}$ullivan's Hollow burned that night. Big Roan's spattered blood and brains, his trailer, his garbage dump, his junk, his old truck, everything. Of course it wasn't an accident. Daddy and my brothers and our relatives did it, but nobody said so.

The next morning Daddy trailered the farm's bulldozer over there and pushed every speck of Big Roan Sullivan's existence into the gully at the bottom of the Hollow and covered it over and planted some kudzu vines on top, which is about the most insulting thing a farmer can do to a piece of land. He tore down the mailbox and wiped out the driveway. He erased the *Sullivan* from Sullivan's Hollow forever.

And he meant to erase Roanie, too.

But I didn't know about all that until later on.

"Where's Roanie?" I asked the next morning when Daddy carried me downstairs. It was just him and Mama at the kitchen table. The house felt too quiet, eerily quiet. And it wasn't even morning, I discovered. I'd slept past lunch.

"He and Grandpa went up on Dunshinnog," Daddy said. I watched the careful glances being exchanged.

"Why?"

Mama stood behind me, her hands cupped on my hair, stroking it. Daddy said gruffly, "Just to talk about things." I blinked. This made no sense. It was so strange. My brain seemed to be disconnected. I could think, but the thoughts didn't reach the rest of me.

"For God's sake, Holt," Mama said tearfully. "I gave her some medicine when she woke up. She can't reason this out. Don't try to talk to her right now."

"She understands. She needs to know. Claire, we're trying to decide what's best for Roan to do."

"I'm going up to Dunshinnog," I whispered. "I have to go help him. You know he needs me. 'Cause it's my fault he had to shoot Big Roan."

Mama started crying again. I didn't get to go to Dunshinnog. I didn't get to help Roanie when he needed me. I had to go back to bed. The odd thing was, I didn't mind.

I hurt so bad for Roanie, I couldn't think at all.

My family wouldn't even let Big Roan be buried inside the county, not in Dunderry soil, as if he would seep into our earth and poison it. What was left of him was carted off to some anonymous public cemetery. Grandpa and Grandma had taken Roanie to the funeral, not to Dunshinnog. It was just the three of them and Aunt Dockey, who had volunteered to say some unofficial preaching words since no minister would.

Daisy showed up at the farm later. I heard her screaming in the yard, saying that it was all jealousy, jealousy over Sally that made Roan kill Big Roan, that Big Roan wouldn't hurt a little girl, that we'd put uppity ideas into Roanie's head, had turned him against his own daddy.

Sally made the rumors worse by packing up her belongings and baby Matthew and disappearing in the middle of the night, not even telling Daisy or her other sisters where she was going. Big Roan, dead. Uncle Pete's little boy, lost. Word spread about Daisy's accusations—there was no stopping that gossip, just as there was no stopping the general belief that I was ruined, had nearly been raped, and would be scarred, somehow, forever.

But I didn't hear all that, not then, because I was trapped in my sleepy, aching, drifting dreamworld, nearly a prisoner in Mama and Daddy's bedroom, sheltered for my own good, they decided.

I heard the loud voices downstairs, after the funeral, and I crawled out of bed. Grandmother Elizabeth was on sentry duty in a chair beside me, but she was asleep. My legs were weak. I crept down the back stairs behind the kitchen, holding on to the rail with my good arm, the other in its sling, my pink nightgown tangling between my thighs.

Daddy's voice. "It's not a punishment. It's not a jail. It's a group home run by the Methodist church. They're good people. It's just temporary, until everything calms down."

I sank onto the bottom step, catching my breath, blinking hard. My head throbbed. My sprained shoulder ached when I so much as twitched my fingers. *Group home? What?*

"I'm not good enough for you." Roanie's voice, fierce and broken. "That's all you're sayin'. I won't ever be good enough. Everybody's calling me a killer, and you think about that every time you look at me. And even if I did what I had to do, and you know it, and you say it's all right, deep down you're thinkin', 'His old man was gonna do something terrible to Claire. We can't have that kind of evil in our house.'"

"Roan, there's nothing but suspicion toward you *outside* this house." Mama's voice. "Please try to understand."

"I trusted y'all. I worked as hard as I could. I did everything just the way you wanted it. You can't send me away. You can't."

Send him away?

I don't know what kind of sound I made. I staggered through the kitchen door, weaving, crying. "What are y'all *doing* to him? No. No." There were Mama and Daddy, Josh and Brady, Grandpa and Grandma. And Roanie, with his fists clenched, standing all alone in the center of them.

He stared down at me. Oh, he looked awful. Wounded from the inside out, his face like stone, the expression in his eyes so devastated and lonely that I felt shattered. I dodged Josh, who tried to grab me, and ran to Roanie and threw my good arm around his back and held on. I wanted to crawl inside him and make sure his heart kept beating. He sank to his knees and held on to me, leaning his head against mine.

Everybody was crying then. "You can write to him, Claire," Mama said. "I promise."

"Don't send him away! We're his *family*. You can't send him away! It's not fair!"

"It won't be forever," Daddy said, squatting down beside us.

"I'll take care of Claire," Roanie begged. "Please. I tried to before. I'll never let nothing happen to her again. Please."

"Don't," Daddy said hoarsely. "There's a time to let go and a time to pull back. We all need that. You need the time, Roan. Look at her. She's sick. She's hurt. You know we don't blame you for what happened. The church home—that's just for a few months. You've got my word on that."

"I'll die if you make him leave," I sobbed. "I don't want to write to him! I want him here!"

"It's going to be all right, honey. Believe me," Daddy said, taking me by my one good hand. "Come on now, let go."

But I wouldn't. I threw my head back and looked at Roanie. "I won't let anybody send you away. You'll see. They're just confused, that's all. You tell 'em. You tell 'em you love me and we're gonna get married when we're grown up!"

I probably clinched it with that announcement. And when he bent close to me and whispered, with bitterness and misery and determination, "I won't never forget you, I won't never forget any of this," I knew he was going away and I couldn't stop it.

I kissed him. My swollen mouth against the corner of his bruised one. He didn't flinch, he didn't kiss me back, he was like a blank rock.

That was what we did to him. We closed him up inside himself forever.

Daddy and some of my uncles took him away the next morning.

No one wanted me to know when he left, but Grandpa wouldn't have that. He came into Mama and Daddy's room and got me out of bed. He sat in a chair by the window, holding me on his lap, and told me. I didn't know what to do, I was beyond hope. I pressed my good hand to the windowpane as I watched Roanie walk to the car.

He would look up. He would know somehow.

He didn't. Or wouldn't. He was gone before he left.

His room empty. His voice beyond my hearing. His smile beyond my horizons. That church home they sent him to was somewhere in Tennessee. Not so far away, just another state. But I'd never felt such agony, such emptiness. General Patton and I slept on his bed every night.

Mama gave me the address of the home. I wasn't speaking to her. I wasn't speaking to anybody. Violet and Rebecca came to visit me, but I didn't have anything to say to them either. I had changed. They thought I was pitiful and ruined, but I was wrapped in bleak fury. I think they were glad when Mama told them they could only visit me for a little while.

I had my plans. Roanie would be back home in a few months at the most. I had letters to write as soon as my arm worked again, and I sat staring out the windows, thinking about what I'd say.

We'll go swimming. We'll shoot off some fireworks up on Dunshinnog. Everybody's already forgetting what happened. They don't talk about it at all. When you come home, you and me don't have to talk about it either.

A week later, I started writing to him. A week passed and he didn't write back. I could feel something terrible in our house, something sad and secretive beneath the silences. "I should call him," I announced to everyone finally. "I'll just call him on the phone. Okay? When can I call him? How about right now?"

Finally, after stalling me and making up excuses for a few days, Mama and Daddy told me the truth. He'd run away from that home in Tennessee the day after they sent him there.

And nobody was able to find him.

Even then I didn't believe he was gone forever. I kept writing to him. I don't know what the people at the home did with my letters; they probably threw them away. I waited all summer. There was shame and regret in my family; it curled around us like a hot, sour wind. I eavesdropped on the endless, torturous discussions at family dinners; I fed on my parents' good-hearted misery and believed that Roanie would sense it somehow, that he would know they wanted to make it all up to him, if he would just come home.

They hired a private investigator recommended by Uncle Ralph. Sheriff Vince sent out notices to sheriffs and police chiefs in other states. Aunt Bess talked with other social workers across the South. They were searching for Sally McClendon and Uncle Pete's little boy, too.

None of it did any good. Both Roanie and Sally had spent their lives learning how to hide from the good intentions of people they didn't trust.

Grandpa, who suddenly looked very old by autumn, finally took me up to Dunshinnog. I hadn't been out of the house much in months. I huddled on the ledge, sobbing, and Grandpa stroked my hair with trembling gnarled fingers.

"Look what I brought," he said gruffly, pulling a green wad of leaves and roots from a pocket of his trousers. "We'll start something up here, Claire Karleen. We'll fix a little place."

I knew those baby plants. They had sprouted around their parents at the end of summer, along the slatted white fence of Grandma Dottie's flower beds, and by spring they would bulge upward in mounds of big, soft leaves and thrust tall spikes into the air, and the spikes would be layered in slender, bell-shaped pinkish-lavender blooms with freckled spots in their throats.

Foxgloves. The foxgloves had been in bloom when Roanie was sent away. "Magic," Grandpa was saying. He thought Roanie would come back someday if there were foxgloves up here to soften his step. I helped Grandpa plant them in the soft earth of the meadow because they are strong, because they have Irish fairies to watch over them, because, even left alone on a mountaintop, they always come back.

But one morning not long after that, just before a cold, frosty dawn, I woke up after a bad dream, and I felt that Roanie must be freezing somewhere, that he would die somewhere, all alone, and I couldn't help him, and how would I ever know?

I went downstairs and got Mama's scissors from her sewing room and went back up to my bathroom, and I very carefully cut all my hair to small nubs, maybe an inch long. I found some tweezers and plucked out all my eyebrow hair, and I even cut off my eyelashes.

Mama came up to get me for breakfast, took one look at my crew-cut head and naked, rebellious eyes, sat down on the floor, and put her head in her hands. Daddy walked up soon and found us, her still sitting there, me staring at them both with a brand of stony anguish that was tearing my heart out of my chest. He squatted between us wearily. "We'll get over this. We'll keep looking."

It has been a long time since then.

Part Two

HE CARRIED A LADDER

ALMOST EVERYWHERE HE

WENT & AFTER AWHILE PEOPLE

LEFT ALL THE HIGH PLACES TO HIM.

—BRIAN ANDREAS

February, 1983

    Dear Claire,

    I write you letters I won't ever mail. You probably don't need to hear from me. Or want to. You were so little and messed up because of me when your folks sent me off. And now there are things I have to take care of. Something I've got to do for your sake, and mine, and for other reasons. I don't hate your family. Won't trust them or expect anything again, but am not too bitter. Had to get around that to do what I need to do. So that's not why I've got to do this the way I am. I'm keeping the faith. Have to. You gave it to me. Have to prove I'm better than my old man.

    Been keeping track of your stories for a long time. Sent off for a subscription now that you are reporting for the college paper. So I can read every word you write. Read all about your awards, too. You sure got a way with words. But I always knew that anyhow. Easy to figure you're not a kid anymore. You or me. If you could see me you might think I'm still pretty rough on the eyes, just bigger and filled out okay. Came out all right after some hard knocks. Got responsibilities. How to tell you? Don't know how to say what happened to me. How crazy it turned out. What the bare truth would do to you and your folks.

    I had to get a look at you. Drove to Georgia like a fool. Nearly froze in the cold. Hunted for you at your school. I got no interest in college. Hell, I can make money without it. But I DO read. Promise you. Read, think, study, make money. Listen to smart people. You taught me. You know me. You always did.

    So I just waited outside your dorm house. Just to see you. Watched you walk across the yard. Just wanted to see how you grew up. You walked so smooth. God, your hair, it's pretty that way. Thought I'd never see that color red again. Your eyes are so big and blue. You looked in a hurry and strong and slick. You looked so good. The way you moved. The way you turned out. Nineteen and stacked like a—forget it. I couldn't dream you any better than you are. I'll put it that way.

    What was that funny name you made up for me that

time you wrote that story? Dirk DeBlane? You said it was romantic. I wish I knew how you would want him to say all this.

Here goes. One look and I wanted to grab you. No, I mean hold you. Okay, grab, then hold. Hell, you won't ever read this anyway. I wanted to kiss you. I wanted to do everything to you. Won't spell it out. But we're not kids anymore, and the feelings are different.

I wanted to love you. All right, I mean it like that. Take you off with me and make love to you and kiss your hair and hear you say my name and smile because we're still special but in a new way. Crazy. You don't know me anymore. Won't ever know me, probably. Probably don't want to know me. You grew up and I have, too.

Sorry I came to take a look at you. Now I'm sure how to go on picturing you in my mind. It hurts. Bad.

But I'll be watching. Reading, anyway. And if you ever do need me I'll know. I'll be there. Promise. If you ever need me. I'll be there.

Roan

1

1995

$\mathcal{L}$ife turns in large cycles, too large to notice until they bring you back to some touchstone, to home, to fractured memories of a sanctuary you thought you'd never need again.

On a balmy northern Florida morning in early March, I headed for lunch down a side street that bordered the peach-colored building of the Jacksonville *Herald-Courier*. The morning edition was still on display in banks of newspaper boxes along the curbs. The lead story, beneath a color photo of a Marlins rookie pitcher, enticed with a new baseball season's hopes. Beside it, in a column of teasers outlined in bright blue and gold, a promotional blurb blared:

TERRI CAULFIELD—FROM FEAR TO HOPE

Her story of marital abuse, courage, and triumph touched readers across the city and state last year. Terri Caulfield plans a bright future in an update by staff reporter Claire Maloney, whose award-winning series turned the young Jacksonville woman's struggles into a public crusade against domestic violence.

I walked on, pleased. Terri Caulfield hadn't had many opportunities to be noticed or fussed over. Abused by the uncle who raised her, beaten and then stalked by the husband she'd divorced, she was only twenty-two, scared, depressed, and willing to talk.

I'd met her while researching an article on Jacksonville's battered-women programs. When I got back to the newspaper offices and told my editor I'd found the perfect case study for a series about domestic violence, his face lit up with a bourbon-on-the-rocks glow. "You could follow her through the system," he mused. "Show how it works."

"It doesn't work," I countered. "Her ex-husband violated two restraining orders in the past year. He gets out of jail, he stalks her again. He shows up at her apartment, at her job, wherever. Last month he set fire to her car. She's hiding in the women's shelter because a judge granted him bond on the arson charge. He threatened to kill her if she testifies against him. Publicizing her story might make him back off."

"Hmmm. Am I going to like her? Am I going to root for her? She's not some welfare-queen drug addict with a houseful of illegitimate babies?"

I chewed my tongue. The Herald-Courier had hired a team of media consultants to shore up sagging circulation. The newspaper was flailing for attention in a world dominated by the National Enquirer and tabloid TV. The consultants advised a strategy they called When Bad News Happens to Good Readers, which, bluntly translated, meant that middle-class sex crimes, murders, and torrid family dramas sell more newspapers to middle-class readers. I understood the economic realities of journalism.

"She's a nice white dental hygienist," I said sardonically. "At least she used to be a dental hygienist until her pathological ex-husband showed up at her job one time too many. She's been on unemployment since she got fired. And get this: She wrote a letter to the governor last fall asking for help. His office sent the wrong form letter back. 'Thank you for supporting our state parks.'"

"Oh, shit." My editor grinned.

After a meeting with the rest of the editorial staff, he said happily, "Run with it. If she's lovable we'll make her the friggin' poster pinup for spousal abuse."

Six months and six articles later, I'd turned Terri Caulfield into a minor celebrity throughout northern Florida. She and I appeared together on a local PBS issues show. We were interviewed on public radio as well. A tabloid show picked up her story and paid her two thousand bucks for an interview. My series on her ran in syndication nationwide.

Hammered by public sympathy, a judge slapped her ex-husband with a heavy sentence on the arson charge. The ex had been in prison ever since.

The city rumbled and sang around me, the bright Florida sunshine glinting off parked cars with saltwater beach rust coating their fenders and palm-tree air fresheners hanging from their rearview mirrors. I had lived and worked here on the Florida coast since college. Seven years. I was only a day's drive from Dunderry, little more than an hour by plane, but I hadn't been home for a visit since Grandpa died, a year ago that spring.

Still, it felt like a good day, everything under control and moving smoothly. This was the year my life was supposed to begin making sense to me. Great-Uncle Fen Delaney had told me so when I was thirteen.

We had visited him in South Carolina for his granddaughter's wedding. Tall, thin, ostrich-shaped, Fen was a Reagan Republican and owned a chain of grocery stores in Charleston, but under his conservative hide was a peculiar streak. He believed in numerology, UFOs, and Bigfoot.

He called me out for a walk. He knew my troubled status in the family, of course. We sat on the low, aged stone of Charleston's waterfront park, watching shrimp boats and pelicans. "Six is your number, Claire Karleen," he told me. "Six letters in your name. And you're one of five children, and six times five is thirty. So I predict you'll be thirty years old before you really understand who you are. Important changes will happen to you that year."

I hoped he was right. I'd tried to make my life seamless with the uneasy glue of ambition and long hours at work. Loneliness got shoved under the clutter of my cubicle in the newsroom, my small apartment, the endless parade of people and events I covered, picking apart other people's lives and motives like a hungry crow. "You live on the edge of something," Violet had said not long ago when she and her preschool daughters spent a weekend with me. "Is it exciting? Everyone wonders. Your folks, Claire. They worry so much—"

"Life is short," I'd tossed back glibly. "Work hard, play fast, and never look back or down."

"He's always out there, isn't he?" she'd asked quietly. "Roanie Sullivan."

I had looked at her with simple denial. "He's probably dead. I try not to think about him."

Lies, lies, and damn lies. I nearly convinced myself.

I turned a corner past a taco stand and a T-shirt shop, striding past my own image in store windows that cast me back in muted shades of blue skirt and gray blazer, damned fine bare legs stepping along in white mules, a mane of wavy red hair pushed back under a rolled white scarf, my cloth tote bag bulging with notepads and a miniature tape recorder. Off duty I favored pipe-legged old jeans and T-shirts; on dates, occasionally, a black cocktail dress or formal gown. Not much jewelry, not much makeup, a

sturdy wristwatch, ink-stained fingernails and a thumb callus from scribbling notes on a reporter's pad.

I'd topped out at five foot nine, nothing voluptuous about the package
but all the padding in perky order. Not a bad combination of sturdy
Maloney bones and delicate Delaney proportions. A truck driver whistled
at me. I gave him a thumbs-up.

"How you doing today, Emilio?" I said to the tattooed street vendor
hawking Cuban sandwiches from a cart. He grinned as he sang out as
always, "Hot mama, when will you write about *me?*"

"When you give me free food." I grinned, reaching for a paper napkin. He laughed.

As I stood there waiting for my sandwich, a taxi stopped at the end of
the block ahead. I gave it an idle glance as the passenger door opened. A
tall, dark-haired man got out. I almost glimpsed his face before he strode
into a nearby café. "Where you going?" Emilio called. I stuck a five-dollar
bill in his hand, then ran up the street with my shoulder bag bouncing
wildly against one hip.

I darted inside the café, took a deep breath, and halted behind the
stranger, who was leaning against the hostess stand, waiting to be seated.
"Roan Sullivan?" I said in a low voice.

He turned. His eyes were blue, not gray, and his face had nothing
familiar about it. "Excuse, please?" he replied in a thick, unidentifiable
accent. He arched a brow and looked me over with the beginnings of
unwelcome appreciation. I turned and walked out, squinting tightly in the
sunshine, one sweaty, shaking hand clamped around my bag.

I had done this kind of thing a thousand times over the past twenty
years. I kept waiting, kept watching, stayed on alert. Many years ago, when
I was a sophomore at the university, I'd thought I glimpsed Roan in front
of my dorm. I was walking across the lawn and something made me glance
over my shoulder, and I could have sworn I saw him in a truck parked
behind some hedges along the curb. For one irrational second I was convinced it must be Roan—as if I knew exactly what he'd look like as a young
man—but by the time I turned completely, the stranger was driving off. I
ran a good quarter-mile trying to catch that damned truck.

I'd been running after ghosts too long. This self-humiliation had to
stop. I promised myself it would. I was getting too old for fantasies.

A week later some bureaucratic clerical error allowed Terri's ex-husband a
sudden and mistaken release on parole. He immediately left a strangled kitten
in her mailbox with a note tied to its neck. *You are next, you lying bitch.*

That night, terrified, she sat on the couch in my living room, dressed in a pale yellow T-shirt and old jeans. When I brought her a cup of hot tea, she sipped it like a nervous canary as she watched me double-check the bolts on the duplex's front and back doors.

"You'll be fine here tonight," I promised. "Off to Miami tomorrow, living it up in a nice hotel. Drink margaritas, work on your tan. The cops'll round him up so fast you won't even have time for a hangover or a sunburn." I was laying it on thick, praying my optimism was justified.

"Why are you doing all this for me?" she asked wistfully.

I waved my mug of beer toward a wall dotted with Florida Press Association awards. "You're my ticket to a Pulitzer nomination maybe. You sell newspapers. You're a good story."

"Oh, come on. You're always writing about homeless bums and run-away kids and beat-up women. But you don't make any sense to me, Claire. How come you care so much about strangers but you don't have a husband and kids?"

I laughed. "I'm too cranky to be a wife, and too distracted to be a mother."

"I could use some distractions right now." She wandered around my apartment, shaking her head, studying framed museum posters and stacks of books, refinished flea-market furniture and an antique mahogany desk Grandpa had left to me. On it, beside a portable computer and a fax machine, sat a stack of family photo albums. Mama sent a new one every year for my birthday. A challenge, a plea, and pure, guilt-inducing senti-ment. If I wouldn't come home to visit often, home would come to me.

Terri carried the stack of albums to the couch, began gingerly picking through them, and looked awed. "Are all of these people *relatives* of yours?" she asked.

"Those are my brothers," I told her, as she pointed to one page. "And their wives. I've got eleven nieces and nephews. That's my oldest brother, Josh. His wife died when their daughter was born. That's her in the picture with her cousins. Amanda. She's about ten. She lives with my parents."

"She looks like you. I bet she's a cutup."

"I don't know. Probably."

Terri looked at me oddly. I went on, telling her that Brady was a real-estate developer, Hop and Evan were in the construction business together, and Josh was a state senator.

"Jeez," she said.

I shrugged. "He's planning to run for lieutenant governor in the next election. Conservative. Rush Limbaugh school of philosophy."

"He looks important."

"Hmmm. He's busier than he should be. Traveling, making speeches. He's also in the family poultry business. My father retired a few years ago, after my dad had a mild heart attack." I nodded toward a pair of stoneware vases on the coffee table. "My mother's a potter. It used to be a hobby; now she's selling her work through a few shops. Daddy stays busy with some llamas he bought."

Terri turned a page and smiled at a snapshot of the llama herd. "They look like little camels covered in shag carpet."

"He says they spit when they're annoyed. I think he loves them dearly."

"What a great family. You visit home a lot? You must miss them, living down here in Florida."

"I moved out when I went to college. Haven't been back much."

"Well . . . why?"

Twenty years of quiet estrangement couldn't be summed up easily. Or painlessly. "We had some disagreements," I said. Silent accusations on my part, that sad mixture of love and retaliation that runs like a cold stream under some families' surfaces. Their regrets made the current no less chilling.

Terri sighed. "If I had a big family I'd go sit in the middle of them and count my blessings. You're lucky."

"You're going to have a family. A good husband, and kids someday, and a good home. I promise."

"Claire, I never believed anybody's promises before. But now I know I can get through this"—she glanced nervously out a window—"because I know people really will help. Because you care."

I grunted. "All you needed was a little publicity and a push in the right direction."

Suddenly we heard the slam of heavy footsteps climbing the stairs outside my second-story landing. Terri's face turned white. She clenched the albums in her lap. I laughed. "It's just the accountant who lives next door. Relax."

"He walks hard for an accountant."

"Maybe he's carrying tax returns." I set my beer down. "Look, your ex won't find you here. He has no idea where you are."

The footsteps grew louder, faster. "It's him, Claire," Terri said frantically. I dutifully went to my small kitchen, brought back the loaded pistol I kept in a drawer by the sink, and flipped the safety off. The footsteps stopped. Someone pounded on my front door. "I know you're in there, you little cunt!"

Terri leaped up. "We've got to get out of here!"

Fear produced an odd, icy calm. I planted myself between her and the door, the pistol held in front of me. "Pick up the phone," I ordered in a soft voice. "Call 911."

The door shook with blows. "I told you I'd find you! Little whining liar! Open this goddamned door!"

"He'll get in. He'll *get* me." Terri was frozen behind me.

"He won't get in this apartment. I'll shoot the bastard if I have to."

The door vibrated with a flurry of violent thuds.

"Call the police," I repeated. Terri fumbled for the phone on a lamp stand. "Nine one—" An earsplitting blast cut me off. My door spewed flecks of wood. A shard stung my arm. I stared at the ragged hole he'd shot in the middle of my door.

Terri snatched my Jeep keys from a dish on the coffee table, then ran for the back door to the fire escape. I yelled for her to stop. Her ex-husband rammed a shotgun barrel through the hole.

I pictured Terri blindly plowing my Jeep into the flock of kids who played basketball at night under the streetlights of the parking lot. I ran after her, hearing the final crash behind me as her ex burst through the front door.

I should have shot him. Running was our worst mistake.

Terri crouched on the Jeep's passenger side, wild-eyed, peering over the seat at the stream of headlights behind us on the old Florida highway. Pines and palmetto grass flashed by on either side under street lamps casting white shadows on the shell-speckled concrete. The air was muggy and oppressive, the dank smell of swampy ditches pouring through my open window.

My pistol lay on the console between us. I threw my car phone in her lap. "Call the police," I repeated uselessly, because she clung to the headrest of her seat with both hands and continued to search the traffic behind us. I wove through slower cars at a hundred miles an hour.

"There he is!" she screamed. I glanced in the rearview mirror and saw an old sedan dodging wildly from one lane to the other. Other drivers flashed their headlights. Horns shrieked. The sedan was closing fast.

A pair of gas tankers lumbered ahead of us, blocking both lanes. I curled the Jeep onto the emergency lane and passed them. We whipped by a string of convenience stores on the right. The city's skyscrapers gleamed against the night sky.

Suddenly the sedan loomed beside me. I glanced over and recoiled.

Driving with one hand and lifting the other, Terri's ex-husband pointed the shotgun at me. Everything telescoped into eerie slow motion: I slammed on the brakes. "Oh, Jesus," Terri moaned. My half-raised window exploded. I threw up a hand instinctively as glass sprayed me.

Chaos. Tumbling. The world turned inside out. I was grabbing, yelling, "Got it, got it, got it," until everything collapsed around me. Silence. Bright lights. My right leg in a vise. The Jeep's steering wheel inches from my throat. I stared weirdly at the bent steel power pole that bit into the Jeep's mangled front end like a flexible drinking straw; a cloud of radiator steam hissed hideously. We were tilted in a ditch. A neon sign flashed green from the parking lot of a gas station.

Terri slumped in her seat, twitching, her blood spraying the dash. "I'm sorry," I whispered to the young woman I'd promised to protect. Pain swept over me in dark, nauseating waves. I sank under, lost, my thoughts swirling in loose patterns like water cycloning down a drain.

Death and failed intentions came back to Roan, to me, to us. I had brought them like a curse again.

"Who do you want us to call?" they asked me at the hospital. I was in a panicky stupor punctuated by blurred faces that appeared by my bed—doctors, nurses, cops, a fellow *Herald-Courier* reporter who slipped into the emergency ward and began making notes. "Who do you want us to call?" they demanded. A female surgical resident methodically assured me that I wasn't going to lose my right leg. I was numb—didn't know, lying there drugged on some morphine derivative, if I even had a body attached to my thoughts. I was one large mind, churning out half-formed fears, failures, confusion, horror.

"The leg," I echoed. "What about Terri?"

"Please try to understand. Ms. Caulfield was shot. She didn't make it. I'm sorry."

I was told later that her ex-husband stood beside the Jeep, his sawed-off shotgun wavering at me, before he changed his mind and put the tip of the barrel in his mouth and pulled the trigger.

Didn't make it. Understatement. Terri was dead in the Jeep a second after the shotgun blast hit her. All my fault. What a dangerous fool I was. Tilting at other people's windmills. Just like before.

"Who do you want us to call?" the surgical resident asked patiently.

Who was I? Who had I always been?

"Maloney," I said.

"Family," the surgeon noted. "Who exactly?"

I couldn't reconnect to myself, but I had never been disconnected from my people. Not really. *Mama and Daddy. Marybeth and Holt Maloney in Dunderry, Georgia.* I mouthed the phone number. "Tell them I'm okay. Don't scare them."

I was awake that night when Mama and Daddy arrived. My father gathered me in his arms and my mother sobbed bitterly with her cheek pressed to mine. I wanted my family, desperately and without judgment, for the first time in twenty years.

Claire,

Writing this on a plane headed east tonight. I thought I'd lose my mind if I didn't try to "talk" to you even though of course we can't really talk. Two hours ago I heard what happened to you from an investigator I hired in Florida. Hired him last year when you started the series on Terri Caulfield. Dangerous situation, I thought. My sixth sense. Men like her ex-husband remind me of my old man. Couldn't stand to just read about it. Worried me, goddammit. Goddammit. God—

I let you down. Should have been there for you. Should have done something before now. All these years, trying to stay away, for good reasons—what difference does any of that make right now? Nothing matters but seeing you again. Making certain you're going to be okay. Then it'll all be up to you. I can't throw the truth at you until you're stronger, though. Too many people could get hurt.

Please be all right when I get there. Please be all right. Please.

☙

2

As I recovered after surgery—awake and fully alert for the first time in two days—irrational ideas moved through my mind.

". . . torn ligaments, torn muscles," the surgeon was explaining to Grandma Dottie, who sat beside my bed. "A minor fracture of the femur . . . reconnected the soft tissues . . . some nerve damage . . . recovery in about six months, though her leg won't be the same for a long time after that. A year at least."

"Was anyone here?" I asked after he left. Grandma Dottie was still sturdy, but white-haired and arthritic. A copy of *The Wall Street Journal* lay in her lap. She folded it carefully as she watched me. "Was I alone at night?"

"We were all here," she answered gently.

"All the time? Every minute?"

"No, not every minute, honey. But we've been watching over you like hawks. Half the family has come down to Florida to take turns."

"No one saw anyone . . . strange?"

She peered at me through her bifocals, bewildered, obviously, and a little alarmed. I was alarmed, too, secretly. "You think somebody strange was here?" Grandma ventured.

"I . . . don't know."

Mama and Daddy came in, carrying more flowers and fruit baskets to add to the dozens of arrangements around the room.

"She thinks some stranger visited her room last night," I heard her whisper to Mama and Daddy. "I suspect she was just dreaming while the anesthesia wore off." Mama took one look at me, saw that I was finally alert enough to talk, and began crying. So did I, but not for the same reason.

Because I thought I'd had a long conversation with Roan.

When I was younger I'd cultivated a fantasy that one day I'd look up and Roan would be standing there. He'd walk up to me with a glow of more than recognition in his eyes. He'd study me, up and down, amazed, and he'd say, "You're beautiful. I always knew you'd be beautiful."

Or he wouldn't say anything at all, but I'd know, from the look on his face, that nothing about me disgusted or disappointed him, that he'd forgotten that battered little girl on the floor of Big Roan's trailer with her overalls pulled down.

But what happened that night at the hospital had to be a drug-induced dream. I was floating in and out, I didn't remember parts of it later, and parts I remembered word for word, like an overwhelming physical bath of details.

The light in one corner was never turned off. Nurses came and went; I'd been checked more often than a holiday turkey. I was caught up in nightmares—the car, the accident, Terri's head sagging bloodily against the crumpled dash, the blank stare in her eyes—and older nightmares, too— Big Roan lurching over me, his head flowering red when Roan shot him. The panicky horror and violence, the sadness and fear were all objective in my mind—it was as if I were idly watching closed-captioned videos. *And here I felt sick and there I felt terrified.*

I heard footsteps on the room's hard, antiseptic floor—soft clicks, then the settling of a hand on rustling sheets, then its careful pressure on my shoulder. Blinking, I opened my eyes. I was down in a warm tunnel—looking sideways from my dark place into the light, the way the big barn used to feel when Roan and I sat inside the hay loft on a bright day.

A hand—fingertips—brushed my hair from my forehead then feathered over my cheek. I looked across the pillow without moving my head. I saw silvery eyes glittering with tears inside a weathered face that had achingly familiar features—yet different—older, harder, settled forms on granite bones, all hooded by ruffled dark hair. A handsomely rugged man in a pale leather jacket and an open-collared shirt. The lingering scent of tobacco was burned into his fingertips.

My heart contracted. That mental picture was captioned with relief and adoration. "Claire," he said in a low, deep voice.

Time was confused. It had never passed us by. I was pleased. "They're not going to leave you at that boys' home," I told him. "They know they were wrong. Don't worry. Oh, Roanie, I love you so much."

"I thought," he said as he bent close to my face and stroked my hair, "that you'd forget. That you'd want to forget." His voice was hoarse.

My concentration faded, then returned. The mental channels changed. Twenty years had gone by. "Roan," I murmured thickly. "I'm the reason Terri died. Like Big Roan. I'm sorry."

"My God," he whispered. He moved his head closer to mine. Those gray eyes shimmered in my dream, fierce and anguished. "I know all about you," he said. "What you write, what you've done. It wasn't your fault. Not then. Not now."

And then he sat down in a chair he pulled close to the bed and he talked to me—for minutes, hours, or days, or years—I couldn't be certain. I watched him from my dream soaked dimension, hearing his voice, not the words but their essence was soothing. Finally I said, "You don't need help with your grammar anymore," and he bent his head in his hands and said nothing for a while. I talked to him while he sat there—about what, I couldn't be sure.

I felt fine and certain and serene because I hadn't completely failed him; he'd drawn on our memories to come back to me. I'd understand it all later, somehow, and he'd understand that no one had meant for him to hate the family, to disappear out of shame and betrayal. "I still love you," I repeated.

He got up, carefully ran his hands over the cast that covered my right leg from hip to ankle, then kissed me on the mouth. His breath was warm, as if he were real. "I still love you, too," he said. "And when you see me again I'll prove it."

I insisted on attending Terri's funeral. Mama and Daddy gathered the family from Jacksonville hotels. We arrived at the cemetery in a caravan of rental cars, under an overcast Florida sky that pushed heavy, ocean-scented air down on us, and my father rolled me in my wheelchair across the grassy grounds with a wedge of my relatives around me.

"Oh, my God," I said groggily. The crowd at the graveside service numbered at least a thousand people. Picket signs rose around the edge of the throng like strange flowers.

MALE GOVERNMENT EQUALS DEAD WOMEN
GUNS KILL—TELL THE NRA
WOMEN OF COLOR ARE THE REAL VICTIMS
FIGHT FOR ANTI-VIOLENCE EDUCATION IN OUR SCHOOLS

The Jacksonville police were directing traffic. A news helicopter hovered overhead. Camera crews from several Florida television stations prowled the scene; a reporter spotted me and headed my way at a trot. A couple of cops recognized me and opened a path.

Aunt Jane, sparrowlike and still peeping, asked loudly, "Is this a funeral service or a political convention?"

A minister's voice boomed some sort of preliminary welcome over speakers set up at the periphery of a huge mortuary tent. The advancing camera crew tried to push past my brothers, who blocked them, Josh in front. "Claire, it's Mark Creeson from Channel Three! Just give me ten seconds on tape!"

"Keep that television man away," Mama hissed. Daddy stopped my chair and stepped in front of me. Violet and Rebecca flanked me on either side. Grandma Dottie clutched my shoulders from behind. I began to tremble. Sweat trickled down my face, over bruises and into the raw cuts that speckled across my cheeks. My cast-encased leg, propped straight out in front of me on a wheelchair footrest, began to throb. Groups of curious people curled away from the gravesite and pushed up to the human barricade of my family. Strangers craned their heads to peer at me. "Can I have your autograph?" a woman yelled.

"I have to get out of here," I said. "This isn't for Terri. This is a circus and I'm responsible for it."

"We're trapped," my cousin Rebecca moaned.

Two burly men in dark suits pushed through the family. Daddy confronted them with an icy, bulldog look on his face. "We're here to help, Mr. Maloney," one of them said politely. "We'll clear the way back to your car."

"Who the hell are you?" Daddy thundered.

"Personal security. Hired by a friend."

"A friend of who?"

"Your daughter, sir."

I heard all this dimly, because I felt faint. What friend? I thought vaguely as my family and I reversed direction and the two security men plowed through the crowd without the least diplomacy. Hop and Evan lifted me into the backseat of a car. The security men disappeared before I could ask who'd sent them.

I felt that if I could just unravel the confusion and remember who I was, I wouldn't lose my mind.

"I'd like to go home," I said.

3

*S*o I came home to the blue-green mountains, the family, the farm, the big, rambling house where generations of Maloneys had thrived, surrounded by the constant activity of family events and family business— farmhands who tromped in and out of the kitchen as they had when I was a girl, plus dozens of people who called or visited Josh, because as a state senator he represented ten mountain counties. There was also a daily stream of locals conferring with Daddy, who had been elected county commissioner after he turned the poultry business over to Josh, and flocks of women involved in Mama's various art societies and charity projects. Josh's daughter, Amanda, lived with my folks because Josh traveled so much. She became my constant companion.

So there I was, helpless, gawked at every time I crept out in a wheelchair. I was the only nonmoving part of a well-oiled machine.

I'd left for college when I was seventeen, vowing I'd never live in Dunderry again. My father had had his heart attack a year later and I couldn't bear to stay away, so I returned for a summer. My mother took antidepressants for a year after I moved to Florida after college. I came home when Josh's wife died after giving birth to Amanda; I came home when Grandma Dottie fell and fractured a hip; and when Grandpa died. But I made certain everyone understood that it took birth, death, and illness to force me back into the fold each time.

Finally, now, I'd broken the cycle by contributing to it.

Mama put me in Roan's old bedroom because it was on the main floor and near the kitchen. Hop and Evan hung one of those trapezelike bars over the hospital bed Daddy rented and another from the ceiling of the bathroom shower. I could ask for anything and be pampered without question. I called for help using an air horn Aunt Irene brought me.

As spring unfolded, I hid as well as I could on the veranda or at windows, drinking in the sights, seeing everything with mystical clarity, pushing guilt and anger down under layers of familiarity.

I wanted to forget who I'd been before the accident. I wanted to stamp out the driven, ambitious, reckless woman who risked other people's lives. I wanted to subdue the Claire who'd treated newspaper work like games of intrigue, snooping into the private problems of others, bribing, charming, and manipulating my way into confidential relationships. I'd been the kind of reporter who put on a tight, low-cut black dress and sneaked into the governor's inaugural ball, where I danced provocatively with one of the governor's fresh-faced junior aides. I let him ogle my cleavage while I asked him whether the governor had taken campaign contributions from several developers who opposed a network of community centers for the homeless.

The aide was such a political babe-in-the-woods that he assumed he was answering questions off the record. He also assumed he'd get laid that night. I didn't hang around the party to honor either assumption.

So I got the story and won another press association award. The aide got fired. A lot of heads deserved to roll in the governor's administration, but that nice, harmless guy was the last person I should have used to swing the hatchet.

In short, I now wanted to erase the Claire who hadn't always made the kindest, wisest choices. Who couldn't be trusted with the care and protection of her sources. The Claire who was still so caught up in childhood fantasies and nightmares that she had hallucinated a detailed conversation with a man who had been driven away because of her reckless efforts twenty years earlier. I kept trying—hopelessly—to remember everything Roan had said that night at the hospital and everything I had said in return.

As if he had been real. But Roan, unlike me, would never find his way home again.

Renfrew still worked for my folks and so did Nat Fortner; the whole, broad clan still gathered for Sunday dinners; much had changed, but much had only ripened.

The roads into town still passed old farmhouses with red-streaked tin roofs, pastures and barns with the land molded so intimately around them that deep footpaths and dirt driveways were natural features rubbed into the hills. Dunderry still wore its old farmsteads like a soft cotton shirt.

Uncle Dwayne and Aunt Rhonda had lost most of their drugstore business to a Super K mart on the interstate fifteen miles away. So they refurbished their grand marble soda fountain, added a gourmet coffee bar, and filled the old pharmacy shelves with tourist geegaws and knickknacks.

Aunt Irene became co-president of the Performing Arts Association along with Mama. They headed a drive to buy and renovate the old Dunderry cinema.

The dime store had become an antiques store. Uncle Eldon moved his hardware store outside of town and expanded it to include a plant nursery and home-decorating center. The old Dunderry Diner now served fried green tomatoes with salsa. And avocado sandwiches. And cheesecake. The county built new administration offices on the edge of town, so the white-columned little courthouse at the center of the square was turned into a welcome center and art gallery. Mama sold some of her pottery there.

The county had voted in a beer-and-wine ordinance after a heated religious war. The Methodists were neutral, the Baptists dead-set against, the Catholics and Episcopalians all for it, and everyone else just hoped they could stop driving to Gainesville to buy a six-pack or a bottle of table wine.

Aunt Jane resigned from the library to open a bookstore and tearoom in partnership with Cousin Ruby, in the shop space where Ruby used to sell the best polyester pantsuits in north Georgia.

Rebecca, like Violet, married a nice man and had nice children. She ran a boutique in town called Dunderry Irish Imports, selling Waterford crystal and linens. Tula Tobbler inherited the apple business after her grandfather, Boss, died. Her brother, Alvin, did exactly as she prophesied—he played pro football for almost ten years, for the Dallas Cowboys, before his legs gave out. Tula invested Alvin's money in Tobbler Apple Treats, opened a shop, started a catalog business, and prospered. When Alvin quit football, he came home and joined the sheriff's department as a deputy. Two years ago, after Vince retired, Alvin was elected sheriff.

There was now a Historic Preservation Committee in town that squabbled over every inch of ambiance around the square. Rebecca had mistakenly planted pink impatiens in the windowboxes of her shop and an hour later, Aster, who chaired the committee, pulled them all up by the roots.

"Red and white is the floral color scheme this season," she'd told Rebecca. "Didn't you read the resolution?"

Since then Rebecca has called it the Hysterical Persecution Committee.

The Christmas nativity, with its old log manger and painted-plywood figures, had been replaced each December by a life-size and live tableau, with volunteers dressed in costume, two real sheep and a donkey, and a trio of camels that were trailered over from a Gainesville petting zoo.

Daddy volunteered some llamas the year Aunt Dockey chaired the nativity pageant committee. "There were no llamas in the Holy Land, Holt," she'd said, fuming.

"Well, the Christ child wasn't born in a manger on a vacant lot next to Dwayne's drugstore either," Daddy had told her.

The merchants' association had taken control of Dunderry's Christmas atmosphere. The shop owners decorated with all-white lights, plus all-natural and occasionally edible wreaths and garlands. There would be no more plastic Santas, no fake snow, no silver metallic Christmas trees revolving over blue-and-pink lamps.

Uncle Eugene finally retrieved his cojones and ran off with the secretary at his Ford dealership. Aunt Arnetta survived, and was still a county home economics agent. Carlton went into banking, moved to Virginia, and was arrested last year for embezzlement. Uncle Ralph marshaled some high-priced lawyers up there and got him probation.

Neely Tipton married one of my cousins. I heard that their son hid behind the doors at the elementary school and jerked girls' hair. He never, however, touched any Maloney or Delaney female.

Uncle Pete died in a hunting accident. His son Harold was killed in a stock-car race at Talladega. Arlan moved to New Orleans and we rarely heard from him. Everyone in the family was relieved about that.

Daisy McClendon and her two remaining sisters had moved to parts unknown not long after Roan ran away and Sally disappeared. There had never been any word about Sally.

The family absorbed all the births, deaths, losses, and scandals the way it always had, with tolerance or shunning, quiet effort and loud brickbats of debate.

But no one ever discussed Roan or Big Roan. At least not in front of me.

Mr. Cicero, my old editor at the Dunderry Shamrock, came to visit me. He had a face as wrinkled as an accordion, he wore trifocals, and he kept his

thin white hair side-combed over a large bald spot. He'd been a wire-
service correspondent in Europe during World War II and then a crusading
editor of a large Mississippi newspaper during the civil rights era. He
proudly showed me a photo of the newspaper's new offices and one-truck
distribution center. He'd mortgaged his house to build it.

The structure resembled a small concrete bunker at a NASA radar station. Mr. Cicero had installed a huge satellite dish on the roof so that he
could watch CNN during the day, as if he had to be up-to-the-minute on
any world news that directly affected Dunderry. Plus he tracked one of the
national wire services on a computer network. His subscriber and advertising base barely paid his bills, but his dreams were global.

He had always called me "girlie." "Girlie," he said, "you wrote for me
all through high school. And I couldn't be prouder of what you've accom-
plished since then."

"Mr. C., I look at you and think maybe there's still something to be
proud of."

"Of course there is! Why do you even say something like that, girlie?"

"I started believing my own credentials. I guess I wanted to be
famous."

"Foo! You got caught up in a story that nearly killed you. You didn't do
anything wrong."

I pointed at the television set across from my bed. "I've been watching
the news. They just segued from a story about a double murder to a fluff
feature on the new baby gorilla at Zoo Atlanta. They didn't even have the
decency to stick a commercial in between. Nothing's sacred, shocking, or
significant. It's all just entertainment. I started thinking in those terms, too."

"Sure you did," he said sarcastically. "You know we need more
exploitation and cruelty in folks' lives."

"We need more shame and guilt," I said seriously. "Reporters stick
cameras in the faces of people who've just survived some horrible tragedy
and we show 'em sobbing for the rest of the world to peer at, and we tell
our audience it's important news. But it's not. It's voyeurism."

He squinted at me angrily. "You ever see a picture like that in the
Shamrock?"

"Of course not. But you know what I—"

"I know there're problems around here that need somebody younger
than me to keep a hard, close eye on 'em. Greedy old-timers and greedy
new-timers prowling around, the old farmland gettin' carved up into little
pieces, zoning voodoo. There're important issues coming up this fall,

girlie—your brother's campaign for lieutenant governor, for one. For another, the church folk are planning an attack on the school board. There's gonna be more arguing over teaching evolutionism and creationism than you can shake a monkey at. I could use you at the paper."

"I'm not leaving town. But I'm not making any plans to go back to work in journalism either."

He got up to leave and said softly, "Looks to me as if you're not making plans to do anything but sit on your behind and feel sorry for yourself."

> *Claire,*
>
> *Your Grandpa Joe said there are two types of people in the world. The ones so damned stupid they don't know enough to worry about anything, and the ones so smart they know there's nothing worth worrying about.*
>
> *I try to stay busy and not worry about you. You could say I arranged to get access to your medical records. I bought them from people who specialize in information. Sorry, but I need to know how you're doing.*
>
> *My information says you're not doing well. Could I make you feel worse by showing up now? Probably.*
>
> *When you're better, I'll be there to help you. I'll take you anywhere you want to go, get you set up with your old job again or any kind of media job you want. Hell, I'll buy you a little newspaper to run if that's what you want. I won't let you sit there at the farm and forget everything you accomplished. If you're blaming yourself for what happened and giving up on yourself, I'll change your mind. I swear to you.*
>
> *I know we'll have to get reacquainted before all this big talk of mine makes sense, but I'm working on that.*
>
> *Don't give up. You never have before.*

Six months, the surgeons predicted. In six months I'd be walking without crutches. I was lucky; my leg showed every sign of a fast recovery. The reattached muscles twitched energetically. Beneath the cast the surgical scars tingled with healthy blood flow. Rejuvenated nerve endings radiated needle-sharp pains. I took a lot of pain pills and could barely get out of bed.

This misery was the definition of a *good* recovery.

I began to let the yellow blooms of April daffodils hypnotize me; the smell of jasmine creeping over the veranda lattices was almost too beautiful to bear. Dunshinnog rose in a natural cathedral of white dogwoods against a dark blue sky.

It belonged to me now. Grandpa had left me the mountain in his will. He'd walked up to the top last spring to see the foxgloves in bloom. When he hadn't returned, Daddy had gone after him. He'd found Grandpa sitting with his back against a tree, endlessly gazing across the valley where he'd been born, and lived, and died. I missed Grandpa so much, and marveled at the way Grandma Dottie stayed busy with her grandchildren and her great-grandchildren, her stock-market investments and the tennis matches she watched on television. She slept in Grandpa's flannel shirts and wore his wristwatch.

I remembered as a teenager asking Grandpa why Grandmother Elizabeth and Great-Gran Alice spent so much of their time by their bedroom windows, looking up toward the mountain. "They'd sit up there if they could," he told me. "They're busy with their memories. The old gals like to see as far as they can."

I suppose, like him, they finally saw far enough. When I was about fourteen both of the Old Grannies died in our house, in their beds, on the same night. After all the years they spent feuding over who would outlast the other, neither had had the last word.

I found Grandmother Elizabeth when I went to wake her for breakfast. She was perfectly organized, lying on her back as if still asleep, but her eyes were half open, and her face looked, in the relaxed state of death, so much younger. I knew what was wrong the moment I saw her.

I touched her cold face, sat down on the floor, and went into something I recognized later, when I was older, as a trance of quiet shock. It wasn't until Mama ran into the room—having just discovered Great-Gran Alice dead in the bedroom down the hall—that I jumped up. "Don't look," I said, but Mama sat down beside her mother's small body and clasped one of her hands. "Oh, Mawmaw," she whispered. "You just couldn't best Granny Alice, could you?" She began to cry, and when I stood beside her, crying, too, she took my hand, so we formed a chain, grandmother to mother to daughter, until Daddy burst in and said "Oh, my lord, hon, I'm sorry," and wrapped Mama in his arms.

Grandpa sat with his mother, Great-Gran Alice, that morning, son and mother, him patting her shoulder; she was curled on her side, looking younger, like Grandmother Elizabeth, and for the first time in my life I saw Grandpa cry, with Grandma Dottie bent over him, hugging his bald head and crooning as if he were a child. There was learning and comfort in seeing the lines dissolve between me and other generations; it made me realize I was part of a journey, the next step. I thought of that now.

It was peaceful at the farm, and I looked out the windows at a spring palette of greens. Shaggy llamas dotted the fields. I hurt constantly, ate badly, slept as much as possible, cried often when I was alone, and obsessed about how I'd failed Terri Caulfield.

Most depressing of all, I spent many furtive hours in my bedroom using my cellular phone to call Florida. I questioned nurses, doctors, orderlies, and security guards who'd been on duty the night after my surgery. None of them recalled seeing a man who fit the description I gave of Roan.

Some parts of me weren't healing at all.

My niece Amanda, redheaded, freckled, tomboyish and naturally charming, brought me fresh-baked cookies; she carried new puppies—descendants of General Patton—into my bedroom. She asked my opinion on little-girl subjects; she drew stars and flowers on my cast and stuck unicorn stickers on it.

She was desperately lonely, motherless, idly neglected by Josh; she sucked in every breath of attention from her doting grandparents, her cousins, uncles, aunts, and me. And I loved her immediately because she needed me.

I didn't know what I needed yet. I used sensation for consolation. "What are you doing out there?" Mama called from the back porch one night. And my voice came back, disembodied and methodical. "Digging in the kitchen herb garden."

"Digging for what?" Mama asked reasonably.

"I'm planting a row of lemon mint."

"It's dark."

"I don't need to see. I need to plant."

One afternoon I fell down trying to sit on the commode in my bathroom. Renfrew hurried in to help me. Renfrew's hair had gone gray under her black hairnet. She'd given up smoking some years ago but had taken up chewing. She spit tobacco juice in a small Spam can she carried in her apron. She had been known to spit at my nieces and nephews when they provoked her. She hadn't spit at me yet.

"Get me a teacup, Miz Mac," I said sarcastically. "I believe I'll sit here on the floor and piss in it."

"You watch your mouth." She hurled the words back at me, flicking the air with her stringy hands. "I ain't kowtowing to you like the rest of this bunch. I always told your mama you'd be all right if we could just get you home. But you cain't mope around like this. Act like a lady."

"I was never a lady, Miz Mac. And this is a helluva way for me to come home."

"You better straighten up and fly right!"

"I can't straighten up," I yelled, "and I can't fly."

"Then you just pee on the floor," she said, and left.

After the cast was removed, I staggered around on crutches. My right leg was strange—just *there*, swollen but pliable, as if it had been attached to me without my consent, as if part of me had come home after a long visit to another person's body. I knew I was healing, that recovery was just a matter of time and exercise, but I felt uninvolved.

Sweet, pleasant Violet, an athletic little auburn-capped woman, was a physical therapist. She wore pink jogging suits and smiled cheerfully. She took charge of my daily rehab sessions in the garden room Mama and Daddy had added to the back of the house. I flexed the leg, practiced my balance, even began lifting weights.

But Violet said one time too many "Oh, you'll be as good as new," and one day when she turned her back I picked up a needlepoint throw pillow from a wicker sofa and hit her as hard as I could.

She sprang around and stared at me. *"Claire?"*

"A woman's *dead* because I couldn't do enough to help her, but everyone around here expects me to forget about all that. I'm supposed to pretend it never happened and recuperate merrily. Chirp at me again and I'll knock you down. My leg might be *as good as new*, but the rest of me is totally *screwed*."

This quirky assault on the sweetest of souls provoked a family conference. "I understand you, sis," Josh said patiently. "I know where you're coming from. Ideals don't mean a damn thing, do they? You made a mistake. All right. Get on with it."

Brady hunched in a chair with a briefcase on his lap. "Your story's worth money," he said. "There could be book deals, Claire. Four production companies want to buy the rights for a TV movie. And talk shows . . . Look, I have an agent's contract right here. Uncle Ralph and I went over it. It's solid. You ought to sign it. Strike while the iron's hot."

I looked at Mama and Daddy, who seemed sour on Josh and Brady. They'd never say so, but we had wisdom in common now, my parents and I. Good intentions don't always do the job.

"That damned lousy husband would probably have killed the young lady no matter what you did," Daddy noted. "You did all you could for her."

"I used her, Daddy. That's what it comes down to. I sold out. I sold her."

"The point is," Mama announced angrily, "that you nearly got killed trying to help the poor soul and now a bunch of vultures want to make money off her—and off you. And one of them"—she glared at Brady—"is your own brother."

"Oh, this is all philosophical," Brady said with urgent control, not understanding a thing. "Sis has a right to benefit from the publicity—sell her story . . ."

"I don't have any right to make money off Terri Caulfield's life." I struggled upright in bed. "Let's resurrect her and give her the good news. How everybody plans to make money off her. How much I can make if I want to. She'll be happy. Dead, but happy."

Brady gaped at me. Josh chewed his lower lip and watched me with narrow-eyed contemplation. Aunt Dockey, who had become a Unitarian minister, was called in. "You did the right thing and it wasn't enough. That's not your fault. Time to get on with life, Claire Karleen. You're a grown woman. A good-looking and smart woman. What do you intend to do—devote yourself to eccentricity?"

"I don't know what I'm going to do. But I don't want to hear how lucky I am."

"Are you much for praying?"

"Hell, no."

"Well, how about a hobby?"

"No."

"How about a good swift kick?"

I laughed. She didn't.

Mama unpacked my journalism awards. "Why don't I hang these on the wall across from your bed?" she asked.

"That's not my life anymore," I told her. "Put them all back in the box."

My mother, who is a strong, straight-backed woman, a woman who was invited to England to study glazes at a seminar sponsored by Wedgwood, looked at me as if I had turned her into fragile greenware. "When do you win the right to be happy?" she asked. "When will there be time for someone to love? For a home, a husband, and children?"

"I don't need what you need, Mama."

"Liar. You've dated some fine men. Violet and Rebecca used to tell me about each one you'd introduce to them when they visited you."

"Dating a man and marrying him are two different things."

"Nobody's ever measured up to Roanie Sullivan. That's it. Admit it."

"Mama, I was ten years old when he left. I didn't even know what to measure then. So, no, that's not the reason—"

"If Roan Sullivan came back, if he walked in and said 'Marry me and go away with me,' *you'd go*."

"He'd have come back years ago if he cared that much. Either he doesn't care or he's dead. Either way, I'm not interested in marrying anybody else."

"See? Anybody *else*."

"*Anybody*. Marrying anybody, I meant."

"I don't want you to stay here because you haven't got the heart to make a life for yourself."

I looked away and said nothing.

Once, when Aunt Jane was clucking over me as she helped me take a bath, I muttered fiercely, "I feel like the centerpiece of a Mongolian cluster fuck."

Aunt Jane leaned back and gaped at me. "What did she say?" Aunt Irene asked from outside the bathroom, where she was changing my bed. I had no privacy left.

"She said she was . . . was 'as flustered as a duck,'" Aunt Jane lied.

Daddy and I sat on the tailgate of one of the farm trucks out in a back pasture, with velvet-lipped llamas crowded around us, nibbling kernels of corn from our hands. He'd driven me out there to name one of his new babies. She stood on spindly legs beside her shaggy mother, her tiny head perched on the periscope of her neck regarding me with solemn dark eyes.

"Dolly," I said. "She's the Dolly Llama."

Daddy rubbed his fringe of gray hair and laughed. The hot spring sun beat down on us, gleaming on his scalp, and the scent of lush, growing grass rose up like perfume. His laughter faded. We sat in silence for a while, llamas touching their mobile mouths to specks of corn dust on my jeans.

"You givin' up on writer's work completely?" he asked.

"I don't know, Daddy. I really can't think."

"Mr. Cicero wants to retire from the *Shamrock*. He says he'd make you a fine offer if you wanted to take his place as the editor and publisher."

"I can't imagine it right now."

"Things have changed around town. More tourists, more neighbors. People moving in from Atlanta. From all over. We talk about it at the county commission meetings. Another few years and the regional planning hon-chos are going to list the county as *exurban*. I don't like the sound of that."

"It's just a ten-dollar term for suburban with fresher air and less traffic."

"Mr. C. already has to compete with a couple of little weekly papers published by newcomers. He says they're just advertising circulars, but I've seen 'em. They publish articles along with ads, like real newspapers."

"I doubt I'm the right person to save the *Shamrock* from competition."

"You could make a down payment on it with the money your grand-pa willed you. Your mama and I'd invest. So would your brothers. And not just because we want you to stay around here. Because we'd be proud to do it."

I squeezed his hand. "I'll think about it. You know what? I love you. You and Mama. Everybody."

I studied the relief on his face, and my misery sank down deeper inside me. He squinted up at Dunshinnog. "When you get married someday, you and your husband can build a fine house up there."

I doubted I'd ever get married. I was beginning to doubt I'd ever leave home again.

I had a promotion and a raise waiting for me at the *Herald-Courier*. In late May I told my editor I wasn't coming back.

So you quit your job. I have sources for this kind of information, so I heard. I'm trying to analyze you, Claire. Are you running scared? That's not like you. I'll be back there soon—everything's almost taken care of—and I hope you'll explain it to me.

Watch the mountain at night. God, I'm telling you as if you're reading this. I'll have a hard time talking to you face-to-face at first.

It's all I can think about. Seeing you again.

4

I heard loud voices in the living room. I struggled into my robe, hobbled in there on a pair of crutches, and found Mama and Daddy embroiled in a shocked conference with Hop and Evan.

"Wilma's daughter put Ten Jumps up for sale," Evan repeated for my sake. "And it looks like she's got a buyer. We don't know who, but we heard she's sold the property."

Wilma was the Minnesota relative who had inherited Ten Jumps. Her daughter had inherited it from her.

"She swore she'd do it someday," Mama said ruefully. "We should have believed her."

"Somebody has to take me out there." My voice sounded thin and distant. Stares. I wobbled closer, absorbing them. Bold talk for an invalid recluse. "Why?" Daddy asked with anxious gentleness.

"I just have to go out there. Hop? Evan?"

"If you want to go," Evan answered slowly, eyeing me and stroking his beard, "I'll get my Land Rover. Rained last night. We may end up pulling ourselves out of a gully with the winch."

"Good. We'll need a pry bar and a flashlight, too."

And with that mysterious show of bravado, I teetered back into my bedroom, hoisted myself into my hospital bed, and stared, dry-eyed, at the ceiling.

We made it to the lake, Evan and I and Evan's unshakable wife, Luanne. The Land Rover's running boards dripped mud by the time we reached the lake cove, where the cabin sat, surrounded by a thicket of blackberry briars that grew in ten-foot-tall mounds the closer they were to the lake's edge.

"Amazin'," Luanne said. "How come that cabin hasn't fallen down after all these years?"

Evan nodded his appreciation. "Logs a foot thick and a double-tinned roof lined with teak planks. And the stonework's strong enough to hold up Buckingham-damn-Palace. Look at that chimney. Look at those columns under the porch."

"Good lord. This isn't a cabin. It's a two-room boat that beached on high ground. It's a little-bitty Noah's Ark," Luanne said.

"It's a shack with a pedigree," I countered.

We got out. I sat in the Land Rover's open door while Evan fetched my crutches. "It's pretty here," Luanne noted. "Wild and quiet. I like the lake."

Evan helped me perch on my crutches. "All right, sis, you're here. What's this all about?"

"I'll show you when we get inside. Maybe it's full of termite holes. Maybe it's fallen to pieces. Just let me look first."

I struggled through the briars as Evan and Luanne held them aside.

"Snug as a bug in a rug," Luanne said, surveying the cabin's musty, rain-weathered interior. She knocked on a wall, then stamped her sandal heel on the thick teak floor. "Solid."

"Lots of bugs," Evan added, slapping at a spiderweb. He flashed the light across deserted wasp nests and shards of acorn shells left by squirrels. The summer wind moaned in the deep maw of the chimney.

"Back there." I nodded toward a doorway. "The back room."

With Evan lighting the way, I thumped into the second room on my crutches. "There." The beam of light fell on a narrow opening with shreds of some dank cloth still hanging from the top. "You came to see a *closet?*" Evan grunted. He ripped the cloth down. Dust flew. He shone the light into a tiny space, peered inside briefly, then looked at me with morose expectation. "Yep. It's still a closet, sis."

I angled past him into the space, leaning heavily against the cool log wall behind me. I twisted. "Flashlight." Evan handed it to me and, holding my breath, I raised the light to a section of plank just above my head. "This is what I want," I said.

Evan shouldered in beside me, craned his neck, and looked. "My God, sis," he said gruffly.

Carved on a board, hidden in the dark recess of a place no one had bothered with for many years, the simple inscription said: *Roan and Claire.*

"Roan carved it," I explained. "I found it after he left."

I took the board home and put it in my dresser drawer.

No one said a word.

"You're going to live here from now on, aren't you?" Amanda asked during a Sunday gathering as we hid out on twin wicker lounges in the garden room. "Aren't you?" she repeated. "Going to stay here forever?"

"I don't know. But I'll be here quite a while."

Amanda twiddled with a soft pink flower on the potted impatiens between our chairs. "But I can count on you being around to do stuff with me, huh? 'Cause Grandma's always busy with her pottery and Papa's gone all the time. And Aunt Luanne and Aunt Ginger and Aunt Simone, they've got jobs and their own kids and stuff. But you don't have a job anymore, and you don't have any kids, so . . . so we can do stuff together, can't we?"

"You betcha. I'll always do stuff with you, and when I'm an old lady, I'll come live with you and your kids can pretend I'm an extra grandmother." I swept cupcake crumbs off my jeans. My fingers splayed over the deep gouge of a scar hidden under the denim. "And when I die, you can have my money."

"*Okay!*" She grinned. "I don't even care if you have any money. Great-Aunt Arnetta says you won't be worth a penny unless pigs learn to fly. What's that mean?"

I just shrugged. "It means I need to practice my oink."

"Papa says we gotta be patient with you. I heard him talkin' to Grandpa about it yesterday. Papa is kinda mad 'cause you hurt Nana's feelings."

My mother is "Nana" to all my nieces and nephews.

"I didn't mean to," I answered. "Your Nana has a chest full of baby clothes for babies I don't have. I told her she should get rid of them."

"Why?"

"Ohhh, let's talk about something else."

Amanda frowned as she licked the filling from a piece of apple pie. We're eaters, both of us, usually gnawing off more than we can chew. "I'm not supposed to eavesdrop on Papa," she whispered to me, "but I couldn't help it."

"So what else did he and your grandpa say about me?"

"Grandpa said we gotta make allowances for you. 'Cause a sad thing happened to you when you were little and you never got over it. And you're a whole lot worse now, he said. I gotta know. How sad was it? What happened?"

An emotional ambush. I tightened all over and felt two decades burning in my chest like hot coals. "It was only sad because of the way it ended." I gauged my words carefully. "It was wonderful before that."

I told her about Roan. From the St. Patrick's Day carnival to the day he was sent away. About the good Christmas we spent together and the necklace he gave me. About Big Roan. About Sullivan's Hollow, which is grown over with pine trees and doesn't exist anymore, the way Roan doesn't exist. I left out the harsh details. I didn't tell her Roan disappeared because my parents, her kindly, beloved Grandpa and Nana, had shipped him off to a church home. She wasn't old enough to understand how good-hearted people can commit terrible mistakes in the heat of the moment.

"Roan moved away," I told her. "And that was the last time we saw each other. When your grandpa says I never got over it, well, it's like what you tell me about your mother sometimes. How you dream that she's on the other side of a canyon and you can't quite jump far enough to reach her? That's what happens when somebody you love goes away. There's always a little part of you that's whispering 'Jump' even though you know it's too far."

Amanda stared at me with her mouth open and her eyes dewy with romantic grief, the way little girls look when they're watching Camelot for the first time and have just realized that Guinevere isn't going to get to keep Lancelot.

"Oh, Aunt Claire," she whispered. "Roan Sullivan will jump back over for you. I just know he will."

That's what I get for sharing. A kick right in the solar plexus. Firefly lights in front of my eyes. And then, with a deep breath, sanity returned. "No, sweetie," I said calmly. "Sometimes people change. They grow up and move further away from each other, until they forget how to jump." I didn't mention the obvious. I couldn't jump if I wanted to. "I'm not a jumper," I concluded. "I'm a sitter."

Her blue eyes flickered. She looked at me as I would have looked at me when I was young and obstinate and sentimental. "Sometimes I think you don't try very hard," she accused softly. "Don't get old and strange on me, Aunt Claire."

My throat closed up and I couldn't say another word. Wait until I started talking to tomato plants and knitting sweaters for cats.

I jerked awake that night, not just crying but yelling, and beating the bedcovers with my fists. I hobbled to the closet and dug through a small, lacquered wooden box I've had for years. I store mementos in it, the kind I can't bear to look at but can't bear to throw away. I pulled my old, faded shamrock pendant and its chain from a tiny cloth bag. I wore the pendant for so many years the green rubbed off and the chain lost its gold plate and turned the color of a tarnished nickel.

I couldn't count the hours I've spent in public places gazing intently at men walking by, the birthdays and holidays when I sorted hurriedly through my mail, thinking, This year there'll be a card from him. All the times the phone rang, the doorbell rang, and I thought, for just an instant, It might be Roan. It *might* be.

I had nearly forgotten the girl who had been tough enough to stand up for a boy no one else wanted.

I couldn't sleep. I sat in the dark by my bedroom window. Dunshinnog was encased in thick clouds that scudded across a full moon and the mountain disappeared into inky black night as devastating as my own thoughts.

I saw a light. Small and flickering at the summit of the mountain. I blinked and it was gone. I wasn't imagining this. There it was again.

Somebody was up there on my mountain, dammit. By the time I woke the household and marshaled their attention, the trespasser might have vanished. There'd be a new round of worried whispers about my emotional stability.

I threw a windbreaker over my nightshirt, then crawled out the bedroom window. It was more painful than any physical therapy session, and by the time I landed in a heap behind a row of camellia shrubs, clutching my crutches, I was panting for air.

I made my way around the house, gazing up at Dunshinnog as I did. The light remained. I levered myself into a battered old farm truck parked beyond the barns, cranked the engine, and drove awkwardly, using my left foot on the pedals.

When I got to the meadowy gate at the top of Dunshinnog along an old, rutted logging road that winds up the mountain's southern flank, the truck's headlights glanced off an unfamiliar car with a rental tag. Flames leaped from a small pyramid of brushwood and tree limbs on the stone ledge overlooking the valley.

Astonished, I struggled toward the fire, glancing around wildly. I saw no one around it, no hint of who had dared wander onto my property during the night. The moon and stars had disappeared completely behind thick clouds laced with heat lightning. I smelled rain in the air.

"Who are you?" I yelled. "Where are you? This is private property! *Private!*"

I tottered barefooted among the foxgloves, offspring of those Grandpa and I had planted twenty years before. Watching, listening, swaying. I suddenly hated the foxgloves for surviving, for making promises they hadn't kept, for letting some stranger wander up here. I began smashing them with one crutch like some furious, wooden-pronged animal. "Come out of the woods!" I screamed toward the forest on either side.

Rain began to fall—cold, dense, a torrent that poured down on me. The fire sizzled and coughed billows of white smoke. I slipped on the ledge and fell down.

The next thing I knew, a pair of thick, strong arms were lifting me into the air.

I didn't know who had me or *what* had me. It was dark, and cold rainwater flooded my eyes, and I was dizzy from the fall, floating, shivering, against a foreign wall of clothed flesh and bone. It was too much like a nightmare. I began to struggle.

"*Claire*," a deep voice said raggedly.

That was all it took. I swung my drenched head toward it, lightning snapped above the mountain, and I saw his face carved out against the night, his eyes boring straight down into mine, holding me.

"*Roan*," I whispered in the middle of booming thunder that shook the air out of my lungs.

Roan.

·5·

$\mathcal{I}$ lived through that night as if I were drowning, and many of the details may never come back to me except in foggy symbolism, trying to see through a glass darkly.

The rain whipped us. Lightning split the torrent and thunder reached across the valley in deep bellows of celebration. The fire—a signal? some kind of primal claim for attention?—sank inside billows of smoke that floated around us as Roan carried me to the rental car. I didn't ask where we were going; I didn't care at the moment.

He drove and I braced myself against the passenger door, studying his profile as best I could during the lightning flashes. An airline ticket folder was crumpled on the floorboard; a sleek leather portfolio had been jammed into the crevice between the driver's seat and the center armrest console. The cold half of a long cigar lay in the open ashtray.

My voice was frozen inside my throat. Rainwater slithered down my face and plastered the bottom of my nightshirt to my legs beneath my windbreaker. My bare feet were muddy; I didn't know where my crutches were.

He's alive. He's come home. He didn't forget me.

Not long afterward I realized the car was struggling over rough, unpaved terrain, bucking and fighting his guidance. Limbs whipped the roof and muddy water sprayed up on the windshield, washed aside in wide streaks by the slap of the wipers.

"Are you kidnapping me?" I asked.

He glanced my way. I couldn't read his eyes, but I saw the flash of his smile. "Hell, yes."

"Roan." It was both plea and thanks.

He jerked the car to a stop suddenly, then vaulted out into the rain and came to my side. In short order he lifted me in his arms again, then carried me through a thicket of some kind, on uneven ground. A lightning flash uncurtained the darkness and I glimpsed the old cabin. Ten Jumps. He'd brought me to Ten Jumps. I wound one hand in his shirt. His skin and hair smelled like summer rain. His chest felt hard and deep against my side.

Nothing made much sense. He climbed the sagging porch steps, caddied me sideways through the doorway that had lost its door before either of us were born, into that tough shell of teak and shipwood. Wet wind sang through the square hole where a single window had been, but the overwhelming sensation was of having ducked into a protective cave.

He put me down on the floor, though something beneath me had give to it. I couldn't see him; I heard him moving. I leaned askew, the bad leg and the good one haphazardly tucked, bracing myself on my hands. There was a sizzling sound, then a flood of light. Roan squatted beside a camping lantern. I was sitting on an air mattress. An ice chest and a bulky duffel bag shared a dusty corner of the small, bare room.

Over the years I'd fought restless dreams in which a faceless stranger reached through fire for me; intuitively I knew he was Roan, but because I couldn't see his face, I couldn't take his hand. All solid evidence of him had disappeared, reduced to stories others told.

You'll be thirty years old before you'll really understand who you are.

And there I was, with all that history behind me, thirty years old, my heart aching, waiting to see what prophecy had brought Roan back to me.

He dropped to his heels beside the mattress, one hand bent against his chin; in the eerie white light of the camping lantern he looked like weathered marble except for those gray eyes as intense and quick as mercury. There was no point in talking; shock took up all the words. Like wild animals we gauged the dangerous situation with unblinking scrutiny.

Finally, after twenty years of unexplained absence, he said with more sorrow than sarcasm, "Home sweet home."

I looked into the face of the boy I remembered, now a grown man with scalding eyes hooded in a man's features, dark hair slicked back wildly from wide cheekbones and high forehead. "Yes," I said softly. He raised his hand to my face. His fingertips smoothed rainwater from my eyes, my mouth, curved under my chin, focusing me. "I know you," I whispered, dazed. "I still recognize you."

"I wouldn't be here if I thought you didn't want to see me again."

Thunder shook the cabin. In my fevered imagination the world was ending and beginning again, past and future colliding with wild pressures that shoved the only truths up from bedrock.

He jerked a red and white blanket from beside his knees and swooped it around my shoulders. I finally realized I was shivering. But he moved too fast, with the unsettling grace of lean, male muscles. Maybe he saw the startled reaction in my face; he frowned, sat back on his heels, then glanced around my ancestor's cabin as if regretting some idea. "I bought this place," he said.

Silence again. I needed time to mull over the fact that somehow he'd made that much money, that he used it in secretive ways, and that his purpose had to do with me.

Rain beat on the roof. I imagined the lake rising, flooding up beyond the blackberry briars and shaggy oaks, until we floated away. The Cherokees' stepping-stone turtles might come in handy.

He sat down, drew one knee up, and propped his arms on it. My leg had begun to ache. Suddenly I was exhausted and dizzy. The fall on the ledge had left a fresh, sore throb on one side of my face. I was so incredulous, I felt numb. "I have to rest," I admitted.

"I don't want to take you back to the farm tonight," he said. The words took the gentleness off his face. "Do you want me to take you back there?"

He wouldn't assume *want*; he phrased my family as a duty. I couldn't begin to explain my complex retreat and return to him; he owed me explanations, too. "No. I'm not going to let you out of my sight. I'm not even sure you're *real* yet."

He reached out, carefully, and I stayed still with marginal willpower. He laid his hand along my cheek for an instant. "As real as you are," he whispered.

Twenty years. I didn't have to say that out loud; his eyes darkened; he nodded. Keeping the blanket firmly around me, I lay down on my side as gracefully as possible, which wasn't too graceful. From somewhere he snared a thick pillow cased in fine blue linen. He laid it within my reach like a mating present. Everything seemed symbolic in my state of mind. I tugged the pillow under my head. Feathers, plush downy feathers. On an air mattress in a cabin with no amenities, in the woods, without another soul but him knowing where I'd gone.

He turned to the lantern, silhouetted; his hand moved in slow sequence, twisting a knob. Inky darkness, scented with the rain and damp earth, enclosed us. For a split second I was disoriented. "Talk to me," I said quickly. "Tell me anything that matters to you. I want to hear your voice."

"I'm sitting beside the mattress," he replied in gruff tones. "Listening to the rain. Listening to you breathe. This is the most peaceful moment I've had in years."

A contented fog began to slide over me in the wake of his voice—strange, because I already knew that deep down I was bitterly angry with him. He had been watching me all these years and never let me know. "I dreamed you came to the hospital," I whispered finally.

"I did."

Early morning sunshine whitewashed the cabin's spartan interior. A pair of hummingbirds were fighting over the fluted orange flowers of a trumpet-creeper vine that had latched on to the ledge of the broken-out window. I heard the rustle of fragile wings colliding in dive-bombing swoops. My mood was a strange mixture of despair and excitement.

Roan.

Clutching the walls and the door frame to steady myself, I half staggered onto the porch. My crutches lay propped against a broken section of porch rail. I hadn't realized that Roan had brought them with me the night before.

Roan stood in a small clearing fifty yards away with his back to me. Older, thicker, prime. That uncanny stillness he'd had as a boy, predatory but also defensive, gave me an impression of spiritual strength now. He seemed engrossed by the blue morning sky and the platinum surface of the lake.

He's here. He's really home.

I studied the terrain between Roan and me. Clods of sopping-wet weeds, a narrow deer trail through briars, the sturdy clumps of young pokeberry. Grandpa had always boiled poke greens to eat in the spring; the rich, fibrous greens gave him his spring cleaning, he swore. Later in the season they matured and turned poisonous.

I pushed myself step by step. Roan's blanket slid down my arms. I shoved at briars, balancing wildly. I was wearing a nightshirt with a flaking appliquéd palm tree on the chest, a yellow windbreaker, and no shoes. Panting, cursing under my breath, I lurched into the clearing. Roan pivoted at the sounds and held out his hands. At the moment of victorious arrival I stubbed one tip of my left crutch on a rock.

He caught me as I started to fall forward. I was livid with embarrassment until I noticed the dark circles under his eyes and forgot my own awkwardness. "Nice catch," I said hoarsely.

"Glad to break your fall. I wish I'd been there for you two months ago."

"You were. Everything I've done for other people has been a substitute for what I couldn't do for you twenty years ago."

"Then we're alike. I've tried to live my life in a way that could make up for what happened."

All the unanswered questions, all the years, so many changes, and yet so few. "I can't think straight right now," I offered. "I just need to look at you."

This seemed to please and worry him. He hunched his shoulders and watched me with chin tucked, his hard, pewter eyes boring into me. "Why don't you tell me what you see?"

I could sum up the parts but miss the point. He had *texture*: rough khaki trousers, hiking boots with black laces, an old gray cotton shirt with rolled-up sleeves. And he had context: a heavy gold wristwatch, thick dark hair that was slightly longish, drying into unruliness, his hands looked callused, and he had a fine peppering of dark beard shadow on his jaw and over his mouth.

"You're perfect," I said. Instantly aware of the pale, thin leg with surgical scars, I pulled his blanket closer around me. His gaze slipped down to the hidden leg, then back to my stare. We guided each other with invisible signals.

"You're the most beautiful woman I've ever seen in my life," he said quietly. "Let's get that point settled right now." There's power in a man speaking like that, not just in the words but in the music of tone and depth. I studied him intensely. Everything about us, every small discovery, was like water puddling on hard-baked ground; it took time to sink in, to soften and find the old channels.

"I was always afraid," I said slowly, "that one day I'd see you somewhere—in a shop, a restaurant, someplace public. And I'd recognize you. I'd walk up to you and say your name and you'd look at me without the slightest idea who I was. I'd have to explain. You'd be polite but edgy—maybe even cold—because the last thing you'd want was to dredge up ugly memories. I'd try to tell you how much you meant to me when we were kids, but it wouldn't mean anything to you. And that's when I'd realize how much of it had been a little girl's sentimental fantasies about an older boy."

"The way I pictured it," he said slowly, "I'd walk up to you and say your name and you'd step back. You'd ask me what the hell I wanted. You'd ask me why I wanted you to remember. You'd look at me but see my old man."

I sagged a little. He pulled a folding chair from beside a camp stove, where a kettle bubbled over blue-gold flames. I sat down weakly. He poured me a mug of coffee.

I set the mug aside, then rested my head in my hands. "How have you been?" I asked. Almost polite. Like a stranger. It was painful and absurd.

"When I saw you at the hospital, when I knew you needed me, that was all I cared about. I just wish, for your sake, it had gone a little different."

"Differently," I corrected. It just popped out; old habits are hard to break. He and I looked at each other with strained humor. He leaned over me, his dark, unkempt hair nearly brushing my forehead, and there wasn't any innocence between us. The scent of him, the scent of me, was like that of wounded animals and heat. "It's easy," he murmured. "How we are together. No one understood it when we were kids, and they won't understand it now."

I leaned back. "How do you know so much about me?"

"I've read every article you've written. Not just from the *Herald-Courier*, but going back to when you were editor of the student paper at the university. And before that. Issues of the *Shamrock*. You've never published a word I haven't read."

We were quiet for a long time. The lake shimmered; the season's first dragonflies darted above the surface. A small doe stepped from the forest on the opposite shore, watched us, then slowly wandered back into the woods. When I looked at Roan, I thought he must be as numb as I was, his eyes and mouth weighed down by isolation.

I said slowly, "I developed some peculiar ideas over twenty years. Such as assuming that since I never heard a word from you, you'd either forgotten me or you were dead."

"When I sat beside your bed that night at the hospital, you said you'd ruined my life. That you blamed yourself for Terri Caulfield the way you blamed yourself for what happened to me." Roan jerked his head in the direction of the Hollow, east along the treacherous ridges and gullies he'd followed as a boy to get to this sanctuary. "Is that what pushes you? I know what I see when I look at myself. I see my old man. Is that what you see?"

"No. You should have at least let me know you were alive and well."

"I've dealt with my old man's history as well as I ever will. I won't let his demons eat you alive, too."

"Dealt with it?" I whispered fiercely. "You bought all this land secretly. You wouldn't step forward at the hospital and tell the family that by

God, you'd come to see me. Why? *Why?* I don't believe you're ashamed of who you were. Who are you now? Where have you been? Do you hate the family so much you had to go to Dunshinnog first to prove you—"

"You asked me to do that."

When I gazed at him in disbelief, he said, "You don't remember. At the hospital. You told me the first thing I had to do was let the mountain know I'd come home. Something about foxgloves. I didn't understand it, but I promised you I'd go up there and build a fire."

"Did I also tell you to buy this property?"

"No." He squatted beside me. "I own a lot of property. Buy. Sell. It's natural for me to buy my way into a situation. Very uncomplicated that way. And I wanted this place. It means something to me. I don't want the cabin to just sit here and rot. I'll have to decide what to do with the place later. In the meantime, I intend to do the same thing for you that you tried to do for me when we were kids."

"And what is that? Meddle in my problems, promise me everything'll be fine if I just learn to trust you, then hurt me? That's what I did for you."

"You gave me something to believe in. I believed in you, and I never stopped believing."

The sunshine burned my eyes. I swept a blinded gaze at the scene around us. "You couldn't come back until you could buy this land? Make some statement about possession and control? Is that it?"

He didn't comment on that. "I called home for you," he said abruptly. He rose to his feet, frowning. "From my car phone. I called the farm at dawn. I may be a cold S.O.B., Claire, but I told your parents you were here and all right. The amazing thing is that they haven't shown up here to intervene. I think they're in shock."

"You don't know how much they've wanted to find you all these years."

"That doesn't matter to me."

"It has to matter. I . . . need answers. You're asking me to believe you're only here to settle old scores. I don't want to be treated like a debt you have to pay off. I don't understand you. There's something you're not telling me. I want to know everything about you."

He went very still, his eyes as dark as the wide-open lens of a camera, like mine on him. We pinned each other inside an invisible maze of smoke and mirrors, searching for each other along separate paths, opening doors, twisting, turning back, edging forward in stark, motionless silence. He reached inside his shirt and brought out a piece of wrinkled, yellowed notebook paper that had been folded for so many years that the creases looked as soft as old skin. "I wrote this to you the first summer," he said. "I have more letters you might like to read, but just read this one for now."

My heart in my throat, my hands shaking, I took the fragile paper. The words on it were scrawled in faded pencil; my eyes blurred with tears.

> *You got words that come easy. I never had no words that come that easy. But I will practice writing to you the way you wrote to me that time I was so by myself at 10 Jumps I wanted to die. Feel like I could die from being lonely right now. Can't half spell. Can't half write. Hard to think good tonight. You are inside my heart.*
>
> *Leaving this shitty church home tonight. Running away. Sorry. It hurts so much. What my old man done to you. What your folks done to me. Sorry. I will learn to be somebody new. I will be better than my old man. I will prove it some way.*
>
> *If I ever get to see you again I won't never hope for nothing but that you have forgot what my old man done to you. If I go away maybe you will grow up okay and not be the girl Big Roan Sullivan hurt that way. You are still a little girl, you hear me? You forget about what happened and about me and you will be okay. Fight for people like you done for me. Don't be scared of regular boys because of me and my old man. Don't blame your folks for sending me away. I had to go. I knew it, deep down.*
>
> *But I love you, little peep. And there is not nothing nasty or sexy about it. It is the only easy thing I have done in my whole life.*

I folded the letter and clutched it tightly. I was crying. "I want to read all of them," I said. "Every letter. Every one you wrote to me. I have to understand why you couldn't come back before."

He held out his hands. "Just for this morning, be a kid again. The one who didn't need answers before she'd take a chance on me."

My mind slid close to the edge of a razor. I glimpsed some hard exit, desolate but honest, in us both. I took his hands.

*H*e owned a twin-engine Cessna. Considering my history with airplanes, this meant more to me than the simple fact that he could afford a private plane.

My mother grew up helping care for her paternal grandmother, Quenna Kehoe Delaney, who as an elderly widow lived with Mama's family in the big Delaney house in town. Quenna spoke in a lilting, old-country brogue, was a staunch Catholic, and had a morbid, gothic nature that she insisted was true Irish.

The Kehoes had been a prominent Irish family; they'd immigrated to Boston when Quenna was a teenager, under relatively luxurious circumstances. This was in the 1890s, more than half a century after the pioneering Maloneys, Delaneys, and other Irish refugees settled in the Georgia mountains. Quenna had two brothers; one was a priest. A misguided Catholic diocese sent him south to the wilds of Dunderry because it was assumed that a town founded by Irish families and bursting with their descendants sorely needed a parish. Quenna and her other brother Ryan came with him.

Father Kehoe quickly discovered that he was dealing with third-generation Southerners, mostly Methodists, who were not infrequently hostile toward Yankees, even Irish ones. He stoically organized a tiny parish and built a church, which still exists, but eventually he went back to Boston. Quenna married Thurman Delaney, my great-grandfather. Ryan Kehoe married an O'Brien woman, who was a first cousin to Maloneys, and the two of them established the Kehoe clan in Dunderry.

When Mama was a little girl, in the early 1940s, her Grandma Quenna traveled by plane to Boston for a Kehoe family reunion. All went well until my great-grandmother flew home to the Atlanta airport, which was then little more than a dusty provincial operation. The pro-pellered passenger plane hit a flock of stray Rhode Island Red chickens on the runway during landing. Great-Grandmother Quenna refused to set foot on an airplane again and spent the years of Mama's impression-able girlhood telling and retelling the exact, horrifying details of her air-plane disaster: how the propellers flung chopped-up hen carcasses back along the passenger portholes so that Quenna never forgot the sight of bloody entrails smacking her window.

Whether Mama was brainwashed into a phobia about flying by that grotesque story, or had a dollop of Celtic superstition in her personality, we had never been sure.

But Mama has always been terrified to fly. She'll do it when necessary because she has a merciless scorn when it comes to what she perceives as character weaknesses, her own or anybody else's. I had watched her march onto commercial jets several times when I was a teenager, her legs shaking, her face as pale as an egg. I think, because I wanted to be even stronger-willed than my mother, I became almost cavalier about flying.

Once I flew to Tallahassee on a reporting assignment, bouncing all over the hurricane-threatened Florida sky in a claustrophobic commuter plane. The other passengers gripped their armrests and drank heavily. I read a novel and fell asleep. The next year I wrangled a dozen flying lessons from a boyfriend who ran a charter service.

At the tiny airfield outside Dunderry—two asphalt strips, four hangars, and a tower—I sat beside Roan in the cockpit of his blue and gold Cessna with tears welling helplessly in my eyes and my chest aching with pleasure. "Is it me, the plane, the situation?" he asked as he donned a radio headset and slipped dark aviator glasses over his eyes.

"I like to fly. Thank you."

He handed me what I assumed was a guest pair of sunglasses. I dully wondered what guests—female, male, business, or pleasure—he took with him regularly. I covered my eyes with the glasses.

"You didn't know the airport manager," Roan said once we were soar-ing over the green landscape and had leveled out. "I'm surprised."

"I don't know everyone in Dunderry County anymore. I haven't been around much since college. There're a lot of new people. It isn't the way it used to be."

"Good."

A few minutes later we were soaring through air currents in brilliant sunshine and a cloudless sky. "Any destination?" I asked.

"Just a local tour."

"You want me to say I'm impressed? I'm impressed."

"Bought the Cessna a few years ago. I use it for business trips."

"Where?"

"Out west."

"How far west?"

"West of the Rockies."

He flew low over Ten Jumps. A flock of mallard ducks scattered across the lake, casting shadows like fleeing ghosts. We skimmed along the ribbon of Soap Falls Road. To my right I saw the farm, far away, and Dunshinnog. To the left the deeply wooded ridges led west from Ten Jumps to the Hollow. The Hollow was a cluster of scrub pines draped in kudzu vines, a jungle on the edge of a handsome forest. What could I say for his godawful memories and my own?

"You had to see it from above, didn't you?"

Jaw clenched, he circled the area, banking sharply as he looked down. "Put it in perspective," he said.

"Go on. Get away from it. I turned my head for years, every day, when I rode the bus to school. When I got my own car, I never drove past it again. I don't want you to think about it."

"It's always there. Always will be."

I felt sharp-edged with too many emotions, as if I had broken glass inside me. I framed my gaze on open sky for a minute until I realized we were swooping over Dunshinnog, then down into the broad green valley of the farm.

Putting it all in perspective. Reducing it in scale.

The house was big and fine nonetheless, the yards around it quilted in gardens and shrubbery, the yard oaks spreading green canopies over the private architecture of roof and family.

We were no more than a hundred feet above the house. My parents and Amanda hurried out, plus an assortment of relatives I didn't have time to identify. There were a dozen cars in the yard. Visitors on a weekday, Amanda not in school. An event. The return of Roan Sullivan.

I waved gamely. Everyone shaded their eyes and squinted up. Amanda butterflied her arms wildly in response. "Feel better?" I asked as the family and valley disappeared below and behind us. "What are you trying to show me? What is all of this really about, Roan?"

"Just my point of view."

We flew north, toward town, above new houses dotting the hillsides, the new roads, a strip shopping mall and supermarket that had been built in recent years. Many newcomers.

"Let me fly this plane," I said suddenly. "I've had some lessons."

"I know." He glanced at me, one brow arched above the dark glasses. "The charter pilot. You wrote a feature article about him a few years ago. I thought you made him sound more interesting than he probably was. I thought *that* was interesting. That you went to the trouble."

"Well," I said. "It's a good thing I didn't write about the other men I dated."

He sat back and rested his hands on his knees. Startled, I grabbed the control on my side. The plane nose-dived briefly, then I got it leveled. We had to work together—his feet on the rudder pedals, my hands on the steering control. "Watch this," I said between gritted teeth. I swung low over the town square, then across back streets lined with big, gracious old homes with wide yards. I made two passes just above the elaborate roof of a Victorian. Finally a stout, gray-haired woman strode out into the yard and shook her fist at us.

"Aunt Arnetta is now officially warned that you're back," I noted. When I looked at Roan, he was watching me quietly with a thin smile on his lips. "Did you lose the tooth again?" I asked.

"What?"

"The tooth that Uncle Cully repaired. Must have lost it. You don't show any teeth when you smile."

Slowly he parted his lips. "All there."

My hands trembled. I felt ashamed of the giddy excitement but also addicted to it. He'd done that for me already.

"You trust me," he said. "*Claire.*"

I guided the Cessna out over the countryside. The tiny air strip appeared on a plateau among hay fields. "Do you trust *me?*" I asked. "I've never landed a plane before. I might get us . . ."

"Land it," he said.

And I did. Not very well, but he didn't flinch. When we were racing along the narrow asphalt runway, I turned the controls over to him and he brought the plane to a stop. He let out a long sigh. I was soaked with perspiration and gulping air. "Do you remember my mother's stories about her Grandma Quenna?"

He frowned and rubbed a hand over his jaw. Of course he wouldn't remember. He'd been deluged with Maloney and Delaney stories when he lived with us. I was sorry I had asked the question because I wondered if all those quirky family stories had seemed to exclude him, had made him feel more alone. He tilted his head back and eyed me with quiet affection. "You made a perfect no-chicken landing," he said.

So he did remember and in minute detail. He'd kept the faith, whether he'd wanted to or not. "Oh, my God," I whispered. "Whatever we're getting into, I have to say something. If you disappear again, don't come back. You'd break my heart."

He put his hands over mine. "That isn't the option we have to deal with. You may wish I'd never come back or tell me to get the hell out of your life."

"I don't think so."

He raised his hands and slid them into my hair, a tight grip, his thumbs rubbing heat into my cheekbones. There were tears in his eyes and a lot of them in mine. I'm not sure what we said. Not much, maybe nothing. He didn't just look at me, he *absorbed* me, my eyes, my face, my humiliating predicament. And I absorbed him.

And then, because I still marched to the drumbeat of the old, young, take-no-excuses Claire Maloney we'd both known once, I took a deep breath and choked out sternly, "I ought to skin you alive, *boy*."

He'd rescued me and I'd given him a lecture. He began to laugh. It was just like old times, but not remotely the same.

He returned me to Dunshinnog to get the farm truck I'd deserted the night before, but the truck was gone. Daddy had probably sent dutiful old Nat to retrieve it, not out of concern for the truck but to make certain Roan had to deliver me to the house in person.

I stood, still barefooted and dressed in the nightshirt and windbreaker, balanced between my crutches in a sea of lavender-tiered foxgloves shimmering in fresh, pink-tinted sunshine. They swayed heavily in small breezes that curled into the vise between the towering walls of oak and beech, sweet gum and white pine. I told Roan why Grandpa and I had planted them. "He was right," I finished. "They brought you home."

Roan walked among the flowers, bell-shaped blooms brushing his hands, the spires dancing in place as they let him pass, the foxgloves presenting him to me. It was a picture I set down permanently in my mind. He halted in front of me, looking from me to the foxgloves around us and back to me. There was a tortured sweetness between us that no amount of unexplained misery could erase.

Twenty years. A grown man, a grown woman. No more little-girl innocence, no more big-brotherly resistance. A thousand unanswered questions, but pulsing underneath the shock was an unpolished current, ripe
and provocative.

"Please, kiss me," he said.

I leaned forward and kissed the edge of his jaw. I kissed one corner of
his mouth. He bent his head. We shared a breath. Very slowly, we came
together. First it was gentle, but then it became a frantic welcome, con-
suming the hot, smooth, liquid world between us.

He held me by the arms, his head bent to mine. I touched his cheek
and he turned his face toward the caress. I pulled my hands into a tight,
controlled fist against my chest.

Suddenly we heard wild rustling noises in a thicket of tall laurel that
skirts the forest. Amanda burst out, her red hair tangled with twigs and
leaves, a pair of binoculars dangling from a leather strap around her neck.
She was dressed in sneakers, overalls, and a T-shirt as pink as her face. She
halted at the edge of the meadow a dozen yards from us, her hands rising
to her mouth in awed scrutiny. "Aunt Claire, he *did* come back! I *told* you
he'd come back! Everyone's waiting to see him! Oh! He's just perfect!"
Then she turned and darted back into the laurel, scrambling down the
slope until she disappeared from sight.

"You told her about me," Roan said softly. "Your niece? You told her
about me. When?"

"Not long ago."

"Why?"

"Because she needs to believe in magic." So much for maintaining control. I turned away from the look in his eyes, desperately. "I think we've
been ambushed by a fairy," I said.

The mountain's old logging trail comes out on Soap Falls just above the
driveway to the farm, and we turned in past the familiar oversize rural
mailbox with MALONEY FARM painted on its sides in square white letters.
Twenty years after his helpless expulsion, Roan made his face a mask as he
guided the sleek gray rental sedan back down the graveled road between
wide spring hayfields and acres of corn. A mixed pack of fat farm dogs ran
out to meet us, barking and wagging.

Mama and Daddy waited on the veranda. I hoped Roan saw them as
I did—so much older, only human, not the icons of authority they had
been in his boyhood. My father was turning into Grandpa, complete
with the bald head and lumbering stance of an old bear; my mother was

vulnerable in the graciously preserved aura of youth, slender in beige slacks and a gold pullover, her shoulder-length hair tinted in expensive shades of brown and copper, her blue eyes fanned with lines at the corners. Grandma Dottie sat royally ensconced in a white rocking chair, and Roan could surely see that she had become a thin little old lady despite the coy blue leggings she wore and a long Pavarotti T-shirt she'd ordered from the public TV catalog. Smoke curled from the tip of a long, filtered cigarette she'd tucked into one corner of her lipsticked mouth, and her bifocaled eyes were wide with hope.

Amanda, on the veranda's broad stone steps, swayed from one foot to the other as if caught up in the thrall of an inner song. I saw Renfrew peeking from an upstairs window, a tall feather duster clutched under her chin so that she looked like the hairnetted centerpiece of some strange flower arrangement. Nat gaped with gnomish delight from among camellia bushes in the side yard, potbellied in overalls, wisps of his gray-blond hair dancing atop his head in a warm breeze. The visiting cars were gone. My parents had wisely cleared out the rest of the crowd.

I had no idea what to say or how to handle the reunion. My stomach was tight under my breastbone. Roan stopped the car beside a lawn border of old rose shrubs bursting in full red bloom. Before he could open the car door I reached over and stopped him with my hand on his forearm. Below the rolled cuff of his shirtsleeve his muscles were bunched in ropy lines. I believed, at that moment, that he could easily have slammed his fists into a brick wall. "The day my father took you away in the car I stood at a window and watched and cried until I couldn't breathe," I said. "With Grandpa holding me up. I don't need anybody to hold me up this time, and I don't intend to cry. All you have to do is listen to whatever they say to you, just listen, and don't forget that I was here then and I'm here now."

He said nothing and abruptly got out of the car. I slung my door open before he could reach it and struggled to my feet, hanging on to the door frame and searching Mama's and Daddy's faces. They had the dumbstruck look of old grief and awkward concern; it was a painfully humiliating confrontation for all concerned. My horror was that no one would say a word, that this was beyond words.

Roan took my crutches from the backseat and helped me get situated on them, closed the door, and then stepped ahead of me and halted. He stood stiffly, as my parents did, not speaking, his head up, his hands hanging by his sides.

Everyone studied him as if he'd emerged from a cloud of sulfurous smoke. And at me, in my nightshirt and barefooted, hair tangled madly, as if I'd been rolled in strange dough.

Daddy held up his hands and walked down the veranda steps to us. Mama followed him hurriedly. "Your mother and I can't tell you what to do," he said to me. "But we can tell you there's no reason for you to take sides. Roan's welcome in this house. You hear me, Roan? That's the truth."

Roan inclined his head slightly, accepting and rejecting.

Mama said, "Claire needs peace and quiet and rest. I'm not sure you understand that."

"You think the worst," Roan countered.

"No, Roan. No." Her face was pale. Her eyes glittered. "You think what you want, Roan. I don't blame you. If you're even *half* as honorable as the boy we were stupid enough to send away, you don't need to explain a thing to me or anyone else."

"I came here to do what I can for Claire. I'll help her any way she'll let me. I don't expect anything from anyone else."

"We have faith. I will say it, and say it, and say it—everything I should have said when you were a boy. I'll say it until you believe it. You're welcome here. You still have a home in this community and people who never meant to lose you."

"That's really not important to me now." Roan turned to me. "I have work to do at Ten Jumps. Plans to make. So you know where I'll be."

"Don't leave like this. Come inside," I said frantically. "I thought you meant to."

"Yes, please, *please* come in the house," Mama added urgently. "Talk to us. Tell us about yourself."

Roan straightened. "It's not that simple."

Daddy put in brusquely, "Ten Jumps doesn't have much to offer. There's plenty of room for you here. I mean that. It's a sorry invitation, yes, it sounds that way. Pushed out as a needy boy and then asked back as a fine, upstanding houseguest? But listen to me, Roan. We did what we thought was right then. It wasn't meant to be the end of you with this family."

"This"—Roan swept my folks, the house, the valley, Dunshinnog, the whole farm with a burning look that settled finally on me—"was everything I cared about. I still care. But on different terms. My terms."

"This is how you're going to handle it?" I asked, stunned. I gaped at him. I wanted to shake him. "Don't set terms. People get ruined by setting their own *fucking* inflexible terms."

Anger and frustration colored the mood far darker than the obscenity had; as soon as I said it he touched my face with the tips of his fingers, scalded me with a look that said I'd betrayed him by not understanding, then walked back to his car.

Suddenly I saw myself the way he must be seeing me for the first time—clearly, in bright, brutal sunlight—my need for family, the incontrovertible evidence that I was a willing part of people who'd hurt him.

Blind with fury and confusion that rose up within me like a tidal wave, pushing me against my will, I stumbled after him. "It's not a *choice!* You're part of us! *You are still part of this family whether you like it or not! You have to be willing to forgive them!*" I reached the row of raised stepping-stones that bisected the front yard. The tips of my crutches caught and I tumbled hard.

On Dunshinnog the night before, then nearly falling at Ten Jumps, and now this. I wanted to sink into the flat fieldstone beneath me, taking every gulp for breath, every aching joint and furious thought of helpless disgrace with me. I heard Mama's gasp, I heard her and Daddy running toward me.

Roan was beside me, kneeling. "Easy, easy," he said. He took me by the shoulders.

"Don't touch me. I told you I don't need anyone to hold me up. Not even you. I won't be caught in the middle again. This is stupid. You've come home. You didn't make that effort without good reason. You can't turn it into a standoff *now.*"

"Holt, stay back. Let them—" Mama said tearfully.

"I'm lettin' 'em. But this isn't very good for her. This isn't helping. Roan, dammit, you traipse her around the countryside and bring her home like a rag doll—"

"Holt!"

My father went silent.

Roan said, "Look at me."

I tested the inside of my lips, worked my jaw, then raised my head and gave him a level, brutally honest stare. "I can't *chase* you," I said.

He gave me the most unwavering scrutiny, heartbreaking and mesmerizing. He lifted a devastatingly familiar hand, big-knuckled, with strong fingers, and gently brushed my tangled hair from my eyes. "You have to try," he said. "If I don't make you try you'll keep sitting here like a goddamned invalid." I shivered. His accent had boiled down to smooth, dark amber tones. "I remember a girl who never let me hide unless she was with me, to make certain I was all right," he went on, tearing me apart. He slowly slid his arms around me and pulled me to him. I stiffened more inside his embrace.

He bent his head next to mine. "How many times did you see me in trouble, and filthy, and hurt, and alone?"

"It's not the same."

"Do you want to be helpless?"

"No."

"Then get up. You can do it."

I gripped his hands. My legs felt like a lead weight under me. I struggled. Sweating, breathing hard, my eyes never leaving his, I wavered on my knees, got one bare foot under me, and swayed desperately. My nightshirt tangled between my thighs. Roan's grip tightened on my hands, I felt his calluses, his thick, gentle fingers sliding down to my wrists. He clamped firmly and pulled. I shoved myself upward with every ounce of strength.

I stood. I *stood*. No crutches, wobbling, light-headed, my teeth gritted, but I *stood*. Some unspeakable devotion and challenge moved between us. "I want those letters you wrote to me," I said. "I want you to bring them here right now and sit with me while I read them. All of them."

He arched a brow. "If you want the letters you'll have to come to Ten Jumps."

I stared at him. He wouldn't give an inch. Amanda bolted to us. "Ask him to stay and visit! Ask him, Aunt Claire!"

"He's been asked, sweetie." I braced my knees. "He understands that I don't move around very well. He'll come back to sit with me and visit."

Roan smiled thinly at my ploy, but he bent to my niece with gentle regard. That subtle but stunning shift had an effect on all of us. I know it nearly broke me. "Has your aunt ever told you how to *sugar* people?" he asked Amanda.

For a second she clamped her hands to her mouth, too overwhelmed to answer him. The legendary Roan Sullivan, cool and powerful—he not only deigned to notice her, he did it with great charm and kindness. "Yes, sir," she said in a small voice. "She says tell 'em what they want to hear and they'll eat right out of your hand."

"Yellow jackets used to light on her hands," he murmured. "She was scared, but she'd never admit it."

"Because she sugared 'em," Amanda whispered back.

He nodded. "I think she's practicing to sugar yellow jackets again. You keep an eye on her and let me know."

"Oh! I will!"

Roan looked at me. "I'll be nearby. You can find me if you want to."

"That's something new, anyway," I said. "Being able to find you."

Watching him drive away was one of the hardest things I'd ever done.

Behind me, my parents said nothing, individually or in unison, and when I turned to them they looked shaken but resolute.

"We'll work on him," Daddy said.

"He expects too much from you," Mama said, "and not enough from us."

"He thinks you're sweet." Amanda sighed. "He thinks you're full of sugar."

She'd missed his point, thank God.

Turned thirty this year, Claire, and put my first million in the bank. What would you think of that? I think you'd expect it. Money is power. I hope you'd be proud. I'm writing this on fine linen stationery. Twenty-five dollars for a little box. I use it to write thank-you notes for the parties they invite me to. Big business. Big parties. Money. Land. Opportunity. Women . . .

The women. I hope to tell you about them someday. Whatever you want to know. You'll tell me about the men you've been with. And then we won't talk about that part of our past again, either of us, because it was only loneliness and plain human need.

I'm learning to play golf. Picture that! It's a ritual, Claire. A way of fitting in. I learned about rituals with your family. You play a certain way, you fit in. You don't play, you don't fit. Human nature, I guess.

Golf's a sucker's game. It looks easy but winning is hidden in the fine points. I respect that, don't get me wrong. I like the game. It's precise. But my God. Me dressed in golf shirts and khakis and shoes with cleats. Spending thousands of dollars to play a game. I look at it as a business investment. Everything is business to me. I'd put on a goddamned monkey suit if that's what it took to make deals with the other monkeys. . . .

Strange stuff, these letters. I talk to you on paper and lock the letters in a box. Nobody who knows me now would believe I do anything this sentimental. But then they don't really know me. What a damned waste. Twenty-five dollars for writing paper.

But I would write to you on pure gold if I could.

∞

7

I was barely able to move for several days. The knee and ankle of my healing leg swelled, were hot to the touch; every muscle in my body punished me for sleeping on the air mattress at Ten Jumps, for falling twice in less than one day, for standing on the leg too much. Emotionally, I felt as I once had when I was assigned to cover a hurricane in Florida. Scared, excited, and holding on as hard as I could in high winds.

"Roan's come back for revenge," some in the family said.

"He deserves to take revenge on us," others replied.

Lurid, uneasily recalled stories resurfaced in the family and among the oldest friends—about Big Roan and Jenny, the Hollow, Roan and the McClendon sisters at Steckem Road, Uncle Pete and Sally, Roan and my family, Roan and me. People sorted rumors and tidbits of truth about us as they lounged on their front verandas in the rose-scented spring air, and over their morning biscuits and cream gravy at the diners, and in the shops and the fields and the offices. And I heard that Roan had made his money in drugs or in gambling; I heard he planned to build a public park and dedicate it to his mother and that he had bought Ten Jumps to develop condominiums, apartments, industrial warehouses, a shopping mall, or a horse farm.

I heard he had taken me away from Dunshinnog against my will the first night, that he had offered me a lot of money to leave town with him, that Mama and Daddy wouldn't let him set foot on the farm, that my brothers had threatened him if he tried to see me, and that his homecoming had caused me to have a nervous breakdown, which was why I was pale and nearly sleepless and had kept to myself since Roan returned.

The gossip was as good as any story I'd ever written.

During my newspaper career I'd picked through countless strangers' lives, presenting their heartaches and hopes and failures for other strangers to read. Journalism is a noble but cruel right in a free society. I'll always defend the principles behind it, but theory doesn't sink in like the reality of knowing your own life is the object of rabid scrutiny. I wanted to spare Roan all the lies and speculation that swirled around me.

And I wanted to make him come to me because I was furious and hurt. For twenty years he'd let me suffer, worry, and hunt for him while he watched me neatly from a distance. He owed me explanations.

Josh arrived from the legislative session in Atlanta, where he leased an apartment in a downtown high-rise. Brady came, and Hop and Evan. The family gathered in the living room one evening after Amanda was in bed. Josh said brusquely, in the strange way he had of turning other people's misery into his own problem, "I can understand how a person can search for someone he cares about and not forget the loyalty and not give up, but Roan's always known where you were. Why did it take him twenty years to come back?"

That was the excruciating question on everyone's mind.

I felt my face growing hot. "I don't know."

Josh pursed his mouth. "He wants to prove a point to the family. He could have contacted you—a phone call, a letter. What stopped him? Instead he *spies* on your life, and when you're vulnerable, he bulldozes his way back in. Just when you've come home, when you're getting settled. Because alienating you from the family again would be the ultimate payback. I understand how he might have worried about a reunion—always wondering if you'd want to see him, if he'd done the wrong thing when he left here as a kid—but on the other hand, you may just be some kind of trophy to him, sis."

"Not much of a trophy," I said wearily.

"He came to see you at the hospital but waited two more months to see you again. I think you're hurt and mad as hell about that, and I think you want answers he won't give. Tell me what you think he wants from you and the family, sis, since nobody else has been forcing you to consider the issue."

"I don't know yet."

Josh leaned forward, his ruddy hands on his finely trousered knees. His general intensity bordered on rabid determination at times. It was as if he were always after something. He would have made a good reporter. "I'm not trying to cause trouble for him," Josh went on, "but I know too many men who've clawed their way out of the gutter by means they won't admit, and their biggest ambition is to punish all the people who kicked them when they were down. It's standard philosophy in politics, and not much different elsewhere: Help your allies, hurt your enemies; compromise to get what you want, *and never admit your true intentions.*"

Daddy scowled. Mama drew up tightly. "Son," she said in a low, even gentle voice, "you should spend less time with politicians and more with decent human beings. I think you see ugly motives and conspiracies behind every rock."

This interrupted the flow of conversation temporarily as everyone waited for the angry moment to fade.

"Let's not jump to conclusions," Brady said finally. "Maybe Roan's interested in the investment opportunities around town. I could talk to him about that."

"Brady, for God's sake," Evan retorted. "Have you got a dollar sign tattooed on your—"

"Roan has no reason to give any of us so much as the time of day," Hop put in gruffly. "But I can't believe he's come back to cause trouble. I believe he's got Claire's interests at heart."

"I go along with that," Evan added, stroking his beard.

I listened dimly as the family launched into a discussion of the situation, my brothers and father arguing my business like a clan of old-world patriarchs, and on a stronger day in my life I'd have accepted it politely from my father, as was his due, then rounded up my brothers in private and scorched the piss out of them with a few choice words. But I had no strength for small battles.

"One thing's clear—Roan's never let go of Claire any more than she's let go of him," Mama concluded.

I limped outside to the veranda and sat in a rocking chair with the first fireflies of the season blinking yellow around me, gazing toward the Hollow and Ten Jumps, separate from everyone and alone.

I watched Dunshinnog for the lure of another light. There wasn't any. I was almost relieved. He expected me to follow him everywhere, just as I had when we were kids. Away from the family this time, away from home, never resolving the betrayals and regrets on either side. I was afraid he'd ask me to leave with him.

And that he already suspected that sooner or later I'd go.

Claire, I'm very aware of what I was. That's why I try to make a strong impression on people. A certain one. There can't be any doubt they're dealing with someone to take seriously.

When I was a kid, you were the only one who looked at me without seeing only what I came from.

I've spent a lot of time thinking about how your parents treated you and your brothers. The teaching, the discipline, the respect. I try to decide how to do it the way they did. Or how your Grandpa Joe would. Strange thing, Claire. I try to see the world the way they did, to learn from them. I learned more than I thought.

I'm trying to pass it along to my boy.

☙

8

"*H*e bought a box of Earl Grey and a box of English Breakfast tea from me," Aunt Jane relayed to Mama and the other sisters during a Saturday brunch in the dining room of Hawks Ridge Country Club, Brady's golf-community development about ten miles south of town. Hop and Evan are two of the main residential contractors for the development, building half-million-dollar homes on lots barely wide enough to mow the sodded grass. There are no more hawks around Hawks Ridge now, and the ridges have been scraped clear of trees, and neither my mother nor any of her sisters play golf, but these ironies paled in comparison to Roan buying tea from a member of the family. "He was very polite but not very talkative," Aunt Jane confided. "Still, I consider it a fine sign that he remembers me so kindly. I believe I was one of his favorite people."

"Good lord," Aunt Irene retorted. "I was the one he'd ask for extra help-ings at Sunday dinners. And he sure didn't speak to anybody else at those dinners."

"Y'all are worse than Arnetta," Mama told them. "She's insisting that she tried to talk Holt and me out of sending Roan to the church home. That's not how I remember it. God forgive us all."

"Our memories are kinder to us than the truth is," Aunt Jane admitted wistfully. "I suppose all he wanted was to buy some tea." There was con-siderable silence at the table after that.

I soon realized that Roan didn't really need anyone's good references, including mine.

He brought in his own crew to renovate the cabin at Ten Jumps. Uncle Eldon told us about it the day he sold the crew's foreman a tractor-trailer load of lumber, plumbing, electrical supplies, nails, screws, concrete mix, and assorted other necessities.

Then Uncle Winston, who had purchased a motel franchise in town, where the crew had taken rooms, reported that Roan and the dozen men were working day and night at Ten Jumps. "They got a couple of big electrical generators," Winston told us, "and enough high-powered lights to hold a football game. You look west over the trees late at night, you can see the glow."

He was right. I sat outside on the veranda, with a huge gathering of family, and looked that night. The horizon over Ten Jumps was bright.

The crew immediately cleared, scraped, and graveled the dirt road that led to the lake and cabin, then built a pair of stacked-stone columns where the dirt road ended at the paved public road and hung an elaborate, stately set of black iron gates. Everyone was flabbergasted. "I don't know what to think about that gate," my father said to me angrily. "Roan's thumbing his nose at us. What are you going to do about it?"

"What are you going to do about him?" Mama added more specifically. "Because he's not coming back over here. That's obvious."

"If I go I'm afraid I'll lose something," I said, shaking my head at my own vagueness. "I'm afraid he'll make me choose sides and that it'll be forever. And I don't know which side I'd pick. I don't want him to ask me to choose."

My parents stared at me, unsettled by that honest information.

"Make up your mind quick," Daddy insisted. "Before he starts building a fort around his place."

Mama came to me in private later. She said she had missed so much of my "young womanhood," because I went away to college and stayed so busy—we both knew the truth, that I'd rejected her and Daddy as soon as I was old enough to leave home—but she told me how much she'd missed all the mother-daughter part of that time and I admitted I'd missed sharing it, too. She brightened immediately and got straight to the point. "I never even knew when you had sex the first time," she said. "I assume you've had sex."

I stared at her. My face grew warm. "Yes," I managed to say.

"My point is, I'm aware you're in an awkward circumstance, living at home, a grown woman. If you want to buy some birth control . . . just go ahead and don't feel you have to sneak around. I'll get it for you." She paused. "Of course, we're not going to tell your daddy about it."

I wanted to laugh at her, but I also wanted to slip down low and hug her around the waist with my head on her breasts. To be small again and give us both a second chance at those years we'd missed.

I took her hand. "I don't intend to have sex with Roan anytime soon, if at all. But thanks. I love you."

She thought for a minute. "I expect he'll supply his own, but I'll get you some condoms just in case," she announced.

I dreamed at night of faceless women who danced naked, and cats who slept on hard pillows, and other more blatant symbols that included myself, and Roan, and made me forget that my leg ached when I moved.

Food. Of course. Like the old days. I would send him food.

I enlisted Hop and Evan, Uncle Winston, and some of the cousins to take it to him. With the assistance of Mama, Renfrew, and various aunts and cousins, we put together boxes and ice chests filled with enough food to feed him and an entire army of construction workers for several days. Food is a primitive gesture of welcome; food is apology; food is a sacrament. There is more generosity in pies and casseroles than in a thousand pious words. We knew those facts by heart; I hoped he remembered.

I went through some of the storage boxes from my apartment in Florida. I found the large paperbound road atlas, one of those oversize, colorful editions with each state's map on a separate page. The pages were worn and curling at the corners; the major cities and towns of each state had black lines drawn through them.

I wrapped the atlas in tissue paper and enclosed a note:

> *It took me a lot of years and who-knows-how-much money in phone bills, but every black line represents a place where I called Information and asked for the telephone number of Roan Sullivan. I called each one. It was never you. Is it you now?*

"What did he say?" I asked after my stocky, placid brothers returned from delivering the food. We sat in the living room with Hop's kids watching a cartoon video in the corner near the piano. "He looked pleased, I guess," Hop said, frowning. "You know something? I remember his stare when he was a boy, and he's got that look honed to a hard edge. He's got that Clint Eastwood/Dirty Harry thing goin' when he levels a look at you, and you can't tell if he's likely to smile or take you by the throat. I told him he shouldn't have brought in outsiders, that me and

Evan would have sent a crew, but he just shrugged. If he hadn't shook our hands I'd have been a little antsy. Him and that crew're working like they got no time to spit. You ought to see what he's done with the place in a week's time."

"That's what Roan said," Evan interjected. "'Tell her to come see for herself. I wanted a nice spot for us to get to know each other again. It's almost ready. She can come anytime.'" He nodded fervently. "After he looked at that package you sent with the food, he got a funny expression on his face. You hit him somewhere soft, sis. He gave me something to bring back. That's a start." Evan presented me with a large, bulky manila envelope.

I laid it on my lap, ripped the envelope quickly, and pulled out a half-inch-thick portfolio bound in leather.

I hurriedly scanned the handsomely printed columns and lists on the pages inside the binder, cupping one hand to my throat as I did. I saw an address in Seattle. On the other side of the country. Seattle, of all places. Why there? Hop and Evan peered blatantly over my shoulders.

Land. Houses. Apartments. Warehouses. Buying. Selling. Leasing. Several states, several cities. Good lord. I was stunned by the enormity of it, set down on paper. He was proud of himself, but this ambition was part of a bigger mystery that had kept him away for two decades.

"Good lord," Hop breathed. "This is some kind of prospectus on his property holdings and investments."

Evan exhaled loudly. "He's telling you what he's worth, baby sister. And he's worth a fortune."

Roan had also sent a note. Written on pale gray stationery, it said:

> *Your Grandpa Joe told me once that he and your grand-mother traded gifts for six months before she'd see him without a chaperone. He had a bad reputation. She'd send him apple pies and he'd send her flowers. Finally he bought her some records for her Victrola. Classical music. "I don't recollect what kind of dog howl it was," he told me. "But it had lots of violins and she went nutty over it and me."*
>
> *So here's a gift in return for the food. In return for the atlas. Now you owe me another gift. You see, I remember how traditions stick in the family. I never forgot the best. Or the worst.*
>
> *I think I know what you're afraid of.*

I'm going to get you out of that house, out of your bed, Claire. By God, you're going to get over here and take care of your own situation. Nobody to blame but me now. I'm real now, not an unlisted phone number anymore.

I took out the piece of old wood he'd carved with our names. I wrapped it in handsome gift paper, with a bow, and Hop delivered it to Roan with my note:

I don't want your résumé. I don't want to know how much damned money you have or that you deal in land and houses or that you set up housekeeping on the Pacific. I want to know everything that happened to the boy who cut his name and mine into this board. Until you've got the cojones to SHARE THAT BOY WITH ME, nothing else matters. COME HERE AND BRING YOUR LETTERS.

He didn't offer any answer at all in response.

I got up at dawn the next day, dressed in my white terry-cloth robe and jogging shoes, went to the sunroom, and stepped very slowly onto a treadmill Violet had sent over after I hit her with the pillow. I had written her a long letter of apology, and she said she had forgiven me, but she wouldn't risk being walloped again; she told me to walk.

Josh strode into the room; he'd arrived from Atlanta well past midnight in the staid, gray Town Car that said he was prosperous, conservative, and didn't believe in bucket seats. The click of my oldest brother's shoes on the sunroom's rust-red tiles—custom-made for Mama by a potter friend in Mexico—made my nerves pop.

We brusquely exchanged good mornings. He sat in a wingback wicker chair with his coffee cup perched on his knee. He's built like a barrel with legs; his red hair has receded into a V that sweeps back from his forehead. I call it his *Republican mohawk*, and when I do, he has enough humor to laugh at himself.

He flicked invisible wrinkles from his white dress shirt and pinstriped pants, adjusted the knot of a silk tie with one hand, and held the coffee cup in the other. He told me he had a full week planned: speeches, meetings, the care and contrivance of his state senate district. He still used his old bedroom at home, plus a second one he had converted to an office. But he was away three weeks out of four, either traveling or attending legislative sessions in Atlanta.

He dated an administrative assistant from the state department of transportation. Her name was Lin Su; she was working toward a master's degree in political science at Georgia State. She was also only twenty-five years old, born in America but Vietnamese by heritage. Mama and Daddy kept asking to meet her, but Josh insisted she wasn't significant.

"I've got no use for Roan if he's here to cause trouble," Josh said finally. "He's made his money, but money's not the same as family. He can't buy family."

"Don't preach at me," I said.

"You've lived away from the family. You and I are the only ones who've really seen what the world is like on our own. Brady sees the world as one big cookie jar. Hop and Evan don't have the imagination to worry about the bigger picture. Mama and Daddy secretly wish Eisenhower was still president."

"Cut to the chase, big brother."

"It means so much to Mama and Daddy to have you back home. To be close to you. I don't want the family torn apart over you and Roan."

"Then don't take sides."

"Mama will say what you want to hear because she wants you to forgive her. Daddy prides himself on being fair; he'll bend over backward to right an old wrong. The rest of the kin will keep their mouths shut for the most part, out of respect. All I'm doing is playing devil's advocate. Somebody has to."

"I have no intention of tearing the family apart. Roan redefined this family," I panted. "Brought out the best and the worst in us. Now it's time to prove we've changed for the better."

"You think I'm a hypocrite."

"On the contrary, I think you're desperate to believe the world isn't completely screwed up. That's why you're afraid to get close to your own daughter. You're afraid to care too much. I understand how that is."

"Don't change the subject. How do you plan to deal with Roan?"

"I plan to do everything in my power to make him feel welcome in this family. To make him believe it's possible for him to still be part of the family."

Josh craned his head. "You talk as if you're planning a future with him. But he's a stranger, Claire."

"He's not a stranger to me. He never will be."

"Face the fact that Roan may not want to resolve anything. Face the fact that you could let yourself get . . . *attached* to him and then be forced to make a choice that would hurt you for the *rest* of your life."

"That's not going to happen. I won't let it."

"Listen to me." Josh leaned forward. Speaking softly, in a voice pared down to a hard monotone, he said, "When I was on duty one night in Saigon I saw a lovesick bar girl pour alcohol over her head and strike a match. It happened so fast I couldn't stop her. She burned like a goddamned Christmas tree. Ten seconds, maybe, and what was left of her face didn't even look *human*. Was it my fault? Hell, no. If I'd sat around for years asking myself what I could have done differently, I'd have ended up contemplating a bottle of booze and a box of matches myself."

I stumbled off the treadmill and took several queasy breaths. My oldest brother had revealed more about himself in that story than I'd ever understood about him before. "We all come home from our wars with scars we can't forget," I said softly. "Is that why you blame Amanda for being born? You lost a wife and got a daughter in return, and you can't forgive the trade? Is that why you sleep with a woman who reminds you of Vietnam but you won't let her be part of our family? What are you ashamed of?"

His head jerked up. "There's a lot you don't know about me, sis," he said softly. He fumbled with his tie, got to his feet, and walked out.

Another woman just told me I was a lost cause. She said she catches me looking through her as if she's not there. I like her, and I'm sorry we had to end with her feeling that way. But she's right. Part of me isn't finished. Isn't there. I know it makes no sense to believe I'd be different with you. I know none of this makes any sense after all these years.

We won't have a future until the past is torn apart and settled between me and the family, Claire. Until you and I look at each other and decide how many people we're willing to hurt. I'm always hiding something. I listen to other people talk about the way they grew up, about their folks and all their good times, and I know I'm blank except for the time I spent with you and your family. It's as if you helped me just invent myself one day. Like a Frankenstein. I'm made up of pieces that other people gave me.

I won't get close to other people because I don't want to tell them about myself. I killed my own old man. That's not the kind of thing you tell other people. I'm always separate.

I want something good to remember, Claire. Something I can hold on to, something that erases what happened. If you see me someday, maybe all you'll remember will be the bad part— what's broken.

I want you to talk to that kid I used to be and tell him it's okay to come home. That you still love him.

And I want you to tell my boy he can be proud of me.

9

*A*manda was furious with me. The next afternoon we collided in the front hall. "I'm not speaking to you," she said. I wheezed from the impact. She looked at me with absolute despair. "Why won't you go see Mr. Sullivan?"

"Sweetie, you don't understand. We have to get to know each other again, very slowly and carefully so that—"

"Grandpa and Nana told me. They told me they sent him away a long time ago, and it hurt your feelings, and it hurt his feelings, too, and they're sorry about it, and they're doin' their best to make it all right. But you gotta help."

"I'm trying to help, sweetie. But when you're older you'll understand that grown men and women have to be very responsible about their friendship. They have to move slowly. They need to be very honest with each other and they need to agree on a few rules about their—"

Her eyes filled with tears. "You sound like Papa. He thinks about makin' rules and laws so much, he forgets I'm even around."

"Your papa's just busy. He loves you so much."

"No, he doesn't. He won't say so, so he must not love me. He won't get married again and gimme any brothers and sisters because he doesn't even *like* me. Just like you must not love Mr. Sullivan 'cause you don't even care enough to *tell* him."

"Sweetie, I love Mr. Sullivan in a certain way. But sometimes even when you love somebody you don't really know what to say to that person. You almost wish they'd stay away until you do know what to say."

"You kissed him! On the mouth. Right after he came home! You kissed him and he kissed you back for a long time!"

"People kiss for a lot of reasons—"

"I told him about you." She glared at me victoriously. "I was at the Pick N' Save with Aunt Luanne yesterday, and he was there buying a newspaper, and everybody was staring at him, but I went up to him, and I said, My Aunt Claire is pretty, isn't she? And he said, She's the prettiest, smartest, strongest woman I've ever seen. And so I said, Well, if you don't come to visit her, you're not ever gonna see her 'cause she won't even go to town. And he said, I bet I can make her go to town."

"You are so much like your papa. You're a little politician. When you get to be president I'll come stay in the Lincoln bedroom and I'll steal the pillowcases."

"I told him all you told me about him! How you said he was wonderful, and you never forgot him, and how sad you looked when I said I was sure he'd jump back for you!" She flailed both hands in the air. "And I told him you've still got his shamrock necklace in your jewelry box!"

I shut my eyes. "And I get to steal Lincoln's sheets, too," I said.

I watched Alvin Tobbler on television today. Saturday, wet and cold even for Seattle. I sat there on the couch with a fire in the fireplace and watched Al Tobbler play football somewhere on the other side of the country, thinking about how many Friday nights I watched him at the high school stadium in person and about that night you and I lost our teeth.

That was the night your family took me to the farm. I'd never been in a bed with nice, clean sheets before. The bedroom smelled like flowers. I couldn't believe I was there. That your family cared the way you said they would. That anybody cared except you.

Today I wondered if you were watching Al's game, too, and I thought about the ways you are part of my everyday life, as if you were sitting beside me.

Alvin Tobbler, Mr. Tobbler's grandson, Tula's brother, ex–Dallas Cowboys linebacker, my distant, dark-side cousin, and Cousin Vince's successor as sheriff, came to see me. Tall and barrel-chested in his crisp uniform, he sat on the veranda with me.

"I went out to say hello to Roan. Shook his hand. Gave him a welcome-home gift. Sister put it together. Fried pies. Jelly. Apple cookies. You know. Samples of the whole inventory. She's always looking for new customers."

"Thank you."

"I just thought you'd like to know. He visited Mr. Leroy the other day."

After Alvin came home from the big leagues, his knees ruined, his fortune made, his wild oats sown, he'd married Mae Brandy Walker, the first black cheerleader in the history of Dunderry High School football, his old sweetie. That Mae Brandy had put up with his absence, outwaiting the groupie women he'd dated, had been a story of considerable local victory. The Walker pride ran deep in perfecting the finest pit barbecue ever set on a restaurant table, and her father, Mr. Leroy, had run Mr. Leroy's Pit Barbecue Eats on the town square until he retired and sold the building to Aunt Jane.

"What did he want with your daddy-in-law?"

"Mr. Leroy used to make sure Roan got fed," Alvin explained gruffly. "You know, back when Roan was little, before your folks took him in. Well."

I leaned toward Alvin, stunned. He nodded. "Roanie'd slip up to the restaurant's back porch and steal leftovers from the tables. Mr. Leroy started leaving sandwiches for him. Never said anything. Just left 'em out." Alvin studied my face. "You didn't know that, did you?"

"No."

"Roan came over to Mr. Leroy's house the other day. Told the old man he intends to take him out to dinner at the best restaurant in Atlanta." Alvin smiled somberly. "That's the kind of man Roan Sullivan is. He doesn't forget anybody who was good to him. We don't forget either. You know, my granddaddy thought the world of Roan, too."

I was quiet, remembering Boss Tobbler and his strict kindnesses, how he and my grandfather had shared the instinct for humanity that is bred in old men who've survived war and intolerance. Alvin gazed into space, then said quietly, "One of my uncles, over in Alabama, he marched with Dr. King in the sixties. Got chewed by police dogs, hosed down by cops. Things weren't ever like that around here, but they weren't so good either."

"Alvin, I know. Nobody talked about it openly, but we all knew."

"The worst game I ever played, though, we were in Pittsburgh—"

"When you tore up your knee the last time?"

"Yeah. I was laying there on the field, feeling like somebody had jabbed hot pokers in my leg, but all I could hear was about a thousand Pittsburgh fans chantin' 'First and ten, hit him again.'"

"Al, I'm so sorry."

"Damn Yankees." He chuckled, then flattened his brows and stared at me. "That was when I knew I was going home. That Dunderry was still home. I told Roan why I came back, and I told him how it's changed. No place is perfect, but some are special."

"What did he say?"

"He said he couldn't afford to be sentimental."

"That's all? He didn't explain what he meant?"

"I don't think he does much explaining to anybody, Claire. I think the man's got some secrets."

A chill ran up my spine. "I hope you're wrong. I'm afraid you're not."

Alvin slid his Stetson back on his head, eyed me with a frown, and sighed one of his thick-chested, worldly, all-encompassing sighs. "You work on him. And keep working on yourself, too." He thumped his knee. "Legs heal. And about that woman—that girl you—"

"Terri. Terri Caulfield. I can't let her be anonymous. I'll spend the rest of my life reminding people about her somehow or other."

"You do that. I refer women to the shelters over in Gainesville all the time, Claire. They've got one thing in common. They think nobody cares. That they're in it alone. Well, you cared, and they know about you. They've got some of your articles on the bulletin boards. They don't think you did anything wrong. They think what happened to her would have come sooner or later, no matter what you did."

"Thank you for telling me."

"Family takes care of its own."

"Hey, maybe we should go on *Oprah*," I said, broaching the subject that always simmered beneath the surface with Tobblers and Maloneys. "You and me. Tula. Be a helluva show."

He rose to his feet. He tipped his hat to me. "I'm not going on TV and admit Tobblers have some lily-white third cousins once removed." He paused. "Especially a little lily-white woman cousin who's wastin' time sitting out here on her skinny *veranda* instead of takin' care of her *business*, if you know *who* I mean."

He left. I sat on the veranda, pushing at morning glories with my fingertips, watching them close against the heat.

Roads around Dunderry weren't named frivolously. They pointed travelers to the oldest family properties, to geographic wonders, to practical needs and whimsical desires. Road names not only told where a person was headed but *why*.

"A little to the left," I said. The sun beat down on me. I sat on the tailgate of a yellow county maintenance truck parked beside Roan's elegant new gate. I was shaded by a wide straw sunhat and dark glasses. I sucked on a blade of grass. My father, who sat beside me, shook his head. "Left's the side you wear your watch on, Nat."

Nat squinted at us as he nudged the tall metal signpost in place. "Oh." Oliver Kehoe, a young cousin of mine who was fresh out of college with a degree in civil engineering, hummed as he poured concrete into a hole around the post's base. My father scowled at the padlocked gate a few yards behind us. "I'm going to *assume*," he said grimly, "that Roan put that gate up to keep nosy no-accounts from trespassing. Not the rest of us."

Oliver and Nat finished. They stood back. I looked up at the slender green sign that now stood at the entrance to Ten Jumps. "Thank you," I said to Daddy, who filched a cigar from his pocket and dismissed the project with a soft grunt. "Just his due. It's good to be the county commissioner. Get things done."

SULLIVAN ROAD, the sign told all.

"He's official now," I said.

He put up a gate. I put him on the map.

The small gold box was delivered by Roan's foreman, a burly, middle-aged man who put a hand over his heart as he stood under the yard oaks gazing from the house to me, Mama, and Renfrew on the veranda. "I don't know which is lovelier," he announced with unexpected courtliness. "You ladies or the workmanship on this place. Mr. Sullivan should have warned me."

I leaned on a cane I'd borrowed from Grandma Dottie. Roan hired a bullshit artist, I thought, chewing my tongue. "Have you worked for Mr. Sullivan before?" I asked.

"Here and there over the years."

"What kind of projects?"

"Oh, this and that."

"I see. Here and there. This and that. No ifs, ands, or buts. You're a discreet man."

He smiled. "I'm a well-paid man, and I like working for Roan Sullivan, and I've already heard that you used to be a newspaper reporter, so I suspect you're trying to charm all sorts of information out of me."

"I'm rusty. I'll have to be more devious."

"You'll have to ask Mr. Sullivan for any details you want."

Mama nodded shrewdly. "Mr. Sullivan," she mused.

"The boss man," Renfrew intoned.

They refused to budge while I frowned deeply and opened the gift package.

Inside a long, slender jewelry case was a delicate gold chain and a small, filigreed shamrock pendant dotted with shimmering stones. A shamrock to replace the cheap dime-store original. My breath caught in my throat.

"Good God Almighty," Renfrew murmured. "Those rocks ain't made of glass."

"They're emeralds," Mama said with troubled wonder. "And diamonds." Roan was trying to rebuild, erase, or upgrade everything about our past.

"Would you like for me to take a reply back to Mr. Sullivan?" the man asked.

I hesitated. Mama looked at me firmly. "I didn't raise you to run off without a backward glance the way I did with your daddy, or for that matter the way your Grandmother Elizabeth did when she met your Grandpa Patrick in London during World War One. But then it can't be denied that you come from two generations of women who couldn't resist a dare. The dare turned out fine for your grandparents, and it turned out fine for me and your daddy. So if you go over to Ten Jumps and Roan gets you off balance, just promise me you'll eventually come back home and make him come home, too."

I felt as if Mama and I had finally come home ourselves, back to the trust we'd had between us when I was a child. I nodded. "I promise." Then I turned toward the mercurial-looking foreman. "Tell Mr. Sullivan," I said as calmly as I could, "that I'll be over to see him in the morning at first light and I intend to trade this necklace for the letters he owes me."

"Well, will wonders never cease." Renfrew sighed.

Mama hugged me.

I exhaled as if I'd been holding my breath for years.

10

*W*hat he and his crew had done to Ten Jumps in less than two weeks would become the stuff of local legend.

He'd built a dirt landing strip for his Cessna. The small plane sat there with the cocky assurance of one of the large dragonflies that perched on ferns at the lake's edge.

He had rebuilt the old cabin—a new roof, a new porch, doors, windows, wiring, plumbing; he'd added a handsome kitchen at the back and a low, large deck that stairstepped down the slope toward the lake, narrowing to a stone walkway that led to a gazebo under the water oaks.

When I arrived in the pinkish light of early morning, I was dressed for a construction site, not a handsome scene that could have served as background for the L. L. Bean catalog. I eased from one of the farm trucks in my jeans and T-shirt and hiking boots and was confronted with an elegant little Eden filled with men who were installing squares of sodded grass along smoothly graded earth, where the blackberry thicket had been.

"It's perfect," I whispered, just before Roan reached the truck, cupped his hands under my elbows, and gave me a quick, hard kiss on the mouth. "It is now," he corrected.

The kiss happened so fast—the feel of him imprinted on my lips; I was dizzy and the breath went out of me. A dozen men were gazing avidly at us with chunks of grassy earth in their hands.

I cocked my head in the direction of the cane I leaned on. "Borrowed it from Grandma. No more crutches."

"And no more excuses?" Roan asked quietly.

"Who's dodging reality? Me or you?"

He arched a brow, then slid his arm through mine as cozily as an old pal set for a stroll, except for the fact that his arm was warm and hard and covered in rolled-up blue cotton sleeve and that he brushed his forearm, deliberately, I thought, along the side of my breast. "Let's both ignore reality a while," he countered with a fine, casual smile, and he was as handsome as I'd ever imagined him and I felt soft inside and scared.

He'd taught himself so many sugaring lessons over twenty years. He knew exactly what he was doing.

"They're finishing up this morning," he said about the crew, as if the project had been no problem at all. "They'll be leaving by noon. I've got the cabin completely furnished inside, too." He paused. "Would you like to take a tour inside?"

"No," I replied. Nearly barked it at him. "No, thanks," I added in a more normal voice. "Maybe later."

We sat in the gazebo at a picnic table covered in linen and decorated with a silver vase filled with red roses. A boom box broadcast Mozart from atop a stack of lumber on a flatbed trailer.

"From this angle," Roan said, "you don't even notice the cabin has an addition on the back."

"Grandpa would be glad you bought the place."

"Are you glad?" Roan asked.

I looked at him for a few seconds. "You know I am," I said finally.

"I wish you'd worn the necklace."

"I did." I pulled it from under the neck of my T-shirt. It was the old one, the color in the pendant worn thin and brassy.

Roan studied me with narrowed eyes. "I want you to wear the new one."

"I want the letters you wrote me. They're mine."

He nodded and gestured calmly toward the cabin. "I told you all you had to do was come here and get them. But I'd appreciate it if you'd wait until the crew's gone. The letters are private."

We traded polite, stilted nods of agreement. It was an excruciating deal.

Roan introduced each man in the crew to me. Wolfgang, the middle-aged foreman who'd delivered the necklace, bowed to me. He wasn't actually a foreman; he was an independent contractor; the crew were his employees.

Roan said Wolfgang had taken up contracting to support a wife and five children, but before that he'd been a disc jockey at a small radio station that broadcast classical music; Mozart was his favorite. He owned the boom box, and the crew made a running joke of hiding his Mozart tapes and replacing them with Snoop Doggy Dog and Hank Williams.

There was so much familiarity and affection in these descriptions, so many people and events in Roan's history I hadn't shared, and the same was true for what he knew about me. "I thought you bought and sold land," I said. "What do you need a building contractor for?"

"I started by buying tract houses in poor neighborhoods. I bought one, made all the repairs myself, sold it for a profit, bought two more. Renovate, resell. Buy more. Wolfgang handles the renovations for me now. It's a sideline."

"You do it just for the money? I don't think so."

"Money and satisfaction," he said, shrugging.

"Tell me more about your business. And tell me how you ended up on the West Coast."

He turned his chair to face mine. I clasped my hands between my knees, shoulders folded in, compressed and tight. I was creating a narrow focus for absorbing information. "I find land in opportune places," he said carefully. "Potential for commercial, industrial growth. I study zonings and planning prospectives; I read local newspapers, research the market trends." He paused. "I slip in and buy land before it's worth much, hold on to it, then sell when it's worth a lot more."

"Buy low, sell high. Take what nobody suspects is worth having, prove it's special."

"It's all about looking closer than other people will and looking farther. I learned that from you."

The mood was tender, electric, and strangely serene between us. But because there was no easier way to do it, I asked quietly, "Are you married?"

"Good God. No."

"Why do you say it like that?"

"Because you could think I wouldn't tell you if I was married."

"Why aren't you married? You've never been married?"

"Never," he said slowly, searching my face. "Why aren't you married?"

"I've been around. I just never cared enough."

"Same here."

"There's a lot you still haven't told me."

He reached beneath the table, retrieved a manila folder, and handed it to me. I opened it and skimmed more documents. Properties he owned on the West Coast. There was a business address under the name Racavan, Inc. I shut the folder and laid it aside. "You still think this is what I'm most interested in? How much money you have?"

"I just wanted you to know that part first."

"You mean you wanted the family to know."

"All right. I wanted them to know." He filled two crystal glasses from a bottle of champagne he'd set to chill in a bucket crusted with dried concrete. "My serving style isn't fancy," he said with a droll curl in the words, "but the champagne is one of the best." He handed me a glass and then clicked his to mine. Holding his glass against a ray of morning sunshine and studying the sparkle of crystal and liquid, he added simply, "I don't drink very often, and when I do it's for quality, not quantity."

He's hard on himself because of Big Roan's drinking, I thought. I started to say so, and from the look on his face he wished for the right words, too, but finally we settled for the ritual tap of fragile glass against glass again. I cleared my throat. "I haven't had a drink since before, well, before that night—"

"The night of the accident. Just say it. Get past it."

"It was no accident. I don't know what to call it."

"It was as much an accident as everything else life throws at people." Roan leaned toward me intently. "The only part of my life that feels like destiny, not just plain dumb accident, is *you*."

I bent my head. I didn't want to cry in front of him for some reason. I didn't want to be that vulnerable yet. "Go ahead and indulge," he whispered. "You're safe with me."

Safety had nothing to do with us. Desperate togetherness, tense kindness, something darkly sexual and politely remote, twenty years of space between childhood and adulthood, squeezed together like a time warp.

I drew back, swallowed my champagne, and stared blindly at the pods of several portable construction toilets nearby. One was set off by itself behind a sweetgum shrub and bore a hand-lettered sign that said LADY ONLY. "Thank you for hiding my personal outhouse behind a shrub. You've got indoor toilets by now, I guess."

"I wanted to be ready if you visited sooner. I didn't want you to feel like you were on display."

"I was hoping to avoid that, for both our sakes."

"We can't. I knew that when I came back."

Jenny Sullivan gave her son a face that escaped godawful comparison with his father's blunt, fleshy features. Big Roan gave him the height, the thick shoulders and heavy chest and dark hair, but Jenny gave him the large gray eyes and handsome mouth. And he had made himself into a man, with all that implied. "You look untouchable, but I know better," I said. "And I want to touch you, but I don't want to hurt you."

"That's how I feel about you."

I sat there, blinking helplessly. We were both desperate to get beyond these cautious formalities, but we didn't know how yet. "What does Racavan stand for?" I asked.

He took a pen from a dusty breast pocket of his workshirt, pulled the folder between us on the table, and wrote *Rathcabhain.* "Irish," he said somberly. "I'm . . . sentimental. Like Maloneys and Delaneys. I boiled the words down to Racavan."

"*Rath.* Fortress." I squinted, struggling to translate the second term.

"Hollow," he said. "The fortress of the hollow."

The crew left just before noon; I'd watched them come to him with questions or suggestions and he had the easy confidence of a man who was accustomed to being called "sir," though none of the crew were that formal with him.

"You need lunch," Roan said when we were alone, and before I could say, *I want to read the letters now,* he bounded to his feet and left me sitting in the gazebo while he disappeared into the cabin. A few minutes later he carried a wicker hamper back and set out white china plates, heavy silverware, white napkins, and tall etched glasses that he filled with ice from a small insulated container. And then he produced ceramic bowls and as neatly as a schooled waiter dished out boiled shrimp and colorful salads and croissants. He finished with a flourish, pouring cold white wine from a tall bottle.

I stared at the spread. "Is that hamper bottomless?"

He inclined his head. "No, but my intention to take good care of you is unlimited. You always brought food to me. Now I want to bring food to you."

"Well, then, I'll just have to eat it," I said softly, singing inside, helplessly.

The letters, my common sense whispered.

We talked all afternoon.

The day grew more peaceful with each glass of wine; the sky's blue seeped down into the air until the light had the quality of prisms through a stained-glass window; and the clean scent of water and woods and the raw clay of the cleared earth combined with the wine and the emotions to make me suddenly turn close to Roan, grasping his hands and looking at him tearfully. There was nothing deceptive about him as I'd worried; there was kindness and a brand of troubled restraint, as if he had to measure every word and gesture.

I told him I was anchored and so was he; we came from the same people, even without a direct bloodline. My line of conversation clearly dampened the mood, although his large, strong fingers stroked my hands urgently. Frowning, he said I thought that anyone who had Irish roots was related, and I said of course they are, I'm being philosophical from the alcohol, just listen.

He knew how it was with my family. The kindest things they say to one another are rarely said out loud: they bring food and personal support, small gifts and photographs. I took a photo album from my bulky cloth purse and laid it open on the table. "There," I said, thumping the album. Parades, ceremonies, reunions, garden club initiations, Civitans, Kiwanis. Church, state, community. "You're part of all that," I told him.

"You don't see me in the pictures, do you?" he countered wearily.

"If you hadn't run away from the church home you'd have been brought back to the farm. Everything would have been all right. If you'd only trusted me more."

"Trusted you? Peep, you're the only person I did trust. But you couldn't change what happened to me, no matter what you think."

Peep. Tears slid down my face. I brushed them aside angrily. "You will feel at home here soon," I insisted. "I'll bring you rootings from shrubs in the yard at the farm. Offspring from plants my great-grandparents cultivated from cuttings their grandparents were given by kin and neighbors."

"Rootings?" he echoed with a ferocious half-smile. "I've got enough Maloney influence around me."

I went on urgently, telling him that polite compromise can be a virtue; feuds are traded in silence, because nothing is more important than preserving the root. We remember how we came here, I insisted; your Sullivans must have settled the same way—alone and poor, strangers in a mountain wilderness where a soul could freeze alone in the winter, a widow and her babies could starve unless people worked together.

Now we move away and around; the roads are fast, the satellites bring distant peoples into our lives, there are planes to take; the world is much smaller than it was when he and I were kids, and much closer. My father and his brothers sit in the town diner discussing computer software and the Internet. Mama corresponds by e-mail with potters all over the country and elsewhere. Daddy's llamas forget how far north they've come from their Peruvian homeland; Daddy files their hooves with an iron rasp forged by his blacksmithing grandfather before he was born; Josh squires visiting Japanese officials to dinner in Atlanta, then comes home to the farm and sits in the dark in the bedroom where he slept as a boy, smoking a soapstone pipe one of our great-great-grandfathers purchased from a Cherokee as soldiers marched the last of the Indians away from their homeland, these mountains.

And because Roan was born with my parents' help, because my mother held him in her arms before his own mother did, he was ours. We had let him down once, but there was hope for the future. I told him so.

He said very little, but something shifted and settled between us. "You don't really believe I've come back here to stay," he said. "This isn't permanent. I'm setting up housekeeping just long enough to persuade you to leave with me."

"You'll stay," I said. "And right now I can't stand to think about you being out here alone at night. Come to the house. You've been invited. Come on. Make the effort."

"You're a grown woman. You don't have to be discreet. Stay here. Keep me company."

"I'm living under my parents' roof. That was my choice. I don't want to upset them or make them think badly of you."

"I don't care what they think of me," he countered quickly. "If you won't stay here tonight, then how about this? We'll get in the plane and I'll fly us over to the coast. We'll find a hotel right by the ocean."

"Are you trying to seduce a woman who only has one good leg to stand on?"

"If I seduce you, you won't have to stand on it."

The rush of sensation was addictive. To *feel* again—the leftover memory of his mouth, the relaxation of the champagne, the May warmth, the delirium that hadn't sorted everything out yet and sought to make sense. I got up, took my cane, and made my way along the lake's edge, just moving because I needed to move. He walked beside me, between me and the lake; it wasn't much of a stretch to worry I'd fall in. "I've got a lot on my mind," I said. "The rest of me has trouble getting my attention."

"All right," he said, moving around to my left side and offering me his arm. "I'll give you an arm, you loan me the rest of you, and I'll show you around the cabin."

I looked from him to the cabin, sitting beautifully in its new, pristine state. Renewal. Trust. Comfort. The lure of privacy between us. The fear of intimacy between us, because there'd be no room for common sense then.

I should leave. Keep my distance for now.

Bats and swallows flitted overhead, through streams of late-afternoon sunshine. An evening mist began to gather on the lake; a lone mourning dove flew into the forest, as if headed across the ridge that led to the Hollow.

The Hollow. Suddenly we were connected to the same earth as the Hollow; the terrible memories were too close by and I saw them in Roan's eyes and felt them in my own. "Stop thinking about it," I said suddenly, as much to myself as to him. "You're not alone here now."

He looked at me gratefully. I slid my hand around the crook of his elbow, and we walked slowly up the slope.

I sat with queenly luxury in an overstuffed armchair in the cabin's refurbished main room, next to the fireplace, my feet propped on a plush ottoman. Roan moved among the room's brass lamps, heavy woven rugs, and dark furniture with a kind of charming masculine vagueness about the decor. *That's a chair, that's a table. They're made of wood.*

"You're almost as bad as I am. You'd never cut it as an antiques dealer," I said gently. "That thing in the corner's an armoire, not a *clothes box.*"

"Good God." He tapped a knuckle on the armoire's heavy doors. "So that's why it cost so much."

"You're not talking to Martha Stewart here, believe me. I can only say that you have some nice sturdy old-fashioned furniture, and you don't go in for froufrou, and it looks like mostly pine and oak to me, maybe Shaker or country style, and I like that floor lamp with the iron vines around the base."

"They never let you write for the home section of the newspaper, did they?" His mild teasing brought up a bad subject—my discarded career. I smiled but quickly focused my attention on an old rug spread under my chair. "Turkish," I said lamely, pointing. "Or some type of English Victorian design."

"I don't know," he admitted. "I liked it because the pattern was green and white." He angled between a thick coffee table and a deep, plush couch, then went to the door to the second room and gestured inside. "You should see the bedroom," he said. "And I'm not being coy, I mean you should see how good it looks."

I got to my feet, went to the door, and peered in at a large bedstead of thick square posts in pale wood, possibly pine. The bed's mattress was cov-

ered in dark green sheets and a voluptuous green comforter. Roan studied
me quietly, his hands on his hips. "I like green," he repeated. "Wolfgang's
wife got it all together for me last month. To bring here. She's a decorator
in Portland. I described the cabin and told her I liked plain and I liked green.
But the first time I sat down on that comforter I felt like a big damned rabbit in an Easter basket."

I laughed, then thought of Easter baskets, the McClendon sisters and
Big Roan, Uncle Pete's bastard son, the violence that Easter at Steckem
Road. I turned and went back to my chair, sank down in it unsteadily, and
looked at him. He came over and dropped to his heels beside my feet. We
studied each other in acute silence for a few seconds. He picked my feet up
and placed them back on the ottoman, then removed my hiking shoes and
my socks as I stared, speechless and enthralled. He curved his hands around
the foot of my injured leg and pressed gently with his fingers, massaging.
"I've got no plan other than a foot massage," he told me. "I want to help,
if you'll let me, because you keep shifting your leg as if it's aching."

Scattered warnings moved through my thoughts, but they couldn't
overcome the power of temptation. His hands felt so good. "The muscles
twitch sometimes. The surgeon told me to expect it. He says it's the nerves
test-firing while they get their act back together. Growing pains." Hurting
and healing. We couldn't have one without the other.

Roan molded his fingers around my scarred ankle. The sunset-streaked
sky felt closer outside the enormous frame of a large new window in one
wall; the warmth spreading through my breasts and belly became full, rich,
and urgent. I closed my eyes to block him out, but that only magnified the
stroking pressure of his hands.

I was letting him have his way with me, so to speak, poised on the
chair with no willpower to stop him. He not only knew what he was
doing, he was caught in the same spell. "I don't know what to do about
you," I whispered. "I'm just so glad you're alive."

He went still; a chasm opened, mocking the charade of his restraint.
He bowed his head slowly to my foot cradled in his hands, then rested his
cheek against the pink line of scar tissue. "I almost lost you forever. I don't
want to let you out of my sight again. I don't give a damn whether anyone understands how we can be this way with each other so fast. I want
you."

I was shaking. I feathered my hand over his hair, traced the outline of
his features with quiet devotion as he raised his face to my touch. It was
incredibly intimate, the rush, the energy we shared. Tender, shattering, the

acceleration of emotion, a stark, sexual prowling unleashed by invisible signals. He got up, bent over me, and we kissed in long, smooth sequences of exploration. "Let's be simple tonight," he whispered as he reached for my hands. And I had my arms halfway up, to slip them around his shoulders, when I remembered how many years he'd let me agonize over him.

I pushed back from him. "Don't do this to me. This isn't fair and you know it."

Roan gazed down at me with bitter amusement on his face. "Has our situation ever been fair?"

"I love you," I yelled. "I know I do, whether it makes sense to love a man I haven't seen in two decades or not. I love you. And if you're using me to prove you can own me, I'll still love you, but I'll never touch you again." I was pulling at him violently. "If you can't tell me why you disappeared for twenty years, then what we are to each other is a lie."

He straightened slowly. There was a stillness between us filled with challenge and expectation. Then he turned and walked into the bedroom. I moved to the edge of my chair and grabbed my cane, planning to follow him, but he returned carrying a deep metal file box, dented and rusty at the corners. He set it on the ottoman in front of me, then dropped to his heels beside it and spun the dial on a small combination lock dangling from the lid clasp.

He looked at me for a moment without speaking. His jaw worked. "You may not want to touch me after you read these. There are more boxes. This one is just the letters from the early years."

He opened the box and riffled through bulging file folders until he pulled out several wrinkled sheets of paper marked with a red tab. "This is a letter you need to read first," he explained, laying it on my knees.

My hands shook. I looked down at yellowed sheets of old business stationery with RACAVAN, INC. printed across the top. Slanted, passionately haphazard handwriting filled the pages as if Roan had put his thoughts down in a flood of emotion.

> *He nearly died this week, and now I understand what I've got to do, Claire.*
> *It's been extra cold and wet this winter, like the ocean is moving in one cloud at a time, and I got a lot of work to do on a couple of rundown split-level ranches I bought last fall at a*

government auction. I always bring him with me to work every day after he gets out of school and I give him some tools to learn with. I been teaching him to saw angles on moldings with a miter box. He's real good and he works hard, but he'll never go into my line of work. He's not interested in property. He's crazy about animals. I guess he was born to be a farmer or something like a farmer. Born to be. He's great with all kinds of animals. We got a dog. He takes the dog everywhere we go. It's almost funny, if his natural ways didn't remind me so much . . .

Anyhow. He got sick to his stomach the other afternoon while he was working with me, and that night he started running a bad fever and I took him to the emergency room. It was his appendix. They had to take it out, and I walked the floor like a wild man while he was in surgery. I was so scared he might die. I couldn't stand to be that alone in the world again.

When he woke up after surgery, he grabbed my hand and held on like he did when he was just a baby. He said he wasn't scared because I was there. I got him up in my arms and rocked him and promised him I'd always be there.

That's when I knew how much I loved him and he loved me. I can't risk somebody taking him away from me. Give him what they think is a good home. Not with me. Hell, I know what I look like. Trash with big dreams. And not even old enough to raise a kid.

I can't put him in the middle and let strangers fight over him. I can't take the chance that nobody wants him because I know how that feels and what could happen to him. If I never do anything else good with my life I have to raise him—make sure he's happy, and educated, and solid. I can be the kind of daddy I never had, and maybe that can make up for what my old man did to you. And I can do for my kid what you tried to do for me, Claire. Never let him down.

But see, I know now that I can't tell you where I am. I meant to do that. Been thinking and planning ever since I left. But if I get in touch with you the family would find out sooner or later.

I can't have that happen, at least not until he's old enough to take care of himself. And so I'm missing you worse than usual tonight. I'm broken up inside. I don't know if you'll ever want me; I have to believe we were meant to be together someday, and that it will be so fine—special—when we are. Some people have crazy hopes. That's mine. My hope. I'm going to raise this boy because I love him and he makes me think of you, because he's like a bridge to you.

You'd want me to do this, I think. Because if you knew what I know about him you'd understand why your family's not ever going to want to know.

And you might wish I'd never come back.

I couldn't breathe. I lifted my gaze to Roan's stark scrutiny. "You have a son?" He hesitated, then nodded. My heart twisted. "You could have told me."

His eyes held my fixed gaze. "I adopted him."

"All right. Then you knew his mother? You must have loved her. Who was she?"

"I didn't love her," he said flatly. "I lived with her and the boy for a few years. The years right after I ran away. Then she died. The boy was only about seven then."

"Why couldn't you tell me? Why couldn't you risk having the family find out where you were and that you were raising a child? Did you really think I'd reject you because you—"

"Claire, listen to me." Roan's face was brutal in the shadows sliding into the old cabin. "His name's Matthew."

I blinked. "Matthew?"

Roan put a hand over mine and gripped hard. "Sally McClendon was his mother."

I sat back, stunned. The truth sifted through me. "*Matthew,*" I whispered. My cousin. My Uncle Pete's son.

Roan had raised Matthew Delaney.

11

The moon was a high, white coin in the night sky, its light cast down as shimmering silver on the lake's black mirror. Frogs sang their high-pitched chant in celebration of the new season, fresh, urgent life seeking company in the darkness. A soft, sweet-scented breeze moved through the water oaks. Deceptive serenity.

I sat on the edge of the new porch of the cabin. Roan stood on the thick carpet of sod in the yard, his hands shoved in his trouser pockets and his shoulders hunched. We'd hammered facts into meaningless strings of words; it was time to be still, be quiet, sort through the labyrinth of emotion.

There are brands of jealousy too primitive for reason; I remembered Sally so well, the big-breasted, hard-eyed teenager from the shacks of Steckem Road. She and I had recognized everything that was special about Roan when we were growing up. She deserved sympathy, but I sat there scalding myself with images of her wrapped around Big Roan and then Roan. *Did you? With her?*

As a boy he'd listened to Sally talk about her daydreams; when she left he had ideas about where she'd gone. He found her living in a small apartment and working at a strip club in some town he didn't name.

And she took him in, hid him, and he stayed with her for the next few years.

"I'm glad Sally helped you. Thank God for that," I said.

Roan came over and sat down on the porch steps beside me. "I'm no saint," he muttered. "But I didn't sleep with her. Room and board. That's all it was. She knew I was always remembering her and my old man."

"I was thinking you were only human. And you owed her."

Roan turned and eyed me quietly. "I didn't owe her that kind of debt. My old man had already made a few payments."

"I'm only saying—"

"I know." He scrubbed a hand over his face wearily. "But she didn't need anybody else pawing her. She got plenty of that at her job. She needed me to be her friend and baby-sitter."

I nodded, relieved. Sally got him a job, the only job where no one asked questions. He worked in a back-alley garage, a chop shop, dismantling stolen cars. He was good at that, very good, the boy who had a way with mechanical things, and could make a lot of money at it.

"I went out with the Jacksonville cops one night," I offered, "when they busted a chop shop." It was a lame effort to convey empathy. I hesitated. Then, "I don't give a damn if you cut up stolen cars. It doesn't matter now."

"I've reformed," he answered with a certain bleak humor.

I felt feverish. "What happened to Sally?"

"She was killed."

"How?"

"Drugs, booze. She got stoned and picked up the wrong guy at a bar one night, and he beat her to death in a motel room."

"How old were you then? How long had you been living with her?"

"I was about nineteen, so I'd been with her and Matthew for maybe four years. Matthew had counted on me for as long as he could remember. Hell, Claire, I'd changed his diapers, fed him, taught him games, read bedtime stories to him. Sally loved him, she really did, and she was as good to him as she knew how to be, but she'd disappear sometimes. I took care of him. I always did."

"You could have asked me for help after I was old enough to make my own decisions. And the family—"

"Don't tell me that. I'll never believe it about the family. Your folks wouldn't publicly admit Matthew was their own blood kin, much less take him in to raise. They'd have turned him over to foster care just like they did to me. They wouldn't have let me raise him either."

"You're wrong. They'd have loved him. They'd have welcomed you and him back. They wouldn't have made the mistake they made before, when they hurt you."

"I'm not going to argue a useless point. It's done. I pretty much stole him after Sally died. Got him a fake birth certificate, changed his last name to Sullivan, and we headed west as far as we could go."

"Oh, Roan." A man accustomed to extremes of loyalty and rejection doesn't deserve a glib assurance that there's nothing left to fear or a promise of simple solutions. He hadn't stolen Matthew, he'd saved him. When the family learned what he'd done, he'd be showered with more love and admiration than he could imagine. And so would Matthew. "We have to tell them," I said desperately.

"They don't want him. And believe me, he doesn't want them. He knows all about his history. He's not bitter, he just understands that there's nothing for him to come back to."

"Oh, *Roan*. There's so much, and so much has changed. Uncle Pete was killed years ago in a hunting accident. Harold was killed on the stock-car track. Arlan's pretty much deserted the family. He's in Louisiana and he's not coming back. You don't have to deal with any of them."

"I know all about Pete and his boys," Roan said darkly. "I made it my business to find out about them over the years. About the whole family. There's not much I don't know."

"I see." Silence. "I can't promise that the whole Maloney-Delaney clan will throw open their arms to Matthew, but I know my folks will—"

Roan laughed harshly. "You're wrong. I'll take any shit anybody can dish out, but I don't want him treated like shit, Claire. And I don't want you put in the middle of a mess either."

I moved around in front of him on the steps, pushing his thighs apart and balancing on the knee of my good leg, leaning into his chest with my hands curved around his face. "You'll feel better when we've talked all this over a few times. We can resolve this. It will be all right."

He covered my hands gently. "I've wanted to see you every day for twenty years. I didn't know how in the hell we could deal with what I had to tell you, and I still don't know. But I do love you. Don't ever doubt that."

I put my arms around him. For twenty years he'd hidden the truth from everyone, even me, when I could have been trusted, I would have helped him. But no one had given him many choices. He had offered an incredible act of devotion and sacrifice to protect a child's innocence in return for the innocence he and I had lost. And we had lost each other for twenty years because so much trust and hope had been hammered out of him.

"I've never cared what other people said about us," I whispered. "All that matters is that I know *who you are* again. Hello. *Hello, boy.*"

His eyes glittered. He laughed hoarsely and then kissed me, and we were frantic with relief, clinging to each other. He stroked my hair and face, the years fading and shifting, sugar between our tongues, children's memories burned away in a flash.

"You want simplicity?" I asked. "Then stop talking and do something."

He carried me inside and put me on that deep green new bed in the old cabin. Slowly, while I watched him, he removed his clothes and then, slowly, he helped me undress. "Well, here we are," he said quietly, looking at me in ways that brought goosebumps to my skin.

I touched him between the thighs with my fingertips. "This is about the only part of you I never got to see when we were kids."

"Explore all you like," he answered, and carefully cupped his hand over me. "As long as I get the same opportunity."

Breathless, I placed kisses down his body and he did the same to mine. We lay together, naked, our hands moving over each other. We were trembling, both of us, caught up helplessly in the sensations and newness of each other's sexuality; it was awkward at moments, intense, blindly compelling to share, signaling with touch and breath, small sounds and movements, lost in a place as hot and emotional as a summer night filled with lightning. His eyes darkened to the color of old pewter, endlessly searching my face for clues. "We would have been like this years ago—the first time—if we'd had the chance," he said softly. "Not a whole lot of grace to it, but plenty of love."

"A little grace and a lot of love is all I need right now," I told him. "This is our first time. *This is our time* tonight."

He eased a pillow under my injured leg; it didn't hurt, I told him, and he swore he'd be careful, and I knew he would be. He made my body bend like a flower. When he was poised between my thighs, I curled my fingers around him, my other arm draped around his neck. I urged him gently forward. He put his arms under my shoulders, cradling my head, his mouth just above mine. "Help me go where I belong," he whispered.

And I did.

12

*T*here was room for hope and reconciliation. I would coax Matthew McClendon Delaney Sullivan back home. I would bring him back—Uncle Pete's abandoned boy, my grown cousin, Roan's adopted son, a testament to our faith in each other and to Roan's own large heart. All of Roan's mysteries would be explained, and anyone who had ever doubted him would be ashamed of themselves. I felt more serene and hopeful than I had in months. In years.

I took so much for granted.

My parents had formed a protective wall around their children when we were small, and Mama always told me that someday I would be big enough to see over her and Daddy and then I'd climb out and move beyond them. But the thing about parents, she said, is that their wall would always be there, backing me up, no matter how old and ignorant and small I might think they had become from my view outside their boundaries.

"Thank you for calling last night to let us know you'd be home by morning," Mama said briskly when Roan and I returned to the farm at dawn. "We appreciate the courtesy."

"Roan and I had a lot to talk about," I answered, which at least proffered a dignified alibi. "And I read some of the letters he wrote to me over the years. There are a lot of them."

But Mama and Daddy stood there sphinxlike in their bathrobes, both of them obviously struggling to deal with the fact that we were adults who had spent the night together, probably committing acts they didn't want to imagine. Mama expected it, of course, and was just relieved we hadn't left town.

Daddy looked unhappy but all he said was, "I'm sure y'all talked up a storm."

Roan stepped ahead of me, facing them, and I put a hand on his shoulder. "I asked Claire to visit the West Coast with me for a few days," he said quietly. "Seattle."

Mama's face turned white. Daddy thrust out his chin. "Seattle?" he barked. "You're taking her to your place in Seattle? Why?"

"It's all right," I said gently. "Don't worry. It's just a trip we need to make."

"You promised," Mama reminded me.

"We'll be back," I repeated. "And we'll bring y'all a gift."

By early afternoon we had flown more than halfway across the country, turning back the clock in more ways than artificial time zones. There'd been little debate about the choice of travel: Roan's Cessna was out of the question—I wasn't up to a couple of grueling days spent airport-hopping from coast to coast in a cramped private plane. We flew first class.

My voice was a hoarse croak, and Roan's deep, faded drawl had the rasp of a too-tightly-strung cello. My leg throbbed from negotiating the cavernous terminal and concourses at the airport in Atlanta. I refused to use a wheelchair.

His mood was brittle. So was mine. At that moment it was hard to believe we'd been in bed together not many hours earlier, as close and intimate as two people can be.

"What's in the bag?" Roan asked, gesturing toward the heavy zippered canvas tote I'd stuffed under my seat.

I sipped a Bloody Mary and eased my stiff right leg back and forth. "Photo albums and family histories."

We traded a look—mine firm but apologetic, his resigned. "He'll be polite about it," Roan said, "but he really won't be too interested."

O ye of little faith, I thought.

We spent that afternoon in Seattle. Actually, in a town just outside Seattle. The town reminded me of Dunderry when we were children: one main street and no stoplights, a lot of pickup trucks, a pretty municipal park with benches. For a few seconds we watched a college-age couple who sat on a blanket in the park. They were dressed in hiking clothes and a pair of backpacks lay beside them. They were absorbed in each other. He played with the tips of her hair; she rubbed the small of his back. It was a peaceful, simple, indelibly erotic scene.

"When we're here again and have more time," Roan said, "we'll sit over there and do the same thing."

"But we could do it better at Ten Jumps," I replied. "We wouldn't have to wear any clothes."

He eyed me narrowly. I rubbed the small of his back.

I thought there was significance in the town. Roan had chosen a place so similar to home.

Racavan, Inc., was based in a four-room suite in a small brick office building next to a coffeehouse. He introduced me to Bea, his assistant and the manager of the three-secretary staff. She was motherly and efficient and wore a jumpsuit with rhinestone flowers embroidered along the neckline. She was the kind of woman who used snapshots of her grandchildren as a screensaver on her computer. The kind of woman who could manage the paperwork on a portfolio of real estate properties with one hand and bake cookies with the other. She bear-hugged me and gave me a steaming hot mocha latte to sip. "You're in coffee country now," she said. She had long ago nicknamed Roan by his initials.

"R.S. warned me about you," she added cheerfully.

Roan said to me in a dry tone, "I told her you were probably the mysterious *businesswoman* who called last week pretending to be looking for commercial property. You can't hide your accent."

My face turned hot, but I shrugged. "I'm a journalist. When I get a little information, I naturally try to get more. I was just curious about your business. What kind of people work for you. Nothing sinister about that." For the first time I talked as if I still thought of myself as a reporter.

"R.S. said you wouldn't be able to resist," Bea told me.

"He's too smart for his own good."

She laughed. "Thank God. That's what pays the bills around here."

"Not to change the subject too quickly, but do you know Roan's . . . Matthew . . . very well?" I asked abruptly.

Bea's brows shot up. "Of course. When he was growing up, he stayed with me whenever R.S. traveled. He and my grandsons are good friends. They played basketball at school together. Matthew was on the debating team, and the soccer team, and in the chorus, and an honor graduate. And he just graduated from the university this spring with honors. And he married the sweetest girl in the world. But you know all that."

"Of course. But thank you."

"He's married?" I said to Roan when we walked outside a minute later. "That wasn't worth mentioning to me?"

"I had to be at the wedding and the graduation this spring," Roan answered. "It's why I couldn't get back to you sooner. I don't like to talk about it because it was hard to be torn two ways."

"You were right to be at his wedding and graduation," I said quietly. "You're his family. I understand."

"I know you do," Roan said, and put his arms around me.

Roan's house sat off on a wooded backroad a few minutes' drive from town. Roan said he bought it when Matthew was twelve or thirteen, before the big money started to come in, and so the house wasn't anything grand, but it had been home to them for the past ten years. It was a handsome cedar two-story, refurbished with copper trim and fine stonework and a few acres of shady, hilly, landscaped land filled with tall fir trees and floored with ferns and vines. The setting had a cool, misty, Pacific rain-forest atmosphere. A stone-and-board fence bordered a winding cobbled driveway.

"Hearty," I said, looking appreciatively at iron pots filled with flowers on the wooden floor of the front porch. "It's a good, hearty house with a basketball hoop over the garage. I like it."

"You might like living here," Roan said as we entered a hallway done in heavy woods and tapestry wall hangings. He moved fast and deliberately inside his own territories. I had noticed that already at the office, and he did it at the house, bounding into a large, vaulted den off the hall, turning on heavy brass and copper lamps, adjusting the thermostat on a wall covered in a huge, framed topographical map of the coastal states.

I limped into the den uneasily, using my cane. "I'd enjoy staying here when we're visiting Seattle."

We looked at each other sadly and the subject died.

But I picked up some good details about him that day. He drove a late-model black Suburban with a CD player that had only one CD in it, a reissue of an old Creedence Clearwater Revival album. The radio was set on an all-news station. The Suburban was immaculate except for cigar ashes scattered here and there, but stuck on the dash was a dog-eared, sun-faded decal of Donald Duck that looked as if it had been peeled off a series of dashboards over the years.

"Matthew got it when I took him to Disneyland a long time ago," Roan explained with a casual flick at the decal's frayed edges. "I keep meaning to throw it away."

I nodded, my throat aching. "I'm sure you do," I said gently.

Roan cherished a supply of hand-rolled cigars he kept in a slender wooden humidor on his bedroom dresser. The bedroom was hearty, too—big furniture and bold colors—and it overlooked a rock garden and a pond with a simple fountain. When he opened the windows the water sounds made a soothing melody.

In his large closets there were fine suits and shoes and several bags of golf clubs, but also a row of unpolished western boots so lovingly worn that they sagged at the heels and curled up at the toes. Floor-to-ceiling shelves were filled with novels and reference books, and in an alcove off the bedroom he had a computer, a printer, a fax machine, and a copier, all crowded on a large antique oak desk.

"Sleep. Work. Work. Sleep," I joked softly, pointing from the office alcove to the bedroom. It was late afternoon by then. I was exhausted and frazzled. Roan looked tired, too. I took his hand. "We've got a long flight tomorrow. What would you rather do? Work or sleep?"

He picked me up. "You know what I'd rather do right now."

"Smart man," I said. We went to bed.

We lay spooned together in the pearl-soft shadows that night, Roan curled against my back and hips, his left arm under my head like a pillow, his right one around me, me holding his hands in mine, against my breasts, our fingers twined tightly. Trembling, sweet, satiated. There had been moments when we got past everything and found the children inside us, playing gently, knowingly, with each other, in awe of the new entertainment.

He flexed against me; I flexed back. I felt him harden and relax. His bare chest was damp against my bare back; he sighed, unloosened his hands from mine, and stroked them over me. I had the taste of him in my mouth, and my scent was on his hands.

"I watched you sleep once when we were kids," I whispered. "Not long after you came to live at the house, I slipped into your room one night and watched you sleep."

He rose on one elbow, over me, and smoothed the hair from my forehead. "I knew you were there, and it scared the hell out of me."

"Why?"

"Because you were a little girl and I was five years older. Every-thing female made me uncomfortable. It felt provocative and danger-ous."

"I was too young to know how a teenage boy automatically responds. I'm sorry."

"I'd rather have died than be like that around you."

I squeezed his hands. "You were my best friend. You were my love. It had nothing to do with physical ages."

"I'd never have touched you when we were kids. I wouldn't even let myself think about you that way."

"I know that. That night I thought, He hogs the covers. He sleeps in the middle of the bed. When we're grown-up and sleep together like Mama and Daddy, he'll squash me." I laughed. "That was how I watched you sleep. For practical purposes."

Roan gripped my chin in his hand, made a guttural sound low in his throat, then rolled away from me. I turned over and watched him retrieve his robe from the end of the mattress.

He flung the robe around his shoulders, then walked to the open win-dows and stood with his hands by his sides, silhouetted by a half-moon. I sat up in bed with my hands knotted in the jumbled sheets. "What worries you so much?" I asked.

"I don't want Matthew to visit the family," he admitted bluntly. "It's not going to be good for anybody."

I sighed. He wouldn't relax. Everything was going to be fine. "But you won't interfere while I sugar him," I teased carefully. "Will you?"

"I'll try to keep quiet," he said. "Anyway, I think you'll change your mind once you meet him."

No, I won't, I thought, but simply called him back to bed.

Never let it be said that I don't try to make calculated first impressions on people. Plain brown loafers for practicality and intellect, a calf-length black-denim skirt to hide the funky leg and give me the essence of casual elegance, a delicately patterned green sweater to give the illusion of, well, delicacy, and an ugly yellow rain slicker with a Seattle logo, which I pur-chased in a shop at the Seattle airport before we boarded our Alaska Air flight, because apparently it rarely stopped drizzling in either Seattle or Alaska year-round.

Roan, in creased khakis, a blue chambray shirt, hiking boots, and a brown leather aviator jacket, looked like a darkly rugged individualist who belonged in the Pacific Northwest. I looked like a rejected model for a Seattle Chamber of Commerce ad.

"I'm so nervous I feel sick," I said.

"You're perfect. Matthew will be impressed," Roan answered.

"Impressed and won over?"

"No. Just impressed."

"I'm his cousin, Roan. We'll be okay with each other."

"You're a meddling stranger to him, peep."

I chewed my tongue for a moment. "Well, I'm obviously successful at meddling." And I looked at Roan pointedly. "I got you back, didn't I?"

The Alaskan mountains were huge, wild, snowcapped monuments compared to the comfortable old blue-green ranges where we were born. Below the descending jet, the ocean channels looked deep and far more frigid than any Georgia waters. I decided Alaska was a state of extremes. What had Roan taught my cousin Matthew? Independence, strength, confidence, a spirit of adventure? Or Roan's own isolation?

I expected Juneau to be a full-fledged city because it is the state capital, but from the air I saw no skyscrapers, no expressways, just the patchwork of a sprawling, unassuming town clustered between mountains and water at the edge of the continent. We're not all that far from Russia, I thought, or the Arctic Circle.

Roan held my hand as the small jet landed smoothly across the channel from Juneau. The sun was out; steam rose from the runway. I strained my eyes as the jet taxied toward a small terminal building, searching the handful of people beyond the metal barricades. Roan leaned over, looking along with me. "Don't point him out," I ordered, my heart in my throat. "Let me see if I can recognize him."

But the jet nosed into a berth on the tarmac that angled away from the waiting area. Frustrated and nervous, I watched Roan get up and retrieve our bags from the overhead compartment. "No gate ramp," he said brusquely, his tone distracted as he jerked the bags free. "Let me go ahead of you down the stairway. Take your time. I won't let you fall. Let's wait until the other passengers get off. Don't try to rush."

"Do I seem that frantic?" He glanced at me over the Seattle tote bag he held in his arms. I realized I was tapping both hands on my legs and jiggling one foot. "Never mind," I said.

We waited. When we stood at the top of the stairs, outside in the brisk, damp air glistening with cool sunlight, I was able to look across at the waiting area. "The young guy like a bodybuilder," I said. "With the brown hair. That's Delaney brown hair. That's Matthew."

"One step at a time," Roan said tensely. A flight attendant carried the hand luggage down for us. Roan moved in front of me, patiently, holding my cane for me. I braced one hand on his outstretched arm and clutched the staircase rail on my bad side, peering over him, searching. I tripped on the last step and Roan caught me quickly, cursing under his breath. Unconcerned, I held on to his shoulders and continued gazing past him.

A tall, lanky young man with sandy hair strode purposefully across the tarmac. He was dressed in dark gray trousers, a plaid shirt, a blue cardigan, and hiking boots. Hurrying beside him was a short, plump, sweet-faced young woman in nearly identical clothes. Her dark blond hair flew back from her face like loose wheat straw. She took two light steps to each of his long ones. The pair looked wholesome and ruddy. Pioneers. The last of the fair-haired pioneers lived in Alaska.

I craned my head to look past the couple, still hunting for Delaney hair. He, however, had disappeared with his arms around two of our fellow passengers.

I frowned. Roan put an arm around me, and we faced the advancing pair. My bewildered gaze settled on them, their somber faces riveted to Roan and me, and I stared at the young man. He walked up to us without hesitation, his green eyes shifting defiantly from me to Roan and back to me. He towered over me, but was maybe an inch shorter than Roan. Then he smiled.

For once in my life, I was speechless. Matthew. The baby surrounded by violence and ludicrous Easter charity at Steckem Road. Denied by my uncle, orphaned by his mother, abandoned by his McClendon aunts. But because of Roan—and only because of Roan—he'd grown up healthy, successful, and forthright.

He thrust out a brawny, capable hand. It trembled. Beside him, his wife clasped her hands to her smile and began to cry silently. Roan's arm tightened around me. I felt the electric tension in him. *I won't let you down.*

"I'm not going to shake your hand," I announced. "I'm not a stranger. I'm your cousin. You're part of my family." I gazed steadily at the teary young woman beside him. "And your wife is part of my family, too, even if we haven't been introduced yet."

"I'm Mildred," she said, almost sobbing. "But everyone calls me Tweet."

"Hello, Tweet. I'm Claire. Your cousin-in-law." Then, to Matthew, who was gaping at me, I said, "I'm going to hug you, if at all possible." I lurched at him, hugged him voraciously, and after a stunned moment, he hugged me in return, carefully, as if I might crack. Then Tweet and I hugged each other, and finally I turned toward Roan, who stood as unmoving as a windswept statue on a summit only he could guard, his expression shuttered. I grasped his hand. *See,* I urged silently.

I thought the hardest part was behind us.

$\mathcal{P}$eople not only choose to live where they're comfortable, they choose places that give them comfort, and my first goal was to learn what had drawn Matthew to Alaska. Matthew showed us around in a mud-spattered Bronco with the tip of a whale rib dangling from the rearview mirror. From my poor vantage point in the backseat beside Roan, I struggled to examine every detail about him, his wife, and the scenery, making mental notes.

Cold, gray oceanfronted Juneau and wilderness backed it; the city was secluded, to say the least. A summer honeymoon in Alaska had been one of Roan's wedding gifts to Matthew and Tweet. Roan had bought a small vacation house in the city when Matthew was sixteen. Matthew loved to hike, photograph the wildlife, and fish for salmon. Roan simply liked the wildness of it all.

He had told me during our flight that everything in Alaska, except for a few dots of civilization, was backcountry tucked among ocean channels, cold rivers, or mountains. Where else would the suburbs include bears, moose, wolves, whales, enormous glaciers, and untrackable wilderness? "I like the honesty of places where a person risks getting bitten or eaten," Roan said with a certain dark pleasure. "It keeps me from getting careless."

Roan's distrust of easy comforts was deep and pervasive. I began to worry that he was hiding something else from me but convinced myself he wouldn't do that.

I couldn't see Uncle Pete's pugnacious face in Matthew's large-boned features, and had no strong recollection of any distinctive McClendon traits to pinpoint except Sally's hard emerald eyes. There was something

Delaneyish about the bulldog set of his jaw maybe, but physically he was a troubling cipher. I tried to shake the inventory from my overwrought mind. Sullivan. Matthew Sullivan. That was what Roan called him. What he called himself. That was how I'd think of him.

Dr. Matthew Sullivan and Dr. Mildred "Tweet" Sullivan. Both of them were veterinarians, fresh from the state university in Washington. Smart and motivated, obviously. Young, compassionate, hardworking, and not afraid of getting their hands dirty. Roan's adopted *son and daughter-in-law*. But I couldn't really imagine Matthew as Roan's surrogate son. At twenty-four he was only eleven years younger than Roan. Only six years younger than me. If he ever called me *Mom* I'd thump him on the head.

Roan radiated satisfaction every time he discussed Matthew and Tweet with me. He'd confided that they were conservative and a little shy. They went to church, did volunteer work, and they planned—seriously—to have a half-dozen children. "Dr. Sullivan," he had emphasized more than once. "I raised Matthew and now he's a doctor. And he married a great, smart girl who's a doctor, too. Isn't that something? Sullivans who are doctors. It made me proud of the name finally."

Such honor for the disgraced Sullivan name. I wanted to shake him and make him understand. *He* had redeemed his name already.

As we drove, Tweet kept turning to smile at me and wipe tears from her eyes. I felt sorry for her; she seemed so eager to be friendly and none of us knew quite how to act. I reached between the front seats and tapped her shoulder. "I hear that you and Matthew are veterinarians."

She swiveled and peered at me gratefully, nodding. "Brand-new doctors! This summer in Alaska is our combination graduation-and-wedding present from Roan, but it's a working honeymoon, too. We're sorting out our options. We're going to set up a practice together. Matthew's big animals. I'm small animals."

"How do you feel about chickens and llamas?"

She gave me a puzzled look. "I'm planning to specialize in house pets. But Matthew wants to work with livestock. Why?"

"Just curious," I said, and smiled.

"We're hoping to intern with an established vet for a couple of years first. Maybe in Oregon. Or Washington. We're doing some volunteer work for a conservation group up here this summer. Wildlife rehab."

"Rescue work," Matthew added crisply. "Eagles who've swallowed fish hooks, wolves hit by cars, that kind of thing."

I glanced poignantly at Roan. He nodded almost imperceptibly. He was very proud.

"I'll tell you the major reason we picked this place for the summer," Matthew said. "Roan said he'd probably have to tell your family about me, and I wanted to be someplace where it wouldn't be easy for them to find me unless I wanted them to."

Painful silence. Tweet faced forward and clamped a hand over his forearm atop the Bronco's center console. The way her fingers dug in, I assumed she was urging him to keep his cool.

"The plan was my idea," Roan told me quietly. "And I never meant it to exclude *you*. Which is why I brought you here."

"I see." I swallowed hard and nodded. "You deserve to make up your mind your own way and to keep your privacy, Matthew. Just keep an *open* mind, please."

"I'll see what I can do," he agreed tightly.

Tweet swiveled and forced a fresh smile. "Claire, we hear that you're a newspaper reporter."

"Used to be," I said, and stared out the window.

"I, hmmm, we . . . Roan told us all about . . ." Her voice trailed off. Uncertain and blushing, she looked toward my legs then quickly away. "What you were doing was very heroic. I hope you're . . . recovering okay."

"Doing better. Can't complain."

I didn't deal well with discussions like that. Roan took one of my hands and cradled it in both of his. "I know what I want," he announced. "I want Claire to have a little longer tour of town." He rubbed my hand with soothing motions. "Drive around for a few minutes, Matt. Just keep it simple."

"Simple?" Matthew repeated grimly, as if nothing could be simple now that I had found him. But he swung the Bronco up a tree-shaded street that climbed gracefully higher.

Matthew drives as badly as Evan, I thought, as he nearly sideswiped a mailbox. Evan's driving habits had remained notorious in the family since his teen years. Matthew whipped the Bronco along narrow streets that snaked up steep, crowded hills. My head swam. Roan and I had been traveling for hours, fueled by adrenaline, airport food, too much coffee, and uneasy catnaps. Dazed and bleary, I leaned against him in the backseat of the Bronco, my loafers off. He lifted my feet onto his thigh and slid his hand under the hem of my long skirt, massaging my ankle and knee, squeezing and releasing with silent communication. His dark hair was wildly ruffled; his mouth was set in a perfunctory line of control.

"Tweet and I got the guest room ready for you, Bigger," Matthew announced, darting a clumsy look at us in the rearview mirror as he downshifted up a hillside where tiny flower gardens clung desperately to maniacally terraced yards. "It's nothing fancy, Claire, but it has a private bath-room and a big . . ." His voice trailed off.

"Big what?" I mumbled. "Bigger what?"

Tweet pivoted in her seat, blushing again. "A bed that's big enough for both of you," she finished. Her face was very red. "And *Bigger* is Roan's nickname."

I glanced at Roan. "My goodness, R.S., how many nicknames do you have?"

"When Matthew started elementary school he figured out that I wasn't old enough for him to call me his *dad* around the other kids," Roan explained with gruff exasperation. "And *brother* wasn't exactly right. So he decided to call me his *Bigger*. It just stuck."

"*Bigger*," I repeated softly. "It's good. It sounds funny, but it suits you."

"I didn't think it sounded *funny* when I was a kid who needed somebody to look up to," Matthew said with a sudden edge in his voice. He studied me in the rearview mirror and I saw anger in his eyes. Okay, under his polite exterior he was tense and defiant. No surprise in that. "As far as I'm concerned," Matthew added stiffly, "he'll always be the biggest man in the world."

Roan leaned forward, his jaw set. "Take it easy," he ordered quietly. "Claire isn't here to—"

"Believe me, Matthew," I interjected. "He's the biggest man I know, too."

Roan settled back, frowning. Matthew exhaled sharply. "I'm sorry, Claire. I just don't know what to say to you. You came here because you care, and I appreciate that, but Bigger and I've done pretty well on our own all these years without anybody's concern."

"You said hello to me," I replied softly. "You made me feel welcome. That's all I need right now, and all I expect."

"You need to rest," Roan said.

He was worried about me but also probably none too eager to promote a full-blown discussion. There was so much tension in the air. I took deep breaths to find oxygen. "I hop around like a one-legged duck. Until a few weeks ago I was a basket case. I spent more time in bed than anywhere else. Roan changed all that. I may not be Wonder Woman yet, but if you feed me dinner and give me a place to prop my feet up, I'll answer any questions you want to ask about our family, Matthew."

"Your family, not mine," Matthew countered.

"Your family, whether you like it or not."

"I don't have many questions. They didn't want me. They didn't want Roan either. He's the only family I care about. Him and Tweet. So why should I want to learn anything about the Delaneys? I'm sorry, Claire. You're welcome here because Roan loves you. I know all about you. He told me. But about me . . . If you came here just for my sake, you came a long way for nothing."

"We'll see," I said. I watched Matthew scrub a hand over his hair and then tug at both earlobes as if settling his head firmly on his shoulders, and I thought with amazement, My brothers do that when they're worried. So does Mama. So do I. It's obviously an inherited Delaney trait. I was certain then that I could coax him home to Dunderry, and he would sit on the veranda and eventually he'd smile a Delaney smile. "But you know," I said suddenly, all charm and patience, "all I really want to do right now is hear all about the two of you."

"What a sweet thing to say!" Tweet exclaimed, turning in her seat again and reaching back to grasp my hand on her shoulder. Tweet was a frequent crier, apparently. She was teary-eyed every time she looked at me. "I'm so glad you're here! You're Matthew's cousin! His cousin! It means so much to . . . we really do want to know about you, too! We do! Matthew does, he really does!"

"It's okay to dislike me, Matthew," I said patiently. "I understand what I represent to you."

"I don't . . . dislike you," Matthew said, tugging at his ears again. "I'm even glad to meet you. You'll always be welcome in my home."

"Thank you, that means a lot to me," I said. I realized I had begun tugging on my ears as I spoke.

I glanced at Roan, who was watching me closely through narrowed eyes. I smiled innocently. He lifted one hand and tapped his forefinger to my right earlobe, then my left. *He'd caught on. He remembered.* I was planning to sugar his boy, and he knew I'd made up my mind.

Juneau was more of a big, picturesque, old-fashioned town than a metropolis. Quaint old buildings shared the streets with modern state government offices. The original waterfront district hugged a broad plaza dotted with benches and tourist kiosks, merging with long concrete docks where two megalithic cruise ships were berthed. Turn-of-the-century shops crowded the streets near the docks, catering to the cruise-ship tourists.

Almost everything farther inland was uphill; the Governor's Mansion was set above the city in a neighborhood of pleasant houses with manicured yards, tall fir trees, and pretty flower beds; I studied a cluster of bleeding-heart plants in one yard, their long, delicate green stems dripping rows of the tiny red and white valentine blooms. The Governor's Mansion was amazingly humble: a pleasant, large house with no security walls around it, no gates, not even much of a yard. A pickup truck was parked under the porte-cochere in front, and I could have walked a few yards off the tree-lined street and peered in a downstairs window if I'd wanted to.

So I decided Alaska had practical priorities to Matthew and Roan, very little pomp and circumstance about its human habitation; the grandeur was all in the *place*, and that appealed to me. Bald eagles swooped in flocks over the scraps from a salmon cannery on the waterfront. People took bald eagles for granted there.

The house was a wood-shingled bungalow perched a good hundred feet up on a steep hillside above a steep street. A wooden staircase zigzagged in three long sections through brave, high-altitude-loving shrubbery, and at least a dozen bird feeders clung precariously to the posts of a friendly porch draped in hanging plants.

I leaned on my cane, stared up at the three tiers of almost vertical wooden stairs, and felt Matthew watching me to see what kind of stuff I was made of. "Bigger and I can carry you up between us," he said.

"Oh, I can climb these stairs on my own, but thank you."

Nobody, not even me, believed I could make it up those stairs. Matthew and Tweet gave each other embarrassed looks. Roan took my arm. "You probably need a little more time before you start mountain climbing," he grunted. "Even though I'm sure you could do it." He guided me a few yards along the edge of the narrow yard and we studied a wooden platform about three feet square, set on a base of steel-pipe supports that rode a wooden monorail and cables straight up the hillside, to one end of the porch. "You can ride up on this," Roan said. "We use it to haul groceries and furniture—"

"She might fall off," Tweet called anxiously.

"No, I'll climb up beside her."

"It'd be safer if Bigger and I carried you, Claire," Matthew repeated. I met his eyes. Green eyes. Sally McClendon's eyes. Full of challenge. "*Nobody's carrying me*," I said. "If y'all can winch my ass all the way up on this low-rent freight elevator, then do it."

Tweet whooped. "I'll turn the crank!" She trotted up the stairs, her short, sturdy legs pumping and her trousered rump undulating athletically. Envy tightened my chest; I was tired of being an invalid.

"Honey, don't let the dogs out yet," Matthew called after her. "You know what happens when they see you cranking the platform."

"Dogs?" I said. "What happens?"

Matthew feigned melodrama. "They jump all over her and sometimes she lets the crank slip."

"So the platform plunges down the hill, eh?"

He arched a brow. "Yeah, but you probably wouldn't fall more than a dozen feet before you were knocked unconscious."

I flicked a hand. "No problem then."

"He's yanking your chain," Roan said.

I surveyed the multitude of bird feeders planted above us. I looked at the tiny platform jutting from its crude rail. I was scared of the damned thing but wouldn't admit it. "Give me a chunk of raw salmon to wave and a thousand bald eagles'll probably swoop down and fly me to the porch. It'd be patriotic, too. Bald eagles. Oh, all right, I'll just take your elevator. But let me off at the housewares floor. I need to buy a hostess gift."

Matthew contemplated me intensely, his sandy brows a flat line, some new edge dawning in his appraisal. Then he stepped over to Roan, threw an arm around him, and gave him a quick hug. Roan slapped him gently on the back. Matthew nodded to me. "Bigger told me you never back down and never give up. I see what he means."

We'd established the first round of respect then. Roan helped me sit gingerly on the contraption's platform. As Tweet cranked a handle-and-gear device from the end of the porch, the platform jerked roughly up the rail. Roan and Matthew climbed on either side of me, plowing through the shrubbery, each extending an arm in front of me to block me if I went off headfirst. I didn't flinch, didn't bat a nervous eyelash. I finally realized how much I'd inherited from my Grandmother Elizabeth's regal and obstinate English dignity. A person can hide a lot of fear and worry behind an aristocratic posture.

She would have been proud of me that day, and proud of Roan, and proud of Matthew, her lost grandson.

Matthew and Tweet had two dogs, one big, one little, shaggy mixed breeds, who wagged and slobbered and flopped on the main room's braided rugs with their bellies exposed for me to scratch. A multilevel collection of perches sat in one corner of the living room over wide wooden trays filled with kitty litter. Two large green parrots, two cockatiels, and two parakeets fluttered on the perches, squawking and relieving themselves with a cheerful bawdiness that reminded me of Grandpa Maloney's pull-my-finger jokes.

My newly found cousin and his bride had a deceptively spartan honeymoon lifestyle—from a pair of expensive kayaks strapped to the ceiling of their back porch to the clustered diamonds of the wedding ring Tweet wore on her pragmatic little hand, they were enjoying the Eddie Bauer version of newlywed pioneer adventure, thanks to Roan.

It wasn't that I thought they were naive and pampered. They'd both worked as veterinary assistants during college, and Roan had told me how he'd taught Matthew as a boy to manage money and make money. I knew that during the early years he and Matthew had lived in a lot of cheap apartments and in dilapidated houses Roan had bought to restore and resell—not exactly a luxurious upbringing for Matthew. But then Matthew hadn't grown up hungry, neglected, and tortured, fighting bullies in the neighborhood and a bad-tempered alcoholic father at home.

I knew I could pry more personal information about him from Tweet. Reporters develop an instinct for the easy interviews, and she was one of the most openhearted people I'd ever met. While Matthew and Roan shared God-alone-knew-what-kind of dark discussions over salmon-grilling duties on a back porch beyond the kitchen, I sat down with Tweet in the living room.

The house was tiny—living room, kitchen, two bedrooms—adorable, and filled with comfortable furniture, bookcases stuffed with veterinary textbooks and novels, and funky craft-show lamps and knickknacks, mostly depicting animals. I curled up on a plush gray couch with an afghan draped over my legs, chilly enough in the Alaskan June evening to like the cover and the fire burning in a soot-stained stone hearth near the couch. The afghan's woven motif was a tree filled with songbirds.

"Maybe I'm reaching here," I said to Tweet, as she nuzzled each of her bird flock and told me their names. "But I'd bet money that your nickname—"

"Yep," she confirmed, grinning. "I love birds. I always have. I've raised every one of these from babyhood. This one"—she stroked one of the parrots, and he chewed her fingertip—"was my first bird. My parents gave him to me. He's an old bird."

I imagined Tweet visiting the farm, strolling among rows of commercial chicken houses. I hope she doesn't fall in love with edible birds, I thought. "Where do your parents live?"

"They don't." She retrieved a glass of wine from a handsome oak table and sipped it. I sipped from my own glass and waited. "They were killed in a boating accident when I was twelve. Near where we lived. Seattle. Out on Puget Sound. I was raised by friends of my parents," Tweet added. She smiled the way people do to put others at ease when a wornout personal grief has to be dispensed. "So I grew up like Matthew. Adopted."

I found that very interesting and let the interest show on my face, which encouraged her to confide more. Tweet tiptoed to the kitchen doorway and glanced furtively across to the closed, glass-paned door to the back porch. Then she came over and sat down beside me. "Roan doesn't know this, he thinks Matthew and I met in a class when we were in pre-vet, but we met in a support group on campus. For adoptees."

I inhaled sharply. "Why haven't y'all ever told Roan where you met?"

"Because he doesn't understand how adopted people fantasize about their biological parents. Look, I knew my parents; I have great memories of them. My foster parents are nice people, but they've never taken my mom and dad's place. Good, bad, or indifferent, your family is a big mystery to Matthew, and he barely remembers his mother or her sisters. So, in a strange way, I'm at peace about my parents because at least I knew they wanted me, but Matthew can't stop wondering about his."

I sat back, blinking in amazement. "I can't believe he's never admitted that to Roan. They're so close."

"That's the problem. Matthew knows how much it would hurt Roan to admit it. He doesn't want Roan to feel betrayed. Roan's always been dead-set against Matthew contacting any relatives. When Roan suddenly told us he was going back to Georgia to see if he could help you, we were shocked. We thought Roan had no good memories about your family. No reason to ever go back. That's one reason Matthew never pushed it. For Roan's sake."

I was stunned. "But Roan was mainly concerned about protecting Matthew when Matthew was underage; he thought my family might find him and interfere. He was wrong—I've been trying to convince him that they would have been good to Matthew and him, too, if he'd let us know where he was. And now, of course, Matthew's grown. There's nothing to worry about."

"Except that Matthew wants Roan's approval," Tweet whispered, glancing toward the kitchen again. "He won't do anything that might make Roan feel discarded. But Roan doesn't appreciate the larger concept of family the way Matthew and I do."

"The larger concept? That's not true."

"Even Matthew says Roan is hard to figure out. For example, Roan enjoys women, he really likes them, they like him, he's been involved with some really nice ladies, and he didn't treat them like one-night stands—I mean, he's always been very gentlemanly and discreet about his female friends—but marriage? Forget it. He's never been interested in marriage or raising more children. I hope you don't think I'm tacky for saying that."

I dismissed the subject with an impatient shake of my head. She was missing the point. "You're talking about a man," I emphasized slowly, "who devoted himself to bachelor fatherhood when he was barely grown himself. Family means everything to him."

"I know, I know, it doesn't make sense. I'm sorry. That thing about women—he certainly doesn't feel casual about *you*. There's never been anybody like you. For one thing, he's never brought a woman to, hmmm, sleep over, around us before."

"I'll take that as a compliment. *Listen to me.* If Matthew wants to meet the family, Roan will support his decision. He'll do what's best for Matthew. You have to believe that."

"Don't get me wrong. Roan's been wonderful to Matthew. And to me. When I lost my scholarship during my third year in pre-vet, he paid my tuition. He's done so many things like that. Not just with money, but . . . accepting me. Including me. Treating me with respect." She tapped her wineglass to mine. "Baccarat crystal. You should see the complete set. It was one of our engagement presents from Roan. And the day after we picked out our china and silver—you know, set it up with a bridal registry—the store delivered everything we listed to our apartment. One of Roan's wedding presents. And you should have seen our wedding this spring."

This spring. Roan had visited me in the hospital but couldn't stay. He had to be at Matthew and Tweet's graduation from the university and at their wedding. Trying to do the right thing for me and for them. Two sides of an impossible situation.

"You look upset," Tweet said anxiously. "I upset you. I'm sorry. I'm better with animals than I am with people."

"No. Go on. Tell me about the wedding."

"Roan paid for the whole thing. Three hundred guests, an orchestra at the reception. Lots of important people who are business acquaintances of Roan's. I didn't come from that kind of background. It was amazing. It was magical." She dabbed her eyes. Her mop of shaggy golden hair danced in the firelight. One of the parakeets swooped across the room and sat on her shoulder, picking at her hair. "Matthew asked Roan to serve as his best man. Roan was really pleased to be asked, I know.

"But he looked absolutely *miserable* during the ceremony. Everybody commented on it. He hates to be put on display in front of a crowd. That's what he calls it. *Put on display.* In fact, he was kind of strange during the whole spring and now we understand why—he was going nuts over your circumstances, but he didn't tell us about you until after we were married."

Tweet didn't understand Roan's motivations—neither she nor Matthew could understand because they hadn't seen how Roan grew up. He had been put on display too often in his life, and never without humiliation. He had learned to stay behind the scenes. What people didn't know about him couldn't hurt him.

"He didn't want to ruin your special moments," I told her. "You see, don't you? He did what was best for Matthew, and for you, and that's all that matters. Trust me. He knows the value of family loyalty."

"I'm just saying he's not *comfortable* with the whole family *ideals* thing—ceremony, traditions—he's not interested in *that*. I'm just saying he's not sentimental enough to understand that Matthew is *very* sentimental about relatives he's never met."

I chewed my tongue. Roan and I lost each other for twenty years because he committed himself to making a family for Matthew, to prove *he* deserved a family. I'd be damned if I'd let anything or anyone else take more time from us. I wanted to say that to Tweet, but it would only sound bitter. "You look more upset," Tweet said. "I'm sorry. I squawk nonstop. Like a parrot."

"At least you don't shit when you talk." That was a little blunt. I was thankful when she grinned. I exhaled and took a deep swallow of wine. "I'm just trying to sort through everything. About Matthew—you have to realize that Roan only told me about him two days ago. And I'm the only person in the family who knows."

Tweet leaned toward me. "Be honest with me." Her round, sweet face became fierce; her voice shook with emotion. "I don't want Matthew to visit your family if they're going to reject him."

"Matthew's family," I corrected. "And they won't reject him."

"Hmmm. Matthew can see Roan's point of view. After all, his mother wasn't exactly a pillar of the community, and she died when he was little, and apparently his . . . your uncle—"

"Is dead, too. He died in a hunting accident. You'd have to have known my Uncle Pete to appreciate how appropriate that was. And Matthew's half brothers, Harold and Arlan, well, Harold died in a stock-car wreck and Arlan just sort of wandered off to see the world. I know they don't sound very appealing, but—"

"Is most of your family really as openhearted as you? Will they be happy to learn about Matthew?"

"*Yes*. And you'll be doing him a favor if you encourage him to meet them."

"He won't go if Roan doesn't agree."

"He will agree. You and Matthew," I said slowly, "you don't know Roan the way I do. From childhood. He won't let you down."

"We know he was poor, of course. He's told Matthew some things, but he doesn't discuss it much."

"Do you know how my family treated Roan?" I asked carefully.

"He's always told Matthew they were good to him, but that he had trouble getting along with some of your relatives. And that your parents finally decided he'd be better off in a foster home. That sounds pretty, hmmm, cold to me, Claire. That your family could have felt that way."

"My parents have never forgiven themselves for sending him away," I said, weighing every word. "The circumstances were different then. It's hard to describe. You had to be there. You had to know Roan and the family back then. We've all changed. He changed us."

She bit her lip. "Roan must have been a tough character."

"Roan didn't do anything to deserve being sent away, if that's what you're getting at."

"No, no. I just mean—I can see why they might have been afraid of him."

"*What?*"

"Hold on, hold on. He's been wonderful to me and wonderful to Matthew. It's just that—I was afraid of him when Matthew took me home to meet him—before I got to know him. God, Matthew and I were only seventeen. College freshmen. And he took me home with him to meet his . . . surrogate father, who wasn't old enough to be his father, and when he introduced me to Roan all I saw was this big, dark-haired, serious, almost sinister self-made businessman who seemed so old psychologically. So driven. I kept expecting him to say I wasn't good enough for Matthew or that we were too young to be so committed to each other. I expected him to ask me if I was after Matthew's money. But he never did. He was great to me."

"Then you understand that he's not someone to fear. What happened between him and my family wasn't his fault. And, believe me, nobody wanted to lose track of Matthew either. It was just such a mess. So different then. I'm trying desperately to get everybody back together. I need some sense of redemption myself. Roan counted on me when we were kids and he got hurt because of it. And then this year someone else got hurt because she depended on me—"

She frowned. "You sound so much like Roan. You and he are both really into guilt and responsibility. I'm missing something here. I mean—what?" She chuckled. "Was it something they put in the drinking water when you two were kids?"

I stared at her a moment. Then, "You and Matthew certainly know enough about Roan's history to appreciate how hard it is for him to trust people. You know about me, of course, and what happened with Roan's father."

"Oh, yes." She nodded somberly. "You were Roan's only friend. He was poor, you tried to help him, his mother died when he was little—you see how much he and Matthew have in common?—and then, of course, Roan's father was kind of disreputable and he died young, and then Roan was sent away."

Kind of *disreputable?* And he *died* young? That was a benign description of Big Roan Sullivan's life and how it ended. I studied her with growing dread. "Roan's father died when Roan was fifteen," I went on vaguely, trying to draw her out, my heart in my throat. "He died . . . suddenly. But you know that."

"Of course Matthew and I *know* the important details about Roan's past. Do you think he wouldn't share *that* kind of information with Matthew?" She gazed at me impatiently, then counted on her fingers and recited with parrotlike efficiency: "Roan's dad was a disabled Korean veteran. He drank too much. He was moody and undependable. Roan pretty much raised himself." She paused for a breath. "And then his dad died of a heart attack."

Oh, my God. Matthew and Tweet had no idea what a monster Big Roan had been, or how badly Roan had suffered because of him, or even that Roan had *killed* him. Killed him for my sake.

"Oh, come on, let's lighten up!" Tweet exclaimed suddenly. "Everything's going to be fine!" She clicked her wineglass to mine again. "Look how much we've learned about you and you've learned about us already! I feel as if Matthew and I have known you forever! I'm so glad you're here!" She threw her arms around me and hugged me.

I sat there, frozen. I finally understood. If we brought Matthew back to Dunderry, Roan could no longer hide how far he'd come himself or what he'd done to survive.

We stayed up late talking to Matthew and Tweet. I made good on my plan to ask Matthew a lot of harmless questions about himself and he warmed up to me, while Roan watched us with a wary half-smile, aware that I was a professional snoop and an expert at putting people at ease.

It worked. When we said our good nights, Matthew hugged me. And so did Tweet again. I liked them together. They were comfortable with each other, they adored each other, they traded quick pats and reassuring glances. Mama would melt with romantic approval when she saw them together. Everyone would.

I felt sick with worry.

I took Roan's arm and we walked into the guest room. He shut the door. My facade crumbled and I slumped on the bed. Roan sat down in a chair by the window without turning on a lamp. The bedroom was small and cluttered, filled with storage boxes in one corner and veterinary texts stacked in another, with camping gear piled in a third. But the bed was large and covered with a white down comforter, and I wanted desperately to sleep with him and say nothing at all.

He sat very still, one foot slung out and the other back. In his dark trousers and gray sweater and hiking boots, he looked as resilient and all-weather as the spruce tree that brushed rhythmically against the window-panes. He steepled his big-knuckled hands beneath his chin. "When you were a little girl I always knew when you wanted something from me that I didn't want to do," he said quietly. "Your cheeks would turn bright pink and you'd stare straight at me without blinking. Those big blue eyes *never* blinking. I was convinced you tried to hypnotize me. I *felt* hypnotized."

"It works. Great-Gran taught me to do it to people."

"What do you want from me tonight, peep? You've given me the blue-eye since before dinner."

"You need to explain something to me, boy."

He frowned but moved over and sat beside me on the bed. He took one of my hands, turning it, smoothing his fingers over the palm. Then he touched one hand to my throat and slid it gently down to my breasts, stroking with the backs of his fingers across my sweater.

"That won't distract me. Not right now."

"Too bad."

"How much have you told Matthew about yourself? About how you grew up in Dunderry?"

He lay back on the bed and latched his hands beneath his head. "He knows I didn't have much. He knows I worked for your family. He knows I left after my old man died."

"You've never told him the truth about *how* your daddy died. And my part in how he died. Roan, this is really unavoidable. You've got to tell him."

He sat up again. Silence. The tension grew. He shut his eyes for a moment and when he opened them he looked so tired. "I tried to tell him when he was little. I tried when he was older. I've tried to tell him a hundred times, but something always stopped me. He was too young to understand, I decided. Then he was older and having a hard enough time growing up with kids teasing him about not having any real parents. There was a window of time when I should have told him—when he wasn't too young to be confused or too old to resent me for keeping secrets. I missed that chance. To be honest about it, I didn't want to tell him. I couldn't stand to screw up a good thing."

"You wouldn't have ruined how he feels about you. I've only been around him a few hours, but I already see the tremendous love and respect he has for you. Tell him the truth now—and tell him why you waited so long, the way you just explained it to me—and he'll understand."

"He'll pity me," Roan said stonily.

"No, he'll be sympathetic. There's a difference."

"Maybe he doesn't think of me as a father, but he does look up to me. I've been as good to him as I know how to be. I don't ever want him to feel sorry for me. Or embarrassed to be a Sullivan. Not for any reason."

"Embarrassment. That's what you hate the most. Come on, Roan, he'll never reject you."

Roan turned toward me angrily. "After all these years of me saying nothing about myself, now I'm supposed to tell him: Oh, by the way, I blew my old man's brains out with a pistol after I caught him slapping Claire around the floor with her clothes half pulled off."

"If you need to be that blunt about it, yes."

"And tell him how your family—his family, the family that you want him to love—shipped me off because they couldn't stand the sight of a Sullivan in their house anymore?"

"Yes." I was trembling. "Tell him exactly how it was and we'll deal with it."

"You take family loyalty for granted. That's a luxury you can afford. I can't."

"You owe him the truth. Anything less is nothing but a self-serving excuse."

"You think I'm selfish?" Roan countered tightly. "You think I'm only worried about protecting my own goddamned pride?"

"You want us all to prove how much we love you, but you can't even comprehend why we love you."

"I don't want him to see the Hollow. I don't want people to tell him about me—about white-trash Roanie Sullivan who had bad teeth and smelled like garbage. His idea of how I grew up poor is the way he and I were poor when he was little. He thinks it means my old man bought me secondhand bikes for Christmas instead of brand new. He thinks it means shopping on a budget and wearing jeans with patches in the knees. He doesn't know what my kind of poor was like. He doesn't know what I was."

"You were special. You were strong and decent and gentle. Anything ugly that he'll learn will only help him know how special you are because you overcame so much."

"There's nothing I can do about it if he doesn't want to go back. I keep telling you it's his decision."

"Roan. That's not true." I took his face between my hands and repeated everything Tweet had told me about Matthew's attitude and motivation. "He wants to go," I finished. "He's always wanted to see *who* he came from—good, bad, or indifferent. But he's loyal to you, and you have to let him know you agree."

Sorrow, shock, and finally resignation sank into Roan. "Oh, God," he murmured, bending his forehead to mine. "He's never even *hinted*. I didn't have a clue."

"The apple didn't fall far from the tree. You're not the only one who can keep a poker face about your real feelings. He learned it from you." I put my arms around him and we said nothing for a while. "He won't go unless you tell him you want him to go," I repeated. "I know you'll do it."

"I told you I wouldn't interfere when you tried to persuade him," Roan said. "But I never promised I'd help."

Amazed, I drew back and looked at him. "That's not fair. What kind of life can we have together if you won't make peace with the past? You can't keep the truth from Matthew. You can't hide Matthew from my family. It'll all come out eventually, no matter what you do." I paused. "Unless you and I go our separate ways and don't see each other again."

He pulled me back on the bed and bent over me. "You know that's not an option."

"Then trust me."

"We could be happy out here. Washington State. California. Alaska. Anywhere you like. You went for years without visiting home. It's a habit you could cultivate again."

"I don't want to cultivate loneliness and estrangement again. Anyway, this dilemma isn't about *where* we should live our lives. It's about where we *belong* and *how* we should live. It's about being honest, Roan. You've always been honest with me, and you've *got* to be honest with Matthew."

"He doesn't belong in Dunderry," Roan said flatly. "He won't be accepted there. Ever. No matter how bad you want it. And neither will I. Stop counting on fairy tales."

"Badly," I corrected sarcastically. "How badly I want it."

He got up and jerked the comforter over me, then walked out of the room and shut the door.

He came back an hour later and I pretended to be asleep, and he pretended to let me sleep until he brushed against me in bed and then we both sighed in defeat and made love to each other with tenderness and anger.

But we didn't talk.

$\mathcal{M}$atthew and Tweet drove us to the ferry docks on the Juneau waterfront the next day, and the four of us boarded a sixty-five-foot double-decker named the *Ice Dancer*. It was a small tourist ferry that offered an observation deck scattered with lounge chairs on top, behind its pilothouse, and a cozy, gingham-curtained dining room below. The *Ice Dancer* took a payload of two dozen tourists out every afternoon in the spring and summer months, and its five-member crew served gourmet meals on jaunts to the glacier fjords.

Matthew and Tweet had hired the ferry for a private excursion. "It'll take all afternoon, round trip," Matthew explained politely. "You can sit, Claire. Take it easy, watch the world go by."

"I'd pay money to see her take it easy," Roan countered. I squinted at him, then craned my head, feigning an innocent perusal of the box filled with photo albums that Matthew had carried on board. I opened the tote bag I'd brought with me, set a half-dozen books on the linen-draped table where the four of us sat, drinking hot lemon tea while the *Ice Dancer* chugged out of Juneau proper, and said, "We have plenty to do. Sit and look at pictures, and talk."

Matthew stared, bewildered, at the collection of books I had spread on the table. Some were oversize paperback editions, quaint self-published volumes, and a couple of hardbacks with the imprints of small regional publishers on their spines. "Books about the Delaneys, the Maloneys, and the history of Dunderry," I explained with feigned nonchalance. "Nothing fancy. Your Aunt

Jane and my mother, your Aunt Marybeth, wrote one of the Delaney histories. The most recent Maloney update was put together by my Uncle Winston a few years ago. I edited it for him. He writes like a man who's president of the North Georgia Poultry Council. In other words, there'd be a lot of chicken-related stories in the book if I hadn't intervened."

Tweet stared at the books. "How many Delaneys and Maloneys are there?" she asked. "As compared to chickens."

"Enough to crow about each other each time a new generation hatches," Roan told her. He walked out to a lower-level foredeck and stood in the wind, facing the silver water of the channel slipping behind us.

Matthew scowled, red splotches blooming on his cheeks. "Sorry. He didn't have to say that."

"I'm not insulted. Go outside and warn him that I'll come after him if he doesn't cooperate. Tell him I want his input when we look at the Sullivan family albums. We'll look at those first. After we get some food into us."

Matthew frowned and went after him. I smiled at Tweet, who was staring at the books incredulously. She blinked. "How many relatives does Matthew have?"

I counted Delaneys on my fingers. "Twenty first cousins. Four aunts—including my mother—and three uncles. About forty second cousins. And I'm not including great-aunts, great-uncles, or in-laws."

"Good lord."

"About half of them live in Dunderry or within an hour's drive."

"Good lord." She grinned.

Matthew and Roan returned and sat down. I shuffled the books aside as a bearded waiter in blue jeans and a white jacket began setting cups of fish chowder on the table. Matthew's expression grew agitated. He pivoted in his chair and clamped a hand on top of the photo albums. "Claire, I don't think there's much use in showing me a bunch of family pictures." He jabbed a thumb at himself. "I won't find any baby pictures of yours truly." He glanced at Roan. "What do you think, Bigger?"

Roan didn't show me any mercy. "I think you're right. There's no point in it."

"Claire, I don't care what these two say," Tweet muttered. "I'm going to look at the pictures after we eat."

"Thank you," I said with as much grace as I could. I watched Roan throughout the meal. He'd completely dissuade Matthew from ever meeting the family if he could. He wouldn't risk exposing his own history to Matthew, not even if I begged him. He'd let Matthew go on avoiding my family when it could be so different. How could he be that heartless to Matthew? And how could he do it to me?

The glacier ice was blue. An opalescent blue, like the sky behind a frosted window. The *Ice Dancer's* captain idled the ferry at the center of an inlet, where the water had a soft, milky shimmer from the glaciers seeping finely ground ice and rock into it. I sat on the end of a teak lounge on the foredeck, my hands hooked over the deck rail.

Roan stood beside me, his elbows on the rail, and my eyes swept from the walls of striated azure ice to him. His face was silhouetted against the massive ice floes. He glanced at me. "The ice is the color of your eyes in bright sunshine," he said. "Stop looking at me that way." He smoothed a fingertip beneath my lashes.

"Obviously I'm not able to mesmerize you. I can't change your mind. I can't persuade you to do anything until you win the battle with your own personal demons. I can't make you see how disappointed I am. How much you're jeopardizing our happiness, and Matthew's, too. So just ignore the truth. You know how to do that."

We didn't have time to say more before Matthew and Tweet stepped out on the deck to stand with us. Matthew wrapped his arms around Tweet, hugging her from behind, resting his chin atop her head. They were cozy and unabashed; it made me realize how private Roan and I were with each other in public, how we pulled inward together for safety. "Isn't it beautiful here?" Tweet enthused.

Pride came up in me; this world was fine, but Matthew should see our round, blue-green mountains at home. I talked about Dunshinnog, the legend behind its name, how Roan and I had climbed up it to hunt for mistletoe with my grandfather, and that its sides were lush and sprinkled white-pink this time of year, with the laurel not quite finished blooming. "Roan and I loved Dunshinnog when we were kids," I finished carefully. "When you see it, you'll understand why."

Matthew grew more still and less exuberant, with troubled eyes, and my mind turned in weird circles. He's so familiar, but not the way he should be, I thought, which made no sense. Roan shifted beside me, straightened, and slowly rested a hand on my shoulder. His firm grip conveyed relentless disapproval.

As we watched, a slender slab of ice broke free from one of the glaciers with a ripping, deep-pitched groan. "We call that calving," Matthew explained. "When the glacier loses a piece of itself."

The water boiled at the glacier's base. The birthed chunk of ice, compressed and nurtured over hundreds or even thousands of years, sent deep ripples across the water, and the ferry rocked with the motion, so we were part of that amazing moment, which had been coming our way for many generations.

I saw portents in everything.

"I think we should look at the Sullivan pictures first," I said.

"Are you a vampire?" I called to Roan with forced humor.

"What?" He stood across the foredeck from us, and I'd already noticed his restless inclination to pace and smoke cigars during the two hours Matthew, Tweet, and I had spent going over their photo albums. They and I shared my lounge chair, sitting sideways in a row, me in the middle, the two of them offering commentary on each page of each album I spread on my lap.

"You're invisible," I went on. "There are hardly any pictures with you in them. I assume your image doesn't reproduce."

"Someone had to *take* the pictures."

"Bigger didn't like to be photographed," Matthew said drily. "He was afraid someone would steal his soul."

"He was afraid someone would steal *you*," I replied. "Somebody, somewhere, might have recognized him. The family might have found you then. Might have taken you away from him. That's what he believed. I wish he hadn't felt that way."

Roan and I traded looks. He nodded slightly. I turned to Matthew. "But I believe wholeheartedly that both of you could have come home and that you'd have been accepted and loved."

Matthew scrubbed his hands over his hair and sighed. He glanced at Roan and smiled sadly. "Sometimes I'd get totally ticked off with you when I was a kid. You wouldn't pose for any pictures with me. All the other kids had pictures with their families, but I didn't. When I was old enough to understand, you explained why pictures weren't a good idea."

"I tried not to scare you," Roan said.

"I know, but I was scared anyway. I used to have nightmares about the police busting into our house and dragging me away. Why do you think I went through that phase when I tied one of my feet to the bedpost at night and slept with all my dogs on the bed? So the dogs would bark and wake you up, and before the cops could untie my foot, you'd have time to run into my room and save me."

Roan stared at him. From the expression on his face I knew he'd never heard that story before. It seemed to cut him from the inside out—to know that he'd ingrained that brand of nightmarish fear in a child, even with the best intentions.

Tweet's eyes filled with tears. She peered at Matthew. "You still sleep with the dogs on the bed," she managed to tease. "And I thought you liked it when I tied your foot to the rail."

Matthew laughed, but Roan still looked as if he'd been punched. I figured out why the anecdote burned me up.

"This isn't funny," I said between gritted teeth. "Your family," I emphasized to Matthew, "deserve better than a reputation as boogeymen in childhood nightmares. Yes, some of them were petty and self-righteous; yeah, some of them never wanted to admit you were a Delaney; and some of them were too worthless to give a damn about. Pete, your daddy, was like that, all right. Your half brothers were nasty little shits. But most of the other Delaneys are very good people. My mother *wanted to adopt you.* Even Roan will admit that."

Matthew looked at him. Roan nodded vaguely, frowning with distraction, a "what have I done to this boy" expression in his eyes.

I slammed shut the last Sullivan album and dropped it at my feet. I'd seen what kind of life Roan had given Matthew—Little League, soccer, football, academic awards, birthday parties, pets, and friends. But plenty was missing from it, and I was the only one who could fill in the blanks.

I snatched a stack of dog-eared snapshots from my tote bag. My hands trembled. Roan tossed a half-smoked cigar overboard and stood beside us grimly. I had the feeling he'd have gladly taken my pictures and thrown them in the ocean if I'd let him. "Matthew," I said suddenly, softly. "Are you a damned coward?"

He gaped at me. So did Tweet. "This must be a joke," he managed.

"No, it's a serious question." I shook the photographs at him. "These can't hurt you. They can't hurt Roan either. If you want to look at them, have the *cojones* to admit it."

Matthew turned as red as I must be, because my skin felt blistered. He frowned at Roan. "I *would* like to see if I can pick out Pete Delaney without you or Claire telling me who he is."

Roan's jaw worked. He appeared tortured. "If you want to make a game out of it, go ahead."

"I guess I sound morbid, but I need to know if I look like him. If I can recognize him."

I smiled. "That's not morbid. I did the same thing—tried to pick you out of the crowd at the airport without Roan helping me."

"Could you?" Matthew asked hopefully.

"Without any effort at all. You look like a Delaney," I lied. I quickly asked Tweet to hold half the photographs. She took them as if they were precious. I shuffled the others. "I'll choose a few to get you started, Matthew. Your Aunt Marybeth Delaney Maloney, who's my mother, and my four brothers, who are your cousins, of course, on the Maloney side—"

Matthew held out a hand. "I want to see if I can pick out Pete Delaney first. Please."

"We'll be docking in Juneau in a few minutes," Roan interjected. "I say put this away until later."

"Later? Maybe a hundred years or so?" I suggested coldly.

Matthew sighed. "Come on, it's not a major thing. I'll just look and get it over with." He flipped through his stack quickly. Tweet hopped up and handed him the rest, then huddled beside him, one arm stretched soothingly across his lanky shoulders. She peered at the pictures with him, biting her lower lip. I clenched my hands in my lap and glanced at Roan. He'd become a guardian, standing at stony attention. They're only pictures, I urged silently.

"This one," Matthew said. His voice shook. He planted his forefinger on a snapshot. Tweet gasped. "Oh, *yes*, honey, that has to be your . . . Pete Delaney. You look so much like him. I mean, you look *exactly* like him."

In the old black-and-white picture, without benefit of color to mark the contrast between sandy and red hair, the stalwart, crew-cut young man gazing up at us seemed undeniable. He couldn't have resembled Matthew more if Matthew had posed in an army uniform circa 1970. I finally understood what had puzzled me every time I looked at Matthew.

I felt as I had when Terri Caulfield's ex-husband shot at us and I lost control of my Jeep. Spinning, horrified, out of control. I pulled myself together like some chimera built of different parts that fought one another. I said calmly, "No, that's your cousin. My oldest brother. Josh."

I lifted my head and gazed hopelessly at Roan. His eyes were bleak but honest. I shoved another picture into Matthew's hands, then made myself say, "That's Pete. That's your father and those are your half brothers."

"Well," Matthew replied in a gruff voice after studying the photo for a long time. "It's no wonder nobody forced Pete Delaney to admit I was his. Little fair-haired bastard kid. I didn't look remotely like him or his other sons."

And then he tossed the picture in my lap and got up and went to Roan.

The wind was high and cold, and the *Ice Dancer* was pulling into the docks by then. "You were right," Matthew said gruffly. "It wasn't worth the trouble. I only care because—"

"You need to know who you are and where you came from," Roan said with the slow, stunted agony of a man coming to terms with forces he can't conquer. "Even if your old man was an S.O.B., you need to know. I see that. You're not going against my wishes. That's not why I've been a horse's ass about it. I know what you're feeling. I'm scared for you. Because it's hell when you want to love your old man but he makes you hate him instead."

Matthew shook his head. "Maybe the Delaneys were right to ignore me. I don't think I'm a Delaney at all. Not judging from the pictures."

I was reduced to helpless rage. All the failures rose up in me at once: Roan killing Big Roan; Roan being taken away, with me unable to stop it; being in the crumpled Jeep, lost in Terri Caulfield's bloody, violated face; trapped in beds and on crutches and inside my own mistakes.

"You *are* one of us," I yelled at Matthew, and when Roan looked at me like I was tearing his heart out, I put my head in my hands and burst into sobs that made Tweet look like an amateur crier. Roan was beside me in an instant, kneeling down and wrapping his arms around me. "Don't say any more. Not here, not right now," he whispered. "I'm sorry. Peep, believe me. I understand. Sssh." He stroked my hair. I nodded against his shoulder and cried harder. It was not a good day for Maloney dignity.

Now I knew the only secret that mattered, the secret that had always made a simple homecoming for him and Matthew impossible.

Matthew was my brother's son.

When I was ten and Roan fifteen, during the spring when he lived at the farm, there was a huge work party one weekend to restore the Delaney covered bridge. Great-Grandfather Thurman Delaney built the bridge after the Civil War to replace a ferry barge he'd operated; it became a proud monument connecting the rutted wagon road that ran from Dunderry to Gainesville. Delaney Bridge Road was the first road paved as part of a local WPA project in the 1930s, and the bridge was shored up with iron beams then, but by the time I was a girl the bolts had rusted through and the beams showered big, red-brown flakes into the river with the slightest vibration.

The old bridge, a hundred years old then, was a quaint eyesore rather than a crossing point over the Slow Forks River east of town. The state highway department had rerouted the road a few years earlier and built a new steel-and-concrete bridge upstream; the old wooden bridge shed rotten shingles on the rooftops of every car that drove through.

But when the highway department planned to tear the bridge down, a coalition of Delaneys bought it along with five acres of cornfields on either side and, in the way Delaneys have of consecrating their own history, decided to make the bridge the centerpiece for a county park.

Over the long Memorial Day weekend in May, dozens of Delaney kin descended on the site with tools and materials. The event quickly bloomed into a three-day festival complete with picnics, ad-lib entertainment from the family bluegrass musicians, an outdoor church service on Sunday morning, and the wonderful cacophony of unleashed Delaney cousins running wild in every direction from morning until dark.

Roan wouldn't admit to being anything but a hired hand; he approached the weekend as part of his work chores for Daddy and as always kept to himself while I circled from my cousins' orbit on regular swoops to bring him food and talk to him, which earned him snickers from the men. When I finally understood that I was embarrassing him, I kept a morose distance.

Josh came home from college for the weekend. I think Brady went to Tennessee to visit a girlfriend. But not Josh—he took solemn pride in attending to family duties. People were proud of his attitude.

I remembered Roan and Josh sitting astride the bridge's shabby peaked roof, ripping the frayed shingles as if they were performing an autopsy on the spine of some long, large animal. I remembered Josh's red hair highlighted against the brilliant autumn hills above the river valley and Roan's thin, dark contrast to my oldest brother's ruddy maturity. I wanted to be up there with them and might have tried to wrangle it if every Delaney matron in the county, Mama first and foremost, wouldn't have snatched me by the hair the instant I set foot on a ladder.

Uncle Pete chainsawed fresh timbers with a team of men that included Daddy, my Maloney uncles, and Uncle Eldon. People wandered out from town to work and party with us; no one could do anything interesting in Dunderry without it having a drawstring effect; besides, half the families in the county could be counted as Delaney relatives by blood or marriage.

There was a general murmur of shock and embarrassment when Sally McClendon appeared at the edge of the picnic tables. She had Matthew in tow; he was about three years old then, fair-haired and quiet. Sally had ratted her blond hair up on top and in huge curls down her back; in full

Maybelline raccoon-eyes and tight jeans with a spangled T-shirt, she made me think of a tall, dried-out imitation of Dolly Parton. She stood there, a beacon of shame and notoriety, clutching Matthew by the hand.

"Well, our personal whore and her poor little get are here." Aunt Irene snorted. "I guess it's a full celebration now."

Grandmother Elizabeth, ensconced queenlike in a lawn chair set in the bed of a flatbed lumber truck, hooked Mama with the head of her cane. "Remove that creature," Grandmother ordered. "She's come to flaunt herself."

"Delaneys," Great-Gran Alice hooted from her chair next to Grandmother Elizabeth's. "Blood will tell. Why, Elizabeth, that little ragtailed baby boy may grow up to look just like your Pete. Go and give him a kiss."

Grandmother Elizabeth moaned, draping a hand over her eyes. "Either that child and his awful mother leave the premises or I do."

"Hop down and take off," Great-Gran retorted.

"It'd be a sin not to offer food to a baby," I piped up, and I thought Mama would strangle me.

"You budge and I'll tie your fanny to a post," Mama said. "I'll take care of this problem." She bowled through the crowd, her sisters left behind with Aunt Irene marshaling a grunt-mouthed choir of dismay. Uncle Pete turned from his work, saw Sally and Matthew, cursed loudly enough for everyone to hear, then set his chain saw down and disappeared below the slope of the riverbank, pulling a silver flask from his back pocket.

I glanced up from the immediate melodrama and saw Josh staring at Sally from the bridge's roof; Roan handed him a double-clawed crowbar and Josh fumbled it. The bar fell between the exposed rafters, bounced off the head of Robert Kehoe, a cousin who had been ripping boards from the bridge's floor, then fell through a hole into the river.

Everyone looked up at Josh then, startled but without any sinister concern; it was just curious that capable Josh Maloney, college honor student, fraternity president, and Vietnam veteran, had made a careless error. A contingent hurried to help Robert, who was clutching a bloody streak across his forehead, and Daddy called up to Josh, "Pay attention, son." Roan, of course, sat frozen with grim, hyperalert defensiveness, afraid someone might blame him for handing the crowbar to Josh in the first place.

Josh scrubbed a hand over his mouth as if he'd gone spitless and never took his eyes off Sally and her son. Sally stared back at him. I'll never forget the look she gave him—accusing, mean, and helpless. She picked Matthew up, face forward, and held him in the air toward my brother, like a proffered sacrifice. Then she flung him atop one hip and trudged off toward her ancient, duct-taped sedan, with Mama striding along after her making gestures of grudging welcome toward the tables heavy with food. Sally ignored her and drove away.

Josh came down from the roof, jumped into the river, and hunted in the waist-high water beneath the bridge until he retrieved the crowbar. He staggered onto the bank, soaking wet, climbed back up to the roof, and never said a word to anyone.

The memory came back with terrible clarity now.

And finally made sense.

Roan and I had given up twenty years because he'd protected, hidden, and raised Josh's son. The stakes were much higher than I'd ever suspected. No wonder Roan had always believed he couldn't bring Matthew back. No wonder he was secretive.

We went to our room early that night, then sat on the edge of the bathtub with the faucet turned on. We were both a little paranoid about being overheard. I stared at the photograph.

Josh was posed in his army uniform beside Daddy and Grandpa Joseph, standing rigidly in the front yard, so young—twenty-two, twenty-three—with a forced smile and hard eyes—the Maloneys' patriotic veterans, three generations, World War II, Korea, Vietnam. My grandfather had fought enemy soldiers in a noble cause; my father had served honorably, dutifully, without ever setting foot on a foreign battlefield; but Josh had been sent to the other side of the world to police a human sewer of brothels and bars and opium dens and had come home with a brand of cynicism that fed on scraps of self-disgust. Sally must have been either a transition or a confirmation for him.

As a young man, he and Matthew looked so much alike.

Roan spoke, his voice low and empty. "I'm sorry I kept the truth from you, but I had to know if Matthew would pass for a Delaney. If he would pass your scrutiny. Now I know. He won't fool anyone."

"You're sure about Josh, aren't you?"

"Sally told me when I moved in with her. She wanted me to know why she left town. She thought Daisy was going to tell your folks the truth out of meanness after my old man—"

"I remember. What did she say about Josh? Don't be delicate about it. Tell me exactly."

"Josh would pick her up on the road north of Murphy's Feed Mill.

Throw a couple of blankets in the back of one of the farm trucks, park in the woods. Use her, pay her, take her back to the mill road, let her out. She said he barely spoke to her."

"Oh, God. He probably treated her the way he learned to treat bar girls in Saigon."

"Probably. She said he only met her out there a few times. Then he just stopped. Never used her again. It was as if it never happened. She was scared to admit she'd ever been with him. Being with your Uncle Pete was one thing. Nobody expected much from him. But being with your brother—and having a baby by him—she thought your family'd take the baby and chase her out of town if they knew. And believe it or not, she really did love Matthew. No matter how she looked or what she said, she wanted to keep him."

I crumpled the picture and threw it aside. "Mama and Daddy could forgive Josh for fathering a child with her but not for being a coward who turned his back on his responsibility."

"They were able to look the other way when they thought Matthew was Pete's baby," Roan noted quietly.

"You want to argue over degrees of righteousness?"

He cupped a hand around the back of my neck and pulled me to him for a rough, apologetic kiss. I leaned against him wearily and exhaled. "You know what the circumstances were. Mama wanted the family to adopt Matthew, but it was complicated. Would you have approved if they'd dragged Sally into court and taken her baby? You say she loved Matthew. Then she didn't deserve to have him taken away by so-called decent folk. What she needed was *help* and you were the only one who gave her that."

"All right, peep. All right. But here's the problem we've got to handle—you didn't have to look hard today to see the resemblance."

"Josh *knew* Matthew was his," I hissed. "I'm convinced he *knew*."

Roan hesitated. Then, with defeat, "That day at the Delaney bridge—"

"You remember that, too!"

"I've thought about it over the years. Josh didn't want Matthew. It was obvious. That's why I never doubted that I was right to keep him. And I thought *everybody* in the family saw how strange Josh was around Sally and her baby that day. I thought other people saw the truth but still didn't do anything about it. It's what convinced me Matthew wouldn't get a fair shake if I brought him home."

I snatched my cane like a club and hit a pillow Roan had placed on the toilet seat for me to prop my leg on. I pounded the pillow, barely missing my own leg, until Roan's hands closed around my wrists. "I could kill Josh! How could he let our uncle take the blame? How could he ignore his own son? He's the reason you had no choice."

"I still don't have many choices, peep."

"I know. The family's going to find out about Matthew sooner or later. What we have to do is *manage* the process."

Roan uttered a dark sound of amusement. "Maloneys," he said grimly, gazing at the ceiling as if trying to imagine something. "Maloneys being managed."

"It's not impossible. People might comment on the resemblance, but that won't matter. It'll just be talk."

"Just talk. I can't believe you dismiss it that way." Roan looked at me as if I'd lost my mind. "Your brother will know it's not just *talk*."

"If he didn't admit anything twenty years ago, he probably won't admit it now." I paused, grinding my hands together. "I'll deal with Josh."

I didn't want anybody ambushed. I didn't want the wrong things said in surprise; I didn't want to take Matthew blindly into the situation; and for Mama and Daddy's sake I didn't want them to meet a stranger and suddenly, with him in the flesh staring at them, be told that he was not only Matthew but that Roan had found him, raised him, hidden him, and learned the truth about his parentage from Sally years ago. That they were looking at their grandson.

I told Roan I thought I should speak to Josh first. Yell, scream, get it out of my system. Learn what he intended to do about Matthew. Be prepared for him to deny his involvement or reject his responsibility. Then arrange for Matthew to meet him with Roan and me along for support. Let Matthew scream and yell, if need be, let him hear it straight from Josh what Josh felt about him.

But I thought about Amanda and felt sick about the dilemma. Her troubled relationship with Josh would be even worse; what little girl could hold up under the news that her papa had abandoned an earlier child, that she had a half brother she'd never heard of before?

I would simply start with Josh and hope for the best. "This is something between Josh and me," I said in a low voice. "Just us first."

Roan moved to sit in front of me on the bathroom floor, his expression harder than I'd ever seen it. "It's my business, too, peep," he warned very softly. "If your brother doesn't do the right thing by Matthew, I'll hurt him, Claire. I swear to God I'll make him pay."

That was chilling. "So what would you rather do? Tell Matthew the truth right now and have him take off for Dunderry, mad as hell, confronting everybody with no warning? You want to do it that way? To him? To my parents? To Grandma Dottie? To Amanda?"

"No. Of course not. Jesus. I don't know what's best."

"We can ease him into it. Just get him there, get everybody warmed up to Matthew and Tweet and vice versa, and deal with Josh on the side, privately—talk to him, the two of us. It's *his* duty to confess to the family. And to Matthew. That's it. That's the way to do it if we can. Matthew doesn't have to know you've kept his real father a secret from him."

"His real father," Roan repeated quietly. He looked defeated.

I put my arms around him. "I'm sorry. I didn't mean it like that."

"He probably won't go to Dunderry anyway. He was disappointed and apathetic after he looked at those pictures."

I said nothing else and let Roan enjoy that small consolation for the rest of the night. Matthew would go home eventually, with or without the truth to propel him. Like foxgloves, we always came back to where we started.

The next day, after a lunch none of us did more than pick over, Matthew and Tweet cornered us in the living room.

Matthew glanced from Roan to me, frowning. "Look, I'm prepared for the worst, but I'm hoping for the best. Don't try to shield me. All I need is the truth. Just an honest reaction from the Delaneys. I want to meet them."

Roan and I traded strained glances. Honesty. Matthew had no idea. Suddenly Matthew pushed a phone across the coffee table. "Speakerphone," he noted patiently, tapping the console. "Call your mother, Claire. We can all listen."

I froze. "Why?"

"Tell her about me. I know that's a lot to ask, but I want it straight. I want to hear her reaction." He smiled tentatively. "If I'm welcome to visit, I want to know it right *now*."

"Matthew," Tweet moaned. "It's not fair to judge people with shock tactics. You wouldn't do that to one of our patients."

"If I want to know whether a cow kicks, I give her a chance to kick me," Matthew replied. "But at least I stay ready to jump out of the way." He tapped the phone. "Claire. *Please* call my *Aunt Marybeth* and tell her about me."

Your Grandmother Marybeth, I corrected silently. "Can I tell her you compared her to a cow?"

"We're not going to do this," Roan said. "Not this way, Matthew."

"I have to," Matthew said. "Bigger, we agreed yesterday, didn't we? I thought that's what you meant. I should meet these people."

Roan raised a hand. "You should . . . get them out of your system," he said carefully. "But Claire and I thought we'd go back and tell them about you—and how you ended up with me—"

"Roan needs to explain, for his own sake," I put in.

"—plow the field for you," Roan continued. "Plow the field before you plant the seed." When Matthew looked at him askance, Roan added, "It's a saying I learned from Claire's grandfather. Grandpa Joe. He had a lot of sayings."

Matthew's great-grandfather, I thought.

Matthew shook his head. "Bigger, you can't protect me anymore. I'm going to meet my father's family on my terms." He tugged on his ears firmly. "Either Claire places the call or I'll do it myself."

I looked at Roan. We were trapped. Mama, don't fail me, I prayed silently as I reached for the phone.

"Your mama's in the pottery room," Renfrew snapped. "Where are you? Where's Roanie? Come home. You're scarin' everybody. Your mama ain't sleepin'. Your daddy's smokin' too much on his pipe. Rest of the family's all jabberin' about you and Roanie like crows pickin' an ear of corn."

"We're coming home soon," I said patiently. "Would you please go get Mama? I need to speak to her."

"Why? You sound okay. You know I don't never bother her when she's in her—"

"Miz Mac," Roan interjected quietly, leaning over the phone. The four of us were hunched over it as if it were a shrine. "If you'll get Marybeth out of her pottery room this one time, I promise you she'll forgive the interruption."

"Roanie! Roanie, I'm gonna do it for you." We heard her slap the phone down.

"Who was that?" Tweet asked. "And does your mother go in the potty room a lot?"

"Pottery room," I corrected numbly. This was absurd. "And that was the housekeeper."

"Renfrew," Roan said flatly. "She's crazy about me. She used to fight me for my underwear."

"Don't," I begged. "She's Missus Mac," I told Matthew and Tweet. Then to Roan, "Don't get them started on the wrong foot."

"Which foot would that be?" he asked darkly.

"Claire!" Mama's voice sang out of the speakerphone, melodic and

Southern, and urgent. "Is it an emergency? Are you okay? Is Roan okay? Where are you? When are you coming home?"

"We're fine, Mama. We're . . . in Alaska, Mama."

"*What?* Wait! Holt! Holt! Get on the other line! It's Claire. They're in *Alaska!* Just a second, sweetie. Daddy just came in from the barns. He's been out there all morning. He's got a dozen llamas with a hoof fungus."

Matthew and Tweet squirmed closer to the phone. They consulted with each other in frenzied whispers, gesturing in wild patterns. Matthew grabbed a notepad and jotted a pharmaceutical name on it. *Tell him to get this ointment from his vet,* he wrote underneath.

I rubbed my eyes. He was so eager to please. Roan made motions at Matthew. *Calm down. Calm down.*

"Hey," Daddy's deep voice grunted at us suddenly.

"Hi, Llama-papa."

"Hear your mama breathin' heavy on the other line? Tell her to calm down."

It was an epidemic. "Mama, everything's fine."

"Tell your daddy. He's the one who smells like an ashtray."

"I just need to discuss something with y'all. Is this a good time?"

"Oh, for lord's sake, *talk,*" Mama said.

"I don't want a lot of people overhearing. Where's Amanda?"

"She left for summer camp yesterday," Mama said quickly. "And Josh is in Atlanta."

"As usual," Daddy said.

I exhaled. I'd settled a crucial preliminary problem. Josh. We had to get home and deal with Josh in private and in person. "Where's Miz Mac?" I asked. "Still nearby?"

"Miz Mac always eavesdrops," Mama said. "So there's no point worrying about her. Honey, what's going on? You and Roan are coming home, aren't you? Tell me. Tell me and your daddy straight out."

"We're coming back," Roan interjected. "I'm giving you my word on it."

"*Roan,*" Mama and Daddy said in unison. "It's good to hear you," Daddy went on. "We'll take you at your word anytime. All right?"

"That's good to know," Roan replied evenly.

"What's in Alaska?" Daddy asked.

I hesitated. "It's not a what, it's a *who.*"

"Besides Roan?"

"Because of Roan."

Silence. Mama said quietly, "Roan, you wouldn't have asked Claire to meet somebody unless you thought she'd be happy about it. So I'm assuming this *who* isn't a wife."

"Not even a girlfriend," Roan answered in a strangled voice. Mama's approach could be disorienting.

"Then you've got a child. Or children."

Silence. Roan looked at Matthew. "You could say that."

"You're divorced?"

"Never been married."

"I see."

"Hold on," I said loudly. I was shaking. So was Tweet. Matthew was tugging his ears and Roan was as tense as a stone wall. "Mama. Daddy." I took a deep breath. "He brought me here to meet *Matthew.*"

"Who?" Daddy asked.

Oh, God. "*Matthew.* Uncle Pete's *Matthew.* Roan located Sally McClendon years ago. She died and he adopted *Matthew.* That's why he's been so secretive. Matthew." There, in a hard nutshell, was the story.

More silence. Matthew's expression went from hopeful to desperate. "They don't even remember me," he muttered. He dug his hands into his knees and stared at the phone. We all did.

Then came a soft wail of delight. "Is he there?" Mama shrieked. "Matthew? Is Matthew right there?"

Matthew's mouth opened and shut. "I'm . . . I am here," he said, inching closer to the phone. "Hello."

Mama said, "Oh, thank you, Lord," in a soft, high-pitched voice at least a dozen times, and then there were noises, and eventually we heard Daddy in the background calling out, "I had to change phones, she had to sit down on the floor, but she's okay—"

"I don't care how this happened, I don't care what happened, or where or how or who or anything else right now," Mama yelled tearfully, "but y'all bring Matthew *here,* you *bring* him here, you bring him *home* with you."

"Bring the boy home," Daddy said in a gravelly voice. He had obviously snatched up Mama's phone—his voice was clear and rang as beautifully as a brass bell. "It's a miracle. Come home and worry about explaining it later."

Tweet started sobbing, and Matthew had tears on his face, and Roan and I sat there together on the couch, relieved by one small victory but too worried to relax. This was only a beginning.

$\mathscr{I}$ told Mama and Daddy I'd call when we got to Ten Jumps. That we'd bring Matthew and Tweet to the farm for supper. "Don't invite anybody, please," I urged. "Let's not rush the whole crowd at 'em right away. We'd need name tags and a genealogy chart, and it'd just be overwhelming."

"Okay," Mama said too blithely.

Matthew and Tweet transferred their menagerie of dogs and birds to the temporary care of trusted co-workers at the wildlife center, then we packed and caught a jet bound for Seattle the next afternoon. Matthew popped a bottle of champagne during the flight. "To Sullivans and Delaneys," he said. Tweet laughed and pointed at me. "You do that just like Matthew. Only he does it when he's upset."

"What?"

She laughed harder. "You pull on your ears."

Roan and I were astonished and anguished over a chain of events happening too quickly for the facts. What Matthew didn't know would hurt him. The more I brooded over Josh's betrayals, the angrier I became. He could keep his cowardly secret and let everybody go on believing a lie, or he could confess to Matthew and the family.

I almost wished he'd deny the whole thing and we could get away with never mentioning it to anyone. But if Josh denied Matthew, Roan would be more brutal than anyone else; I really believed he'd ruin my brother in revenge.

• • •

We stayed in Seattle overnight, at Roan's house, but were besieged by phone calls from home—conversations with my parents, with Grandma Dottie, with all of my brothers except Josh, who was still out of town, and with cousins, aunts, uncles—they were all excited and pleased, and many of them wanted to talk to Matthew, and to Tweet, who grew so flustered by all the attention, she retreated into a discussion of viral poultry diseases with Daddy.

I asked Mama and Daddy to warn the family that one subject was *absolutely* off limits in these conversations: Roan. He listened to the rest of us chatter on the phone and I think he felt his happiness was being carved away from him in painful slivers; his biggest fear at the moment was that someone would mention his past to Matthew.

Thankfully, everyone seemed so humbled by what he'd done—taking Matthew to raise, doing so well by him, and bringing him back, to boot—that it was embarrassing to mention the past. I'm sure no one was eager to tell Matthew, a former outcast himself, how the family had ignored Roanie Sullivan, then warily embraced him, then discarded him. It was easy to warn the family off that subject, at least during the first flush of home-coming.

Matthew was ecstatic. "It's turning out to be so easy," he said to me out of Roan's earshot. He had a bewildered expression. "I don't under-stand why Bigger worried so much all these years. I think he's so cynical about people that he twisted this family thing out of perspective." Matthew sighed and nodded wisely. "You know, I've decided he was just born with the kind of personality that looks every gift horse in the mouth."

I almost said, *He's got good reason to believe that behind every gift horse there's a horse's ass,* but I didn't want to encourage the discussion. Roan deserved to explain himself to Matthew in his own way, when he was ready.

Ready or not, he'd have no choice soon.

"I need a stiffer drink than this tonight," Roan complained in the shad-ows of a small balcony outside his bedroom door. "And I don't say that very often." He tossed the remnants of a beer away. I sat between his bare legs on the balcony's cedar floor, naked except for the large Navajo blanket we shared. I tried to meditate on the slow chuckle of the fountain in his gar-den.

"Here, you can have the rest of mine." I twisted inside the blanket and his arms and held my shot glass of bourbon to his lips. He took the rim between his teeth and tossed the bourbon into his throat. "No hands," I noted as I retrieved my glass. "You learned that trick in a bar."

"No. I learned it when Matthew was still in diapers. Change enough dirty diapers and you can learn to drink, eat, or sign your name without using your hands. You'll learn not to forget and put your fingers near your mouth."

I tried to laugh, but I could imagine him all too well, fifteen or sixteen years old, a rough-looking, skinny, hulking teenage boy taking care of a child. "I love you," I said simply. "I love you more now than I did when we were kids, and more than I did when you came back a few weeks ago, and more than yesterday. And more than this morning."

He curved his head around mine and kissed me. "Are you a little bit drunk?" he teased gruffly.

"Maybe. But that only makes me clear on what I really feel. I need to make you believe we'll be okay back at home. Matthew will hear about Big Roan. About the past. About us. There's no getting away from that. But we'll be okay."

"I don't ask for many guarantees. I'll tell you what I want. I want to laugh with you. Sit and look at you. Wake up with nothing to think about but how warm and smooth you feel against me. I want us to be peaceful with each other. Be together and make a life together. All of this has been worth it, if we can have that."

"We can. I promise you. Sometimes it takes me a while to make good on my promises, but—"

"I'm not as good at waiting as I used to be," he said. "And I'm not looking forward to tomorrow."

"Me neither," I said.

Grandpa was waiting in spirit, spectral and supportive, directing me to take Roan and his lost great-grandson home.

The metallic green DOT marker proclaimed the J. H. Maloney Memorial Intersection where the four-lane ended in the foothills and the state route turned west. This was the path first taken by pioneer Maloneys and Delaneys along an ancient Cherokee trail toward Dunderry. Sitting stiffly beside Roan in the backseat of a limousine we'd hired at the Atlanta airport, I watched Matthew and Tweet, who sat across from us. He hadn't stopped gazing raptly out his window since our driver turned off the interstate. "Which Maloney was J. H.?" he asked.

Your great-grandfather, I thought furtively.

"My grandfather," I said. "Grandpa Joseph. He and some of his brothers planted the grove of willows over there behind that convenience store. Their great-grandfather built a stagecoach inn there in the late 1800s. Not long after Grandpa Joseph and his brothers planted the willows, the inn burned down, and they built a gas station and general store. He and his cousin Harriet O'Brien ran it for a few years. It was the only gas station in the county then. Daddy bought Mama a Coke at the gas station when they had their first date. Nobody suspected they were dating because he was eighteen and she was only fourteen, and your Great-Grandmother Elizabeth Delaney would have locked Mama in a cellar if she'd known about them. Daddy hid Mama under a blanket in the front seat of his Ford and—"

"Are there as many Maloneys as there are Delaneys?" Tweet asked weakly.

"More Maloneys, actually. Anyway, Grandpa Joe always claimed he knew Daddy had Marybeth Delaney stashed in the Ford, but he pretended not to notice. Daddy took Mama down to the willow grove and they drank Cokes. It was a dangerous romantic rebellion at the time."

"I need a chart to keep track of all the Delaneys," Tweet noted, laughing. "I'll have to memorize Matthew's family tree."

"Oooh, we've got charts. Lots of charts." Just not the ones you expect. She poked Roan's knee. "Tell us something interesting about the Sullivan history."

I clasped his hand, supportive and protective, and wondered if any of this was worth what it would tear down. Roan's eyes narrowed as we flashed by the Chamber of Commerce's large, handsome wooden sign set among a carefully landscaped island of azaleas and begonias.

WELCOME TO DUNDERRY, GEORGIA! A LITTLE BIT OF IRELAND IN THE MOUNTAINS! POPULATION 15,287. INCORPORATED 1839. IRENE DELANEY BOGGS, MAYOR, CITY OF DUNDERRY, HOLT T. MALONEY, DUNDERRY COUNTY COMMISSIONER.

"Bigger?" Matthew prodded, because Roan had not offered a word in response. Roan finally said, "My old man won a Silver Star in Korea."

Matthew gaped at him. I did, too. I'd never known. I don't think anyone knew. Matthew shook his head. "Why haven't you ever told me that? I mean, I knew he lost a leg in the war, but I didn't know he was a hero. What happened to his medal?"

Roan stared out the tinted limousine window, tucked my hand against his chest, gripping tightly—*A hero?* I could imagine him thinking. *They probably confused my old man with somebody else.* "I buried it with him," he said.

We weren't even home yet and the past was already catching up with him. With all of us.

Roan's crew had finished transforming the muddy, mile-long trail to Ten Jumps into a perfectly graded and graveled lane with pretty wooden bridges over the two creek crossings along its path. Small Latchakoochee EMC markers designated the new, buried power line along the road's right shoulder, along with a small sign designating an underground phone line.

I faced forward tensely as the limousine lumbered down the narrow road. A hawk sailed along in front of the car for a few yards; a woodpecker swept across the road at one point and then a half-dozen fat wild turkey hens ambled from a huckleberry thicket in front of us. It was as if every species of fowl sensed the arrival of a bird-loving friend. Tweet opened the limousine's sunroof and stood up, pounding the rooftop with her hands as she clucked at the turkey hens. "Matthew, look," she called. They traded places. "There's a couple of deer," he said, pointing. He dropped back into his seat. "Bigger, this place is incredible. I love it."

"Wait until you see the cabin and the lake," Roan said quietly. "You'll never have to ask anybody in this neighborhood for a place to stay. I fixed up the cabin so you'd have something to call your own, if you came here. If you and Tweet really like it and you want it, it's yours." Roan looked at me. I nodded, finally comprehending another reason he'd bought Ten Jumps. A person needed to own land, he thought, to be taken seriously in Dunderry. He'd bought status for himself—and more important to Roan, he'd bought status for Matthew.

"*Roan*," Tweet said tearfully, gently. Matthew reached over and affectionately shoved Roan on one arm. "This is your property, Bigger. You've always told me how you loved to explore around here."

Hid here, tried not to starve here, I thought miserably. But Matthew didn't know that history either. "No, Dunshinnog is Roan's place," I said, meeting Roan's somber, mercury-quick gaze. "The mountain. Up high. The long view. That's our special place."

When we reached the cabin, a flock of mallards rose from the lake and a tiny spotted fawn bounded after a doe who'd been nibbling the expensive sodded grass of the yard.

Matthew and Tweet exclaimed over it all and rushed from the car. They hurried down to stand at the lake, talking excitedly and gesturing at the scenery—a sanctuary of water, purple-and-gold sunset, and forest rising on mountain slopes. I wished we could lock it around us.

Roan tipped our driver and the limousine pulled away. Roan and I stood beside the luggage, sharing unspoken dread and a sense of the inevitable. The hot, soft whisper of the evening breeze crept over us. He looked at the cabin and then, for answers, at me.

More had been done since we left, and not by Wolfgang's crew. A field-stone pathway led to the porch and the yard was a kaleidoscope of freshly planted shrubs and flowers. Four white rocking chairs sat on the porch, behind hanging baskets lush with ferns.

"The family's been here." I nodded toward a late-model sedan in the yard. "You needed a car here, so Uncle Eugene sent one from his dealership."

Roan's reaction pulled away all the years for a split second and suddenly I saw him as he'd been on his birthday, the time we surprised him with a cake and gifts. The brief flash of surprise and appreciation was quickly shuttered.

"Mama and Daddy left a few gifts in the cabin, too," I told him. "I loaned them the key you gave me."

He said nothing as we went up the walkway. The door was unlocked, and when we stepped inside, we found an enormous vase of white daisies set on the fireplace hearth and the room smelling of fresh pine and cedar sachet.

We went into the newly added kitchen and I opened the refrigerator door. It was packed with food. I opened a cupboard. The shelves were stacked with handsome earthenware dishes colored in whirls of burgundy and gold. "Mama made this set of dishes. She finished them last month. She says they're the best work she's ever done. They were promised to a fine-crafts shop in North Carolina. One of the boutiques that sell her work. But she wants you to have them. 'From my hands to his heart,' she said." I faced him. "They did this for you. It's just one of the small ways they can show how they feel about you and what you did for Matthew."

He leaned against a countertop and ran his hands through his hair. We gazed out the window, watching Matthew and Tweet by the lake. "Your family may wish they'd burned this place down after they learn the truth about him," he said.

I turned away. "I need to call the farm. Mama and Daddy are waiting."

We heard the sound of a car. "They're not waiting for a call," Roan said with a tired smile. "They probably had most of the family stationed near the main roads with binoculars. Probably had Alvin's deputies hidden in the woods. They knew the second we got here."

I sagged a little. "Probably. But it's good. They're enthusiastic."

We walked outside. Mama and Daddy had just stopped their car in the yard. "I was right," Roan said. "They couldn't wait until—"

His voice trailed off as the car doors opened. Mama got out and stared, emotionally riveted, at Matthew and Tweet. Daddy stood with his legs braced apart on the cabin's new lawn, looking from them to us.

And Josh walked down the slope to the lake, toward Matthew, who gazed back along with Tweet, half smiling but obviously puzzled by the stranger headed his way.

His father. No. Not here, now, like this.

I felt as if my heart had stopped.

Roan moved so quickly, he was striding down to intercept Josh before I realized I was stumbling forward without my cane, murmuring frantically under my breath, "He doesn't know, he doesn't know," as if I could stop time with an obvious plea on Matthew's behalf.

"Mama, what do y'all think you're doing?" I called out. She reached one hand toward me and the other, ineffectually, toward Josh's back as he advanced toward Matthew. Her eyes lit up with joy and anxiety. "Honey, it'll be all right," she called to me. "We couldn't keep Josh away after he heard about Matthew, but, hon, I promise that you and Roan will understand why he's here with us after you learn the real story—"

"You know?" I stared at her. "You and Daddy already know about Josh?"

Mama stared at me in return. Then her hand rose to her mouth. She pivoted and went to Daddy. "Holt," she said urgently. "Roan and Claire know about Josh and Matthew."

Daddy shot a hard, shocked look at me, then at Roan. "Oh, my God," Daddy said, and hurried down the slope.

"You deal with me," Roan said as he reached Josh and blocked his way. "Goddammit, you talk to me first."

Josh halted, blinking. He looked dazed. His face was flushed. Larger, older, heavier than Roan, he brushed at him with a benign shove of one hand, then tried to sidestep him. He simply didn't seem to have interest or time for anything but Matthew, who stood, openmouthed, a few yards away.

Roan raised a fist and I knew he would hit my brother. I yelled something, limping forward as quickly as I could. Daddy got there first and planted himself between them. Mama went to Matthew and Tweet, holding out her graceful hands to them. "Please don't think we meant to ambush you two. This is all getting out of hand, but it's because we care so much. And there's no easy way to do this."

Matthew gave her a blank look, then bolted to Roan and Josh, shouldering in beside Daddy. "*Bigger*, I don't know what's going on, but calm down." Roan pulled Matthew aside and stepped in front of him. Daddy clamped both hands on Josh's shoulders and held him still. Josh simply continued to gaze at Matthew.

I was the one who suddenly became unhinged. Twenty years. Twenty years Roan had sacrificed for Matthew, for the family, for Josh's pride and cowardice. Twenty years lost. When I reached Josh, I grabbed his shirtfront. "Don't you dare," I ordered furiously, forestalling any rejection he might offer. "How could you? Why? *Why?*"

Josh barely flinched. Never taking his eyes off Matthew, he shook his head slowly. Mama and Tweet tried to defuse the situation, begging or ordering restraint and retreat as they pulled us all away from one another. We were a human tangle of people staggering in a tight group, trying to shield, avoid, or attack one another, until Daddy tilted his balding head back and thundered, "This is a helluva family reunion. Step back or I'll start tossing you bulls into the lake. And you, too, daughter."

Some sense was restored. We all stepped back a few inches, breathing tensely. "*Who are you?*" Matthew asked Josh.

My brother struggled to speak. "Josh," he said finally in a gruff tone. "Josh Maloney."

Slowly alarm dawned in Matthew's expression. His chin rose. "You're the one in the picture. I picked you out of an old photo Claire brought."

Painful surprise showed in Josh's eyes. "You did? God! I was right. I can just look at you and know. And you recognized *me*."

Roan spoke bitterly. "You don't owe him a damn thing, Matthew. Remember that. He has nothing to do with who you are. Don't forget everything I taught you. Nobody can take you down."

Matthew held up both hands. "Nobody can take me up, down, or sideways," he yelled, "*because I don't understand what the hell is happening here!*"

Josh nodded. He reached past Roan and clasped Matthew's shoulder. "I've tried to find you for years. This isn't the way you need to hear about it, but I couldn't wait to see you. You're not Pete Delaney's son. *You're my son.*"

Beside me, Roan sucked in a breath as if Josh had stolen his air. And in that shocked moment, that welcome we'd never expected, I saw the unexpected joy in Matthew's eyes.

Roan, dear God, saw it, too.

$\mathcal{R}$oan believed the family he'd created for himself was destroyed, almost by whimsy, in a bizarre turn of events we'd never predicted; he was a man who guarded against every possibility, but now he and his vigilance were suddenly unnecessary. In a terrible way, the best for Matthew was the worst for him.

Mama and Daddy celebrated Matthew, their firstborn grandson, in style. I knew it was an event when relatives began arriving with food and guitars. Everyone said what a blessing the reunion was and they thanked Roan, who had come full circle in their minds, sacrificing once again for the family, taking and bringing back.

A kind of break-your-heart generosity flowed. We sat in the living room, Roan and I with my parents. Mama perched beside Roan on the main couch. She clasped his hand in both of hers and he looked sadly uncomfortable about her doing it.

"I expect to be your father-in-law," Daddy told Roan. "As good, I hope, as the father you've been to Matthew."

"You couldn't be more dear to us, Roan," Mama said softly. "I know you don't believe it, but we're so sorry you thought we'd turn you and Matthew away."

"You might do it yet," Roan said.

"Stop it. Don't you ever say that again!"

I sat on Roan's other side, hardly able to take my eyes off him. He met my gaze. In him I saw that hard inner frame he'd kept from his childhood, and I think he saw the same stubborn strength in me. Roan looked at Mama and Daddy, his head up, his face strained.

"He's my family," Roan announced gruffly, holding his fist over his heart. "I never tried to make him hate anybody here, but I told him the truth. I told him the good as much as the bad. I taught him to build his own life so he wouldn't ever feel empty if he came back here and found nothing and nobody who cared about him. So he doesn't hate any of you. He just doesn't know you. Whether he decides to hate you—that's his business."

"He'll be fine," Mama insisted, "if we give him a chance. And so will you, Roan."

And so a mostly unspoken understanding was settled between my parents and Roan.

Matthew responded to his homecoming welcome with blind fervor. Suddenly he and Tweet had more family than they'd ever imagined, and they were both drunk with pleasure. So was Josh.

Many people said Josh had suffered enough for denying Matthew years before—his guilt, his shame, his worry. When his wife died after Amanda's birth, he felt cursed, I suppose, and he withdrew from Amanda's affection because what man could take himself seriously as a father to one child when the memory of a rejected one burned in his conscience? We finally understood his coldness and his moods.

But I didn't sympathize. Matthew had nearly been lost because of him. Roan was the only reason we had him back. Roan had suffered for his dedication. I had, too, in different ways. All because of Josh. "When did you and Daddy first suspect?" I asked Mama that night.

She bowed her head. "You remember the time we had the big work party to restore the Delaney bridge and Sally showed up with Matthew? Well, I'm sure you were too little to pay attention to Sally and Josh, but your daddy and I watched her stare at Josh as if she wanted to scald him. And she held Matthew up toward Josh, and Josh was so upset he nearly fell off the roof of the bridge. He dropped the tool he was holding . . ." Mama went on about our cousin Robert getting hit on the head. I said nothing.

Mama and Daddy couldn't believe what they'd witnessed meant what they feared it meant, and for a while each was too uncertain and too upset to admit the fear. Then it was too late—Sally disappeared in the aftermath of Big Roan's scandal and Josh confided the truth, and for years they'd quietly helped him search. They'd hired investigators through Uncle Ralph's legal contacts, but no information had ever turned up.

They had always looked for Sally and Matthew McClendon, of course, or Matthew Delaney. Never for Matthew Sullivan.

On the night we brought Matthew to the farm, lights glowed from every window of the house, cars filled the yard and the driveway, and dozens of Maloneys and Delaneys gathered on the porches and under the trees, deep in conversation. The other grandchildren swarmed around Matthew, some shy but all curious. From teenagers to toddlers, they were all introduced. Amanda was the only one missing. She'd gone with Rebecca's daughters to summer camp, a few hours' away, for a week. The issue of how Josh should tell her about her half brother had been thoroughly debated already.

And how to thank Roan—that was debated, too.

"I know what brand of honor it took for you to come here after all this time and risk this," Daddy said to him. "You were armed for trouble and instead you got a kick in the stomach you never expected. But nobody's turning their backs on you this time. Not Matthew and not us."

"We kept Josh's secret because he grieved over it and wanted to make it right," Mama told him. "We're not washing our hands of his guilt. We know who did right when it counted. I'll never look at Matthew without knowing the truth. Everything fine about him is your doing."

"We'll do everything we can to make up for the time he's missed," Daddy added. "And we'll do the same for you."

Roan, who was quietly devastated, said, "I only want one promise from you. From the whole family. I don't want anybody to tell him anything about me. Nothing. Don't tell him about my old man, the Hollow, what happened, nothing. I have to be the one to tell him."

Mama and Daddy promised.

"We have to work the boy out of his loneliness," Daddy said to me in a private moment. He and Mama were upset. "Get him talking about the past. Get it settled. Get that poison out of him. And out of us, too."

In the meantime, Matthew had a fine homecoming party.

It was already clear that he and Tweet could fit into the pattern of the family as tightly as a new seam. Every Maloney aunt and uncle came to the same conclusion that night—summed up out loud by Arnetta, who had not given many compliments inside the family since Uncle Eugene divorced her to marry his secretary at the car dealership. "The boy couldn't have turned out any better if he'd been brought up here by his own people," Arnetta announced in front of Roan.

His own people. An embarrassed hush followed that statement. Roan smiled thinly and walked outside. "How could you?" I said to Aunt Arnetta. And to the rest, "I'm ashamed of you all."

I followed Roan to the veranda. "Time to regroup," I ordered, snagging his hand as I shoved aside the curious farm dogs with my cane. "We're going to the barn loft."

"Just like old times," he said.

He had to carry me up the staircase, but we made it. I sat on a bale of hay. He stood, leaning against the door frame, looking out at Dunshinnog under the stars. "The view hasn't changed." He sounded defeated.

"You're wrong. Nothing's the same, and it's because of you."

"I raised Matthew. I fed him, put clothes on him, educated him, stood up for him, and now I bring him here and it's as if I never existed."

"No. Give everyone time to sort through it. Nobody meant to patronize you tonight."

"You can't change their reaction to me," he said wearily. "I don't doubt I did the right thing by bringing Matthew here. They want him. They don't really want anything to do with me, but they want him. And God knows it's clear he's where *he* needs to be. He found out his old man didn't really desert him. That's powerful medicine."

"*You're* his old man."

"No. I never was. I forgot that fact sometimes, but it was always in the back of my mind."

"You think he'll blame you about Josh? You didn't know Josh was looking for him. Matthew won't fault you for not telling him about Josh."

He turned, dropped to his heels in front of me, and took my hands. "I wish I had your faith." He lifted my hands to his face, kissed the palms, rested his cheeks against my fingertips.

I kissed him. "You're in so much pain you don't know what you wish."

He bent his head to my knees and I slid my hands over his hair. We heard heavy footsteps on the loft stairs. Roan stood quickly.

Josh made his way among the tiers of stacked bales and stopped by the door. He and Roan were both silhouetted by stars. "Roan, I believe you'd give me a fighting chance before you pushed me out this loft door," he said in a big, jovial voice. "But I think Sis would push me from behind and never shed a tear."

"You're damned right," I said slowly. "Are you turning this into a joke?"

"No, just trying to ease the tension with humor."

"Stop it. I know a shit-eating politician when I see one. I used to interview guys like you. All mouth and no action."

Josh shifted angrily. "That's enough, sis."

"Enough? We're supposed to hug and smile and stand in a prayer circle holding hands because you had the guts to welcome your own son home after Roan took care of him for two decades?"

"I'm not asking for any parenting awards. Roan, I give you full credit. I'll never be able to do enough to thank you."

Roan moved quietly, warningly, toward my brother. "I don't want any thanks from you. I want answers. Tell me why you used Sally. Besides the obvious reason."

Josh leaned against the loft door, his head down and his hands shoved into his pockets. He gazed blankly into the night sky. "Sis, do you remember the night I came home from the army? When the family came down to Atlanta to pick me up at the airport?"

"Yes." I remembered Daddy carrying me on his shoulders down the Delta concourse, a crowd of Maloneys around us, and that we were dressed up in the middle of the night. I felt so proud because Mama had given me a long-stemmed red rose to hand to Josh, and Grandpa had whittled the thorns off with his pocketknife. I was so excited I waved that rose at everyone we walked past. I was so proud of Josh. We all were.

"As I was getting off the plane," Josh went on, "one of the other passengers asked me if I'd been in 'Nam. When I said yes, he spit on me. Called me a killer."

"What did you do?"

"I wiped the spit off my jacket so the folks wouldn't notice."

"Oh, Josh."

"I respect your support of Roan. I'm ashamed to admit I was one of the ones who agreed with the folks when he was a boy, after he killed Big Roan. That he'd be better off somewhere else. I didn't want him to be spit on for doing the right thing. Now it looks like he's the one who intends to do the spitting."

"I'm not here to prove any point," Roan said. "And I'm not here to listen to your self-pitying stories. People misunderstood you, so you treated Sally like dirt? Is that it?"

"I didn't know how to act around the family anymore." Josh spoke in a low, strained voice. "I couldn't talk to anybody about Vietnam—the things I saw, the way I lived. I had habits I wasn't proud of, and bad dreams, and . . . But when I came back home everybody expected me to want one of the nice girls I'd dated in high school. I didn't even remember who I was, though, for a while. Sally seemed . . . uncomplicated. But after a few times my mind started to clear. I looked into her eyes once and saw that she *hated* me. Despised me. Like the bar girls in Saigon had. That's when I realized I was trying to make life as ugly here as it was there, so I'd have excuses. I knew I had to get myself under control, try to figure out a new place for myself at home. I had to forget."

I snorted. "You could have done better than forget you had a son."

He pivoted toward me. "Look, sis, at first I wasn't even certain he was *mine*. I'd been careful with Sally. Not perfect, but careful. I thought there was a good chance he was Pete's boy, like everyone assumed. He might have been. I told myself that. And Sally had other . . . customers, too." Josh paused. "I told myself he could be Big Roan Sullivan's son."

"I wish he was," Roan replied flatly. "He'd be my half brother. I'd have a blood tie to him. I wouldn't have had to hide him. I could have brought him back a long time ago. I could have told Claire, and Claire and I . . ."

Josh nodded. "I understand what you say, Roan. If he was your brother, you could tell us all to go to hell. And you would."

"Yes."

I hunched forward. "You were *sure* about Matthew that day at the Delaney bridge."

"I was sure, sis. Yeah. I was sure. I spent too much time debating what the embarrassment would do to Mama and Daddy. And to me. My plans. A lot of gutless debating," he added sarcastically. "I did manage to tell the folks. I did that on my own, sis. But I told 'em after everything went crazy around here that summer. Big Roan . . . Daisy McClendon screaming nonsense about Sally, threatening to say what she knew . . . and Sally had already disappeared with Matthew."

"Lucky for you," I shot back.

He tossed both hands into the air and yelled, "There hasn't been a goddamned day since then that I haven't thought about him, sis. Wondered where he was, if he'd starved or been hurt, if he was in prison somewhere, or dead."

"Good. *Good*," I yelled back. "I spent twenty years torturing myself over Roan for the same kind of reasons. I'm glad you know how it felt."

Josh's arms sank limply by his sides. "I couldn't look at Amanda without thinking of Matthew."

"What are you going to tell her now?"

"That she's got a half brother. That he's terrific. That no matter how he came into the world he's part of the family and we're going to love him." Josh pivoted slowly toward Roan. "And we're going to do our best to convince him to stay in Dunderry."

Roan went absolutely still—that lethal quiet I remembered so well. "He's got friends on the West Coast," he said finally. "That's his home turf. I doubt he'll change all his plans."

"I'd just appreciate it if you wouldn't try to influence him."

"Don't you dare," I said in a low, furious tone. "Don't you *dare* lecture Roan and dismiss him like a deliveryman. As if he's been some kind of hired surrogate whose job is done and now we can all just go merrily—"

"That's not what I meant, sis, goddammit, and you know it. *Roan*. You're going to have to do what I did when I came home from the army. Make a new place for yourself. I want you to do that."

"I don't need your permission."

"Oh, hell, you're welcome around here. You don't want to believe it, but you are. Ask Claire to marry you. Settle down. You'll be close to Matthew. Keep being what you've been to him. But understand that we'll have to come to terms about that. You've known since he was a kid that I was his father. Accept the new situation." Josh tapped Roan on the chest. "You're not his father. I am."

Roan swayed, his fists clenched by his sides. Josh thrust out his chin, and they stared at each other. I lurched to my feet and nearly fell over as I slammed a hand into the meaty hummock of my brother's shoulder. Roan caught me by the arms and pulled me to him. He wrapped his arms around me because I was struggling to get at Josh. "You want to threaten somebody, big brother? Threaten me."

"Claire, for God's sake." Josh sighed.

"Come on. *Come on*."

"You knew." Matthew's voice came out of the shadows. Josh, Roan, and I turned quickly. Matthew stepped into an aisle between walls of hay bales. "I didn't intend to spy," he said in a strained tone. "It's just that you were all so busy arguing, you didn't notice when I walked upstairs."

My heart twisted. He moved forward, his arms rigidly crossed over his chest, his shoulders hunched. He halted before Roan, who released me. I moved aside but watched Roan worriedly. Matthew stared at him. "You knew Pete Delaney wasn't my father, and you knew Josh Maloney *was*," he accused. His voice quivered. "You knew when I was a kid, but you didn't tell me. How could you lie to me like that?"

Roan grabbed him by the shoulders. "Listen to me. I thought there was nothing worth coming back to here. I thought it was kinder to let you think your old man was dead. I thought it was safer."

"*You lied to me*. Nobody deserves to make that decision for another person. I trusted you. I always trusted you. But you let me think I had nobody but you."

"Matthew," I said hoarsely. "Don't jump to conclusions—"

"One phone call," Matthew went on, his head tilted back. He studied Roan in anguish. "Or even one letter. That was all you needed to write. You could have found out I was wanted here. We could have come back."

"This family might have taken you away from me. I had no legal rights. Josh could have shipped you off to a foster home. Or put you up for adoption. It's easy for you to stand here now and say he wouldn't have done that, but that's not a risk I was willing to take."

"You couldn't risk it? You couldn't risk some simple contact with the Maloneys to find out *for my sake?* What did they ever do to you to deserve that kind of judgment? *Nothing.* You taught me to trust people, to give them a fair chance to prove themselves, but *you've* never trusted anybody. You never gave this family a chance to prove anything to you or to me."

"You see them a different way than I do. Good. I want you to. Hindsight is easy. Enjoy it."

"That's not an answer."

"That's all you're going to get right now."

Roan still gripped Matthew's shoulders. Matthew shoved his hands away. "There's no excuse for what you did to me. You could have told me who I was when I was old enough. You could have let me decide whether I wanted to meet my biological father. But you didn't want anything to do with these people and you made the same choice for me. *Let's get this straight. You don't have the right to make choices for me anymore.*"

"Make your own choices then. Tell me what you intend to do."

Matthew inhaled sharply. He looked miserable, but I didn't feel sorry for him at that moment. He had hurt Roan for unwarranted sins, and he didn't understand the depth of that betrayal. "Tweet and I are going to get to know the family. My grandparents. My little sister." He looked at Josh, who seemed subdued by victory. "And my father." Matthew stared at Roan. "If you don't like that, you don't have to be a part of it."

Tell him, I begged Roan silently. *Tell him why you lost faith in the family. Tell him what happened to you and me.*

But Roan stood there offering nothing, no excuses or apologies, while the starlight over Dunshinnog faded in Matthew's unforgiving eyes.

17

*M*atthew and Tweet settled into a big corner bedroom at the farm, a room that was part of the oldest core of the house.

I was right about Tweet. She loved chickens, but she ate them, too. Matthew loved everything that walked, crawled, swam, or flew on the farm. He and she were outdoors half the time, exploring.

Mama and Daddy pulled out all the stops to surround them with the largesse of that sunny room in the main house of the Maloney clan. There were dinner parties with my brothers and their families, all done up in their prosperous best, the wives smelling like the latest Neiman Marcus catalog.

Matthew and Tweet were made the center of attention among the glimmering antique silver and crystal and china of the dining room, summer flowers bursting from vases at every turn, generations of well-kept heirloom furniture and knickknacks polished for inspection, a family story waiting to be told with each one.

Roan and I stayed away.

My brother proudly introduced Matthew around Dunderry, wined and dined him constantly, and showered him and Tweet with presents that ranged from a set of Depression-glass bowls Josh had inherited from Great-Gran to fifty acres of prime land in the north end of Dunderry County and a full membership at the country club.

"It's embarrassing," Daddy told everyone angrily. "He's trying to buy instant respect from the boy." Mama told her sisters Matthew obviously appreciated Josh's sincerity but wasn't impressed by money. "That's because

Roan raised Matthew around money, with money—it's nothing new to him," I emphasized to everyone who'd listen. "He's not a hick. He's not going to be dazzled. Josh can buy his attention, but he can't buy his love."

To which Renfrew replied dourly, "But your brother sure is makin' a down payment on it."

Josh took Matthew and Tweet to Atlanta, where they were the guests of honor at a cocktail party Josh threw for them at his apartment. He didn't tell Matthew about his longtime relationship with the Vietnamese-American Lin Su, who was out of town on business. She wasn't a fatherly subject to share with a new son—a girlfriend who was only slightly older than he. Instead Josh squired Matthew around the state capitol, introducing him to his legislature cronies, to the lieutenant governor, and finally even to the governor.

"Matthew handled the meeting beautifully," Josh reported to Brady, who told me. "I couldn't have been more impressed. He's well-spoken, well-informed, good with people. And so's Millie." Josh didn't refer to Tweet as Tweet. I guess he thought her nickname was undignified. "My son's a natural-born people person."

Natural born. Josh really didn't want to believe that Roan had done a good job raising Matthew, a better job, probably, than he himself would have done. I took grim satisfaction in telling Brady to mention that Roan's social circles included a senator and two ex-governors of Washington State. That Matthew hadn't grown up in a cultural vacuum.

But nothing really mattered except the silence and distance growing deeper every day between Roan and Matthew.

Roan walked the woods obsessively. My leg wasn't strong enough for me to go along, and he didn't want me to, anyway, which hurt me. He said he had to be alone, and I told him he was forgetting we shared the same past and future. We didn't have much else to say to each other during those days. I was worried and depressed.

He couldn't be still when we were at the cabin together. He didn't eat much, he didn't sleep well, and when we reached for each other in bed we were wild, hurried, explosive together, but miserably quiet afterward.

Every day he roamed from the lake to the Hollow and all the land he owned on either side, stretching from Cap's Ridge on the west to Soap Falls and the Hollow on the east, to the back of Uncle Bert's farm on the north and the boundary of Kehoe property on the south, a huge block of wilderness pushing into the settled territory around it. He lost himself in the creeks and springs, the gullies and ridges and rocky overhangs, and the Hollow, with its buried corpses of junk.

"What are you looking for?" I asked gently, knowing that he was try-ing to make peace with what he'd been and what he'd done as a boy. What he had to tell Matthew about himself.

"Answers," he said.

He brought me wildflowers and turtle shells, birds' nests and interest-ing rocks, as if we were still kids. I cooked food we didn't eat and read box after box of his wonderful but emotionally exhausting letters to me, years of conversation to fill the void. I sat at a table in the gazebo with the boxes scattered around me, stacks of letters anchored by turtle shells and rocks, my chin propped on one fist while I read for hours at a time, tears stream-ing down my face.

He caught me at it once, and the scene upset him worse than anything I could have said. Not knowing how else to help each other, we lay down in the shade of the water oaks and eventually made love. He owned his mis-ery and he owned mine.

The next morning Josh brought Amanda home from summer camp and told her, during the drive back, about Matthew. When Josh introduced them, Matthew presented Amanda with a beautiful gold bracelet bearing a small, round charm inscribed LOVE TO MY SISTER. Tweet wasn't the only one who cried sentimental tears over that.

But Amanda shook her brother's hand formally and offered him and Tweet nothing warmer than the crystalline, blue-eyed stare I had taught her that spring while I was bedridden, and an hour later, when Josh and Mama checked on her in her upstairs bedroom, her window was open and she was gone. I'd also made the mistake of telling her how I used to climb down the jasmine trellis when I was her age.

She left a note on her pillow.

Dear Papa,
You never show off for me like you do for Matthew. You never tell everybody how proud I make you. I guess you have just been waiting to get Matthew back. He's a boy. Now I understand why you don't love me. I'm not good enough. I'm not a boy.

Good Bye and Best Wishes,
Most Sincerely,
Amanda Elizabeth Maloney

· · ·

The entire family spent the next six hours frantically searching for her in the woods and the roads around the farm. Alvin called in sheriff's deputies from all the neighboring counties, horseback teams, search dogs, and forest rangers. Roan and I went up in the Cessna and scoured every pasture, meadow, and mountaintop in a ten-mile radius.

Late that afternoon we landed on the small dirt airstrip Roan had installed at Ten Jumps. Amanda was sitting on the cabin's front porch.

Her face was swollen from crying. She clutched a cellular phone and a pink knapsack in her lap. She was dirty and disheveled, wearing sandals, denim shorts, and a striped T-shirt; her bare arms and legs were streaked with red lines from briar scratches, her red hair was snarled with twigs and leaves. She had a look of intense little-girl desolation, but when we reached her, she peered up at us with a flat, resolute mouth. "You won't tell anybody I'm here, will ya? This is a safe place." She focused on Roan. "Aunt Claire says this was always your safe hiding place. So you won't jinx it by telling on me, huh?"

"It'd be wrong to turn a needy girl out of Ten Jumps," Roan agreed solemnly. "You can stay here as long as you want."

I glanced at him reproachfully as he helped me sit down beside her. I put my arm around her. "I liked your running-away-from-home letter," I said. "Polite but to the point. Good technical skills as well as a snazzy style. I think you're ready for a promotion. You're ready to write a coming-back-home letter."

Roan sat down on a porch step below ours with one leg drawn up, and Amanda gazed at him tearfully. "I heard you wrote a lot of letters to Aunt Claire. Did you write her a coming-back-home one?"

A child's sincerity in unhappiness brings memories of corrupted innocence. Roan and I traded somber looks. "Not yet," he said.

"Then I won't write one to Papa. You don't have a kid anymore. So I'll stay here and be your kid."

I nudged her gently. "What did your papa tell you about Matthew?"

"Papa said he had a girlfriend a long time before he met my mama and they made Matthew together, but they weren't married, and she went away when Matthew was still a little boy. And then she died and Roan took care of Matthew. And Papa's sorry he didn't take care of Matthew himself and now he wants to."

"Then you understand why you have a brother?"

"Yeah. Half a brother. We've got the same papa. I get it." She fumbled with the phone and the bag. "Papa's all excited about him. He doesn't need me anymore."

"Oh, honey," I said. "That's not true."

"He's never gotten all excited about *me*." She gazed at Roan with her mouth trembling. "Don't you want Matthew anymore?"

"That's not the problem, and of course I . . ." Roan halted, and looked away, clearing his throat.

"In a way, Matthew has two fathers now," I finished quickly, my own throat burning. "He has Roan and he has your papa. But I'm sure he wants to have a little sister, too!"

"Doesn't need a little sister," she replied with a wild shake of her head. "He's got two papas. It's not fair. I don't see why he's stayin' with us when Roan's his papa. You got him first," she said pointedly to Roan. "Why don't you keep him?"

"He needs to spend time with his family."

"I thought you came back for Aunt Claire because *she's* your family, and that means *all* of us are your family, and so you oughta spend time with Matthew, too. I think you oughta take him someplace else and spend time with him. Then Papa and me could visit him. I think that'd be the right thing to do. Great-Grandma Dottie says he'll feel like a stranger till it all gets straightened out anyhow."

I hugged her. "Everyone's looking for you. May I at least borrow your phone and tell your papa you haven't been kidnapped by space aliens?"

"I don't want to go back." She cried softly. "I really do want to have my own daddy, just mine. If people can switch around like y'all say, then I'll switch, too. Because I bet Roan's a good papa. Matthew looks like he got plenty to eat and all that. So I'm going to live with Roan." She looked at me. "And you can be my mama. I know you like me. I won't be any trouble. I promise."

"I have to call your papa. He loves you. I'm sure he wouldn't let anybody else in the world have you."

"He let Roan have Matthew. For a *long* time."

"He didn't know I had Matthew," Roan told her slowly. "I thought it was a good idea for me to take care of Matthew, but I didn't understand that his . . . your papa was looking for him."

"I—I don't care. You need a kid. *Somebody* oughta need *me*. Don't you?"

This was tearing our hearts out and getting us nowhere. I warned Roan with a glance. Then, brusque and helpful, I told Amanda, "All right, we'll let your papa know you're going to live with us. But since you don't want to see him anymore, we should probably go live somewhere else. So you can forget about him. Where should we live, Roan?"

He nodded. "Oh, I don't know. Why don't the three of us get in my plane and I'll fly us, oh, north. Canada. I've heard Canada's nice. I'd say it's far enough away that Amanda couldn't get back home even if she changes her mind. Hmmm. Canada."

Amanda gaped at us, swinging her attention from him to me. She broke down in sobs. "I thought we could j-just live here! I don't want to go to C-Canada!"

I rocked her in my arms. "Maybe you should think about it—at home—and decide later."

"Maybe Papa might want me to stay. He wants Matthew to stay."

"He wants both of you," Roan said. "Just the way I would, if I was your papa."

She threw herself at him, and this man, who had raised a child and exuded more paternal sweetness than he'd admit to and more than Matthew remembered for now, carefully folded her in his arms and picked her up, then held out a hand to me and helped me up.

And we took her home.

Our arrival brought Josh running from the house with a forestry-service map in his hands. "Here she is!" Daddy bellowed from the door of his office in the main barn. Mama ran out onto the veranda with a phone still clutched in her hand. Matthew and Tweet climbed out of a muddy truck and ran to us, looking more lost than found themselves. Matthew's face was stern and gaunt, and so much like my brother's that I couldn't bear to watch Roan watch him.

"Why did you leave home?" Josh growled to Amanda, dropping to one knee before her. She stood at attention, her tote bag hanging from one shoulder like a soft pink animal she'd captured. "Roan and Claire said I could live with them. I could be Roan's little girl. But Aunt Claire said I oughta think about it some more."

Josh fired a furious look at Roan and me. I shook my head slightly. Roan offered no reaction other than a thin smile. "You scared me," Josh said to Amanda, taking her gently by the shoulders.

A tremor went through her. Her eyes widened. "I did? How?"

"I haven't been very nice to you, have I? I know it. I felt so . . . worried about where Matthew was when he was growing up, because I didn't know if he was all right and it was my fault he was lost. I didn't tell everyone he was my son when he was a little boy. If I had, his mother wouldn't have taken him away. I made a mistake and I felt bad about it."

"So I wasn't good enough to make you not feel bad?"

"Baby, you've been so good I was afraid I didn't deserve to have you. I loved your mother so much, and I was afraid I didn't deserve her either. That doesn't make any sense, does it?"

"I didn't want to make you afraid."

"Now I have a chance to be a good daddy to you and Matthew. I'm going to try."

"Because you want Matthew to forgive you for losing him."

"Yes, I do. But that won't be enough if you don't try to forgive me, too. If you'll promise to try, I'll promise to be better."

She wavered, then suddenly exploded with smiles. "I promise." She put her arms around him and he hugged her with a fierce affection he'd never shown before. "But—" Amanda turned a crumbling expression up toward Roan. "What's gonna happen to Roan? I promised him—"

"No, no," Roan said quickly. "It's all right if you change your mind. I understand."

"But you oughta have—"

"Let's discuss this later," Mama said with alarm. She hurried over and held down a hand to Amanda. "Come on, hon, let's go get your face washed. You come inside with me. Come on."

Josh kissed her cheek. "Okay," she said, and went with her grandmother.

Once she was safely inside the front door, Josh stood. I said without much sympathy, jerking my head toward the house, "You've got a lot of work to do with her. You only primed the pump."

He scowled. "I know that. Roan, why the hell did you tell Amanda she could stay with you?"

"It didn't happen quite the way she described it."

"I don't care how it happened. That's low, Roan. Are you trying to alienate my little girl the same way you came between Claire and the family? You stole one of my children for twenty years and now you're trying to steal another one?"

Roan punched him. It happened quickly, a recoil and release that slammed into Josh's mouth and knocked him on his back. Roan loomed over him, feet braced apart, his fist drawn back again. "Claire's all I ever wanted from this goddamned family," Roan said.

"Easy, boy, easy," I urged softly, darting glances at Matthew, who leaped forward, slack-jawed with horror as he stood halfway between Roan and Josh. "He deserved that, Matthew," I added.

Daddy said, "All right, all right, that's done." He pushed Roan back carefully. "That needed to be done. Roan, you hear me? He had it coming. But it's done. Back off."

Josh groggily raised a hand to his bloody lower lip. He nodded. "Fair enough," he said.

Roan remained on guard until he noticed Matthew's humiliated stare. When Matthew dropped to one knee beside Josh and offered to help him up, Roan's fist unfurled in defeat.

Roan and I went to Dunshinnog that night, gathered a small pile of limbs on the mountain's stony brow, and sat beside it, watching the fire burn to embers.

"Read this one," Roan said, handing me an old letter he pulled from his pants pocket. "He was maybe ten years old when I wrote it."

You ever hit anybody? he asked me today. He's in trouble for popping a kid in the mouth at school. The kid knows Matthew's adopted. Teases him about it. Matthew had enough. So he knocked one of the kid's front teeth out.

He thought I'd be mad. I had to pretend I was. Did I ever hit anybody? Not since I grew up, I told him. Hell, I was in some ugly fights when I worked at the chop shop, but he doesn't know about that. I lied—wanted to set a good example.

I told him there's only two good reasons to hit somebody. To protect another person from getting hit, or if you've got no other way to protect yourself. I said I have no respect for people who hit for any other reason. Any fool can hit. The people who don't hit—they're the people with real power. They're the smart people. Be one of them, I told him.

I paid the other kid's dentist bill. I told Matthew he'd have to pay me back out of his allowance because I want him to understand that you always have to pay, somehow, when you hurt other people. Even if they had it coming.

And I promised him if he'd never hit anybody without good reason I'd never hit anybody again either. We shook on it.

I learned a lot from you, Claire. I learned what I'd missed, and I learned what I wanted. In a way, your folks taught me how to raise myself and how to raise Matthew. Funny. I learned the most from the people who hurt me the worst. The people I loved.

I put the letter down. "You didn't break a sacred vow today," I said gently. "You didn't even break any teeth."

"I've worked all my life to be different from my old man. Matthew was ashamed of me today. I saw the look on his face."

"You've got to talk to him, Roan. Tell him. Tell him everything."

In the dark, the tip of a cigar glowed between Roan's fingers. Ashes scattered across his shirt and fell. "Next thing he'll do," Roan said slowly, "is change his last name. He'll stop calling himself Sullivan." He threw the cigar in the fire. I put a hand on his chest.

"Warm," I whispered. "A good, solid rhythm. So many people care about this heart."

"You can't imagine how it feels, can you? To not have family. I can. I don't know another Sullivan in the world who's related to me."

"We'll research your family tree then. Believe me, you're related to thousands of Sullivans."

"You know that's not what I mean. Real family. Not names on a chart."

I took his right hand and smoothed the swollen, broken skin along his knuckles. "I do understand. You need to look into the faces of Sullivan grandparents, uncles, aunts, brothers, sisters, cousins, and see yourself."

"I want to be part of a family. That's the hell of it. I want to see someone like me looking back at me."

I sat for a minute, lost in thought. "I want to have children with you," I said finally, softly.

He quickly turned to me and took my face between his hands. "We'll have good children. I know it. I think about it."

"But you want somebody to give twenty years back to you. Erase everything that happened to me and to you. That's not possible."

"This situation isn't going to work out. For Matthew, for me, for the rest of the family."

I drew back, watching him, the dread rising in my throat. I shook my head. "I know what you're trying to avoid. But if you don't tell him the truth about Big Roan, he'll hear it from other people. You *have* to trust *him*."

"I'll tell him soon. He'll never look at me the same way again. I know that. If I stay here, I'll ruin everything for him. We're going to have to make some hard decisions. You and me. Maybe we could travel for a while, let things settle down . . ."

We'll never come back, I thought desperately. I'll never get you back here.

We had to find a way back to achieve a way forward; Roan was not far enough from that boy who'd lived in the Hollow, hiding his fear and pain behind pride, and I was still the shadow of the little girl who'd tried to change his life; we had to get past those memories. "When we were kids," I said slowly, "there were times when I was ashamed for you, but there was never a time when I was ashamed of you. You always fought for me, and I fought for you. Matthew will feel that way once he knows everything."

"If he doesn't—" Roan continued.

I pressed my fingertips to his mouth. "Have some faith," I said.

I went over to the farm to see Mama and Grandma Dottie. "Get Tweet for me," I told them. "Just get her away from Josh and Matthew for an afternoon. We're going to talk." Mama was fired with grim agreement; Grandma Dottie chain-smoked and nodded.

When I met Tweet the next day, we hugged sadly. I drove her up to the top of Dunshinnog. We sat on the rock ledge overlooking the valley. Muggy June heat cloaked the afternoon; I could feel my surgeon's prediction of arthritis in my healing leg.

"Matthew's not too happy about me visiting with you today," she admitted. "He thinks Roan's sent you to ask him to apologize. I'm sorry, Claire, but Matthew doesn't have anything to apologize for."

"Roan's not waiting for an apology. But he doesn't owe Matthew one either."

Tweet shoved her hands into her straw-mop hair as if she wanted to sweep her mind clean. "You don't protect adopted people by hiding their identity from them! It's not fair! It causes more problems than it solves."

I stared out over the valley and quietly told her how Roan grew up. About the Hollow. How Big Roan really died and why. And what the family did to Roan afterward. When I finished, Tweet was pale and dry-eyed. That was the past's powerful effect. It dried Tweet up. She was speechless for a while.

I told her Matthew knew us—the family—well enough now. He could see that we were neither all good nor all bad, that there was kindness and generosity in us. All he had to do was study the proud, ruthless, unsmiling portraits of tough Sean and Bridget Maloney to understand the clannishness that had helped us prosper. But he needed to see the Hollow, too, where Roan had survived to become the imperfect, self-made, endlessly devoted man Matthew wanted to dismiss. He needed to understand the place Roan had won and lost in our family because of the family's pride.

"What do you want me to do?" Tweet asked urgently. "Poor Roan. This explains so much about him. How can I help?"

"You can't. And neither can I. It's up to him. Let's leave it alone a while," I told her. "That's all I can think to do."

"Oh, Claire," she began to murmur. "He's got to tell Matthew." She looked at me with sorrow and sympathy. "Now I understand Roan, but I understand you, too."

I craned my head warily. "My dear Tweetie Bird, there's nothing mysterious to understand about *me*."

"Until you get this resolved, you won't trust yourself again."

"What? Now hold on—"

"You won't really be *home* again yourself unless Roan stays. And if he insists he doesn't belong here, you'll go away with him, because you'll always be trying to make it right for him. I bet you were thinking about Roan when you got involved with the problems that woman—"

"Terri Caulfield," I said tightly. "Look, don't use that to analyze me—"

"You think you failed Roan again, and you'll always feel you failed him if this isn't settled. If you can't keep him here, you'll go wherever he wants, even if it breaks his heart and yours, too."

I felt the blood draining from my face; Tweet was looking at me the way she'd look at a blind owl caged at a wildlife sanctuary, as if I were hopelessly trapped. "He's not going anywhere," I said loudly.

"Oh, Claire," she soothed. She patted my hand.

Josh took Matthew and Tweet on a tour of the local farms. They happened to be at Uncle Winston's when one of his Black Angus cows was struggling with a breech birth and they delivered her twin calves. When Dr. Radcliff—Dunderry's aging veterinarian and a cousin of Mama's—arrived a few minutes later, he was very impressed.

"He's a whopper. She's little but she's strong," Dr. Radcliff raved to Winston and Josh. He was talking about Matthew and Tweet I decided, or perhaps them and the calves as well. At any rate, the event started a series of discussions about the two of them interning at Dr. Radcliff's veterinary practice with an understanding that they'd buy the practice when he retired in a couple of years.

I heard this news and had to be the one to break it to Roan. I talked him into driving to the city park at the Delaney covered bridge. We sat on a blanket in the bridge's shade, our feet inches from the river beneath it. Roan contemplated an unlit cigar in his hand, tossed it aside, and said, "You're tugging your ears and giving me the blue-eye. Just tell me. Whatever it is, just tell me."

I stalled. "Everybody who grew up in this town came here at least once when they were teenagers. It's the oldest make-out spot in the county. But you and I never got a chance. Goddammit, we deserve it." I thrust out one hand. "Come on."

He frowned but took my hand and helped me up. I leaned on my cane and made my way up the grassy shoulder to the road. We stepped inside the shadowy tunnel of fragrant wood and faced each other. He laid the cane aside and latched his arms low behind my back. "It's not much of a notorious place in broad daylight," I began, losing the words when he kissed me.

"How's that for notorious?" he asked several minutes later. We sagged against each other, breathless. "Tell me," he repeated.

I did, and when I finished, with the river bubbling below us, the lazy song of insects droning in our ears, and the hot, ripe sunshine seeping through the fine cracks in the wooden roof over our heads, Roan said quietly, "It's done then. Matthew's staying. There's not a damn thing I can do about it. Except get out of his way."

18

We woke the next morning at Ten Jumps with thunder rumbling in the distance and the air hot and oppressive, charged in the heavy way of summer storms. We dressed hurriedly in old jeans and T-shirts. Roan frowned at the low, bruised clouds above the bedroom's skylight as he knelt by the bed and wordlessly pulled my bare feet onto his thighs. He slid my tennis shoes on my feet while I pushed a dark wisp of hair from his forehead. "We have to talk about the future," he said.

"Let's just deal with the present. Check the weather."

We went to the porch. I leaned on my cane and surveyed the scene, with a knot of concern in my stomach. The birds and insects were silent. There was no breeze. Lightning flickered in short pulses, and the sky to the east was turning an ominous purple-black. "I don't like this," I said.

Roan unhooked the hanging baskets of ferns and set them on the ground along the porch's stone foundation, then put each rocking chair on its forward tips with the headrests against the porch rail. He tapped the flat, deep chestnut logs of the cabin's front wall. "This cabin is built like a concrete bunker. It won't even shiver in a high wind."

How he knew that, from childhood, brought images of him huddled alone inside the dank and cobwebbed haven. "I'm going back in," I said. "I've got goosebumps and my bad knee aches. I'm turning into a human barometer."

The phone rang as I hobbled through the front room. Daddy was calling, with Mama on an extension, quoting the weather reports and urging us to come over to the farm. "What about Matthew and Tweet?" Roan called with strained inquiry.

"They're with Josh. He took them and Amanda to brunch at the club."

Roan's expression hardened; he looked away. "We're fine here," I told my parents, and quickly said good-bye in the middle of their protests. I followed Roan outside again. "Afraid?" he asked with a grim smile.

"No worse than usual."

Roan took my hand and pulled me into his arms; we braced ourselves in the growing darkness. I didn't know how much time passed; the morning light faded into a peculiar dusk, tinted with a yellowish undertone that made a single rose on one of the yard's newly planted shrubs stand out in sharp crimson relief.

The eastern sky churned. Suddenly, a deep wind sprang up and leaves tore from the water oaks along the lake's rim, swirling across the yard. Tiny whitecaps broke across the lake's surface. "Roan," I said uneasily. "This is no ordinary thunderstorm. This feels like tornado weather."

He straightened, his face tightening as he listened to the wind. "Go inside," he said. "I'll watch."

I shivered as a gust of cold air skimmed us. "Watch what? Do what? Fight the wind with your bare hands?"

He released me and stepped into the yard. The wind pushed at him. He staggered. I clung to a porch post. "Go inside," he called again. A limb snapped off an oak and whipped toward him, struck him across the chest, and knocked him flat on his back. I fell down the porch steps and crawled to him. He rolled over on his hands and knees.

Roan snagged me by one arm, and we staggered inside the cabin. He lifted me around the waist and carried me to the doorway between the bedroom and the kitchen, between the old and the new, where we sat down. I curled an arm over his head protectively; he did the same for me.

The wind began to howl; I'd never heard anything like it in my life. Then a limb slapped the bedroom window and the panes shattered. The curtains suddenly streamed like furious white flags; there were thumps and thuds, but submerging every other sound was the wild bellow of the wind. I met Roan's gleaming eyes and began to count out loud, as if the numbered seconds were a chant to ward off danger.

"What are you doing?" he yelled.

"I believe in numerology," I yelled back.

Rain whipped in through the broken window, but the wind began to subside. The light grew brighter. I fumbled for the door frame, trying to pull myself up. "Got to make some calls, call home, make sure—"

Roan vaulted up and ran to the front room. Shaking, I dragged myself up along the door frame and looked at the shards of window glass flung across the bedroom floor and the bed. I went after him. He already had the phone in his hand.

We stayed on the phone for almost an hour, as Mama gathered and relayed information. Arnetta had lost the roof off her garage, an acre or so of Uncle Winston's Christmas tree fields had been flattened, Hop's bass boat and boat shed had been mangled—nothing really serious, only property. Nothing had happened around the country club; Josh had left the brunch to meet with Daddy and other county officials. Matthew, Tweet, and Amanda were fine.

Finally, exhausted, we walked outside. The rain had turned into a fine drizzle and a warm mist rose from the ground and the lake. On the far side of the yard, a swath had been cut through the forest, as if a giant lawn mower had run across the trees, snapping them off halfway up. I felt Roan's hand on mine, gripping hard. The strange, malevolent path disappeared down the ridge, in the direction of the Hollow.

Roan slowed the car as we rounded the curve, driving over small tree limbs scattered across the pavement.

My stomach lurched when I saw the twisted alley of destruction. Twenty years' growth of pines and kudzu had been ripped and strewn, the splayed root balls of some trees pulled out of the earth, pulled out of the buried garbage and the deeply submerged ruins of Big Roan's trailer and pickup truck.

Like a macabre insult, the desecration of a graveyard, throwing bones and open caskets into plain sight, the jumble of downed trees and tangled vines was littered with unspeakable evidence—rotted shreds of cans, the rusted-out hulk of a steel barrel, indefinable bits and pieces of corroded, muddy artifacts. A doughnut-shaped object hung obscenely from the tattered trunk of a split pine, dripping streams of dirty water.

"That's a half-rotted tire hanging in that tree," Roan said.

I couldn't breathe, couldn't speak. I looked at Roan, and his horrified expression broke my heart. His childhood, his shame, had been pulled from the ground and nakedly exposed. I put my hand on his arm, my fingers digging. "I'm sorry," I begged. "This is too much. Don't stop here."

His gaze was riveted to the exposed debris, his hands clenched so tightly on the steering wheel that his knuckles were blue-white. He stopped the car on the road's weedy shoulder, cut the engine, slung his door open, and got out. "No," I said urgently, holding on to his shirt sleeve. He pulled his arm away and staggered down the rain-drenched slope, shoving broken limbs aside, climbing over tree trunks. He pivoted, his eyes stark and agonized, his fists clenched. "Stay back," he called. "I don't want you down in this with me."

I struggled past the door he'd left open, holding on to the door frame, flinging a hand back to grab my cane. "I've always been part of it. You keep me out now, you'll keep me out forever. Wait. Someone's coming. You hear it? A car's coming."

It was Matthew, driving one of the farm trucks. He parked on the shoulder and leaped out, frowning at Roan. "I knew you'd be too damned stubborn to go anywhere safe in the middle of a tornado. I couldn't find you at Ten Jumps, so I've been . . . What the hell are you doing down there?"

"Go get him!" I ordered. "Get him out of there!"

Matthew hesitated, looking from Roan to me in astonishment. "What is it? What's here?"

"Me," Roan said in a gutted tone. "What I was. What I'll always be to everyone who wants to forget. Everything you don't understand."

Matthew shook his head. *"What?"* He bent down and picked up something from the weeds, then straightened with a dented, rust-pocked, muddy hubcap in his hands. He turned the piece of debris, frowning, examining it, then dropped it suddenly and stared at Roan. "Whatever this is about, just tell me. It couldn't be that bad." He clambered down the slope.

Roan lurched forward a step. "Both of you—stay up there!"

Matthew stopped, looking askance at Roan's furious warning. Then he clamped his mouth shut and went on, swinging at limbs, angrily pushing through the mud-spattered vines. "What are you going to do? Is it like the other day—somebody gets in your face and the best you can do is knock him down? Go ahead. *Show me who you really are.*"

Roan snatched him by the shirt and shook him. I screamed, "Roan, don't!" as Matthew clamped his hands on Roan's fists. Matthew lost his balance and fell backward into a pile of branches. Roan leaned over him, still dragging on his shirt. Matthew stared up at him, frozen.

"This is where I grew up," Roan said to him. "In this garbage hole! This

is what I come from! Claire came here for help when we were kids, but instead of helping her, my old man tried to rape her. *And when I got here*—"

"Roan," I called brokenly.

Roan's head sank. He took a long breath, then leveled a brutal, unapologetic stare at Matthew. "I killed him."

19

*T*he three of us sat on the soggy mat of weeds in the roadside by the Hollow, me in the middle, Roan staring straight ahead, Matthew with his arms propped on his knees and his head bowed.

The past had been laid out in Roan's words and mine. The why, the how, a raw portrait of Roan's childhood, Big Roan's unsalvageable violence and cruelty. Listening to Roan tell it all made my skin crawl; the horrors hovering outside an uncurtained window on a dark night had solid form again.

I tried to make Matthew understand why our family had sent Roan away, as I had finally come to accept it, and why he would have to accept and forgive his own treatment as a child. Imperfect and shamed intentions—a hard lesson in the dignities that hold families together, making them generous and ruthless at the same moment, both sanctuary and fortress.

Matthew had said nothing, listening in incredulous silence. He seemed dazed.

Roan and I traded a helpless look. He picked up a tattered stalk of Queen Anne's lace and smoothed his fingers over the flat disk of tiny white flowers. "I killed him," he repeated wearily. "My old man. He hurt Claire, and I killed the son of a bitch. And I'd do it again, if I had to. What happened to me after that had as much to do with my lack of faith as the Maloneys' bad judgment. If I'd stuck it out at the foster home I'd have had a chance to come back here and be part of the family again. I don't like what was done to me, but people make mistakes. I made one when I didn't tell you the truth about me and about who you are."

I bit my tongue, trying to stay quiet and let them settle this, but wanting to shake Matthew and make him see.

Roan snapped the flower in his hand, then tossed it away. "Let's get this straight. Claire and I spent the past twenty years without each other, and I wasn't with her this spring when she needed me. That's the price she and I paid. Twenty years without her—that's the only thing I wish I could change. I'll never let that happen again. I brought you home. You have a family now. You don't owe me anything. Now you know the truth about me. I understand what this family means to you. There's a helluva lot more heritage for you to be proud of as a Maloney than as a Sullivan."

Matthew staggered to his feet, moved in front of Roan, then dropped to his heels and met his eyes. They studied each other for a moment in silence. "You're not a murderer," Matthew said. It amazed me, how he unraveled the issues down to that single turning point. He jerked his head toward the Hollow. "You don't belong here. You never did. And you don't have to deal with it by yourself. You think I'm ashamed of you?" His voice shook. "I'm still a Sullivan, if you'll still have me. Give me a chance to earn the honor again. Sullivan. I'm proud of that."

There were a hundred images of Roan in my mind, pieces of memories—the fierce, accused boy at the carnival; the boy who knocked Neely Tipton down for me; the half-strangled boy carrying my chocolate Easter rabbit away from Steckem Road; the boy who stood atop Dunshinnog with Grandpa and me, listening to an old gospel song on a tin whistle, his eyes glowing. And every time I had surprised him by loving him and fighting for him, everything good he had brought out in me, and everything he had made of himself as a grown man, and for this young man, my nephew, whom he'd cared for and loved and raised as a tribute to what we meant to each other—all of that came together in him now.

"We're going to dig this place up," Roan said. "Clean it out. Get rid of it. If I have to pull every piece of it out with my bare hands. Cut it out and close it up and forget it was ever here."

He scrubbed a hand over his hair, struggling in spite of the powerful words. Matthew scooped up the hubcap he'd examined earlier. His face set, he leaped up and tossed the hubcap into the back of the farm truck. "Okay. Let's get to work then," he announced. Roan stood quickly and helped me up. I carefully jabbed the tip of my cane into a paper-thin scrap of rusted metal in the weeds, then balanced precariously, lifted the cane, and shook the scrap into the truck's bed. "One piece at a time, that's all it takes," I told Roan.

He tilted his head back and shut his eyes. There was a long moment when I didn't know what to expect next. "We'll clean this place out," he repeated. "Clean it out"—he opened his eyes, and his voice grew—"haul it out, and fill it in again. And then I'll *never* set a foot in this goddamned hole again, and neither will anyone else I love."

Matthew draped an arm over his shoulder. Suddenly Roan put one arm around him and the other around me. He pulled us both close, and we pulled him.

"I need chain saws," I said when I got to the farm. "Work gloves, bug repellent, and a water cooler." And then I explained why, with my heart in my throat, and Mama firmly sent old Nat to gather everything. Tweet grabbed a pair of work gloves. "I'm going over there with you," she said. "Roan needs all of us."

I didn't know what pleased me more—her brusque, clinical attitude as she shoved her hands into the gloves or the purely determined tenderness with which she had already claimed a place in the family.

"You know, you and Matthew are going to be fine here," I said.

"What about you and Roan?"

I didn't know, couldn't judge yet. "Let's dig up one piece of trouble at a time," I told her.

It was hard work, and slow work, and that was good, sweating out the poison. I moved around the perimeter of the Hollow clumsily, piling branches and small pine logs into heaps with my free hand, hating my cane. Roan and Matthew, sweat pouring down their chests, flung debris to the roadside, and Tweet tossed the pieces into the truck. Hot sun scalded us, and the damp air became a pine-scented sauna. Gnats and fat horseflies and stinging no-see-ums swarmed mercilessly around our faces. A small black snake slithered from a pile of brush. I captured it gently and held it out to Tweet. "Better carry it across the road and put it out of harm's way," I said. "There'll be more where it came from. And watch out for copperheads. They're not potent enough to kill a person, but if one bites you it won't be any fun."

Tweet accepted the black snake in her hands, hurried across the road and set it down, then trotted back to me, gazing anxiously toward Roan and Matthew. They were mired in a flattened maze of trees. "It'll take *weeks* at this rate," she murmured to me. "This is like four ants trying to move a rain forest."

"Faith can move mountains," Matthew said, grunting as he shoved at the half-fallen pine with the tire hanging from it. "It just can't push this damned tree over."

The tree mocked him by suddenly collapsing, and a thick limb slapped him across the back. He sprawled face-forward into jagged rubble and blackberry briars. Tweet shrieked and started down the bank. Roan dived into the debris. I sighed with relief as he pulled Matthew upright. There were several long red scratches across Matthew's face, and he hunched over, heaving, the breath knocked out of him.

Tweet got to him and frantically ran her hands over his back, pulling his sweat-soaked shirt up to his shoulder blades and probing his spine. "I'm okay," Matthew gasped. "Baby, you're a vet, not a chiropractor. Stop poking my vertebrae."

Tweet's face convulsed. She swiveled toward Roan, flinging her hands out. "I know he wants to do this with you, and I know you and Claire need to make the effort, but this plan is *not going to work!* We're all going to get snakebit or eaten alive by insects or"—she pounded the malevolent fallen pine—"crushed under a tree! You have to accept the fact that this isn't a job for two men and two women, one of whom is staggering around devotedly on a barely rehabilitated leg!"

"Wait a minute," Matthew called. "Listen."

One of the farm's big, one-ton hay trucks lumbered into sight around the curve. Mama, with Amanda in her lap, Grandma Dottie, and Renfrew were packed into the front seat beside Nat, who drove the same way he thought, slowly. Mama climbed down from the high cab and immediately instructed Nat, "Set the sawhorses across this lane of the road." She brusquely tugged at a yellow straw hat that made her face seem like the center of a large daisy. "Carry them back about where that big elm tree hangs down. We're going to block off this lane."

. Grandma Dottie waved her cigarette at Roan from the window of the truck's cab. "Get my card table, Roan. Put it on the pavement and set up my patio umbrella. And put the lawn chairs under it. I'm not getting out until I have a chair to sit in." Renfrew went to the back of the huge, wooden-sided truck, snapped the tailgate down, and bellowed, "I cain't haul none of these ice chests and food boxes out by myself! Roan, get your boy and his wife to stop gawkin' and come help!"

Mama, dressed in jeans and a workshirt, clambered through the debris.

When she reached Matthew, she carefully sprayed him with insect repellent. She sprayed Roan next, and then me, scowling mildly at my sweaty, sunbaked face. She plopped her hat on my head.

Amanda, outfitted in pink sunglasses and a baseball cap, and cradling a small cassette boom box in her arms, wandered to the edge of the road and looked around uneasily. "How come Papa isn't here yet, Uncle Roan?"

Uncle Roan. Roan's jaw worked. "I don't know, hon. We haven't talked to him." He looked at Mama, bewildered.

"I can't speak for Josh," Mama said wearily. "But the others are coming."

As if on cue, we heard a distant sound of large proportions and a minute later a fat yellow dump truck rolled between the steep, moist overhang of laurel and trees, coming from the direction of town. Behind it came four more dump trucks, and then a tractor pulling a backhoe on a trailer, and another tractor pulling a bulldozer on a trailer, then a stream of cars and pickups.

The lead truck grumbled to a halt near us, with the others parking on the shoulders on either side behind it, filling the road with the loud purr of heavy horsepower, then the small vehicles maneuvering for parking space.

Hop and Evan waved at us from the lead dump truck. Brady, Uncle Winston, Uncle Eldon, and several of my cousins climbed out of the others. Their thumbs hooked in the bibs of camouflage overalls, Hop and Evan took one long, unhappy look at the Hollow, then at Roan, Matthew, and me. "Y'all ought not to go huntin' for bear by yourselves," Hop said.

Evan nodded. "Not much of a place for handwork either. Matthew looks like he's been sawin' stumps with his nose."

Roan inhaled sharply. "I don't know how to thank—"

"You've got no need to offer any thank-yous," Uncle Winston said. Uncle Eldon added loudly, "No point in any cussing or discussing. We're here because we want to be."

A line of cars and trucks began to arrive. They came—Maloneys, Delaneys, Kehoes, O'Briens, and Tobblers. Aunts, uncles, cousins, in-laws— topping a hundred people by my count—bearing food and witness and quiet dedication. More chain saws and shovels and axes; boxes of food, ice coolers, guitars, lawn chairs, and blankets.

Daddy climbed out of a car, the hot, damp breeze picking at his thinning hair and plaid shirt. My father seemed to be sunk inside dark determination, the man who had buried the Hollow and sent Roan away unfairly, remembering.

Roan turned to look at me. "Did you ask them to do this?" he asked hoarsely.

Crying a little, I shook my head. "Don't you understand? They're here for you."

The picnic tables were being set up. Music rose from a guitar. This, then, was dinner on the grounds, bringing fellowship to hell's half-acre in the wilderness.

Except for Josh, whom no one had heard from yet.

The Hollow was scalped of trees by late afternoon. Violet and Rebecca goaded me into resting on a blanket with them at the base of the shady hills. The silence that followed hours of roaring chain saws felt heavy and portentous. Neat stacks of pine logs lined the clearing.

Everyone went silent, watching Roan and me. He walked over and squatted beside me. We gazed at a backhoe, manned by Hop. I put a hand on Roan's shoulder and gently massaged a steel-spring knot of tension. He fumbled for my hand and gripped it tightly, then tucked it in the crook of his arm. Matthew and Tweet stood nearby. Matthew looked regretful. "Now that push comes to dig," he said, "this feels pretty gruesome. I'm beginning to wish we could just sing a couple of hallelujahs and go home."

Roan said in a low voice, "Until we scrape the rot out of this ground, this place is home."

It was tough. My skin crawled every time Hop dug the backhoe's claw-scoop into the earth. Shadows fell across the Hollow. Everyone gathered in a large semicircle, their faces trapped in the Don't-look-I-have-to-look expression of spectators at a grisly accident.

Five feet down, the rusted-out hull of the truck's roof appeared. Matthew grimaced, Roan raised a hand, and Hop stopped the backhoe. Roan walked over to the hole and stood, looking down.

No one moved, no one breathed. A minute ticked by and then another one. I began to fear that Roan had lost himself in some time warp. "Help me up," I told Violet and Rebecca. "Hurry."

The backhoe clawed into Big Roan's truck, muddy and rusted; the cab caved in, the twisted metal charred black in spots, because Daddy had set fire to it and the trailer, before he buried them.

The backhoe dragged it out of the clinging mud, and it gave off metallic groans that made people edge closer together for comfort. Evan posed the bulldozer behind it. "We'll shove it up on one of the trailers," he called.

The look in Roan's eyes tore me apart. He stood there in agony, muddy hands jammed onto his hips, his chest rising and falling roughly beneath his sweat-drenched shirt. I knew he was seeing Big Roan in that truck, seeing himself in that truck.

I slid my arms around him. "Let it go," I whispered.

"I can't. I can't stop seeing it."

"Wait." Josh, his expression resigned, stood at the road. We all turned in surprise.

My brother walked slowly, heavily, through the raw clearing. Matthew watched him with troubled eyes. "Let me help," Josh said.

"Papa!" Amanda yelled, darting up the slope to him then halting uncertainly. "I knew you'd come! I told everybody you would! I told Matthew!"

That broke my brother's strained expression and curved his face into gratitude. He scooped her into a hug and lifted her off her feet. "What a prize you are," he said gruffly as she peered at him over her sunglasses, her face flushed and worried, then relaxing into a smile.

Tweet trotted to the truck's carcass, peered at it with her small blond head cocked to one side, thumped one warped door that hung by a single hinge, then looked at Roan solemnly. "Looks like a fixer-upper to me."

Some in the crowd burst into relieved laughter. Roan and I looked at Josh, who held Amanda tighter. She patted his cheek. We hadn't brought him a son with no compromises, but we had given him a wholehearted daughter.

Cans, the battered hulk of a washing machine, rotting tires, mysterious shards of who-knew-what origins—we dug it all up and lugged it away, we scooped it and flung it and dumped it into the big trucks.

Deeper, deeper. The backhoe was sunk so low in the gouge it had made that we could hand Hop a cup of iced tea without reaching up. Water began to seep among the garbage, big, muddy puddles of it from the narrow creek that used to trickle through the gully at the very bottom of the Hollow.

The daylight was fading fast. Several dozen camping lanterns glowed with weird, festive charm. "There it is," Hop yelled as his scoop thudded on a metal wall. The trailer.

"How big was it?" Matthew asked Roan.

"Not big enough," he said, without taking his eyes off the pit below us.

It took the backhoe and the bulldozer working together to wrestle that sunken hulk from the ground. Charred, collapsed, the skull-eyes of its broken windows looking at us, it rolled out of the pit and shuddered upright, like a cardboard box stomped by a giant. It lay there in the flickering lantern light, its closed, battered door dripping grotesque streams of muddy-red water.

And then, through some obscene quirk of physics or fate, the door slowly swung open.

There was a collective gasp as everyone except Roan and me backed away. We stared into that black rectangle jumbled with muddy, rotten, charred furniture. Fetid water trickled over the threshold. I was ten years old again and Roan was fifteen, and the old nightmare came at us.

Suddenly Roan's arms were around me and mine around him, and he hid my face in the crook of his neck, and I pulled his head close to mine and shielded his eyes with my hand.

I heard the door slam shut. Josh and Matthew stood there together, holding it closed.

The rotting trailer was hauled away. The old truck, gone. The garbage, gone. The pit filled in.

We lingered in the darkness, in the lantern light, dozens of us, at a loss for something, I didn't know what, that would sum it all up and send us to our homes with a feeling that it all made sense.

Aunt Dockey, the Reverend Maloney, who had arrived after her Sunday sermon at the tiny Unitarian church in town, stepped forward. "I have something to say." She looked at Roan and me. "If y'all feel the need to hear it."

Roan looked dazed, so I answered, "We feel the need."

We sat down, all of us sat, old, young, in-betweens, black and white, a patchwork quilt of people sharing a network of strong seams. We sat on the muddy ground and Aunt Dockey stood before us, and there was something powerful and dignified about the stocky, graying woman wearing grimy tennis shoes, a mud-flecked blue golf shirt, and a denim skirt with a small crucifix sewn in rhinestones on one hip pocket. She could rant confidently against the darkness and the wilderness.

She spoke in casual commentary, an ad-libbed sermon woven around sound bites from the Big Scriptwriter, and my dazed, exhausted thoughts wandered and came back, faded, then focused.

"'The seed sown by the wayside withers in poor soil. The seed sown on good earth grows, and bears fruit.'"

I held Roan's hand, I wound my arm inside his; he squeezed my fingers in a rhythm of gentle contemplation.

"'. . . and David gave thanks because his soul had been brought up from the grave, he was alive, he would not sink down into the pit.'"

Not ever again.

"'. . . brought me up also out of a horrible pit, out of the miry clay, and set my feet upon a rock, and established my path.'"

Aunt Dockey was heavily into pit analogies, and she picked through the Bible as if it were a cross-referenced book of quotations. But we needed that; we weren't sorting out theology, we were hunting for comfort.

"'Let the wicked be ashamed, and let them be silent in the grave. Let the lying lips that speak grievous things proudly and with contempt against the righteous, let them be silent.'"

There would always be idle gossip about Roan, Matthew, the Sullivan history in general, and me, my part in it, and how I came home and why. But idle gossip is no match for Maloney stubbornness or Sullivan pride.

"'When I was a child, I spoke as a child, I understood as a child, I thought as a child: but when I became grown, I put away childish things.'"

No more nightmares, in the daylight or the darkness.

"'For now we see through a glass, darkly; but then face to face: now I know in part; but then shall I know even as also I am known.'"

Faith looks at faith and understands.

Aunt Dockey paused. Around us, people sat with bowed heads or closed eyes, touching here and there, fingertips to their cheeks. Roan exhaled and put an arm around me. We looked at each other. He smiled wearily, and I saw more peace in him than I think I've ever seen before. I brushed a kiss across his mouth.

And then we realized Aunt Dockey was speaking again, and we faced her. "'Though I walk through the valley of the shadow of death, I will fear no evil.'"

We had walked. We had feared. But we had come out safely on the other side.

And so, that day, that night, Sullivan's Hollow was unearthed, exhumed, autopsied, prayed over, and pronounced dead of the most natural causes.

Faith, hope, charity.

And forgiveness.

．　．　．

Late that night, at the farm, the immediate family—Mama, Daddy, Grandma Dottie, my four brothers, three sisters-in-law, the twelve grandchildren including Matthew—Tweet, Roan, and I sat on the veranda eating cold fried chicken and drinking tea. I listened to the warm, thick honey of their voices, looked at the mixture of old and young, sleek and stout, big hair and no hair—a family it would be a mistake to peg as simple or short-sighted, because they were both wide and deep in a short arc, as most families are.

Roan and I went to the barn but just stood in the lower level, holding each other in the dark. A llama stuck its head through a gate and nibbled on our shirtsleeves. "How about that. There are llamas all over the place," Roan said, as if he'd just started looking.

After the others had left or gone to bed, I met Roan in the hallway between his old bedroom and the guest room Mama had assigned him, meaningfully, nearby. We were clean from separate showers.

We looked at each other for the first time with the freedom of contentment. Nothing left to guard against, or protect, or redeem, or restore. Fully, openly satisfied, we examined each other with a kind of brazen wonder. "There are llamas all over this place," I said. "Hello again, boy."

"Hello, peep."

He picked me up and carried me into his old room. We shared the small bed together. Outside the window the moon winked above Dunshinnog. The stars were fading. "I'm so sore I can barely move," I said.

"I won't ask you to move." Roan pulled the covers over us. "I'll be careful not to take all the covers. I'll never leave you alone in the dark. I'll never turn my back on you. I'll try not to crowd you. You've got my word on it."

"That promise sounds like it covers a lot more than just this bed." I curved a hand around his face, feathering my fingers over his mouth, caressing him. "It could sum up a lot of answers. It could go a long way."

He bent his head to mine. I felt tears on his cheeks. "Just say 'Welcome home.'"

I did.

20

*H*op said to Roan, "Evan and I'll take Matthew hunting this fall." Evan said maybe Matthew didn't hunt; it wouldn't suit his profession.

"Well, we'll take him fishing then," Hop countered. "He's not a fish doctor."

They funneled every social matter through a simple system—go into the woods, commune with nature via fishing rods and hunting rifles, and camaraderie would follow without discussion.

And Brady said, in his smooth, efficient way, boiling his alliance down to dollar signs, "You'll need a stake here, Roan. Partnerships. Some plans. I have two words to say to you. Just two. You think about the possibilities. *Outlet mall.*"

"Oh, I'll think about it," Roan promised solemnly.

We were giddy and carefree, so immersed in the pleasure of being together that we spent days together at Ten Jumps without seeing another soul.

Roan and Matthew began planning to build a barn near the lake. The dogs and birds were shipped from Alaska, and one of Tweet's parrots immediately bit Renfrew.

And so the parrots came to live with Roan and me, temporarily.

All around us July began, the sun grew hotter, barbecue grills were scrubbed, watermelons were iced down, colorful banners went up around the square, the Jaycees set up a stage for the Uncle Sam speeches, and small children began to feel the prickly promise of public humiliation.

The Fourth of July in Dunderry is red, white, blue, and Irish green. The leprechauns were marching.

Our Little People looked like unhappy munchkins in an Irish version of *The Wizard of Oz*. About half of them were kin of mine.

"Why do we have to do this?" Amanda whispered miserably to me, distracted by a loose green feather on the little green leprechaun beret that went with her fluffy green leprechaun dress. "Aunt Claire, I hate this shit."

"Good girl," I whispered back. We stood in the spare shade of an awning around the corner from Main Street, the parade staging area, swamped in a mingled mass of participants: high school band musicians sweating in their uniforms; lawyers from Uncle Ralph's motorcycle club, sweating in their studded, black leather jackets—I kept coaxing Uncle Ralph to have BORN TO LITIGATE put on the back of his, but he wouldn't do it; and about every other strange group imaginable, including four of Daddy's llamas draped with red-white-and-blue banners, which would be tugged up Main Street by four banner-draped Maloney grandchildren.

Immediately around me was a sea of small, flushed faces atop green dresses or green jackets with green knee-pants and green shoes. Mothers scurried everywhere. Violet rubbed an ice cube on her daughter's glistening frown. Tula fluffed the ruffled green collars beneath the stoic brown faces of her two youngest daughters.

"Aunt Claire, why do we have to do this?" Amanda repeated.

"Because y'all need some embarrassing pictures to show your own kids someday. Snapshots and videos." She groaned. I felt a certain gleeful satisfaction. I'd been lucky enough to do my leprechaun duty before everybody in the family owned camcorders.

Josh walked up. He swept Amanda into his arms and beamed at her. "Papa," she said seriously, "I look like turnip greens with red hair."

"You're beautiful," he corrected. "I've never seen a prettier sight. I want you to keep wearing the whole outfit until Lin Su gets here tonight. I want to get a picture of you and her together. And I want some pictures of you with Matthew. Okay?"

"Sure. But Matthew has to wear something green, too."

"Whatever you say, Princess Leprechaun."

Amanda laughed. Josh and I traded satisfied looks. He'd brought Lin Su to meet the family recently. She was smart and charming, she obviously cared about Josh, and she had a good knack with Amanda. Mama was hoping for a marriage eventually. Amanda waved at Roan, who had walked up the street from the Maloney staked-out curbside viewing spot. He laughed as he stood there, large and handsome, and I grinned at him and rolled my eyes at the chaos.

I patted several small Maloney heads and tweaked Amanda's hair. "All right, little people, luck o' the Irish to y'all. Have fun. Believe me, it'd be worse if you had to tap-dance."

Several thousand people lined the town square. Tourists wandered among craft tents on the lawn of the old courthouse and among food stands. A Sousa march blared from speakers atop the fire department's hook-and-ladder rig, which idled a couple of blocks away, waiting to lead the parade from the corner of Main and Delaney Streets.

There were dozens of Delaneys and Maloneys on either side of Roan, me, Matthew, and Tweet. Mama smiled at us over her sunglasses, Daddy fiddled with his camcorder, and a flock of camera-toting aunts, uncles, and cousins parted to let us have choice territory.

This was not how Maloneys and Delaneys ordinarily act when they're all vying for a shady spot under the same public elm tree.

Matthew balanced Hop and Ginger's toddler, nicknamed Erp, on his hip. Erp gnawed a melting fruit pop. Matthew pointed to a gooey splotch on the front of his own shirt. He smelled faintly of Erp-launched peach drool. Tweet sidled in next to me. "Good spot," she announced cheerfully. "Now Erp can hurl at the fire trucks." The hook-and-ladder rig began to creep forward. Roan put his arms around me from behind and latched his hands in mine. The fire department trucks inched by. Hop and Evan are volunteer station captains, so they were among the men sitting on top of the rigs. They yelled and laughed like boys and made a point of pelting the family with green mint candies.

Erp spit a blob of frozen peach pop into Tweet's palm, and Tweet tossed it. Brady stood nearby, and it hit him between the eyes. Evan and Hop laughed so hard, they nearly rolled off the truck.

Dozens of Maloney cameras clicked and whirred.

The high school band marched past, playing "I'm Proud to Be an American." Fronting the leprechauns, a group of my more musical uncles, led by Uncle Dwayne, wandered along playing a high-pitched Irish jig on fiddles and uilleann pipes and tin whistles and a bodhran drum.

I felt enriched with security, confidence, love. Despite the coy new businesses and the touristy atmosphere and the strangers packed everywhere along our shady streets, we were still, at heart, familiar to one another and united in whimsy, like a favorite family story told and retold and much loved.

I thought of us that day at the carnival, of Roanie Sullivan standing below the stage, both of us isolated by our particular brands of humiliation and yet linked by that, too. And I thought about the Christmas parade, that year Big Roan ruined it, and the shame that made Roan nearly disappear into himself. Today we were together, no petty humiliations, no shame, and it was so rich, like a sweet grape bursting on my tongue, that I could taste the happiness.

And then, suddenly, the parade skewed toward me.

Uncle Dwayne's group halted. They stopped playing. Amanda waved her green troops forward. A flock of little people gathered around the musicians, all of them staring and giggling at me, or at Roan and me—I wasn't sure which.

I drew back against Roan. His arms slid closer around me. I didn't sense any surprise in him. I was totally bewildered. "Either they think we're the secret parade judges," I whispered out of the corner of my mouth, "or they think we're hiding their pot of gold."

"Sssh, just wait," Roan whispered.

I turned my head and gaped up at him. Conspiracy gleamed in his eyes. I looked at Mama, at Daddy, and then swept the faces around them. Conspiracy. I looked at Amanda's street-centered grin. Conspiracy. I'd been had.

Uncle Dwayne began to play his fiddle, some old Irish ballad, lilting and sweet. Little people scurried, bumped into each other, rearranged themselves into a line facing Roan and me. Small hands dived inside the collars of green dresses and green shirts. Broad white cards flashed out, an uneven line of them, each one printed with a blocky green letter of the alphabet.

And there it was, printed out for the whole family, the whole town, the whole universe to see.

CLAIRE, WILL YOU MARRY ME?

I twisted inside Roan's arms and looked up at him tearfully. His eyes glistened, too. There was such joy in him, such beauty. "Surprise," he murmured. "You've read all my other letters, so I thought we ought to share this one with everybody else." Bold talk from a man who had spent his life avoiding public spectacles.

I unwound his arms, then limped into the street. I tapped shoulders, rearranged little people, turned some flashcards to the blank side.

When I finished, I faced Roan, dimly aware of a cocoon of laughter and applause around us, but riveted to the wonderful expression on his face as he read the rearranged cards.

I WILL MARRY YOU

He stepped out of the crowd and walked toward me. I met him halfway and he took my hands. We were part of the parade now. Part of it all.

I heard Mama's ecstatic voice. "And the bridesmaids' dresses will be gold and mauve and . . ."

Uncle Dwayne struck up "When Irish Eyes Are Smiling" on his fiddle.

Matthew and Tweet grinned.

From the crowd, Mr. Cicero gave me a thumbs-up. "Good editing," he mouthed.

The leprechauns giggled.

Roan and I gazed at each other without a shred of dignity.

Erp spit frozen peach mush at us.

Everything was absolutely perfect.

21

*A*utumn

The old mountain, it whispered to itself, it drew us up to its brow with the murmur of its seasons, the patient circle of life that it anchors.

We climbed up the old hiking path to the top of Dunshinnog that fall, the day after we deeded Ten Jumps to Matthew and Tweet. They were clearly in love with the lake, the cabin, its birds and animals and its room to grow.

My leg was strong, but the hike up Dunshinnog was a test I hadn't taken yet and I had some doubts I could make it. Couldn't let Roan down though, or myself. I had signed a contract with Mr. Cicero to buy the *Shamrock*. I was a little nervous about the responsibility but excited.

"Come on, you can do it," Roan urged gently as I panted and climbed the last, steepest knob on Dunshinnog. He moved ahead, held out a hand. I took it, and he helped me up on the granite overhang above the valley. I punched his shoulder, then burst out laughing with victory. And he smiled broadly, at ease and pleased for us both.

We examined the small green rosettes of new foxgloves growing among their fading, majestic elders. "Best crop yet," I claimed. "It'll be a good year for foxgloves next spring." We walked along the mountain's crown, found the spot we'd discussed, then Roan pulled a canvas knapsack off one shoulder, taking from it the old plank with our names carved on it. I held the plank high up on the side of an oak while he nailed it in place.

"The heart of the house. Right here," he said. "We'll sit here and look out at the sky. With the family. Friends. See the whole valley. See for miles."

I took something from a pocket of my jeans and held it out on my palm. "This is for you. Grandpa would want you to have it. You remember when we came up here with him the first time and he played 'Amazing Grace'?"

Roan took the old tin whistle between his fingertips. "I'll have to learn to play it, too," he said softly.

"You will. I'm sure. He always knew who to trust with the traditions."

Roan put his arm around me. There was no need to doubt the serenity in his eyes. He was happy. He'd come back to where we both belonged. He'd found his place. He touched just a fingertip to my lips. An old kiss, from childhood. In the slowly gathering dusk, the cool and ripe harvest time of the year, we sat down on the ledge close together. The wind rose gently, a pure song. We shared the view across land and sky, remembering, and looking beyond.

ABOUT THE AUTHOR

A former newspaper editor and multiple award winner for her novels and contemporary romances, DEBORAH SMITH lives in the mountains of Georgia, where she is working on her next novel.